Praise for the Mag

"Maggie O'Malley will not k ___ M000295716 ___
she sets out to prove the innocence of a friend facing a murder
charge...*39 Winks* has is all: characters, plot, pace—from the very
first line to the spectacular conclusion."

– Patricia Gussin,
New York Times Bestselling Author of *Come Home*

"With twists you won't see coming, Maggie O'Malley and *39 Winks*
are sure to keep you up all night!"

– Julie Mulhern,
USA Today Bestselling Author of *Shadow Dancing*

"A page-turner! Smart, fast-paced and surprising."

– Hank Phillippi Ryan,
Mary Higgins Clark Award-Winner, Author of *Say No More*

"This one will have you up all night following Maggie O'Malley on
her search for the truth... If you like a book with smarts, a heart,
and flesh-and-blood characters, don't miss *Protocol*."

– Maggie Barbieri,
Author of the Murder 101 Series

"Gutsy and loyal, Maggie O'Malley finds herself plunged into the
corrupt and chilling world of big pharmaceuticals where trusting
the wrong person could prove as deadly as an experimental drug
side effect. With a page-turner debut like *Protocol*, I can't wait to
see what Valenti cooks up for us next!"

– Annette Dashofy,
USA Today Bestselling Author of *Uneasy Prey*

"A clever and twisty thriller that will grab you from the first
sentence and keep you guessing until the very end."

– Kathleen Barber,
Author of *Are You Sleeping*

AS DIRECTED

The Maggie O'Malley Mystery Series
by Kathleen Valenti

A MAGGIE O'MALLEY MYSTERY

AS DIRECTED

KATHLEEN VALENTI

HENERY PRESS

Copyright

AS DIRECTED
A Maggie O'Malley Mystery
Part of the Henery Press Mystery Collection

First Edition | March 2019

Henery Press, LLC
www.henerypress.com

Trade Paperback ISBN-13: 978-1-63511-467-6
Digital epub ISBN-13: 978-1-63511-468-3
Kindle ISBN-13: 978-1-63511-469-0
Hardcover ISBN-13: 978-1-63511-470-6

Printed in the United States of America

For the readers

ACKNOWLEDGMENTS

When I reflect back on the genesis, creation and completion of a book, I'm humbled by the outpouring of help, support and encouragement I've received along the way.

As Directed is no exception.

This book was a challenge right from the start. I knew I wanted to write a complex story with characters to match. Fortunately, I have a wonderful community of friends, family, experts and readers ready to lend a hand with medical research, literary analysis, ninja-proofreading, adjective-wrangling, hand-holding and coffee-dosing. Because of them, challenge became fulfillment.

I owe a huge debt of gratitude to so many people and communities. Here, I'm hitting the highlights.

My eternal gratitude to my family for their support and ability to feign surprise when I reveal a plot twist at a reading.

My deepest thanks to beta-readers, intrepid commenters and tireless advice-givers Rachel, Valerie, Lisa and Nancy for keeping me on track, inspired and always chasing the power of Better.

My admiration and appreciation to Phyllis for her kick-butt extraordinary proofreading and copyediting skills.

My heartfelt thanks to medical advisors Daymen, Allan, Tabitha and Annette for keeping me on track.

My endless appreciation to the Henery Press team and my agent, Jordan, at Literary Counsel for their wisdom, insight and counsel.

My profound gratitude to author friends who opened their arms and hearts to welcome and support me.

And finally to the readers, my tribe, who believe in the magic of words and the power of pages, who not only hang out with Maggie and Constantine but ask what's next for them, as if they're valued friends hoped to be seen at an upcoming barbecue—I'm so very grateful for you.

To all of you and those whose names I hold in my heart, I offer my many thanks.

As always, any errors are my own.

Prologue

Claudia Warren took too long to die.

She should have been dead when her lungs stopped inflating, when her brain stopped communicating with the rest of her body. But her heart kept beating, even as her cells began to necrotize and the blood pooled in her muscles.

Claudia couldn't even die right.

Then again, she'd never been murdered before, so maybe that was to be expected.

Claudia died alone, as she did most things. She came home from the grocery store, carefully inserted her key into the deadbolt, jiggling it up and down to engage the tumblers, then tossed her purse on the counter next to yesterday's mail. She deposited plastic grocery bags on the counter—she couldn't be bothered with toting around cloth ones—and began to unpack the fruits of her Pick & Save foraging.

A pack of single-serving puddings.

A box of single-serving juices.

An array of Lean Cuisine entrées, the accent capping the "e" an attempt to catapult the food from TV dinner to culinary experience.

Single serving food for her table-for-one life.

Not that she minded living alone. She relished it. She had her rescue cat, Todd, a fat tabby who bumped her chin with his head when she bent to fill his dish, and her work as an advertising account exec, which followed her home every night like a stalker.

Human beings? She found them overrated. They were too critical of her missteps. Too overbearing in their suggestions. Too *there.*

And yet the moment she knew something was wrong, very wrong, she had a sudden and intense urging for that thereness.

Her cheating ex-husband. Her meddling mother. The woman next door who pilfered coupons from her mailbox. It didn't matter. She would've taken any of them. She needed help. She needed someone there.

She needed someone to stop her heart from stopping.

Think.

Claudia tried to cogitate her way into living, to assign reason for her certainty that she would die before next week's work trip to Tobago where she'd nod and smile and pretend to be interested in her client's plans for a new beachside resort.

Claudia's head exploded in a blinding streak of agony.

She put her hands to her temples and dropped a magnum bottle of pinot grigio, the only super-sized indulgence she allowed herself, and staggered against the counter. She broadened her stance as if getting her sea legs and tried to ride out a wave of vertigo.

It didn't work.

She swayed. Recovered. Swayed again. She tried to focus on what was happening. The cascade of pudding packs from counter to floor. The puddling wine. The blackness encroaching at the periphery of her vision like a wolf coming in for the kill. None of it made sense, except maybe—

A new pain, sharp and insistent, seared through her body, blunting her thoughts. She dropped her hands from her head and clutched her neck. She pawed at unseen hands that seemed to close around her windpipe, choking out her breath. Her life. Her future.

She fell to the floor beside the shattered wine bottle and the shards of glass that trailed behind it in a wake of gravity and destruction. The wine ebbed from the bottle. Breath ebbed from her lungs.

Todd nosed Claudia's cheek, his whiskers tickling skin that had already begun to turn ruddy with hypoxia. He bumped her chin. Claudia's head flopped like a doll's. He bumped her again, an entreaty to move, or perhaps cat CPR. Claudia's head lolled again, eyes fixed on the tiny spider webs that her feather duster had missed.

Claudia's vision darkened. Her lungs, burned clean of oxygen, throbbed. Then everything stilled. Her heart. Her mind. Even Todd the cat.

Claudia finally succeeded in dying.

Chapter 1

Maggie straightened her lab coat and examined her reflection in the glass of the medical-grade refrigerator. The new overhead bulbs had turned her skin sallow and transformed her teeth into a shade she imagined could only be called "Beaver Dentin." She dragged her fingers through her hair and mashed her ginger curls into a struggling bun at the base of her neck, then chanced another look in the glass.

She was a dead-ringer for Uncle Fester.

Not that Maggie particularly cared what she looked like. She was more interested in action rather than ornament—what she could do over how she appeared. But still. It was her second day as a bona fide pharmacy tech rather than an intern. She had her preliminary license. She had begun studying for the state exam. She wanted to look professional. Put together.

Not like someone who needed more bilirubin in her bloodstream.

Maggie scrubbed her teeth with her forefinger, examined the yield, squirted hand sanitizer from an industrial-sized pump onto her palm. (She was a professional, after all.) Then she hurried back to the counter, making a mental note to ask Thom, the store's part-time janitor, if he could replace the bulbs he'd just installed with a non-jaundice-inducing variety.

Maggie took her place behind the register and surveyed her new dominion. The little row of conjoined waiting room chairs. The blood pressure machine. The laminated barrier that separated prescription-seeker from prescription-filler.

This was the pharmacy section of Petrosian's Pillbox. Her new professional home. The launching pad of her new career.

She felt a frisson of excitement at the newness, the sense of being reformulated as if she were a bottle of shampoo with more frizz-fighting power than ever before. She was an occupational phoenix, reborn from the ashes of her career in pharmaceutical development.

Goodbye, Maggie O'Malley. Hello, Maggie O'Malley 2.0.

The plan: pharmacy technician today, pharmacist tomorrow—or at least soon. So far, Day Two as a pharmacy technician was going smoothly. She'd pushed pills into bottles, measured out liquid medications, and affixed labels to containers. It was the most independence she'd had since her on-the-job training had begun six weeks earlier. Forget her master's in pharmacology, her award-winning graduate work, her extensive pharmaceutical knowledge. When you worked for Levon Petrosian, pharmacist and business-owner, freedom was tough to come by.

Maggie fluffed her lab coat, straightened her nametag and eagerly awaited the chance to carpe the hell out of the diem. Petrosian had left her in charge of the pharmacy while he ran errands. Phoenix was up for her first solo flight.

The phone rang. Her first opportunity at autonomy. Maggie answered, took Mrs. Duncan's refill order, told her to have a *very* nice day—feeling luxurious in the superlative—and replaced the handset. A movement in her peripheral vision caught her eye. Maggie looked up.

A girl, perhaps nine or ten, was prowling Aisle 5.

Aisle 5 was Maggie's favorite section of Petrosian's Pillbox, a no-man's-land between health and beauty where shoppers could procure gastronomical delights like Vienna sausages, apple juice and hard candies.

The girl circled the Hostess rack like a shark. She surveyed her quarry, picked up a package of Twinkies, ruffled its cellophane edges, then repeated the process with Ding Dongs and raspberry Zingers. With the Zingers, she held the package longer, turning it over, studying the end as if looking for an expiration date. She brought the package to her nose and inhaled deeply, eyelids fluttering. Maggie wondered if the girl could smell the cloying scent of coconut and Red 40 or if she were reliving an olfactory experience.

As if on cue, the girl sniffed deeply again. She looked over the shoulder of her stained Vikings sweatshirt and licked her lips. Then she curled her fingers around the package and slipped the Zingers into her pocket.

Maggie breathed in sharply. A shoplifter?

Before Maggie's mind could tell her body what to do, the girl was in motion, feigning interest in other snack cakes, mulling mini muffins, fingering palm-sized fruit pies, sauntering to the front of the store, one tattered sneaker in front of the other in a silent tightrope walk.

The girl reached the door and pulled. The overhead bell pealed once. An alarm rather than an adieu.

The girl looked up sharply. So did the woman at Register 1. Not just any woman. Francine.

As far as Maggie could tell, Francine specialized in being annoyed.

Ask her where to find the heating pads: Annoyed.

Ask for paper instead of plastic: Annoyed.

Answer "no problem" instead of "you're welcome": Annoyed.

Francine slit her eyes and put red-tipped fingers against bony hips. "Excuse me," she called. The girl froze. "Excuse me," Francine repeated. "Where do you think you're going?"

The girl turned. Her face flamed against the white sweatshirt, mirroring the red-and-white striped Zingers in her pocket. "I was just leaving?"

More than a question. A request for permission.

Francine flipped her hair, a nearer-to-Thee 'do evangelically teased and secured on each side with white butterfly clips. Francine shook her head. "I don't think so, hon. We don't let shoplifters waltz out the door."

The girl's mouth hinged open.

"Thought you'd get away with your five-finger discount, didn't you? Thought you were too good—too *clever*—to pay like everyone else, didn't you?" Francine sniffed. "Well, now you'll pay." She lifted the receiver of the phone at her register. "I'll make sure of that."

Maggie watched as Francine dialed. She took in the girl's matted hair, the ragged jeans that hung on her thin frame, the way her pallid skin sheeted the prominent bones of her cheeks and chin. Maybe the girl was hungry. Maybe she was homeless.

Maggie imagined the girl picking scraps from a trashcan, waiting in interminable soup kitchen lines, bringing home food to a sibling who begged to have a belly filled with something other than hopelessness.

The thought galvanized Maggie. She thrust her hand into her pocket and brought out a wad of wrinkled bills. She rang up a sale, shoved the money in the till then grabbed the receipt.

She hurried to the front of the store, no great feat given the Pillbox's small size, detouring down Aisle 5 for a few sticks of jerky and a can of beef stew.

"Francine?" Maggie called. Her lab coat billowed her around her like a polyblend cape as her walk became a jog. "Hang on a sec."

Francine's head swiveled toward Maggie as if on a spit. The cashier regarded Maggie, angry black eyeliner hooding flashing blue eyes. "What is it?" she snapped.

"Just wanted to give this girl her receipt." Maggie pressed the thin rectangle of paper into the girl's hand then closed the small fingers around the proof of purchase as if it were a visa to a kinder place.

Francine replaced the handset and folded her arms across her navy blue smock. Her necklace of multi-sized red balls pressed against her skin, creating tiny dents in the pale, sun-spotted dermis. "You're saying she paid for the cupcakes?"

"Zingers," Maggie corrected. "And yes. Plus she forgot these." Maggie nodded to the girl, who obediently stuck out her arms. Maggie loaded them with the few foodstuffs she had hastily selected.

Francine made a guttural sound that was half-scoff, half-retch. "She *bought* those?"

"Yep." Maggie smiled at the girl. "Thanks for shopping Petrosian's Pillbox. Come again soon."

The girl stood rooted in the spot, her eyes darting from the food in her arms to Maggie then to Francine. Maggie gave another nod and the girl spun on her heels and shouldered open the door.

"She didn't have a bag," Francine said, as they watched the girl tear across the parking lot.

"I'm sorry?" Maggie said, as the girl disappeared around the corner.

"The girl." A head bob toward the door. "She didn't have a bag. I found that suspicious."

Maggie shrugged. "You know how environmentally conscious this generation is."

"Right." Francine picked her tooth with her pinky and leaned against her register. "I've heard about you. You like to get *involved*." This said like a dirty word. "You're young and pretty and have a background as a fancy scientist. But you're also new here, so here's a nickel's worth of free advice." She keyed in a code and the register drawer sprung open. She picked up a roll of quarters and slammed it against the corner of the drawer. "Stay in your lane."

"I'll take that under advisement."

Maggie strolled back to the pharmacy counter, fingernails digging into her palm, cheeks reddening with anger. A few years ago, she would have blushed with embarrassment, ashamed to have received a scolding, appalled at her own boldness. But that was before she knew her worth. Before she knew how much she could do. Before she'd been made into something harder and more resilient.

Maggie 2.0.

Stay in her lane? Keep her nose out of other people's business? No problem. As long as people like Francine didn't give her reason to do otherwise.

Maggie ducked beneath the miniature Dutch door counter that separated retail space and sacred pharmaceutical ground and snagged a cardboard box. She scooted back out, intent on restocking the shelves and her good mood.

She assessed her task.

Levon Petrosian was particular to the point of rigidity, committed to not just following the letter of the law but alphabetizing each letter.

Drills to create labels and process insurance claims. Early morning runs to restock shelves. Chores that tasked her endurance as well as her patience. Petrosian's training was more like boot camp. The only things missing were pushups next to the *Please Wait Behind This Line* sign and forced marches down the analgesic aisle singing "I don't know but I've been told; the last aspirin has just been sold."

Funny thing was, Petrosian liked his newest employee. "Adored like a daughter," if Polly, her fiancé Constantine's aunt, was to be believed. Another funny thing: Maggie adored her grumpy, taciturn boss right back.

Part of that esteem was born from the events of last year, part from what she had come to learn of her boss. He was a man of integrity, kindness and generosity. Good moods? That was another story. Maggie's father wasn't much different. She had plenty of experience dealing with curmudgeons.

Maggie propped a cardboard box on her hip and popped the lid. She swished her hand inside. Plastic bottles of Pepto-Bismol knocked against each other. She grabbed a smooth cylinder and got to work, starting with the aisle's end-cap. She placed bubblegum pink soldiers against dyspepsia on the white metal shelves. One by one, she arranged the bottles, facing out labels, adjusting placement for reachability, checking that prices were clear and visible.

She rounded the corner, plastic bottle in hand, humming AC/DC's "Thunderstruck," inhaling the pharmacy's signature perfume of cleaner and plastic. And nearly stumbled over a man sprawled beneath the display of Tums Chewy Bites.

Chapter 2

Maggie pinwheeled her arms to avoid a full-body fall onto the man whose prone form occupied the better part of the aisle. She widened her stance to regain her balance then dropped to her knees beside the motionless figure.

She recognized the man immediately. Colton Ellis, a longtime customer known for his sharp sense of humor, love of Lucille Ball, and extensive collection of t-shirts won for eating hamburgers that approximated the size and shape of his head.

Maggie put her fingers to Colton's neck and felt for a pulse. His skin was red and warm, but still, no drumbeat of life beating beneath the surface. She moved her fingers and tried again, tucking her hand in the hollow where the carotid pumped, below the angle of his jaw, beside his Adam's apple, anywhere she might find the Morse code from his heart.

Nothing.

She began CPR and shouted to Francine to call 911.

"Change your mind about that little thief?" Francine called from her register.

"I don't need the cops. I need an ambulance."

The plaintive wail of sirens pierced the silence of the group gathered around Colton Ellis as if he were lying in wait. And Maggie supposed he was. Despite her repeated chest compressions, Colton remained immobile.

Too many minutes later, the paramedics ran up the aisle, boots clacking, equipment clanking. A uniformed woman with white-blonde hair and gray eyes put a hand on Maggie's shoulder. "Can you continue while we get set up?" she asked.

Maggie nodded and kept pumping Colton's chest to an internal soundtrack of "Staying Alive." Moments later, with their equipment in place, the paramedics assessed Colton.

"No pulse," the woman said.

Her partner, a man with a fireplug body and a face to match, produced a defibrillator. He pressed its paddles onto Colton's chest, which was rose white and hairless like a mountain range above the foothills of his wrinkled jeans.

"Clear!"

There was a whine as the defibrillator charged, then a concussive zap as 1,700 volts charged into Colton's heart.

Maggie expected Colton's body to rise from the floor then crash back into place, as she'd seen in countless movies and television shows. Instead he barely flinched, starting as if in response to a bad dream.

The paramedics checked the heart monitor. The woman frowned then nodded at her partner. He pumped epinephrine into Colton's veins. Waited. Reemployed the defibrillator.

Another look at the heart monitor. Another frown.

The female paramedic resumed chest compressions while her partner bagged Colton with a manual resuscitator, a phrase that made Maggie think of Francine at the check-out counter. Then they hoisted Colton onto a gurney, grunting with the effort, and rolled him away like luggage bound for a long trip.

"Is he going to be...?" Thom called out as the paramedics reached the end of the aisle. His hand gripped the wooden handle of his mop, seeming to draw comfort from its solidness. Thom was in his twenties, quiet, sensitive, the kind of man who seemed to take on others' pain as his own. His empathy was working overtime. "Is he going to be okay?"

"We'll do our best," the woman called over her shoulder.

Maggie had a feeling that "best" wouldn't be good enough.

Colton hadn't responded to the jumpstart to his heart. His lungs hadn't re-inflated. His heart hadn't regained its muscle memory, nor did he rise up, Lazarus-like, to proclaim the gospel or ask for a side of fries.

She was certain they were carting off an empty shell.

She watched the paramedics take the same path as Zingers Girl: past the shingles vaccine poster, through the front door, across the parking lot, a feeling of helplessness rising like floodwaters. This time, Maggie couldn't swoop in with her receipt and her jerky and her white-lie deception. She couldn't save the day—or even the hour.

Maggie dug her fingernail into her thumb. *Damn it.*

She liked Colton. He wasn't a frequent flier like some of Petrosian's regulars, but he'd come in often enough to be memorable, an easy joke on his lips, a new t-shirt serving as a badge of beef-eating honor around his bulging belly.

That very morning he had tromped up to the counter, his ursine form swaying between a rack of corn pads and a tower of Toblerone, and grinned mischievously. "Today's your lucky day, new girl. You can stop a man from starving to death." He had rubbed his belly like a restaurant Buddha. "Just make up the antibiotic elixir to cure my strep throat—makes it hard to swallow bacon cheeseburgers—and I'll be on my merry, gluttonous way."

And so she had. And so he was.

Until his heart stopped cooperating and he stumbled and fell, struggling to live as shoppers checked off lists and juggled coupons.

Maggie wondered what Colton's last memory was. The face of a beloved family member? The way she had laughed at his terrible knock-knock joke? The half-full shelf of digestive aids perched above his head as the blood stopped pumping through his veins?

Outside the siren complained once more, perhaps chafing under its new payload, and the crowd began to slink away from the invisible outline of the body that seemed to stain the pharmacy's well-worn floors.

Maggie turned to go, unsure of her destination other than "away."

The front door burst open. Levon Petrosian strode in.

For a small man, Petrosian seemed to fill the doorway. He had a slight frame, thinning hair and black eyes perched above a sharp nose. His thin face was banked by jowls that pulled his cheeks chin-ward.

He looked around the room then he began pulling off thin leather gloves, one finger at a time. Never mind the unseasonably warm spring day. Never mind the 80 percent humidity. Petrosian wore the gloves every time he drove, as if he were Cary Grant about to race the cliffside roads of Monaco. He'd told her they were a gift from his wife. That fact alone trumped the trivialities of temperature and barometric pressure.

Petrosian folded the gloves in his hand. "What happened?"

The question was loud enough to be intended for anyone, but his eyes were on Maggie. She swallowed. "Colton Ellis." She stopped, weighed her words. "Looks like a heart attack."

Petrosian nodded. With Colton's beet-red face, apple-shaped body and assortment of health problems, a heart attack was hardly a surprise. "Where? When?"

"Next to the Tums. I'm not sure when it happened. I hadn't been down that way since we opened. I don't know if anyone had."

She glanced at Francine then at Thom and Nan, a young cashier who had just returned from break. They shook their heads. It seemed that part of the store wasn't frequently trafficked.

Petrosian examined his gloves. "He'll recover?"

"Doesn't look good," Francine chimed in. She gave Maggie a look then popped a hip. "He was probably dead before Red tried to play hero and resuscitate him."

Petrosian turned back to Maggie. "You administered CPR?" She nodded. He quartered the gloves, knuckles whitening. "I had an AED on order," he said, referring to the portable device that would allow nearly anyone to deliver a potentially life-saving electrical shock to the heart. Under Thom's fluorescent lights, Petrosian's skin turned seasick-green. He rotated his head to take in the pharmacy's now empty aisles, the detritus left by the paramedics, the drawn faces of those around him. "I had waited for a sale. It seems my thriftiness cost Mr. Ellis."

Chapter 3

The rest of the day dragged. Maggie's mind kept returning to her discovery of Colton, the way his mouth twisted into an expression that lay somewhere between pain and surprise, the futility of her efforts to save him. At five o'clock, she molted her lab coat, hopeful her headache would follow suit.

The headache had begun not long after her run-in with Francine over Zingers Girl, a niggling ache that started at the base of her skull then colonized the rest of her head, nape to forehead, temple to shining temple. She'd been getting headaches on a near daily basis, some dull, some agonizing, ever since...

Maggie stopped herself.

Nope, nope, nope.

No sense in remembering what happened last year. Memory wouldn't bring comfort, and it certainly wouldn't bring peace.

Maggie rubbed her neck and counted out her drawer. She went through the closing routine, placing checks and cash in the bank bag, logging out of the computers, locking up the pharmacy cabinets. Petrosian had disappeared into his office hours earlier, giving Maggie another opportunity at independence. Satisfied that everything had been completed according to her boss's exacting standards, she doused Thom's zombie-creating fluorescents and walked down Aisle 5 past Hostess products that promised a sugary reward or perhaps for some, a meal.

At the front of the store, Francine stood with her back to her till, a leopard print emery board sawing at her thumbnail. She looked up and smirked at Maggie. She dropped the file on the counter and held out her hand, palm up. Maggie dropped the bank bag and key ring onto the fish-white skin and tried not to bristle at the fact that Francine was in charge of securing the store.

Francine was Maggie's senior, both in age and in tenure, yet had only been at Petrosian's a couple of months longer than Maggie. Maggie took in

Francine's talons, the Barbie pink eye shadow harassed by heavy black liner, the sky-high hair. As far as Maggie could tell, Francine's biggest talent was her ability to back-comb her hair.

Francine unzipped the bag and peered inside. "Everything balance out?"

"Yes."

Francine's smirk deepened. Maggie noticed with a jolt of satisfaction that a smear of lipstick hugged the base of her two front teeth. "Even with the cupcake that little brat stole?"

Add incessant nastiness to Francine's list of talents.

Maggie balled her hands into fists then remembered what happened when she lost her temper at her last job. She eased open her fist. "Zingers. And yes, everything's there. Feel free to double-check."

"Oh I will," Francine sniffed, then made good on the threat by fanning out bills and the register report. She began to count softly to herself.

Maggie turned and looked for a friendly face to say her goodbyes. The store was barren, Petrosian sequestered in his office, Nan and Thom already gone. She twisted the bolt of the front door, which had been thrown the moment the *Please Call Again!* sign was hung, and pushed the metal handle. The door bumped against something. She pushed again. The door gave, but only slightly.

For a moment Maggie was certain that a body was blocking the door, that someone else's heart had given out, turning a prospective patron into a human doorstop. Maggie poked her head around the door, raking back fugitive tendrils that had escaped her bun. No body. Simply a brown box set atop the mosaic of earth-toned tiles that formed a giant mortar and pestle at the apron of the entrance.

She gently nudged the door open, stooped and squinted at the label. USA AEDs.

Petrosian's automatic external defibrillator had arrived.

Chapter 4

Maggie stooped to retrieve the box, irony in package form. She hesitated, considering whether to bring the package into Petrosian. Her boss didn't like to be disturbed once he was tucked away in the sanctity of his office, and she was late for an appointment. She lifted the package from the entryway, tucked it beneath her arm and pushed back through the door. Francine looked up from the fan of money before her, her eyes alight with surprise, her body tense. She recovered. Smirked.

"Forget something, Red?"

Maggie strode to the counter and placed the box next to a collection jar that trumpeted *Change for Riley!* in curlicue font. "This came for Mr. Petrosian. Can you make sure he gets it? I'm running late."

Francine huffed and rolled her eyes. "Anything else I can do for you?" Her voice dripped with sarcasm.

"Nope, that'll do it." Maggie gave a dazzling smile and disappeared through the door before Francine could reply.

Outside, she tried to blot out her irritation at Francine, her heartache over the ironic arrival of the AED, the mental folder of images that had begun to flap open. But one by one, memories slotted into her brain.

Colton cooling on the store's bone-colored tiles.

Her hands on Colton's chest.

Her heart beating faster, harder, as if it to make up for the silence within his chest. She mentally bore down on the memories, on the feelings, pushing them aside.

Colton was in the hospital. Colton was getting better. Colton would be just fine. She just had to ignore the disquiet that squatted on her chest like a living thing and get to her cake-tasting appointment before it ended.

Because that's what engaged people did. They cake-tasted. They wedding gown-shopped. They florist-hopped. At least according to Aunt Fiona.

Maggie smiled, reflecting on the proposal.

There had been no request to Pop for her hand in marriage. No bended knee or diamond ring slipped into a glass of champagne (which Maggie had always regarded as a choking hazard). No tearful reply when Constantine popped the question.

Because Constantine hadn't done the popping. Maggie had—sweating and stuttering as she asked Constantine to spend the rest of his life with her. Even now, she wasn't sure she had actually come out with the proposal. She remembered mumbling, choking on her own saliva then wildly gesturing her question in the world's strangest round of charades.

Four words. First word, one syllable.

It was ridiculous and embarrassing and wonderful. It was the next step in a relationship that had been born in a middle school lunch line, nurtured over conversations conducted only in movie quotes, grown into more-than-friends in the shadow of the past two years. It was everything Maggie didn't know she wanted.

After a lifetime of telling herself she'd never marry, of telling herself that "forever" was the real F-word, Maggie was over the moon at the prospect of marrying Constantine. The bridal stuff was another story.

Maggie hated the trappings of weddings. The poufy dress. The rubbery reception chicken. The vows, repeated by rote, promising a fealty she'd already pledged. All of which meant that she had zero interest in a pre-nuptial cake-tasting. The appointment had been an appeasement to Aunt Fiona.

Maggie thought of the bridal tasks ahead, of being prodded into crinoline, forced into conversations about the merits of place cards, creating a Pinterest board. She could practically feel her skin erupting in hives.

She scratched her neck and tried to think positively. *Maybe I'll get into a car accident on the way there.*

Maggie bypassed Francine's white Oldsmobile with its dueling bumper stickers and arrived at her car. She ran her hand along the Studebaker's shiny custard-hued hood and sighed with vehicular love.

The car was a 1962 Studebaker Lark. Manufactured the year her mother was born. Restored the year her mother died.

Maggie thought back to that summer of restoration, that summer of disintegration, her twelve-year-old hands buffing out dings and polishing away pain. The car wasn't just her daily driver. It was her time capsule.

She slid onto the bench seat, turned the key and steered the car toward Butte Hill, the redundantly named landmark that marked the northernmost boundary of Hollow Pine and the entrance to The Estates, a multi-use neighborhood that was heavy on nostalgia and light on authenticity. A neighborhood that happened to be just a half-mile past the home where Constantine's Aunt Polly had lived and her husband had died.

No, not died. Was murdered.

Kaleidoscope images slid into Maggie's mind once again. A dead man with a wide, wet smile spreading crimson beneath his neck. A woman hunted in the night. A hospital stairwell.

Maggie gritted her teeth and squared her shoulders, pushing away the thoughts that gathered, the feelings that threatened. She used to think of the place where she shoved the uncomfortable, the painful, as the Wall. Now she realized she had added to her repertoire of denial, creating a blister around her heart that encapsulated the feelings and memories she wanted so desperately to avoid.

In the aftermath of all that had happened last year, she vowed to be more open to feelings, less likely to hide behind humor and movies and exercise. Now she decided she'd tackle that particular to-do list later. Much later.

She put the car in third and pressed the accelerator, passing a smattering of replica bungalows until she reached a studio-lot-perfect lineup of stores that tried to out-downtown Hollow Pine's real downtown.

The Estates' mini-shopping area.

Maggie circled the block and found a spot in front of a coffee shop with a burlap sign emblazoned with *Oh BEANS* and killed the engine. Constantine's Datsun B210 was already there. So were the cars belonging to his Aunt Polly and her Aunt Fiona. Maggie frowned. She hadn't remembered inviting Aunt Polly or Aunt Fiona. She hadn't remembered inviting anyone.

Maggie forty-fived into the space and climbed out of the car. She walked the half-block to Let Them Eat Cake! then paused at the door to peer through the glass. She could make out Constantine's unruly mop above a trio of cake stands, but little else. She stepped inside.

The bakery looked like a Candyland waypoint.

Pastel cakes loomed over confectionary-colored countertops. Cupcakes climbed trellises of sunshine yellow, mint green and baby blue. Marzipan works of art glistened beneath glass domes.

Maggie sniffed. The air smelled of vanilla and caramelized sugar. Her stomach rumbled. Well, maybe the *tasting* part wouldn't be bad.

"Mags!" Constantine's voice jolted her out of her reverie. "We're over here."

"Gus!" she said, using the nickname only she was allowed. Her heart leapt at the sight of him. Chisel of cheek. Speed bump of stubble. Chocolate brown eyes crinkling into half-moons. Broad shoulders encased in a t-shirt that read *You Are My Density*. She ducked beneath a *chuppah* of faux flowers and joined the small group assembled in front of a cityscape of cake-toppers.

Constantine folded her into his arms. "The sweet shop just got sweeter." He nuzzled her neck and murmured something about her being a sight for sore eyes—and noses—and for a moment, Maggie forgot that anyone else was there.

Aunt Fiona fixed that.

"Hello, sweetheart," she said, peeping around Constantine's shoulder, eyes avid and bright. "I'm so glad I was able to make it."

"It's nice to have everyone here, isn't it?" Aunt Polly piped in. "You forgot to tell us the date and time. Fortunately, I'm friends with the owner's mother so I was able to find out." She beamed and tossed bobbed hair tinted with her signature Haute Tamale hue.

"After all, how can we help you if we're not here?" Fiona said.

"You've got me there," Maggie said.

A fourth woman glided up to the group. She was fiftyish with honey-blonde hair and biceps that rose above doughy skin in response to toting heavy bags of flour. "Who's my bride?" she chirped.

The aunts tittered. Maggie raised her hand. "That would be me. I'm Maggie."

The woman swept Maggie into a long, tight hug. Maggie looked pleadingly at Constantine. He grinned and gave her a thumbs-up.

The woman released Maggie and took her hands. "Maggie!" she exclaimed, enthusiasm matching the store's exclamation point. "I'm Martha. Please, allow me to give you a taste of the possibilities."

A taste of the possibilities?

Martha hooked a hand through her arm and dragged her to a table shaped like a giant cupcake. She motioned for Maggie to sit. Maggie plopped onto a pastel pink stool and tried to arrange her thighs against the oversized muffin in the least suggestive way possible. Constantine, Polly and Fiona gathered behind. Polly put her hand on Maggie's shoulder.

Fiona did the same to the other shoulder and squeezed.

Martha opened her portfolio book. She gasped at a triple-tiered lemon chiffon cake on the opening page and clasped her hands together. "Isn't it adorable?" she asked, as if the cake was a toddler to be gently chucked beneath the chin. She flipped the page. "Oh and this is one of my favorites." Martha continued to page through the album as if it were a baby book. "Of course, we offer a variety of different options to suit any wedding theme. Last year, we recreated the Millennium Falcon with a flourless tort." Constantine shot Maggie a look and clasped his hands together in prayer. Maggie rolled her eyes.

"So when's the wedding?" Martha sing-songed as she plucked a pen from a faux champagne flute and pulled a form toward her.

Maggie twisted the engagement ring on her finger, a thin band of gold-colored plastic topped by a blob of faux pave diamonds. She had insisted that she didn't need a ring. Constantine had insisted that she did and plucked it via mechanical claw from a vending machine at Dinah's Diner. "Um, to be determined?"

Martha's indoor-pale face fell like a soufflé. "Oh. What about the venue?"

Maggie looked at Constantine. He puffed out his cheeks and hoisted his shoulders to his ears. "Also to be determined?" Maggie said, her voice curling into a question.

Martha sucked her teeth and put down her pen. "I don't suppose you have an idea about how many guests?"

Maggie shook her head. The aunts responded to her lack of planning as if Maggie had confessed to a string of serial murders, clutching their necks, muttering prayers for deliverance.

Fiona reached into a purse that could double as an overnight bag and produced a lace-adorned notebook. "I thought this might happen, so I brought along some inspiration."

Fiona dropped the book on the cupcake table. *Maggie's Wedding Book* blazed across the top in fat gold script.

No mention of Constantine. No consultation with Maggie. No surprise. Fiona never seemed sure where her life ended and Maggie's began.

Fiona began to turn the pages, interspersing suggestions about wedding décor with a homily about the importance of proper planning. As Fiona began a chapter titled "Modest Wedding Gowns," a silver platter was thrust beneath their noses.

"Sample?" Martha asked, grinning above an assembly of bite-sized gluten rafts beached on miniscule plates.

Aunt Fiona put aside the wedding planning book, tabbing a page of quilted cakes with a Post-It note festooned with illustrations of wedding gowns, and took a plate. The others did the same.

Maggie forked through a corner of silver-capped frosting and slipped it between her lips. She let herself be overcome with an ecstasy of sugar and butter.

The culinary rapture was cut short by a sigh at her elbow.

Maggie turned. Fiona stabbed the edge of her cake with a tine, put a morsel to her tongue, swallowed then sighed again. She deposited the glossy white plate on the cupcake table and crossed her arms.

"Problem?" Maggie asked.

"I hate to complain," Fiona began. Maggie bit her tongue. An enthusiastic pessimist, Fiona collected grievances like some people collected stamps. "It's just the fondant. It's pretty, but it tastes a bit...pasty."

Maggie swallowed the cake she had tucked into her cheek with an audible gulp. "Well, I think it has a certain..."

"You're not thinking of using buttercream, are you?" Polly parked her fork at the edge of her plate and turned accusing eyes on Fiona.

"And why not?" Fiona asked tartly. "It's a classic."

"If you say so."

Maggie made an excuse about researching cake fillings and stepped away from the brewing storm. She sidled over to Constantine who had begun building a tower with favor boxes. "I have something to tell you," she whispered.

"If it's that you find me unbearably attractive and ache for my touch, you'll have to find new material. I already know that."

She pushed him toward a display of cupcakes. "Something happened at work."

Constantine looked at her. "Something...not good?"

"You could say that."

He drew his brows together, tiny muscles knitting and purling. "You're okay? Nobody...hurt you?"

It seemed Maggie wasn't the only one haunted by the past.

"I'm fine. One of Petrosian's customers isn't. I found him on the floor."

"Dead?"

Maggie tilted her head. "Don't know. I did CPR, the paramedics did their thing then took him away."

"Damn." The power of understatement. "What was the deal?"

"Heart attack, I think."

A sudden swell of voices caused them to turn. Polly, tiny yet imposing in a blue velour jumpsuit, had anchored her hands on her hips. Fiona's arms crossed in front of her chest, turning her peach floral-print jacket into pressed flowers.

"Magnolia?" Fiona called shrilly. "Magnolia, please come here."

Maggie squirmed, not only at the use of her full name but at what it implied. She chanced a look at Fiona's face. It was pinched and red.

Maggie slunk to her side.

"Maggie," Fiona began, "Polly and I would like to know which icing you prefer: classic and delicious buttercream," she indicated a photo in her notebook with a flourish, "or...fondant." She practically dry-heaved the word.

Maggie looked at the icing options then at the women. Polly winked and nodded at the fondant. Fiona's lips turned up in the I'll-know-you'll-do-the-right-thing smile Maggie had seen her whole life.

It was suddenly clear: she wasn't being asked to choose between icings. She was being asked to choose between aunts.

"Well, I..."

The aunts leaned forward. The room suddenly seemed too hot, too close, too *pink*. Maggie cleared her throat. "Can I think about it?"

Wrong answer.

The older women pursed their lips, Polly's becoming a tiny pale circle, Fiona's imploding into a crater of mauve lipstick.

"Of course," Polly said through her teeth.

"It's your wedding," Fiona muttered. Maggie wondered if she actually believed that. Her aunt clinched her sweater then checked the gold-toned watch at her wrist. "It's getting late. I should go."

Polly grabbed the cane she used when she felt especially frail. "I should do the same." She fluffed her hair and adjusted her bra. "I'm meeting Kenny Rogers for drinks."

Maggie nodded. Dr. Kenneth Rogers, cosmetic surgeon, not country music legend, had become a constant in Polly's life, moving from old friend to romantic companion in the months following her husband Howard's death. Maggie often wondered if they had always meant to be together but hadn't become a couple because of the unjust taboo of interracial relationships when they were younger. Or maybe Polly's multiple marriages were the impediment. In any case, they were together and happy.

The aunts shuffled through the store toward the entrance, Maggie, Constantine and Martha trailing behind them like the world's saddest wedding party. The aunts paused at the door, leaned toward each other to give and receive halfhearted hugs and pecks that missed cheeks.

Fiona patted her cardigan as if it were a rescue Chihuahua. "I have some things in my car for you, Magnolia." Maggie winced. She wondered how long the formal moniker—and Fiona's irritation—would last. "Perhaps you could accompany me?"

"Of course."

Maggie and Constantine walked Polly to her car and bade her goodbye, then trotted to Fiona's Honda Civic. Fiona unlocked the car, mined a box from a backseat crammed with dry goods for Maggie's father's food carts. Fiona backed out of the backseat and plunked the box into Maggie's waiting arms.

"More wedding planning books," she said stiffly, "plus leftover fabric and ribbon from when your mother made her bridal gown. Your father found it among some things your mother had put away before she…" Fiona's voice dwindled. She coughed and thrust the box toward Maggie. "I thought you could use some of it for your own wedding dress."

Maggie took the box, bumped open the lid with her wrist and felt inside. Her fingers danced over the books then coarse tulle and smooth satin. "Thanks, Aunt Fiona," she said. And she meant it. Most of what she had left from her mother existed only in her mind. Pop wasn't big on mementos.

Fiona thawed. She allowed Maggie to buss her cheek and bundle her into her sedan. Fiona lowered her window. "I'll call you in a couple of days. We can discuss this frosting nonsense and make an appointment at a seamstress. A florist, too, for that matter. And I'm sure Father Brian will want to start on Pre-Cana."

Pre-Cana, premarital counseling for Catholics preparing for the Sacrament of Marriage. Which probably didn't apply to Catholics marrying outside the Church. Or any church at all. Maggie and Constantine had discussed tying the knot at city hall or even eloping. They just hadn't gotten around to sharing that tidbit with their families.

Fiona started her car and backed out of her space. Polly, who had just pulled out of her own space three slots down, stopped short and impatiently waved Fiona to go ahead. Fiona's hand shot up, signing her own exasperated thanks.

Maggie and Constantine walked to the Studebaker. Maggie opened the trunk, moved the spare tire to the backseat to make room for Fiona's box of wedding goods, and placed the crate inside. Then Maggie and Constantine watched as the women drove down the street, their shoulders hooked in irritation.

"I think that went well," Constantine said.

Chapter 5

The next morning, Maggie arrived at Petrosian's Pillbox with the sun. It had been a restless night, her dreams filled with gaping mouths and defibrillators that wouldn't charge. She was surprised a fondant-clad cake hadn't made a cameo appearance. The tension between Aunt Fiona and Aunt Polly had transferred to her, clinging to mind and body despite her six-mile run and chipper self-talk that she didn't have to choose between icing or aunt.

The problem is theirs, she told herself. *This isn't about me.*

But she never believed the voice that promised absolution. The voice that admonished, the one that blamed and criticized, always held sway.

Despite the superficial detente of their farewell hugs, the aunts were preparing for war, rattling sabers made of flour and sugar. Their battleground: Maggie's attention.

Fiona had been like a mother to Maggie since she was twelve. Polly had shouldered the mantle of motherhood in recent years when geography and experience brought them closer. It was only natural for the women to vie for Maggie's affection.

Somehow that didn't make Maggie feel better.

She pushed open the door. It was just past dawn, sun massaging earth into a pinkish glow, and yet she knew the building would be open. Petrosian's workaholism was legendary. His aversion to locks suggested he hoped it would be contagious.

Maggie made her way past the empty registers—the other employees rarely took the open-door bait—and through a maze of Easter promotional items, pausing to right a stuffed bunny that appeared to be preparing to consume the Peeps roosting beside him. She found Petrosian behind the pharmacy counter at his computer.

Maggie waved. Petrosian nodded, his eyes never leaving his screen. This passed as a sunny greeting in the lexicon of Lev Petrosian.

He continued to tap. Maggie scooted behind the counter and

unshouldered her purse, a bright, poppy-colored satchel purchased during a forced march through Macy's with Fiona, and pulled out the day's supplies: cellphone, insulated lunchbox and just-in-case running shoes. She squirreled away her provisions in a cubby and waited.

Petrosian turned to her. "I'm afraid I have bad news."

"Oh?" Maggie's stomach twisted. She knew what he was going to say. She didn't want to hear it.

"Colton Ellis died," he said.

Her stomach rotated another quarter-turn. She nodded. "You called the hospital?" Personal experience taught her that the staff at St. Theresa's wasn't overly concerned about HIPAA.

"No," he said, removing his glasses and breathing onto the lenses. "I heard it on the radio."

She blinked. "A heart attack is news?"

Petrosian rubbed the lenses on a small white cloth and replaced his glasses. "It is when it happens in a public place. The story was a rebroadcast from your favorite news personality."

"Russ Brock." Saying the name aloud inspired a nausea born of loathing and disgust. "What did *he* have to say?"

"I didn't catch the whole thing. Just that Mr. Ellis had a heart attack and was pronounced dead at the hospital. Then he covered the signs and symptoms of cardiac arrest."

"Mmm." A pretty innocuous newscast. If it had been anyone but Brock. She wondered what angle he was playing.

Petrosian snaked a hand beneath the counter and produced yesterday's package. He placed it on the counter, patted its head. "Francine said you found this after we closed."

Maggie nodded, but said nothing.

"It's the defibrillator I ordered, the proverbial barn door after the horse has escaped." His shoulders sagged. He laid the box to rest beside his computer and bowed his head, an inscrutable expression flitting through his eyes before his lids shuttered. He was silent for several moments then, without another word, circumnavigated the pharmacy counter and walked toward his office at the front of the store.

Workaholism as coping mechanism.

Maggie stood there, gathering her thoughts, calibrating her grief, then followed suit. She dove into work, checking the store's answering machine for refill orders, logging into email to review provider requests, cataloguing stock to ensure that supply would meet demand. Trying not to think about the growing inventory of bodies that seemed to a find a way into her life.

She checked her watch. Time had passed more quickly than she realized. The store was about to open.

Maggie bustled around the pharmacy, combining the leavings of small wastebaskets into the larger one from behind the counter, and rolled the receptacle through the small stockroom that buffered the antiseptic bubble of the pharmacy from the world that lay beyond.

She opened the pharmacy's back door and stepped into the dazzle of morning. The day had already grown warm in the ninety minutes since Maggie's arrival, and she pulled her lab coat away from her body as she dragged the can to the dumpster.

She lifted the lid and hoisted the trashcan to release its load, her face turned away to avoid the stench that came wafting upward, then released the lid with a bang and turned to go.

The bushes to the right of the dumpster rustled.

Maggie froze. The plants moved again.

Scrape. Scrape. Scraaaaaaaaaaaape.

Wood against wood? Fabric against ground?

Fingers against casket?

An involuntary shudder snaked up Maggie's spine. "Who's there?" she called.

The base of the bush shifted, furtive and sly. Her body went DEFCON 2. Inconveniences like previous attempts on her life made her jumpy.

She felt for her keys, her phone.

Her only accessory was the increasing pace of her heart.

"Come out," Maggie called again, her voice commanding a strength she didn't feel.

The bush, topped with budding leaves that made the plant look as though it was wearing a toupee, swayed. Maggie braced herself for whatever horror, whatever fight, had come her way.

A small dog emerged from the foliage.

He plopped his rump on the ground and ducked his head. Circumflex brows rose and fell above soft brown eyes as he studied her.

Maggie released the breath she didn't realize she was holding. She placed the trash can on the ground and squatted. "Hey, little guy. What are you doing here?"

As if in answer, the dog rose, turned tail, nosed around the bush and proffered a half-eaten sandwich, dropping it to the ground and nosing it toward Maggie. Maggie was pretty sure it was the ham and Swiss she saw Thom chomping in the breakroom yesterday.

"Ah, sampling our buffet." Maggie chuckled softly. "You've got good taste."

The dog cocked his head and wagged his tail, mottled brown and white fur Swiffering the dirt.

"What's your name, buddy?" Maggie approached the animal and put out an exploratory hand to check for a collar, to feel for tags, ready to retract her fingers in case he changed his mind about being friendly. He sniffed her hand then licked it.

Friendliness confirmed.

Maggie ruffled the fur matted at his neck. Lack of tags also confirmed.

No surprise. Though well socialized and pro-people, the prominent ribs and mangy fur pointed toward longtime stray rather than recent runaway.

Maggie rubbed the dog's ear, his neck. Even these areas seemed bony, cartilage tenting against skin. She began a mental list of her lunchbox—cold pizza, snickerdoodles—when the door behind her banged open.

"What in the—?" Francine's nasal drone came drifting on the air like a new stench. She stopped dead, a small trash can in hand, stared at the animal and did the Francine hip tilt. "First the girl, now a dog. You got a thing for strays, Red?"

Francine pivoted her pelvis back into neutral then teetered forward on Mini Mouse shoes—red wedges with bows at the toe. Her foot dipped into an unseen hole, corrected, then continued to carry her forward like a wobbly, top-heavy tank.

She planted herself ten feet from Maggie and raised the trash can above her head. She waved her arms like an Air Dancer outside a car dealership, the can slicing through air. "Go on, you mangy mutt," she yelled at the dog. "Git. Git!"

The dog regarded her curiously then wagged his tail tentatively.

"I said *git!*" Francine waved more furiously. The trash can lapped against her upturned wrist, clanging a chorus of silver-toned bangles. The dog lowered his head but stayed put, continuing to thump his tail.

Francine's mouth sphinctered into a tiny hole. She charged the dog, banging her trash can like a drum. "Go on! Go on!" She raised the trash can over her head, her eyes focused on the mound of fur cowering before her, and swung the receptacle toward the ground like a scythe.

"Francine, no!" Maggie moved to block Francine's blow, but the dog was too fast. He took off, knocking against Francine and sending her out of one of her shoes. The dog scampered around the building and bolted across the street. The path of Zingers Girl, the paramedics and the body of Colton Ellis. The path to escape, both temporary and final.

Maggie rounded on Francine, pulse thundering through her ears. "You—" She could scarcely hear her own voice over the torrent of blood rushing through her skull. "You horrible—"

Francine retrieved her orphan shoe, shoved her foot to the hilt then pushed by Maggie. She emptied her can into the gaping maw of the dumpster then slammed down the lid. "You got your panties in a wad over that dog? I did you a favor. That mutt is just like that girl: you feed it, it's just going to keep coming back. Like I told you before: stay in your lane." Then she turned and flounced inside, the can bouncing against her Polyester-wrapped thighs.

Maggie waited for the fog of rage to clear, quelling an urge to chase after Francine and wrestle her head-first into the dumpster. She took two cleansing breaths and surveyed the area behind Petrosian's. She spied parked cars, a copse of trees, three candy bar wrappers and a crumpled can of Old Milwaukee.

No pooch.

"Here, doggie, doggie," Maggie called feeling vaguely ridiculous.

She had never thought of herself as a dog person. Never thought of herself as a pet person, period, although Constantine's hamster Miss Vanilla proved to be the exception. As a child, Maggie had no pets. Her father proclaimed them unhygienic. Her mother was allergic.

Maggie put her fingers beside her premolars and whistled like Pop taught her, hoping the pooch would magically appear from his hidey hole. The soft purr of Franklin Avenue traffic was the only reply.

Maggie turned and dragged the trashcan back to the building, her outrage at Francine building at each step. She fantasized about marching up to Francine's register. Confronting her. Hiding her can of Aqua Net. The possibilities were endless.

Maggie threw open the door and charged into the stockroom, the brilliance of early day still in her eyes. Maggie slammed the trash can beside the door, auditioning what she'd say to Francine, and walked toward the pharmacy counter.

As she approached the chorus line of chairs in the waiting area, their metal feet akimbo like the Rockettes mid-kick, she saw something tucked beside the blood pressure machine. Knee-high. Lumpy. Beige. She blinked the sun from her eyes again, cursed Thom and his energy-efficient fluorescents, and refocused. It was only when the lump gurgled that she knew:

A woman lay motionless on the floor.

Chapter 6

Maggie dropped to her knees and put her hands on the prone form. The woman shifted in response to the movement, revealing another lump: a teenage girl crumpled at her side.

Calm rolled over Maggie like a mist. She hadn't always been the Hemingway grace-under-pressure type, but time—and the world—had changed that.

Maggie performed the same first aid rituals she'd practiced on Colton: shout for help, assess the situation, feel for a pulse, check for airway obstruction. Except now her efforts were doubled, her hand and ear moving quickly between the two female forms. Determining if they were alive. Trying to keep them that way.

She found a pulse, weak and thready, at the carotid artery of both the woman and the girl. She put her ear to their mouths, shutting out the Muzak rendition of "Dancing with Myself" that streamed from the speakers, and listened.

Nothing.

Then the music of inhalation and exhalation—labored, shallow, hitching—first from the girl, then from the woman.

Maggie smoothed the hair from each face. Their skin was red and mottled, their expressions twisted into masks of agony. Maggie looked closer. She recognized them.

Maggie shouted again for an ambulance—where was Francine? where was Petrosian?—and checked again for obvious injuries. No weeping bullet hole. No gaping stab wound. No blossoming bruise or accusatory abrasion to tell the tale of mistreatment endured and escaped.

Thom sprinted down the aisle and skidded to a stop. He looked wide-eyed at the scene. "Are they—" His question shimmered in the air between them.

"No," Maggie said, "but they might be if that ambulance doesn't get here."

Thom put a hand to his mouth and kneaded his lips. "I just can't—I just can't—"

Before he could say what he just couldn't, Petrosian appeared as if by magic. He looked from Maggie to Thom, skin blanching to match his lab coat. "What's going on?"

"Not sure," Maggie replied. "I found them like this. They're breathing, but not well."

And maybe not for long.

The pulse of a siren cut off his reply. Within moments, the snare drum of footsteps, a tambourine of equipment and keys, clanged through the store. Yesterday's first responders rounded the corner.

The female paramedic looked at Maggie, lifted a brow. So many questions in such little movement.

"I found them like this," Maggie repeated. "They're breathing, but something's wrong." The paramedic gave her a look that said *Thanks, Captain Obvious* and got to work.

Once again, Maggie looked on as the paramedics pulled implements from bags and endeavored to stabilize the fallen. Once again, Maggie wondered what had happened.

Had the women been cut down by heart attacks like Colton Ellis, their hearts arresting in the cardiac version of synchronized swimming? Had they both been stricken by illness—severe food poisoning, fever, or raging infection?

Francine and Nan joined the scene, the former wearing a frown so permanent it was as if it had been tattooed to her face, the latter looking worried and anxious, her long brown hair curtaining the sides of her young, pale face. Together, the group watched in silence as the paramedics stabilized then carted the women away, precious cargo atop yellow Stryker gurneys. In the silence that followed, Petrosian turned to Maggie. "Tell me exactly how you found Mary and Riley."

Maggie's neurons fired. Of course. The Whitleys.

Maybe it was the chaos of the moment, maybe it was the anguish that had twisted their faces. Maggie hadn't immediately pegged the unconscious woman and her teenage daughter as Pillbox customers.

Like Colton Ellis, Maggie had helped the Whitleys during her brief tenure at the pharmacy. Unlike Colton Ellis, the Whitleys were quiet, subdued, nearly invisible in their mother-daughter beige-and-cream ensembles.

"I came back from emptying the trash and found them on the floor."

"Unconscious?" Petrosian asked.

"Yes. Barely breathing, weak pulse."

"So not a heart attack."

"Hard to say." She paused. "It would seem strange—and strangely coincidental—for two people to simultaneously have a heart attack the day after Colton Ellis died of one."

Petrosian nodded, a short jab of his head.

"Does this mean we get the day off?" Francine demanded. "I can't concentrate after all this drama. Not two days in a row."

Petrosian closed his eyes and breathed deeply. "We'll keep the store open, but please feel free to take a personal day if you'd like."

A look of satisfaction crawled across Francine's face. "Great, I'll get my things and be back in the morning." She whirled on her Minnie Mouse wedges and pranced off.

Petrosian looked at the remaining employees. "Anyone else need to take time off?" Their silence was answer enough. "Very well. Let's get back to work and do our best to move forward despite the..." He looked down at the spot where the Whitleys had lain. "Circumstances."

Nan and Thom returned to their posts. Petrosian stepped behind the counter, and Maggie followed, watching her boss. His posture was ramrod straight, but his shoulders sloped. He tapped his keyboard. Shuffled things on the counter. Then he turned to Maggie.

"I'm concerned," he said.

"About Mary and Riley?"

"Yes. And about the fact that in two days, you've come upon three people who've collapsed in the pharmacy."

Panic scrabbled at Maggie's throat. "My discovering them was bad luck. Someone else would have found them if I hadn't." She hated the defensiveness that tinged her voice. Hated herself for the overwhelming urge to justify, to explain, to shift blame.

Petrosian brushed away non-existent dust from his keyboard. "Did you help the Whitleys recently?"

Maggie felt her skin flush. "I—um—" The rest of her sentence disappeared along with her memory.

Had she helped Mary the day before? Or perhaps the day before that? Mary came in weekly to fill prescriptions for her daughter whose poor health was bolstered by a battery of medications, but details of the pair's last visit slipped through Maggie's mind like water. "I don't remember."

Petrosian folded his hands. "And Colton Ellis? Did you help him?"

Maggie nodded eagerly. She knew this one. "Yes, I helped him before he—before..." She stopped nodding.

Petrosian let the unsaid hang in the air then unclasped his hands. "Most of your tasks involve assisting me, helping with labeling, insurance claims, et cetera. Of course, now you have more latitude, more freedom." He paused, his mouth moving as if trying on words for shape and size. "I'm wondering if it's possible that you've made a mistake."

"Mistake?" Maggie laughed, but there was no humor behind the sound. "I may be new at this job, but I'm not exactly a newbie in the drug world."

"I'm no stranger to your storied career in pharmaceutical development, Ms. O'Malley, but this is a different world with a different set of challenges and risks." He turned his hawk eyes on her. "You make a mistake in development before the testing phase, and it's the study that suffers, not the patient."

A flush trellised her neck. "I assure you, Mr. Petrosian, I made no mistakes."

"The timing is just a little..." He consulted his mental thesaurus. "Coincidental. You begin working more independently, three customers fall ill in the pharmacy."

She wanted to continue to protest, to remind him that she worked under his supervision, that the proverbial buck stopped with the man whose name graced the building. Instead she dropped her head. He was right. Colton's heart attack and the discovery of the unconscious Whitleys coincided perfectly with her new independence behind the counter.

Despite her long history as an unrepentant perfectionist, she couldn't be positive that she'd counted correctly, measured precisely, mated the appropriate label to its intended bottle. Hell, she couldn't even remember if she'd helped Mary Whitley within the past week.

She reached back and touched the base of her skull, thinking of the nagging headaches, the persistent fuzziness that seemed to cloud both recollection and reason, the events that had created a hole in her head—and her memory.

Petrosian gave a smile that didn't touch his eyes. "Don't worry, Ms. O'Malley. We'll check the records, do a physical inventory. I'm sure we'll discover that everything is in order."

Chapter 7

Maggie spent the remainder of the day checking the stockroom. Although small, the back room, which housed the employee bathroom and an emergency eye wash station, was crammed with boxes of medication, cases of sundries, extra sales racks and a carton of wrapping paper that looked older than Maggie. As Maggie combed through the boxes, Petrosian mirrored her actions digitally, digging through the computer to compare recent sales with current inventory.

Conclusion one: Maggie had indeed helped Colton Ellis on the day he died, but not the Whitleys, who had been in two days earlier when Mary purchased hay fever medication.

Conclusion two: The pharmacy's inventory, both physical and computerized, jived with prescriptions filled over the past six weeks.

Maggie and Petrosian breathed twin sighs of relief. The collapse of three store patrons had been coincidence rather than error. They could return to work with clear consciences and untarnished databanks.

At six thirty, Maggie grabbed her purse and her lunchbox from the cubby and stood awkwardly at her boss's elbow. Petrosian cut his eyes to the vintage clock that read *Time to Take Your Vitamins.* "Leaving early, Ms. O'Malley?"

The pharmacy had closed ninety minutes before.

"Yes, I have, ah, somewhere to be." She prayed he wouldn't ask where.

Petrosian frowned, as if the idea of a life outside of work was a foreign concept like time travel or attractive pleated pants. Finally he nodded. "Have a good evening."

Maggie jogged to the Studebaker, turned the key and eased the three-on-the-tree gearshift into first. She was late. Make that *very* late. But like the cake-tasting appointment, this was an excursion Maggie wasn't eager for.

Ten minutes later—everything in Hollow Pine was ten minutes

away—she pulled into the parking lot of GymRatz. She cut the engine and put her head on the steering wheel. Maggie was a runner, not a gym-goer, although the events of last year had left her unable to jog more than six miles at a time, forcing her to leave her marathon goals in the dust. She imagined indoor exercise to be the tenth circle of hell, guarded by a leotard-clad Jane Fonda and replete with grunting men who shoveled dry protein powder into their mouths between sets.

She began to catalog possible excuses for ditching the gym when she heard the tickle of nails on the car's window. She looked up. Ada stood there expectantly, her long dark hair looped into a high ponytail, her twenty-something skin scrubbed clean of makeup. Ada gestured to her watch and said something in Spanish that Maggie guessed wasn't well wishes for a happy equinox, then made frantic summoning motions. Maggie nodded, grabbed her bag from the backseat and clambered out.

"What was that, a pre-Spinning nap?" Ada asked once Maggie had emerged, grabbing her elbow and hustling her toward the dumbbell-shaped building. "We're late."

"Sorry, work was—"

"Yeah, yeah, crazy, busy, whatever." She hustled Maggie through the door, snagged a visitor's pass for Maggie at the front counter, then pushed Maggie toward the locker room. "Just be glad that neither of us is still working at Madame Trousseau's Lingerie."

Madame Trousseau's, the employment life raft Maggie scrabbled onto after Rxcellance sank. It was where she'd merchandised camisoles, fitted bras, nurtured a friendship with Ada and discovered her inner rebel. After years of being the good girl, the careful girl, the girl who took up less space and commanded less attention, Maggie followed the path she'd embarked on in the days following the fallout from Rxcellance, standing up not just for right, not just for others, but for herself.

Rxcellance had been the test. Madame Trousseau's had been the proving ground. She thought of Colton and the Whitleys and wondered what Petrosian's would be.

Ada opened the locker room door. The whir of hairdryers and a whiff of baby powder-scented deodorant floated out. "Now, hurry. The Boulder doesn't like latecomers."

"*The Boulder?*"

"As in mightier-than-the-Rock. That's what they call Sloane, the Spinning instructor."

Maggie concentrated on not throwing up in her mouth and made her way into the bowels of the locker room. She shed her work clothes and struggled into a sports bra, tank top and Lycra tights. Then she laced her running shoes—Ada said going sans cycling shoes would be fine, although most in the class would be wearing specialty kicks—and stuffed everything she wasn't wearing into the locker.

Showtime.

Maggie trailed Ada to the Spinning room, her anxiety climbing with her pulse. Forgoing the trail in favor of the gym had been Ada's idea. Since Ada had joined the police academy, she hadn't just become a devotee of the gym but an evangelist, spreading the good word of burpees, box jumps and Spinning tap-backs to anyone who would listen.

"You've got to shred before you wed, chica," Ada had told Maggie.

"Shred?" Maggie had replied, examining her lanky frame. "Shred what?"

Ada rolled her eyes. "Okay, so maybe you don't need to lose pounds, but it wouldn't hurt to firm up what everyone's going to be looking at when you're up there at the altar."

Maggie hazarded a glance at her backside, which hugged the tops of her thighs like a truculent toddler. Even if she and Constantine didn't go for a traditional wedding, maybe Ada had a point.

They followed signs to the SpinCycle, which sounded more like a nausea-inducing theme park ride than an exercise class, and slipped through the door. The entire class, all atop stationary bicycles, turned to look at them. Ada waved. Maggie tried to hide behind the water cooler.

Sloane, aka The Boulder, was a powerfully built woman with slick-backed hair and a headset. She jerked her chin ceiling-ward. "Welcome, new girl," she purred into the mike. "I'll give you one free tardy. After that, you'll have to make up the mileage after class." The other cyclists roared. Maggie laughed nervously, unsure whether the instructor was kidding or whether she'd be made to sit in the corner and pedal. Was there gym detention? Did GymRatz have a principal? Did Ada have a hall pass that prevented her from accruing tardies?

Maggie zigzagged through the maze of bicycles, quickly adjusted the handlebars and saddle, and mounted the bike next to Ada. She put her feet into the pedals' cages and began to pump.

The music swelled. Sloane, muscular and gleaming as she stared at her form in the mirrored walls, roared orders. The cyclists complied, standing to pedal, taking moments of semi-rest, pouring on the steam once again.

"Who's a freak for SpinCycle?" Sloane demanded.

"We are!" the class bellowed.

"Who's a freak for SpinCycle?" Sloane pointed into the mirror. Maggie looked behind her to see who the instructor was talking to. "You," Sloane thundered. "New girl. Who's a freak for SpinCycle?"

"Um, I am?" Maggie said tentatively. "I'm a freak for SpinCycle?"

Sloane pumped her fist into the air. "Yeah!"

Emboldened by the praise, Maggie sat up straighter and pumped her legs harder. Sweat snaked down her spine into the waistband of her tights. Her heart pounded. The blood thrummed through her head. Her legs ached and shook.

In short: she felt great.

Maggie leaned into the feeling, letting rational thought wash away beneath a flood of sweat and endorphins. This was why she exercised. This was why she ran. Not to shed pounds or firm up, but to quiet her mind while her body moved.

She was just getting into the groove, standing on the pedals as the techno beat crested the hill of a crescendo, when she felt a tap on her shoulder. She turned. A blonde with a perfect face and matching physique stood at Maggie's elbow.

The woman thrust a pair of women's underwear into Maggie's face. "You dropped these!" she shouted over the music.

Maggie began to shake her head. Of course she didn't drop the underwear, which were ragged, washed to translucency and nearly as large as her head.

Then she saw it: MO. The initials she had inked into the waistband of every item of clothing, a vestigial habit borne of Fiona's fastidiousness.

"Oh!" Maggie plucked the granny panties from Spinning Class Barbie's perfectly manicured fingers. "They must have clung to my tights when I did laundry, ha ha!"

The woman gave a frozen smile and backed away as though Maggie might be dangerous. Maggie crammed the underwear into her sports bra and resumed pedaling, her face the approximate temperature of the surface of the sun. "Maybe next time I'll bring my whole laundry basket," she muttered under her breath. "Do a little multitasking."

Thirty minutes later, the music ended and Maggie leaned on her handlebars. Ada dismounted and strode up to Maggie's bike. She put a hand on her hip. "So what did you think?"

Maggie resisted the urge to mop her face with the underwear ruffling beneath her tank top. "I think I'm addicted."

"Pretty great, right? You'll have thighs of steel for marching down the aisle. I'm going to hit the weights then head home. Same time tomorrow?"

"Absolutely."

Ada gave Maggie a squeeze around her shoulders then slipped past the army of stationary cycles and jogged out of the SpinCycle. Maggie heaved herself off the bicycle seat. Her right foot caught on the pedal and she came crashing down. She pulled her foot free, momentarily relieved that she was unhurt and disaster had been averted, then watched in horror as her bike tipped onto its neighbor, beginning a chain reaction in which each bicycle slammed into the next.

Bang! Bang! Bang!

The bicycles cascaded down the row like dominos, the clatter and scrape of metal echoing on the studio's walls. Maggie gaped helplessly as her makeshift Rube Goldberg machine continued to chug along. Bike. Bike. Bike. Speaker. Potted plant. Wall.

The silence that rose in the aftermath was almost more deafening than the percussion of metal on metal. Maggie chanced a look around her. The room was empty, save for Sloane, who stood motionless, mouth open, beside her metal steed.

"I am so—" Maggie began, an apology on her lips, a quick calculation of damages running through her brain.

Sloane threw back her head and laughed. "I don't allow kids in here because rug rats are reckless and messy. I had no idea a grown woman could do so much damage. That was the most spectacular disaster I've ever seen."

Spectacular disaster. A perfect summation of Maggie.

Sloane jogged toward Maggie and began righting the equipment. She checked out her perfect form, her sculpted cheeks, her pneumatic lips in the studio mirror, then turned to Maggie. "What's your name, new girl?"

"Maggie."

The Boulder shot out her hand. "Glad to meet you, Maggie. I have a feeling you're going to make my class a lot more interesting."

Maggie took her hand and laughed. She had a knack for interesting.

After a quick shower and a wide berth around a woman who used the locker room hand dryer to dry her nether regions, Maggie changed, collected her things and headed to her car.

The Studebaker wallflowered in the corner of the lot away from the other vehicles, its pristine paint protected by wide swaths of asphalt and gym-goers interested in accumulating steps on machines rather than in parking lots. Maggie stooped to unlock the car. Stopped. Something obscured the lock.

She squatted for a better look. Red viscous liquid dripped from the keyhole. Her car seemed to be bleeding.

Revulsion, sharp and primitive, rose in her belly. A wave carried it up her throat, spilling bitter bile onto her tongue. The possibilities streamed into her head, her own Litany of Saints.

Human blood.

Animal blood.

Accidental injury.

Malicious intention.

No good option.

No escape.

Her head began to thump again and her vision blurred. Maggie grabbed for the handle, her knuckle swooping through the smear of thickening red.

An odor wafted upward. She expected to smell the metallic bite of iron, to feel the coagulating liquid flux beneath her touch. Instead she got a whiff of tomato and vinegar, and the red blob remained congealed.

Maggie frowned. She ran a finger through the globule and brought it to her eyes. She gave an exploratory sniff. Ketchup.

What the—?

Her eyes roved the surface of her car, searching for more insults by condiment. A white leaf of paper peeped beneath the driver's side windshield wiper.

Maggie tugged the sheet from its rubber paperweight, massaged it between thumb and forefinger as if assessing a sheet's weight. Standard copier paper, folded into quarters. Maggie peeled it open, steeling herself for the gruesome fruit she suspected lay inside.

The paper contained a single sentence and a signature.

I'm back! ☺

—Miles

Chapter 8

Maggie felt as if her blood had turned to ice.

Miles. Mercurial. Unpredictable. Dangerous.

He was the son of the president of Rxcellance, the company at which Maggie had cut her teeth in pharmaceutical development. He was the man who had tormented her and others for fun and profit. He was the reason her stomach turned every time she smelled men's cologne.

Maggie had thought his reign of terror had ended along with his job and his freedom. Now he had crawled out from whatever rock under which he had been hiding, from whatever prison cell in which he'd been languishing, to start the game anew.

How he'd found Maggie was a mystery. The why was obvious.

He wanted to hurt Maggie. To punish her. To make her pay for helping put him away.

Maggie crumpled the note and shoved it into her gym bag. She withdrew her sweaty tank top and used it to wipe the ketchup from the lock. She tried to insert the key. It bounced around, dancing in her shaking hand. She swung the gym bag onto her back and used both hands to steady the key. It shuddered up and down, left then right before finally sliding home. Maggie twisted it. The lock leapt up.

Maggie slid onto the bench seat, locked herself in and drove home, her mind on past conspiracies, old grudges and another door: the entrance to her old apartment, inked in blood that would never wash clean.

Home, the third address in as many years to earn that title, was a rented bungalow at the bottom of a cul-de-sac on the town's eastside. Canary yellow with shutters painted a blue-purple that Constantine insisted on calling "blurple," the house had the benefit of being easy to describe to pizza delivery drivers.

Maggie pulled into the driveway and Constantine bounded out to meet her wearing a t-shirt that read *This Attraction Is Closed*. He scooped her out of the car and carried her into the house.

This had become their tradition since their engagement. Maggie would arrive home. Constantine would carry her over the threshold, nuzzling her neck, calling her *"cara mia"* in his best Gomez Addams impression.

"How was work? How was the gym?"

She hesitated, unwilling to start the evening with bad news, unsure if she was trying to protect Constantine or herself. "Not so good. And not so good."

He placed her on her feet in the small foyer and origamied his arms across his chest. "How not so good?"

"Well, two more customers collapsed in the store. And Miles left a love note on my car at the gym."

Constantine gaped. "Miles? As in Miles Montgomery, son of the owner of the company formerly known as Rxcellance? What's he doing here? What's he doing *anywhere*?"

"He's in our little corner of the Midwest to torment me. But that's just a guess."

Constantine's face darkened. "What did the note say?"

Maggie dragged a hand through her gym bag and brought out the crumpled paper. Constantine flayed it open. Read. He looked up. "It's a little light on content."

"But not context. He'd coated the Studebaker's keyhole with ketchup, which happens to look a lot like blood."

Constantine crushed the paper into a wad. "A hemoglobin trip down memory lane. A little reminder of the gift he impaled to your door?"

Maggie felt a shockwave begin at the epicenter of her spine. She rubbed her arms briskly, relegating quakes to tremors. "At least he used a dupe rather than the real thing."

Constantine looked at her full-on. "This time. We know what he's capable of."

She knew, God, how she knew.

"I hate to state the obvious..." Constantine said. "Actually, that's not true. I love to state the obvious. But shouldn't you call up former rodeo clown and current cop Austin Tacious?"

Maggie plucked the furrowed paper from Constantine's hand. "His name is Austin Reynolds," she said of the ex-boyfriend with whom she now shared a zip code, "and he was a bull rider. And, no, I shouldn't. He's a homicide detective, remember?"

"Oh, right. Guess we'll wait until after you're murdered to contact him."

Gallows humor, Constantine's favorite portal to denial, his own Wall behind which he shoved pain and worry.

"Miles isn't going to murder me. He's just going to torture me for old time's sake." She showed her teeth, more grimace than smile. Constantine frowned, his shoulders climbing to kiss his ears.

She put a hand behind his neck and gave it a gentle squeeze. "Don't worry. If I get another condiment-accompanied nastygram, I'll contact the police, maybe get a restraining order."

"Perfect. Miles is a big respecter of paperwork."

Maggie dropped her hand to her side. "What exactly do you want me to do?"

"I don't know," he said softly, finding the runaway hand, knitting his fingers through hers. "Stay safe? Never get hurt again? Live forever?"

Maggie smiled, genuinely this time. "I'll do my best on all counts."

She tossed her purse and gym bag on a battered entryway table and plunked onto a rust and gold sofa overrun with riotous paisley. A hand-me-down from Pop. A reminder of her childhood.

Constantine sank down beside her. "Tell me about the other not-so-good news. You said more customers collapsed at Petrosian's?"

She nodded. "A mother and daughter. I found them lying on the floor unconscious and struggling to breathe."

"Like the other customer—" He waved his hand in the air as if trying to crank-start his brain. "Colton something?"

"Ellis—and maybe. Although I hope it ends better for the mother and daughter." She swallowed. "We got news this morning that Colton Ellis died."

Constantine blew out a puff of air. "I'm sorry, Mags. You did your best."

Maggie wondered about that. Maybe if she'd spotted him a little sooner, pumped his chest a little longer, remembered how she'd handled his medication, he would still be alive.

"The whole thing gives me a bad feeling," she said, her voice whisper-soft. "Like this is all more than a coincidence. Like a mistake was made."

"A mistake? In medication?" Constantine dropped his voice to match hers. "By *you*?"

"Petrosian and I pored over the records, did a physical inventory of what was on hand." Defensiveness had sneaked back into her voice, belying her words, stealing her certainty. "Everything was in order."

"So why does your face look like that?"

"Because I can't remember."

"Can't remember what?"

She pressed her fingertips into her temples. "What I did. What I didn't do. My role on the days that Colton Ellis and the Whitleys came into Petrosian's. I remember helping Colton, broad stroke stuff. But the specifics? It's all a little foggy."

An eleven formed between Constantine's brows. "You've been foggy for a while. Testy, too. In fact, I'd say you haven't been yourself since...since what happened."

What happened.

Both of them euphemized the act, nicknamed it, dancing around the attack that had left Maggie unconscious—and later, unclear. They hadn't always avoided naming the assault, calling out the assailant, railing against the violence and all that followed. Yet as time passed, so did Maggie's willingness to talk about it. It was classic Maggie; if she didn't think about it, maybe it didn't exist.

"You know it's ironic, right?" Constantine said gently. "The founding member of the Hypochondriac Association of America refusing to see a doctor?"

"Cemeteries are full of people who were accused of hypochondria," she said, jutting her chin. "Besides, I'm not refusing to go to the doctor. I'm just waiting for the right time."

"Like your funeral?" He put his hands on her shoulders. "Come on, Mags. You've got to go in, see what's behind the headaches, the fuzziness, the irritability."

"I don't have to do anything," she said irritably, "and I'm not irritable."

"Of course not. I'm just worried about you. Like, really worried." Constantine pulled her in for a kiss. "I almost forgot. I have some good news." He paused dramatically. "I'm gainfully employed."

"That's wonderful! Tell me everything."

"You know how it's been hard for me to find a job ever since I quit Tech Inc. and moved to Hollow Pine?" She nodded. "Well, now I'm consulting for Tech Inc.!"

Maggie tilted her head. "Wait, what? You're consulting for the company you left and swore you'd never return to?"

"Exactly. Except now that I'm an independent subcontractor I get to call my own shots. For example, I can now work half-days."

"And by half-days you mean twelve hours?"

"Well, yes, but I can also work remotely, which gives me more time to hang out with my favorite human."

She opened her mouth to ask more about the job when her phone sounded, a custom ringtone with De Niro's voice from *Taxi Driver*: "You talkin' to me?"

She dashed across the room and spelunked in her purse for her cell. She pulled it free of Post-It notes, Luna bars and expired coupons and checked the screen, certain that Pop's broad, red face would be smiling back. Instead, Levon Petrosian's profile picture popped up.

She tried to remember the last time Petrosian had called her at home. She came up with never. Had he found someone else unconscious in the store? Discovered an error she had made? Decided that her propensity for finding bodies was bad for business?

"This is Maggie," she said in her most professional voice.

"Ms. O'Malley, this is Mr. Petrosian."

Always Mr. Petrosian. Never Levon or Lev, as Polly affectionately called him. He cleared his throat. "I'm wondering if you can come in early tomorrow. I have some things I wish to discuss with you."

She swallowed. "Discuss?"

"Yes, recent events I believe warrant a conversation. Can you come in at six thirty?"

That sounds awful, she thought. "That sounds great," she said. "I'll see you then."

She ended the call and placed the phone on the entryway table, her mind already tabulating the terrible possibilities that were sure to come.

Chapter 9

Maggie was up before her alarm. She kicked her legs over the bed and slipped quietly into the shower, losing herself in the fragrant lather of shampoo, letting the steady beat of the pulsating showerhead drum out worries about Petrosian, Miles, what she had forgotten and what it might mean.

Constantine was still asleep when she emerged, one arm thrown possessively over her side of the bed, the other canoodling the My Pillow Polly had gotten him for Christmas.

She slid open the closet door and reviewed the selection: a tower of jeans in varying degrees of ruin, a stack of old t-shirts and a smattering of items she was certain a catalog writer would christen "corporate casual." She pulled a skirt and sleeveless top from the corporate casual section, holdovers from her days at Rxcellance, and shimmied into the clothes, checking for taco stains and coffee blooms as she smoothed her outfit into place.

She crept to the small dressing table abutting the bathroom door, plaited her hair into a single braid, then gave each eye a swipe of mascara she suspected had expired. Five minutes later, freshly brewed coffee in hand, Maggie bustled through door and into the hard blue of an early spring morning.

She arrived at Petrosian's Pillbox breathless and keyed up not only about the upcoming conversation, but the singular sensation that she was being watched.

She'd taken a circuitous path to work, her eyes glued to the rearview mirror to spot any car that followed too closely, that tailed her for too long. No dice. The only other vehicles on the road were a vintage Cadillac driven by an old woman and a work truck stuffed with four men who already looked ready for a coffee break.

No Miles. No threat. No blood.

That's what her rational mind told her. Her limbic system had something else to say. She'd been dressed for ten minutes and had already sweat through her light cotton shell.

She ignored the warning flares sent up by body and mind and wove her way through the store to the pharmacy counter where Petrosian stood frowning into his computer screen. "Good morning, Ms. O'Malley. I'll be with you in a moment."

Maggie pretended to check her phone for important messages, hoping her veneer of relaxed patience was convincing. Petrosian pushed the keyboard away and cleared his throat. Maggie waited for whatever would come next. A list of her errors. Proof that her actions had harmed three pharmacy patrons. Secrets that her Alexa hub had recorded and then emailed to her boss. Petrosian simply looked at her.

She met his gaze, set her shoulders. "You had something to talk with me about?"

"Yes. It's been on my mind for a while, but your recent behavior has compelled me to go from thought to action."

The glimmer of a headache announced its intention. "I'm listening."

"I've decided to open an additional pharmacy near The Estates. Business has been good and expansion will allow me to work toward a more secure future and, eventually, give me more time with my wife." He paused and sipped *soorj*, Armenian coffee, from a white demitasse. "I need someone to help run this store while I bring the new store online. After what happened with Mr. Ellis and the Whitleys, I think you're up to the task. You showed remarkable calm and decisiveness."

Maggie tried to hide her surprise. She wasn't being fired. She wasn't asked to recount details of the previous weeks in a test of memory and competency. She was being promoted to a position of trust and authority. "Thank you so much, Mr. Petrosian. I'm so grateful." She paused. "But I'm a technician, not a pharmacist."

Petrosian smiled. "I'm aware of that, Ms. O'Malley. I'm also aware that you're taking classes at the university to earn your Doctor of Pharmacy and in a few years' time will be a pharmacist. I'm simply asking you to handle everyday tasks as I get the new store up and running."

Maggie's chest loosened, expanded. Approval from Petrosian was like praise from her father: rare and to be cherished. She basked in the light of his compliment, tilting her face up as if warming it in the sun after months of rain. "Thank you, Mr. Petrosian. I won't let you down."

"I'm counting on it, Ms. O'Malley." Petrosian extended his hand. As

Maggie reached for it, she heard the drumbeat of boots and the jangle of keys.

Paramedics? What this time?

She turned toward the direction of the footfalls. Austin Reynolds, ex-boyfriend and current homicide detective, marched toward them.

Maggie pasted on what she hoped was a pleasant expression. "Austin. What are you doing here?"

He taxied up to the counter and hooked his fingers into his belt loops. "That's a heckuva greeting, Maggie." He grinned, disengaged from the belt loops and dragged a hand beneath his freckled nose. "It's like you're not happy to see me."

"Of course I'm happy to see you." And she was. A chance meeting meant the opportunity to bring Miles's stalking—pre-stalking?—to the attention of law enforcement. "Just surprised. What brings you in?"

Austin opened his mouth then snapped it shut as a woman, fiftyish with close-cropped hair and model-worthy cheekbones, approached. The newcomer landed beside Austin, edged a shoulder in front of him and stuck out her hand. "I'm Gladys Wren." She flashed a mouth full of white, evenly sized teeth that Chiclets would envy. "Lead detective."

A new lead detective for a newly revamped police department. Maggie knew Austin had wanted the position.

"Maggie, Gladys," Austin mumbled by way of introduction. "She's my new...boss." The last word faded with his self-esteem.

The Chiclet smile broadened, but the eyes remained hard. "May I speak with the manager, please?" All smiles. But all business.

Before Maggie could direct her to Petrosian, her boss stepped forward and offered his hand, his long fingers swallowing Wren's slim manicured digits. "Levon Petrosian, owner and pharmacist. How may I be of assistance?"

Wren pumped his hand once. "Pleased to meet you. I just wish it were under better circumstances."

"How so?"

Wren straightened her jacket, a cropped navy ensemble that rode the line between uniform and civilian togs, and removed a small notepad and pen from her breast pocket. "I understand that Colton Ellis expired in your store two days ago?"

Expired. Like Maggie's mascara.

Petrosian shifted. "I heard that he passed at the hospital."

Gladys's mouth twitched into a half-smile. She clicked the pen, made a mark in the notebook. "Ah, yes, Russ Brock's newscast. A bit of fake news, I'm afraid." She paused, the aural ellipses suggesting that fake news wasn't unusual for Brock. Maggie knew that there was no love lost between the news personality and the local police force. Wren's tone underscored the division. "The medical examiner believes that Mr. Ellis died before the paramedics arrived."

"Medical examiner?" Maggie asked.

"Mr. Ellis had a life insurance policy that required an autopsy upon his death." Wren regarded her notepad. "After noting the decedent's florid color, the examiner detected a distinctive smell. Anyone care to hazard a guess?" No one did. "Almonds. The medical examiner smelled almonds."

"Cyanide," Maggie murmured.

Wren looked at her sharply, brown eyes piercing Maggie's green ones. "Very good, Miss...I'm sorry, I don't think I got your last name."

"O'Malley. Maggie O'Malley."

Wren's smile wilted. "Maggie O'Malley? As in the woman who shot—"

Austin coughed. "In self-defense. She was cleared of any wrongdoing."

Maggie reddened. She didn't need Austin to rush to her aid or make her excuses. She'd killed a man to defend herself. Period, end of story. Unless it was Russ Brock's story. Then there was no end. "Yes, that's me," Maggie said.

"How did you know about the cyanide poisoning?" Wren aimed her pen, watched Maggie's face.

"Mr. Ellis was often flushed, but very red skin can be a sign of cyanide toxicity. The almond smell clinched it for me. It could also explain why I found him near the digestive aids. Cyanide toxicity can create gastrointestinal symptoms."

"Maggie's a chemist," Austin piped in. "She used to make drugs."

Maggie's face flamed again. Great. Now she sounded like Walter White from *Breaking Bad*. "I used to work in pharmaceutical development."

"Ah. Right." Wren continued to study Maggie then glanced at her notepad. "Well, you certainly know your toxins. After becoming suspicious, the ME ran some tests and determined that Mr. Ellis did indeed die from cyanide poisoning." She flipped the pad shut. "Now I'm trying to determine his movements the day of his death, including what he purchased or consumed here."

"We have records of Mr. Ellis' purchases the day he was... the day he passed away." Petrosian disappeared behind the counter and returned with the printout he and Maggie had examined during their impromptu inventory. He handed it to Wren. "You're free to examine anything you'd like in the pharmacy, behind the counter or elsewhere."

Wren nodded her thanks and took the paper. "I understand someone else fell ill in the pharmacy?"

It was the question Maggie had been waiting for, her mind whirring with possibilities the moment "Colton Ellis" and "poison" were wedded in sentence. She wasn't surprised that Wren had known about the Whitleys. Despite Hollow Pine's growing pains, it was still a small town.

"Mary Whitley and her daughter Riley were found unconscious here yesterday," Petrosian said.

"Found by—?" Wren's eyes were already on Maggie.

"Me," Maggie said meeting her gaze, determined not to flinch at the fact that she had discovered them, too. "They were non-responsive but breathing. The paramedics were called. I'm not sure what their condition is."

"Critical, according to their physician," Wren replied. She knew the details and was there to test the drugstore staff. "Neither has regained consciousness, vital signs are screwy. The doctor is ordering a tox screen, including cyanide." She smiled at Maggie. "Neither smelled of almonds, but you never know." She gave the pharmacy a final appraising look, then did the same with Maggie and Petrosian. Finally she said, "Thank you for your cooperation. We'll be in touch."

Chapter 10

Maggie watched Austin and the new lead detective clomp down the aisle and sail out the door. She felt a modicum of relief at the news, a selfish sense of satisfaction that she hadn't made a mistake, hadn't cost a man his life. But that lightening of worry, that easing of conscience, was tempered by the possibility that poison had infiltrated Petrosian's.

"How old were you in 1982?" Petrosian's voice sliced through her thoughts.

She looked at him, mind swimming against a current of questions about who had poisoned Colton Ellis, whether the Whitleys had suffered the same fate. "That was about a decade before I was born."

Petrosian made a face at the latest evidence of her excessive youth. "Do you know what happened in Chicago in 1982?" She figured it probably didn't have anything to do with pan pizza and shook her head. "The Tylenol murders."

Maggie's breath caught in her throat. "The Tylenol murders." she repeated. She'd heard of the poisonings from her father, which he'd served up as evidence of humanity's treachery, but knew few details. "I don't know much more than the case's infamy."

"The original Tylenol poisonings were responsible for the deaths of seven people, including, interestingly enough, a twelve year-old girl named Mary, who was the first victim." He moved to the analgesics section of the over-the-counter aisle and picked up a white bottle. "The death toll grew. The authorities investigated. Each of the victims had taken Extra-Strength Tylenol, which had been laced with potassium cyanide."

Maggie's stomach felt as if it were being dragged to her knees. "You think history's repeating itself?"

Petrosian replaced the bottle. "There were copycat incidents after the initial poisonings, although not all of them used cyanide. The police concluded that the tampering occurred on store shelves, which inspired those looking to kill, or simply dying for attention, to try for their own deadly fame and glory." He faced out the bottle's label. Extra-Strength Tylenol. "It also inspired a new era in packaging. We owe tamper-proof seals and indicators to the architect of the Tylenol murders."

"So how did they catch the murderer?"

"They didn't. They had suspects, including a man who was believed to have murdered a client—the body of which he stored in bags in his attic—but there was no conviction."

A body in bags. Plural.

Maggie tried not to think of how many bags there had been or how the pieces had been puzzled into plastic bags like leftovers. Instead she turned her mind to the current poisonings. The why. The how. And, of course, the who behind it all. "You don't think the original Tylenol murderer has anything to do with this?" she asked. "As you said, the murderer was never brought to justice."

Petrosian considered this, dismissed it with a wag of his head. "It's been more than three decades. I would think the killer, if he or she is even alive, would have been active long before now." He frowned. "Although I'm not sure if cases unrelated to the copycat incidents have been reported. In any case, tamper-resistant packaging has made it nearly impossible for this kind of thing to happen again."

"Nearly impossible isn't the same thing as impossible."

Petrosian's frown deepened. "Indeed."

"What now?"

Petrosian adjusted the bottle. Maggie would need a micrometer to measure the change. "We don't know if someone has tampered with our medications. We don't know how many bottles could be affected, how many people could have purchased them, how many people could have a ticking bomb in their medicine cabinets." He looked at Maggie. "But I do know this: until we get more evidence about Mr. Ellis's death and what happened to the Whitleys, Petrosian's Pillbox is closed until further notice."

Chapter 11

Maggie spent the next day playing house with Constantine and trying to distract herself as Miss Vanilla rounded her wheel again and again in a hamster facsimile of Maggie's life up to that moment.

School. Work. School. Work. Maggie knew all too well what it was like to run in circles.

Despite the emptiness of her hours, she was relieved to be away from Petrosian's Pillbox, thankful that she didn't have to wonder if she'd encounter someone struggling to breathe next to the tampons or dead— *expired*—at the register.

She knew that the closure was costing Petrosian dearly. No customers. No income. No guaranteed return of normalcy. Yet she admired his ethics. There was no proof that Colton Ellis and the Whitleys had been poisoned by something from the pharmacy, and yet Petrosian had done the right thing, putting people above profits. After Maggie's experiences at Rxcellance and Madame Trousseau's House of Lingerie, corporate conscience was a novelty.

After a kickboxing class with Ada at GymRatz, Maggie wandered around the bungalow, sending emails to florists asking for consultations she didn't want, straightening piles that didn't need to be straightened, reorganizing Constantine's collection of ironic t-shirts. She changed out of her gym clothes, steeling herself for a return to Petrosian's to retrieve her check. She needed the money. She didn't relish a return to a potential crime scene.

She arrived at Petrosian's, pulled the Studebaker into its usual spot, then rounded the building. She came to a dead stop, her mouth hinging open.

News vans angled in front of the drugstore's entrance. A woman who wore a turquoise pantsuit and perfectly coiffed bob spoke earnestly into a microphone. A man leaned against the front door, hand shoved in his pocket, jingling change. He looked at her, his bright blue eyes boring into her. She felt a charge of familiarity and a quiver of something like fear.

The Hollow Pine media was attracted to bad news like magpies to shiny objects. Maggie itemized all that sparkled: death, poisoning, an entire community at risk. There was more than enough to spark their interest.

Maggie took a deep breath and charged past the media toward the shelter of the store. She grasped the handle and pushed. The blue-eyed man stepped in front of her.

He was mid-forties, tall, gym-built with surfer boy hair and a chin buttressed by implants. "Miss O'Malley?" A booming voice destined for broadcast.

Maggie looked at him, her internal microprocessor scouring her memory banks. "Yes?"

He brought a microphone to his chin and grinned for a camera Maggie just now noticed. "Russ Brock, News Channel 4." He lifted a brow and leaned in. "For the news, for the people."

Realization fell like a spring rain, slowly at first then picking up speed.

Russ Brock who had tried to turn the tide of public opinion against her in the dark days following last year's shooting. Russ Brock, slinger of mud and slayer of reputations.

Maggie wasn't sure how she had earned the reporter's ire, although her refusal to grant him an interview followed by her rebuff of his invitation for a "hot date with the city's hottest reporter" probably didn't help. She also wasn't sure why she hadn't immediately recognized him. Had her mental fog become so impenetrable? Had her denial become so complete, her refusal to think or talk about Brock so full, that she had given herself anterograde amnesia?

Maggie glared at Brock and shoved the door again. It refused to yield. Right. Because it was locked.

She fumbled for the keys Petrosian had given her yesterday, a preview of the new responsibilities she'd enjoy when the drugstore reopened. The keychain tumbled from her fingers onto the tile apron below. Maggie squatted to retrieve them. Brock genuflected beside her.

"Ms. O'Malley." Brock thrust both his face and his microphone appendage inches from her face. "What can you tell us about the cyanide poisonings?"

"Uh," she said.

Maggie O'Malley, pharmacy spokeswoman.

Brock furrowed his brow and bit his lip, taking him from middle-age Ken doll to Concerned Investigative Reporter. "Can you tell us what medications were tainted?" he pressed, inching the mike closer. "How many people are at risk? What Petrosian's Pillbox is doing to safeguard the public?"

"There's no evidence that the poisoning was related to Petrosian's Pillbox," she said, rising to her feet.

"Oh, really?" Brock smiled smugly at the camera. "Then how do you explain the fact that three pharmacy patrons have been poisoned?"

Three? Was there now evidence that the Whitleys had been poisoned?

He read her face. "Oh, you didn't know?" A shellac of concern failed to hide contempt. "Surprising since you found them unconscious in the store." He gave the camera a knowing look. "It's interesting how people turn up dead when you're around. First Rxcellance, now Petrosian's Pillbox. And let's not forget the shooting, still so fresh in all of our minds."

"That was self-defense," Maggie said reflexively.

"Right. Self-defense." His tone put air quotes around the word. "You're lucky the DA saw it that way." The lip-biting recommenced. "I wonder if our viewers did."

Perspiration sprung beneath Maggie's arms. She could feel panic's claws dig into her belly, scuttle up her esophagus. She caught a whiff of Brock's cologne and the body odor that lay beneath it, and felt the world begin to fall away as a wave of dizziness washed over her.

Maggie propped her hand against the door to steady herself. The door swung inward as someone yanked it open from the other side. Maggie stumbled inside, sprawling on a charcoal gray mat embossed with a mortar and pestle.

Maggie's chin hit the edge of the pictorial pestle. She lurched to her knees, tried to reach equilibrium, tried to find her feet. A hand shot down from in front and above. She looked up. Gladys Wren.

Maggie reached up and Gladys pulled her to her feet, slamming the door behind them. Gladys threw the lock.

Outside Russ Brock pounded on the door. "What are you hiding from, Ms. O'Malley?" he shouted, his voice muffled by the glass. "What's your role in these poisonings?"

"Come on," Gladys said, grabbing Maggie by the shoulders. "We don't need any of that noise."

Gladys steered Maggie toward the store office. She stepped inside, hit the lights with the heel of her hand and pulled Maggie after her. The sound of angry voices floated from outside. Wren fluffed her hair, pulled her cream blazer taut. "Persistent, aren't they?"

"The Whitleys," Maggie breathed. "Are they—?" Her voice cracked, the strain of worry sending fissures down her vocal chords.

"They're still in critical condition–not dead." She paused, considering. "At least not yet."

"But Russ Block implied—"

Gladys jutted her chin toward the crowd outside. "He has just enough information to be dangerous. But he's right about the poisonings. The lab expedited the tox screen. It came back positive for cyanide for the Whitleys."

"Three customers poisoned." Maggie sagged against an office desk that screamed some assembly required. She thought of the specter of the Tylenol poisonings, Petrosian's suspicions of something similar. "Do we know if the poison originated here?"

Wren popped an eyebrow at "we," the way Maggie had unconsciously insinuated herself into the investigative team. "No, *we* don't. Just that they've been poisoned and that the common denominator seems to be this store. We have some additional information, which might have a bearing on these events. Lev is down at the station now."

Maggie felt a flash of annoyance at Wren for using her boss's first name, then alarm. Lev Petrosian was down at the police station? Why? And why hadn't he called to tell her?

As if reading her thoughts Gladys said, "He knew you were coming so he asked me to meet you here then lock up." She dangled the keys. Exhibit A. "We were hoping you could join us, maybe answer a few questions."

Answer a few questions.

It was a phrase with which Maggie was familiar and one that never seemed to bode well. She knew she had done nothing wrong, that Petrosian had done nothing wrong. Then why did her stomach feel like it had turned itself inside out?

The whole situation was disconcerting. Wren meeting her here. Petrosian allowing the detective to lock up. The sudden chumminess in Wren's smile.

Wren strode from the office, dousing the overhead light. Maggie trailed behind as though she, not Wren, was the interloper. Wren stopped, a hand aloft, listening. The rabble of the media floated through the air vents. "Is there another exit?"

Maggie hooked a thumb behind her. "Out back."

Wren nodded. "I'll use the front door, you take the back. That'll give you a chance to avoid all that mayhem. Besides," she gave a wicked smile, "it gives me a chance to mess with the press."

Maggie watched as Gladys unlocked the front door and glided outside, her smart cream suit turned into a photograph negative by the flash of bulbs. The detective motioned for the press to back off, then locked the door.

Time to get the hell out of Dodge.

Maggie loped toward the back door, striding past seasonal displays, scooting beneath the pharmacy counter, shimmying past boxes until she reached the door that led outside. She twisted the handle and peered out. Deserted.

She pulled her purse over her neck and shoulder, and jogged toward the Studebaker. Russ Brock leapt from behind the dumpster like a guest at a surprise party. He landed in front of her, feet wide, arms akimbo. She wouldn't have been shocked if he'd punctuated his touchdown with a "ta da!"

"Very sneaky," he said, waggling a finger at her. "Slinking out the back door doesn't exactly attest to your innocence." He took a step closer. Without the benefit of studio lights, Brock looked sallow, his skin the yellow of an old bruise beneath his spray-on tan. She noticed twin smudges of blue beneath his eyes, the way his wrinkled sport jacket frayed at the collar sending filaments of thread skyward. Burning the candle at both ends?

I'm ready for my close-up, Mr. DeMille, she quoted in her mind. *Or maybe not.*

"I have nothing to say to you," she said, marching toward her car.

Brock grabbed her arm. "But I have plenty to say to you."

For a moment, Maggie was transported back to another parking lot. Memories of Miles rose quick and sharp in her mind, blotting out everything but her desire—her *need*—to run. She could feel her nervous system spooling up, her heart beating against her ribs, blood thundering through her ears.

There was an explosion of light and sound. The rest of the press swarmed them, shutters clicking, flashbulbs popping, men and woman shouting questions as they approached in a surge of sprayed hair and primary colors.

Russ Brock's questions at the drugstore's entrance had found its mark. The others smelled blood in the water and circled in for the kill. Reporters hurled questions she couldn't answer, accusations she couldn't comprehend.

She backed against the drugstore door, caught in the limbo between the sanctuary of the building and the escape of her car. She weighed the options: dash inside the store and risk becoming trapped by the throng outside, or make a run for it, telegraphing an aura of guilt as the cameras caught her fleeing to her car.

It wasn't a question of life or death, but it wasn't ideal, either.

Maggie felt for the handle, ready to pull it like a ripcord and parachute away from the encroaching media. Above the din, she heard a high-pitched whine. She turned, squinting into the sun-basted lot. The dog that Francine had chased off cowered against the dumpster.

One of cameramen noticed the animal and lunged at him in a mock attack, causing the animal to shrink against the container. The cameraman grinned at the sound guy. Both men snickered. Maggie wanted to knock their heads together.

On impulse, Maggie charged ahead. She shoved Brock out of the way. He lost his footing on the uneven asphalt and tripped, falling to the ground. "Hey, that's assault!"

Maggie ignored him and pressed forward. She reached the dog and, without any real plan in place, scooped him into her arms.

She expected a reaction from the media, for the animal to struggle. Instead, the reporters looked on silently and the dog melted against her.

She reached the Studebaker, unlocked the door, flung it open and slid behind the wheel. Seconds later, she squealed from the parking lot, bumping over weed-choked potholes that pocked the asphalt, and turned the car toward the police station.

She glanced over at the brown, furry form seated beside her. He returned her gaze then poked out a wet pink tongue and licked her arm as if to say, *Safe at last.*

Chapter 12

The cost of her impulsiveness came due at the police station. She parked in front of the building and looked at the dog. "What am I going to do with you now?"

He panted a smile then crouched down in the seat, putting his nose between his paws. Translation: *It doesn't matter. I'm adorable.*

Maggie considered the interrogation that undoubtedly lay ahead, the rising heat of the day. She couldn't leave the dog in the car to swelter—or worse. But Gladys Wren didn't exactly telegraph a love of, well, anything.

Maggie wavered, weighing her dignity against the dog's well-being, then scooped up the dog once again. She had a long history of embarrassing herself. Might as well add another notch.

Maggie carried the dog into the police station, an Art Deco structure with a gray edifice, dual windows and a single door that seemed to frown down on the populace below. The station buzzed like a phone on vibrate. People slouched on chairs awaiting their turns. Officers, some in uniform, others plainclothed, strode from cubicle to shadowy back rooms to front desk and back again. Phones rang. Someone shouted an imaginative string of curse words. Maggie prayed that the dog would remain silent without the Miranda warning.

Austin spotted her on his journey to the front desk. "Hey, Maggie!" he said around the toothpick lodged between his teeth, a habit picked up from his former boss. "You here to see Wren?"

Maggie answered in the affirmative and he signaled her to follow him. "I wasn't supposed to be on this case, you know," he called over his shoulder, "but when I heard where the poisonings happened, I asked to be assigned."

"Why?"

"I dunno." He stopped midstride, shrugged. "Seems like wherever you are, excitement seems to follow." He resumed walking and nodded at the brown and white lump of fur in her arms. "Where'd you get the accessory?"

"He's...new." Something kept her from telling him that she'd rescued the stray, as if she were guilty of theft. And maybe she was. Maybe he wasn't a stray but someone's beloved lost pet.

"Ah." He frowned. "Hopefully Wren won't have a problem with him being here. She's kinda particular."

She swallowed and held the dog closer as the carpet, worn, brown, polka dotted with coffee stains, passed beneath her feet. She hoped unauthorized canines were the greatest of Wren's problems with her.

They reached a door at the end of the hall. Austin twisted the knob. The door swung open to reveal Gladys Wren, a vision in ivory and taupe, but no Petrosian.

"Come in, come in." She regarded the dog, her lips folding in on themselves in disapproval. "Only service animals are allowed here." Maggie began to explain about the heat of the car, the lack of leash with which to secure the dog outside. Wren cut her off with a hand held aloft. "Never mind. Any trouble with the press?"

"No more than expected." Maggie shifted and looked around the small office as if her boss were hiding under the desk blotter. "I thought Mr. Petrosian would be here."

Wren gestured to an overstuffed chair that seemed more suited to a country club than an interrogation room and Maggie sank into it. Her backside migrated toward the gap between chair-back and cushion and she wriggled forward to avoid getting lost like errant change.

"We concluded our interview with Lev," Wren said, pinching the crease on the leg of her pantsuit. "We thought it was best if he went on his way. You know, so you could speak freely."

Maggie squirmed with a discomfort that had nothing to do with seating. "Speak freely?"

"Well, he is your boss. We thought you'd be more comfortable speaking your mind if he wasn't here."

"Anything I say to you I'd be happy to say in front of Mr. Petrosian. What do you want to know?"

Wren picked up a picture frame from her desk. It was wood shop-hewn and showcased a younger Wren with a boy of about eight. Wren replaced the frame and rubbed a finger across the top. "How well did you know Colton Ellis?"

Maggie shook her head. "Not well. I've only been working at

Petrosian's for a couple of months and only began waiting on customers recently."

"So you didn't know him outside of your capacity as a..." She pulled a yellow legal pad from the desk's blotter and flipped to the second page. "Pharmacy technician?"

"No. I'm new to town."

Wren gave an enthusiastic nod, a game show host encouraging a contestant. "And were you aware of Mr. Petrosian's relationship with Colton Ellis?"

Maggie felt the familiar pinprick of adrenaline as it trickled into her system. "Only as a pharmacist."

"You had no knowledge of the lawsuit?"

The adrenaline poured in. Maggie swallowed. "Lawsuit?"

Wren showed her Chiclet teeth. "Yes, Lev was suing Colton Ellis for breach of contract." She leaned in. "Real estate deal gone bad."

Maggie sat, stunned. Part of her had suspected that Petrosian had disliked Colton. She couldn't help but notice Petrosian's upturned lip at Colton's bumbling entrance into the pharmacy, the way his eyelids slid shut every time Colton told one of his jokes. But a lawsuit? That was news to her.

"It seems that Mr. Ellis had agreed to sell your boss some property." A look at the notes. "Land in that fancy new part of town."

"The Estates," Maggie supplied.

Another game show host nod. "Right. Something about turning it into a second drugstore location." Wren leaned back in her chair and began pushing back her cuticles with her thumbnail. "Apparently Colton Ellis changed his mind. Word is that he got another offer for more money. When he told Lev the deal was off, your employer was most unhappy." She glanced up at Maggie. "Evidently he visited Mr. Ellis at his place of business, said it was a mistake Ellis would pay for."

"In a lawsuit." Maggie said a little too quickly, a bit too loudly.

Wren seesawed her hands in a maybe/maybe not gesture. "It is a bit odd, don't you think? Colton Ellis poisoned in the pharmacy owned by a man with whom he's engaged in a lawsuit."

"He was only found in the pharmacy. There's no evidence that he was poisoned there."

Wren leaned back in her chair, resumed the mini-mani. "Right you are, Ms. O'Malley. There is no evidence now. But that may change."

"What do you mean?"

"We've just requested a search warrant for Petrosian's Pillbox. If the judge agrees, and I think he will, we'll be looking at every inch of the pharmacy to determine whether the source of the poison was in the building owned by a man embroiled in a poisonous lawsuit."

"Mr. Petrosian will welcome that. You heard him. He said that you were welcome to search every inch of the pharmacy, proof that he has nothing to hide."

Wren smiled. "Yes, he reiterated that, even invited us to put up crime scene tape and seal the building, which —" she glanced at her watch "— should be happening right about now." The smile broadened. "We'll likely get that search warrant. Meanwhile, we'll continue our investigation." Wren got to her feet and smoothed the front of her suit. "Please make sure you don't interfere. We'd hate to compromise any evidence or opportunities due to an amateur's mistakes. Austin will see you out."

Chapter 13

Austin yammered his way through the building and all the way to Maggie's car. Other than a story involving a new belt buckle and a discount on Dentyne bought in bulk, Maggie didn't hear a word. Her mind raced the concourses of possibility.

The original Tylenol poisoner who had never been caught. The re-emergence of Miles into her world. Petrosian's lawsuit against Colton Ellis.

It was the last that bothered her the most.

Gladys Wren was right: it was odd. How did Petrosian expect to move forward with the new store if he didn't have possession of the property? Was he sure he'd prevail? Did he think Colton would change his mind? Was he planning to lease the land?

Or did he know that Colton wouldn't be around to pursue the lawsuit?

She pushed that last thought away. Had she become that paranoid? That suspicious?

She mentally tallied the bodies she'd discovered, the murderers she'd unmasked. Of course she was suspicious. She had good reason.

And yet Petrosian was one of the good guys. Despite his unsmiling visage, his gruff manner, his ceaseless demands and perpetual dissatisfaction, he was her mentor, the man who had helped her find the sweet spot in her Venn diagram of medicine and humanity. He deserved the benefit of the doubt. He deserved a chance to tell his side of the Ellis/Petrosian dispute.

Maggie piled herself and the dog into the car, cranked down the window and pulled out her phone. She dialed Petrosian's number. No answer, followed by an outgoing voicemail message demanding that callers leave pertinent information at the tone. She ended the call without leaving a message. This wasn't the time for the voicemail monologues. This was a time for conversation.

She started the car and made a circuitous route home, stopping at the grocery store for dog food (just for tonight) then tooling by Petrosian's (just to see if he was home).

She idled past her boss's home, taking in the white driveway deprived of vehicles, a house flanked by dueling arborvitae and a huge Armenian flag. She squinted, trying to see if she could catch a glimpse of Petrosian through the vertical blinds that sat akimbo in front of a picture window. Nothing. She sighed and turned the car around in an inelegant three-point turn. She'd try again—by phone or in person—later.

Maggie made it home in record time, her foot as heavy as her thoughts. She killed the engine and looked over at the mutt riding shotgun. He'd stretched out on the bench seat, muzzle on the door handle, spindling legs pushing against her thigh.

"All right, lazy bones," she said softly, patting his silky head. "Let's get you something to eat. Then we'll see who belongs to you."

The dog got to his feet. Maggie tucked him beneath her arm, grabbed the grocery bag and her purse, and headed for the house.

She wondered where Constantine and his threshold carrying gag were and put her key in the door. It drifted open. Garlic and off-key humming floated out.

"Gus?" she called.

Strains of an Italian opera stopped abruptly. "Mags? In here. I'm whipping up something magical." There was a crash of pots and pans, followed by a tinkle of broken glass. "Um, be right out. It's a surprise!"

"The surprise will be if it's edible," she said under her breath.

Maggie led the dog into the living room and parked him next to the sofa. He jumped onto a cushion and sat down. "By all means, make yourself at home. Would you like the remote?" She was sure the dog smiled at her.

Constantine sauntered out of the kitchen, a glass of wine in one hand, a highball glass in another. "Vodka Collins for you and swill for—" He stopped abruptly, glasses sloshing in alcoholic tidal waves, and regarded the dog. "If I'd known we were having company for dinner, I would have made something different. Like with savory beef chunks in a kibble gravy." He dropped beside her on the couch. "Who's your little friend?"

Maggie ran a hand over the dog's head. "I don't know. He's been hanging around Petrosian's. He was being terrorized by the press, so I grabbed him and took him with me to the police station."

Constantine's eyes widened. "Press? *Police station*? Alliteration bonus aside, sounds like you've had quite the day."

Maggie grabbed the glass and took a sip, feeling the heat of the booze make its way from lips to belly. "Someone tipped off the press that three customers had succumbed to cyanide poisoning."

"Three people? Last I heard it was one."

"The toxicology report begs to differ. Turns out the women I found had been poisoned, as well. Fortunately, they're still alive." She added a silent invocation they'd stay that way.

"Not exactly positive PR."

"Bad news is the best news—especially if I'm involved. Russ Brock was leading the charge, trying to make out like I had something to do with the poisonings."

A shadow crossed Constantine's face. "That guy is fixated on you."

"And my habit of being around when bodies turn up."

"Everyone needs a hobby. And the police?"

"Gladys Wren, new lead detective, was waiting for me inside the store. She asked me to come down to the police station where Lev was already answering questions." She paused, scratched the dog's right ear. "Evidently there was a tiff between Petrosian and Colton Ellis."

"And by tiff you mean an unfriending on Facebook?"

"More like unfriending in real life. Petrosian was suing Colton for breach of contract." She told him about the pharmacist's attempt to expand his business and Colton's last-minute withdrawal. "The police think it's funny that Lev didn't mention the lawsuit."

"Downright hilarious if the pharmacy is the source of the poisoning. But there's no way Petrosian could be involved, right?"

"Absolutely not." She silenced the voice in her head that reminded her of the many times she trusted the wrong person. "I'm guessing he didn't mention it because of how bad it sounds."

"Ye olde sin of omission. Very popular, except with the police." He took a sip of his wine, made a face then grabbed Maggie's glass for a taste of her beverage. "Think the press knows about the lawsuit?"

"If they don't they will soon. Wouldn't be difficult to suss out. For now, their interest seems to be on me, with Russ Brock crusading to put me under the microscope." Maggie kicked off sneakers dusted with hitchhiking pollen and leaned against the couch cushions. A cloud of dust plumed behind her.

Constantine took her glass and wrapped his arms around her. The dog wriggled between them and licked his face. Constantine frowned. "So what's the plan with Fido? I'm not a dog person."

"What are you talking about? You had a dog for seventeen years."

"Well, yes, but after he passed on to that big fire hydrant in the sky I decided no more dogs. Too bouncy. Too cuddly. Too...doggy. That's why I have Miss Vanilla."

His words were light, but Maggie knew they belied a heavy heart. He was devastated when his dog died. He loved Miss Vanilla, but he never forgot Daisy.

"I'm going to check Craigslist and the paper for lost pets," Maggie said. "In the meantime, how do you feel about him crashing here?"

"As long as he doesn't take my side of the bed." Constantine reached his hand toward the dog's muzzle. The dog sniffed his long square fingers then recoiled in disgust. "I can see we'll be fast friends." He rose. "Any more ketchup capers with the car?" Once again, his tone didn't match his face. Constantine was as practiced as Maggie in the art and science of humor as defense mechanism.

"Nope," Maggie bolted the rest of her drink. "I can't help but feel the timing of the poisonings and Miles's arrival is strange."

"As strange as Petrosian suing the deceased?"

She traced the lip of her glass with her forefinger. "Just about."

"I'll give you that the timing is cute, but so is the thing with Petrosian. Time—and the police—will tell." His voice underscored "police." The message: let the authorities handle this one.

He clapped his hands together. "Welp, I'd better finish cooking dinner. Prepare to be impressed."

"I always am."

Constantine disappeared into the kitchen and the dog looked at her expectantly. She'd try Petrosian again later. Now it was time to do a little canine sleuthing.

She rose, grabbed her purse from the entryway table, dredged it for her phone. She thumbed through the device until she reached the Lost Pets section of her Hollow Pine's Craigslist page.

She had just encountered the second mention of a lost poodle named Larry when the phone sounded in her hand. *You talkin' to me?*

Her heart did a triple-step. Maybe it was Petrosian calling back.

She gazed into the phone's screen as if it were a fortune teller. Her father's broad, ruddy face filled the screen. "Hey, Pop. What's up?"

"My dander," he stormed. "And probably my blood pressure. You know how hard it is to run a business these days?"

Maggie endured a five-minute lecture on taxes, city codes, competition in the food cart lot where O'Malley's Irish Pizzeria parked its three carts, and perpetual disappointment generated by employees. "The only exception is that Ada of yours. She's a gem, a real gem. Too bad she decided to go part-time."

"She didn't just 'decide' to reduce her hours, Pop. She's in the police academy now. She can't do it all."

"What's a nice girl like her want to be a policewoman for? It's unladylike." Maggie rolled her eyes. "Anyway, Fiona wanted me to call about the wedding." His tone suggested the verbal equivalent of a forced march.

Maggie's own interest in the conversation halved. The only thing she hated more than planning her wedding was talking about it. She imagined the topic would be icing. "Yeah?"

"I spoke with Father Brian. He said that it would be fine to hold the reception in the parking lot of St. Matthew's."

"What?"

"He said he'd put some cones out in the parking lot and I could park the food carts there. We'll bring in some folding chairs, maybe a few card tables. And—good news—Sean has agreed to play the bagpipes."

"Um, that's—" Maggie's mind whirred as she tried to come up with the appropriate adjective. She halted the attempt and changed gears. Maybe it was time for the truth. "I'm just not sure we're going to get married at St. Matthews."

"Not going to—" her father sputtered. "What are you talking about?"

"We're, um, thinking of a civil ceremony."

Or no ceremony or maybe a wedding-moon in a tropical locale, she added silently. Constantine had been leaving around brochures for Bora Bora, and she was pretty sure it wasn't just because he liked the name.

Her father was silent. "Pop? You still there?"

"I'm here." He said it softly, but his disappointment boomed through the phone. Her father expected her to be married in a church. Her father had expected her to wait until after the wedding to live with Constantine. Her father expected her to be the person he thought she should be.

His disappointment in her was crushing. Jack O'Malley wasn't exactly effusive in his praise, more likely to dole out criticisms than kudos, but Maggie always knew that he was proud of her. Until now.

"I have to go," he finally said, then hung up without another word.

Maggie sat in the tiny living room. She could hear the clink of dishes as Gus prepared dinner, smelled the earthy odor of dog and dirt. She felt a tightening at her throat, a burning against her eyelids that heralded tears. She hoisted her glass and put it to her lips, but it was empty. It had been hollowed out, just like her heart.

Chapter 14

Maggie focused on her breathing as her body glided into the tunnel. She tried not to think about the cradle that held her head in place or on the narrowness of the tube, which seemed to be pressing in on her. Hugging her. Maybe crushing her.

She knew that people did this every day. That it was no big deal.

Then why does it feel like a big deal? she thought as the machine awoke and began to purr.

"You're doing great." The technician's voice was thin and tinny through the MRI machine's tiny speaker, as if reduced by a shrink ray. *Honey I Shrunk the Radiology Tech.* "Just try to relax."

Right. Relax. She might as well ask Maggie to turn into a frog.

She hadn't wanted the scan, but Constantine was insistent and she could no longer claim that she was too busy. She'd had plenty of idle time now that Petrosian's Pillbox was closed. In a way, the appointment was a welcome distraction. Without work, she felt adrift, bumping from one activity to another looking to fill empty time. She wondered if she'd feel empty, too, after the test was complete.

Maggie closed her eyes and tried not to think of anything as her brain was digitally sliced in an attempt to locate a reason for the persistent and worsening headaches, the trigger-fast impatience, the fog that seemed to roll through her gray matter as if it were an English moor.

It didn't work.

Her mind crowded with her father's disappointment, the poisonings, Miles's reappearance and her conversation with Petrosian.

Her boss had returned her call shortly after Pop had hung up.

"I'm surprised you're interested in this lawsuit," he'd said.

"I'm only interested because the police seem interested. They might see a contentious lawsuit that ends in the death of one of the parties, who just happened to be found dead in the business of one of the other parties, suspicious."

Petrosian sighed. "Yes, it does look...odd." The same word Gladys Wren had used. "Of course, the whole notion of me as a poisoner is absurd. I hope they execute the search warrant. That should settle things once and for all."

Maggie hoped and worried that he was right in equal measure.

"Be still, please," the technician said.

Maggie complied, listening to the din of the machine and the silence of her body. She emptied her lungs, hoping her mind would follow suit. The thoughts continued to roll through like an old-school slideshow of someone's vacation pictures.

A closed sign on the drugstore's front door.

Click.

Petrosian's body ramrod straight in an attempt to bolster dignity.

Click.

Her own father drowning beneath her mother's medical bills.

Click.

The closure of Petrosian's Pillbox reminded Maggie of the near-bankruptcy of O'Malley's Pizzeria, bled dry by treatments for her dying mother and transfusions for Maggie's college fund. It brought to mind her father's face with its empty eyes, deep lines and gaunt cheeks despite the restaurant's bounty of carbs.

O'Malley's Pizzeria had a happy ending. Jack O'Malley retooled and rebooted. She wondered if Petrosian would be so lucky. He had tens of thousands of dollars in inventory laying fallow, and there was no guarantee that customers would relieve him of that supply when—or if—the store reopened.

Fact: people prefer their allergy medication without a side of poison.

Petrosian could recover from loss of business. Could he recover from a loss of trust? The media had already planted the seeds of fear. Even if a search warrant proved otherwise, the damage could be irreversible.

Finally, the machine stopped. Her body was carted out like sushi on a conveyor belt. The technician smiled down at her. "That wasn't so bad now, was it?"

Maggie felt like jabbing her in the throat. Okay, so maybe she *was* a little testy these days. Maggie smiled. "Piece of cake."

She was shown to a dressing room where she changed and scraped her hair into a low ponytail. She considered driving by Petrosian's Pillbox to see if any reporters stood out front, offering grim descriptions of the police's lack of progress and the possible risk to the public.

Then she remembered: the poisonings weren't the focus of the story. She was. Russ Brock had made sure of that.

The apostle of the twenty-four-hour news cycle worked a mention of Maggie into every newscast, his face growing long, his brows knit into a topographical map of concern. He kept to the facts, but wasn't afraid to pose questions, to conjecture.

As far as Maggie could tell, he was obsessed with her. She supposed she offered plenty of fodder. Bodies seemed to turn up wherever she went. Plus, she was twenty-something and photogenic. It was easy to throw her picture on screen, make her the symbol of whatever cause, whatever point of view, the reporter espoused. Axe to grind? Maggie made the perfect stone. And newscast after newscast, Russ Brock whet his blade to whittle her reputation.

Maggie crawled across the radiologist's parking lot to her car. She inserted the key and twisted. Nothing happened. Maggie squinted.

The car was unlocked.

Maggie was sure she'd depressed the lock button. With a few exceptions, she secured her car as a matter of course. Too many opportunities for theft. Too easy for someone to hide in the backseat.

Had she forgotten to lock up, her mind preoccupied by the imaging appointment? Or had someone broken in? The car lacked modern security measures. Breaching the locks would be easy for someone with a modicum of skill and a little ambition.

Maggie pulled open the door and peered inside. Everything seemed in order. She slid onto the bench seat. A slip of paper fluttered from the speedometer. Maggie retrieved it from the floor.

It contained a single word inked in red:

~~Maggie~~

Maggie's heart thudded sickly in her chest. She was the star of someone's to-do list, checked off like a reminder to go to the dry cleaner's or buy more taco seasoning.

No signature. No smiley face. No doubt in her mind that it had been left by Miles.

He'd followed her. Breached her car. Left a note telling her he planned to nullify her.

Maggie crumpled the note and stuffed it into her purse, telling herself she wouldn't be intimidated by a scrap of copy paper scrawled with a

Sharpie. Trying to believe it. Shrouding her growing unease in layers of denial and downplay.

So Miles left a note. Big deal. He simply wanted to toy with her, to elicit a response. She wouldn't give him the satisfaction.

She wiped at the mustache of perspiration that had sprouted on her upper lip and considered her next move. She could allow herself to think about Miles or she could distract herself. She considered the possible diversions—go home and hang out with the yet-unnamed and still-unclaimed pooch until Constantine returned from his service call, hit the gym for a kickboxing stint—and landed on doing something meaningful, something helpful, something active for a man she respected and for her own tattered reputation.

She pulled out her phone, scrolled to Austin's number and dialed. He answered on the first ring.

"Golly, Maggie," he said, "this is a pleasant surprise."

She tamped down a question about whether he'd been watching too many *Bonanza* reruns and a fleeting urge to tell him about Miles. She concentrated on the bigger mystery at hand. "Hey, Austin. I just have a quick question."

"Shoot," she could hear him cringe over the line over the word choice, considering what had happened last year. "I mean, go right ahead."

"I was wondering if you could tell me the latest about the poisonings. There's been a lot of news coverage, but not a lot of actual information."

"Yeah, it has been in the news a bunch." He had the grace not to bring up the fact that Maggie seemed to be the star. "But I really can't tell you anything. Ongoing investigation, you know."

"Aw come on, Austin," she cajoled. "It's not like I'm going to tell anyone. I'm just curious."

"When you get curious, my job gets difficult. Besides, there really isn't much to tell, other than we're working on a search warrant for Petrosian's Pillbox."

"Yeah, I knew that."

"Oh. Right." His voice deflated. He pumped it with the promise of new information. "Well, it also looks like the death toll is going up."

"What? I hadn't heard of any additional poisonings."

"There haven't been, but the mother who was poisoned is not doing well. She might not make it through the night."

"My God."

"My thoughts exactly." He paused in a prophylactic moment of silence. "Hey, listen, I've gotta run. Talk to you later."

Maggie ended the call and dropped the phone onto the seat. She thought of the woman struggling to live, the daughter keeping vigil from her own hospital bed. It brought back more memories.

The rides up the hospital elevator to see her mother. The acrid odor of antiseptic and old coffee that wafted through each floor. The woman in the bed who got smaller with each visit.

At first, her father accompanied her on the excursions to the hospital, his meaty hand enveloping her small one as they walked. Then Jack O'Malley's boss said that if he missed any more work there wouldn't be any more work for him to miss. So Maggie made the journey alone, clasping her own hands together as the elevator ticked its way skyward, then holding her mother's skeletal hand as she lay beneath a maze of wires and tubes.

Maggie and Riley Whitley were members of the same club: children of the critically ill. The difference? Riley herself had leukemia, leaving her unwell, recovering from poisoning and fearful that the woman who had given her life was about to die. As far as Maggie knew, there was no husband, no father in the picture. Riley was alone with her ailing mother, just as Maggie had once been.

Maggie started the Studebaker and eased it into gear. Then she pointed it toward the hospital. Now she had a purpose.

Chapter 15

Maggie pulled into the parking lot of St. Theresa's, anxiety worming its way into her chest. She had spent a considerable amount of time inside the Tylenol-white building last year when familial duty and an unexpected mystery drew her into the antiseptic fold of its walls.

She parked in the spot she had come to call her own, locked the doors (and double-checked them), then whooshed through the automatic doors into the hospital's lobby. The white-haired man who'd commandeered the hospital's new Welcome Center—a sweeping marble counter topped with flowers and brochures featuring photos of people who looked as if they had no need of a hospital—was engrossed in something on his computer monitor. Maggie gave her most dazzling, I-know-where-I'm-going-thanks smile, bypassed a modern statue of St. Theresa that made the saint look a reality TV show contestant, and marched toward the elevators.

She hit the up button and waited, conscious that the old man's eyes were now on her. She wondered if he remembered her from her previous visits. She touched the back of her head and wondered if he'd heard what had happened to her in the hospital stairwell.

The elevator doors parted and she sealed herself inside, thankful for the studied anonymity of the car's other four passengers. She hit the button for the third floor, which was where medical patients were treated after the hospital's recent remodel, and watched the car's lights illuminate her progress upward.

The doors slid open and Maggie exited, bypassing the nurse's station with the same air of direction and confidence she exhibited for the man at the reception desk. She wasn't sure if she would be allowed to see the Whitleys. It was a good possibility that their room—or rooms, if they were housed separately—had an officer stationed out front.

Attempted murder could make people so touchy. She figured she'd bluff her way in and see what happened, put that whole "fortune favors the bold" thing to the test.

She walked purposefully down the hall, using her peripheral vision to catch a glimpse of each room. A man on a ventilator. A woman sitting on the edge of her bed, seeming to contemplate a solo trip to the toilet. A teenager, sweating and restless on the top of the hospital covers. And finally, a room with two women, one middle-aged, one young.

There was no guard stationed at the door, which was angled between open and closed. Maggie brushed it lightly with her knuckles, a half-knock, half-nudge. The door drifted wide. Maggie entered.

Mary lay unconscious beneath an assortment of tubes. A ventilator supplied her lungs with oxygen. An IV fed her a steady diet of saline, sugar and, most likely, a cyanide antidote. A monitor tracked her heart rate, blood pressure, oxygen saturation and body temperature. Maggie felt a jolt of déjà vu and reached out her hand in a reflexive urge to touch the woman's hand as if reaching through the veil of death to caress her mother's skin.

She heard the grate of stiff bedclothes behind her and turned her head.

The mound in the other bed shifted, awakening, enlivening.

Maggie walked to her. "I didn't mean to disturb you," she whispered to the girl. "I just wanted to see how you and your mom are doing. I'm Maggie? From the pharmacy?"

The girl blinked, green-blue eyes huge in the tiny face. She struggled to sit up, then slumped back against twin pillows stationed behind her head. Although she didn't know the Whitleys well, Maggie had watched from a distance as the girl grew frail, her hair thinning, her skin graying. Now Maggie spotted new hair growth on her scalp, tiny hairs that looked like grass seed. Evidently the girl had taken a break from her chemotherapy. Her hair was beginning to return. Hopefully her cancer wouldn't follow suit.

"I remember you," the girl croaked, her voice sleep-roughed, intubating-abraded. "You're the new girl behind the counter. I heard you found us." She swallowed painfully. "Thank you."

Maggie slid into the padded chair beside her. "The biggest thanks will be you and your mom getting better."

At the mention of her mother, Riley's face clouded over. She turned her head and looked out the window. "They said the poison hurt her more because she's a smoker and has diabetes. They said she might not..." A fat tear rolled down Riley's emaciated cheek. "Mommy says it was unnatural for a mother to outlive her child. That's why she fought so hard to get me the right doctors, the right medicine." She looked at Maggie, her face pinched down the middle. "But I want *unnatural*. I want to go first. That way I'd never have to live a day without her."

Maggie instinctively reached out her hand. She felt another sensation of reaching into the past, this time to comfort her twelve-year-old self.

She murmured the same lies she had been told.

Don't worry.

Everything will be all right.

It's in God's hands.

The words felt empty on her tongue, but she couldn't stop herself. She had to fill the void not only in the room but in herself. It was ritualistic. Call and response. She dug deeper to muster something with meaning, something she wished she'd been told before her mother's hands grew cold for the last time. She came up empty.

The hospital door eased open and a head popped in followed by a woman in scrubs. "How are we doing?"

The nurse went against type. Or what Maggie considered nurse-type.

All the nurses she had encountered over the years were straight out of Central Casting: kindly older women with round bodies, line-worn faces and sensible haircuts. Not the image of the beautiful young bohemian before her.

This nurse had blue hair, a diamond in her right nostril and sleeve tattoos that peeked around her scrubs. St. Theresa's was a Catholic hospital, but it didn't share the same love of dress codes as the Catholic schools of Maggie's youth.

The nurse smiled at Maggie. "Awesome, a new friend. I'm Deena, the nurse du jour, or should I say du shift."

Riley struggled to sit, failed, flopped back onto the short stack of pillows. "This is Maggie," she said, "the lady who saved us."

Deena turned wide eyes on Maggie. "Is that so?" She gave Maggie a once-over then nodded approvingly. "Well, congrats, lady. Your fast thinking saved the day, not to mention a couple of lives."

Apparently Deena wasn't a regular connoisseur of the news or she'd recognize Maggie of Russ Brock's creation: pharmaceutical monster, finder—and perhaps maker—of bodies.

Deena checked Mary's vitals and IV site, scanned her wrist band then exited the room. She returned with a vial of medication, which she injected into the IV line.

"Sodium nitrite or thiosulfate?" Maggie asked.

Deena turned, brows raised. "We administered hydroxocobalamin to both Mary and Riley when they arrived. I just administered another medication into Mary's IV to keep her comfortable." She glanced at the oxygen saturation reading on the monitor. "She has several medical conditions, including COPD. Not ideal for someone poisoned with a substance that attacks the organs." She turned toward Riley with a smile. "And this one is a regular at St. Theresa's. Are we going to get you a punch card or what?"

Riley giggled. "Deena's been my nurse before," she said as Deena scooted beside the walker that pouted in the corner and went through the same routine on the girl. "She's awesome."

Deena smiled. "I used to be in ER. I was there when Riley came in for sky-high blood pressure. We even got some crash cart action. Then I became a floater and spent a lot of time on the medical floor, which is how I got to see even more of Miss Riley." She turned to Riley. "I think on your tenth visit, you get a free serving of Jell-O." She stripped off her gloves. "Anything else, kiddo?"

"Nope," Riley said smiling, lips pulled back to expose prominent gums and small misshapen teeth. Even her dentin seemed to be shrinking.

Deena pitched the gloves into the trash. "Then I'll catch ya later, alligator."

Maggie rose. "I'll follow you out." She waved at Riley then followed Deena from the room, taking a long slow look at Mary. Riley's mother hadn't so much as twitched during the entire visit.

Out in the hallway Maggie said, "You have great rapport with Riley."

"She's a good kid. A great kid. Sucks that life hasn't been good to her."

"Hope they'll be okay," Maggie said, fishing without a HIPAA license. "Both of them have such fragile health it's hard to know how the poison will affect them."

"They've been through the wringer, that's for sure. But we have a wonderful team here, and they seem to be responding to treatment." She gave Maggie's arm a squeeze. "There are a lot of reasons to hope."

That sounded an awful lot like "Everything will be okay," but Maggie decided to take it. She thanked Deena and wound her way down the halls to the elevator and eventually out the front door.

Maggie's drive home was uneventful. Her favorite variety. She found Constantine in their home office, a serious overstatement by nearly any estimation.

The home office—or future nursery, as Aunt Polly suggested—had been converted by the catechism of IKEA: a blonde-wood desk fronted by a matching swivel chair and flanked by a pair of vacant bookshelves. The Böring Collection, as Constantine called it. The only items of interest: a *Christmas Story* leg lamp and a bean bag chair forced on them by Constantine's mother, Helena, because "It was Constantine's favorite."

Constantine sat at the computer, his fingers flying across the keyboard, the rescue dog at his feet. "Mags!" he said when she entered the room. "How was your appointment?"

She flopped onto the beanbag, eliciting what sounded like applause in the world's smallest stadium. "Noisy and unnecessary. I should be getting my non-results in a few days."

"There's the positive girl I know and love. Now we'll find out what's wrong with your brain. And see if you have a concussion."

"Ha ha." She struggled out of the beanbag and plopped onto his lap. She nuzzled his neck, feeling the nip of his dark stubble, inhaling the scent of laundry detergent and coffee. "Still working?"

"Between saving the world from malware and trying to find this guy's rightful owner," he pointed at the sleeping dog, whose head lay atop his sneaker, "I've been doing some research."

"On the mating habits of the tsetse fly?"

"Sexy, but no." He reached around her and tapped the keyboard. "On your boss's legal adventures." He pointed at the monitor with a flourish. "It's all there in 1080p. That's the screen resolution, by the way."

Maggie smiled wryly. "Thanks for the tip." She leaned forward and read. "Lev made an offer on Colton's land, Colton accepted then changed his mind when Nigel Roberts offered him more. More detail than Lev gave me when we talked on the phone. So who's Nigel Roberts? The name sounds familiar."

"He's the CEO of Midwest Communities."

"The development firm?"

"The same. He's known for gentrification, expansion and other real estate-related 'ion' words. He also likes rainy days, old movies and long walks on the beach. At least that's what his Match.com profile says."

"Pretty hard for Lev to compete with. The guy's got deep pockets."

"And shallow principles. When he's not developing housing communities, he buys old properties and turns them into everyone's favorite blight: parking lots."

Maggie nodded. "He had eyes on Colton's property because of its location. He probably made him an offer Colton couldn't refuse."

"Maybe even Godfather-style. Word on the street is that Nigel runs high-stakes poker games at Palate du Gourmand downtown."

"Pretty fancy digs for a poker game."

"Pretty fancy poker games. High-value players with high-value pots. We're talking tens of thousands of dollars. Maybe more."

"And you know this how?"

He tapped the computer screen. "Online bulletin boards and social media." He grabbed a pen and twirled it. "You think Colton was a gambling man?"

"Why, you think he owed Nigel?"

Constantine shrugged. "It's possible. Could have made it easier for him to say yes to Nigel's offer. Nigel is power-hungry with money to feed his appetite. He's always looking to expand and exploit. I read that he hiked the lease on a building he owned in The Estates, a restaurant. And wouldn't you know—he plans to open his own restaurant in its place." Constantine got a faraway look in his eyes. "I always wanted to be a restaurateur. I'd call my place..." He made a frame with his hands in front of his face. "Giardia's."

"A restaurant named after a parasite. People will be lining up to throw up. Anything else?"

"That's about it. Seems like it might be worth checking out the gambling angle. Maybe a bad debt led to bad blood that led to bad medicine."

"And the Whitleys got caught in the crossfire?"

"It's possible. I like it a hell of a lot better than Petrosian, killer pharmacist or Maggie, ghoul Friday."

"Ugh." Maggie rubbed a hand over her face. "Russ Brock will not give up."

"He's just trying to make a big story bigger. The guy's a has-been—or maybe a never-was. My guess: he fancied himself as national talent but ended up on the local circuit. He's bitter, shallow and trying to make a name for himself."

"Trading on lies and the misery of others."

"That's the news, Mags."

Maggie rose and walked over to the window. Outside trees bent to the demands of the wind, which beat them with violent gusts and shrapnel of debris.

March. In like a lion...

"Speaking of misery," she said, staring at the threatening clouds overhead, "I went to visit the Whitleys."

"The second poisoning victims?" Constantine leaned forward. "What prompted that?"

"Austin told me that Mary wasn't doing well. I just kept thinking of Riley, sick and alone, worrying about her mother..."

"And you wanted to be there for her."

"Mary is hanging on by a thread, and Riley's there to witness the whole horrible thing while her own life hangs in the balance. She's doing better than her mom, but that doesn't mean much. She's got cancer. Not exactly the poster child for robust health."

"Think she'll—they'll—recover?"

Maggie turned from the window and the storm that had been brewing but had not yet come to a boil. "I sure hope so. And I hope they catch the bastard who did this."

Constantine leaned back in his chair, its joints creaking in protest. "Did our Boy Wonder say if they had any leads?"

"If by Boy Wonder you mean Austin, no. He talked about searching Petrosian's, but that's it. Not too earth-shattering since Petrosian seems eager for it." She tried not to think about the lawsuit between Ellis and Petrosian.

Constantine picked up a pen, clicked it a few times. "Did you happen to mention your chance encounter with Miles and his ketchup packets?"

"No, and I don't plan on it. I can handle Miles." She contemplated sharing news of Miles's latest note with Constantine. Decided she didn't want to cause Constantine unnecessary worry. She said she could handle him, and she would.

Constantine said nothing.

"I just keep thinking about the Colton Ellis and the Whitleys collapsing in the drugstore," Maggie said. "I'd love to check the database to see if they'd purchased any of the same items."

"You can't access the pharmacy database remotely?"

She shook her head. "Server's down. Has been since the store closed."

"There's an IT guy for that."

"Unfortunately, the pharmacy is locked up tighter than Trump's hair care regimen."

Constantine cracked his knuckles. "A lock is no match for my computer skills. Well, sometimes it is, but I can see if I can figure out the server issue remotely." He leaned forward and checked the time on the computer. "Later. Now I'm heading to Aunt Polly's for a reprisal of 'Constantine, World's Greatest Nephew.' Tonight's performance: hanging curtains while she and Dr. Kenny Rogers canoodle on the sofa. Wanna come?"

"Hard pass. Interior decorating and I don't play nice." She picked at the cuticle of her right thumb. "Besides, things have been weird between Polly and me since the cake shop." She hadn't told Constantine about Pop's reaction over her desire for a civil wedding service, the disappointment in his voice, the iciness of his goodbye. "Just hurry back. I haven't seen you all day."

He lifted himself from the chair. "Be back soon, pinky swear. And try to find out who owns this mutt, will ya? He's cramping Miss Vanilla's style."

Maggie peered into Miss Vanilla's cage perched atop the Böring bookcase. She circled the wheel, tiny feet a blur against the metal rungs. "Yeah, she seems really broken up about it."

"She's sublimating. Takes lessons from someone else I know."

Before Maggie could retort, he gathered her into his arms for a kiss. "Sure you don't want to go? Maybe get some sex advice from a geriatric couple?"

"Tempting but no. I'm just going to hang out, maybe catch an old movie."

Constantine stretched, his shirt hiking up to reveal surprisingly defined abs. He reached into Miss Vanilla's cage, cradled the hamster in his hand then popped her into his pocket. She peeped from her fabric lanai and wriggled her nose. "I'll take Miss Vanilla." He lowered his voice. "It makes her feel special. Oh, and there's a bunch of Hitchcock flicks in the queue. Just make sure you save *North by Northwest* for me so you can tell me how much I look like Cary Grant. Meanwhile, just relax and don't get into any trouble."

She smiled. "I wouldn't dream of it."

Chapter 16

A quick tour of the DVR confirmed what Maggie had already known: she'd seen every Hitchcock film. Three times. The curse of a movie buff whose childhood was spent in the creaking seats of a repertory theater.

She spooned Cherry Garcia into her mouth as she flipped through the options on the TV that Pop had given her when the picture on her own television collapsed like a tiny sun.

Shadow of a Doubt.

North by Northwest.

Rear Window.

To Catch a Thief.

Maggie paused on the last one, thinking not of the onscreen fireworks between Kelly and Grant or the iconic Côte d'Azur scenes, but of the promise of the title, the suggestion of capturing—of stopping—a perpetrator.

Maggie licked her spoon and dropped it into the now-empty pint. She'd do one better than to catch a thief. She'd catch a murderer.

Maggie decided that "catching" began with "identifying" and that identifying began with learning more about the victims. She wandered back to the home office, the dog trotting behind her, and tried once more to log into the drugstore's computer system. As expected, the computer flashed a *Host Not Available* message, as if she'd arrived early for a formal dinner and the host had not yet donned his smoking jacket and ascot.

Maggie logged off the computer and grabbed her purse and keys, which she'd tossed onto the pimp-print sofa. She jingled the keys in her hand as she contemplated whether to leave a note for Constantine. Chances were she'd beat him home. Even if she didn't, he wouldn't be able to read her writing, which looked like the chirographic lovechild of a physician's signature and shorthand notes. She could send a text, but didn't want to interrupt his curtain-hanging endeavors. Better just to explain the whole thing when she returned.

She closed her hand around the keys and made for the door. The dog barked. She looked at him. He wagged his tail, cocked his head and looked generally adorable. "You really should stay here," she told him. "Act as our watchdog." The pooch panted, dog lips parted in a slobbery smile. "On the other hand, I could use a lookout. Come on."

Although it was Friday night, traffic was light—maybe everyone was watching Hitchcock movies?—and Maggie made it to Petrosian's Pillbox in record time. She coasted in front of the pharmacy, car in neutral to minimize noise, looking for news vans, cameras and reporters—especially Russ Brock.

The street was deserted.

She rounded the building and parked in her spot, alert for media who may have taken cover in the darkness that gathered in the shadow of the slumbering building. The lot was also vacant.

Maggie plucked the dog from his seat and climbed out of the car. The wind had died, leaving the air heavy with the smell of spring growth and the promise of rain.

She stole to the front of the building and glanced behind her. The street was still empty, but for how long?

As promised, crime scene tape adorned the door. The iconic ribbon didn't look as though it would bar her entry. Other than its command to not cross, it seemed more suggestion than security measure. She pushed the tape aside and inserted her key into the front door, praying that Petrosian hadn't changed the locks.

She turned the key. It stuck. Perspiration budded on her upper lip. She adjusted the dog, chiding herself for not buying a leash or even an infant carrier that would have left her hands free, and jiggled the key in the lock. She closed her eyes then turned it again. The tumblers groaned, then responded with an affirmative click.

She was in.

A car pulled around the corner, its blue-white HID bulbs coring the night. Maggie slipped into the building and closed the door behind her. She leaned against the door, heart hammering, picturing Brock behind the wheel. And then Miles. She put her ear against the door and listened. She heard the car's engine recede into the distance. She released a gust of breath and threw the lock.

"Stop acting guilty, O'Malley," she muttered to herself. "You're not doing anything wrong. This isn't even breaking and entering. It's just...entering." The dog tilted his head. "And no comment from you."

Maggie walked to the back of the store. Every aisle seemed to whisper an implicit promise. Less pain. Brighter whites. More volume at the roots. Less volume in the thighs. She wondered how many oaths the sundries could keep. She wondered how many she could.

Did she really think she could uncover who had poisoned Colton Ellis and the Whitleys? Did she really think she was better suited than the police?

The truth was, she did. Not because she was more qualified, but because she was more driven. The police wanted to solve the crime, right wrong and restore order. Maggie wanted all of that, plus absolution, restoration and vindication. She wanted her good name restored. She wanted Petrosian's back in business. She wanted whoever took Colton's life and Riley's peace to pay.

She stationed herself at Petrosian's computer behind the counter and keyed in her log-in credentials. She waited as the genie who lived inside the server decided whether to grant her digital wishes.

The loading bar crawled slowly to the right, a barometer of progress or failure. Maggie pulled at the collar of her t-shirt. She was heating up right along with the computer.

Then...success.

A welcome page appeared, followed by a prompt asking her where she wanted to go.

"How about happily ever after?" she muttered.

Her fingers danced across the keys as she accessed the screen for prescription history. Her first stop: the youngest victim.

Maggie pointed, clicked and repeated. Riley Whitley's data loaded. And loaded. And loaded.

Despite her sixteen years, Riley Whitley had amassed an impressive pharmaceutical history. In addition to receiving chemotherapy at the hospital's infusion center, she'd been prescribed opioids for pain, antiemetics for nausea, psychotropics for anxiety and depression, and the occasional antibiotic for infection.

Maggie felt something in her chest tighten. She wondered what kind of prognosis the doctors had given. Whether the cancer was abating or lying in wait deep within her bones. Whether Riley thought about boys and ripped jeans and prom, or just blood counts and stem cells.

Maggie shook off her darkening mood. She had to remain objective. She had to focus.

She scrolled to the Whitleys' most recent pharmacy purchases: a refill of Riley's prescriptions for nausea and pain. It jived with what she'd learned during the brief inventory check with Petrosian.

She tabbed and entered Mary's name into the database, then read the results. The list wasn't as extensive as Riley's, but it wasn't fallow pharmaceutical ground, either. From Mary's pharmaceutical profile, Maggie gleaned that she not only suffered from COPD and diabetes, but hypertension, rheumatoid arthritis and insomnia. Neither Whitley female had hit the jackpot in the wellness lottery.

Bottom line: no pharmaceutical crossover between Riley and Mary, but the history did reveal a timeframe well within reason for poisoning symptoms to appear.

Cyanide killed by volume and exposure. Inhale or ingest a lot? Expect seizure, coma or death almost immediately. Exposed to low doses over a period of time? Enjoy the slow creep of persistent, debilitating headaches, vomiting, and abdominal and chest pain.

There was no way to know long it took for cyanide to reach toxic levels for the poisoning victims. The only certainty was the agony each experienced as the poison starved their cells of oxygen and their organs began to die. Mary and Riley both had medical conditions that made them vulnerable to the effects of cyanide.

Maggie tabbed again and searched for Colton Ellis. The list was long, but not overly so: the antibiotic she had helped fill the day he died, migraine medication, a drug to control blood pressure and mitigate kidney disease, and OxyContin.

Maggie stopped scrolling. Reread. The OxyContin had been refilled seven times.

She frowned. She couldn't remember a recent surgery or chronic pain condition that would warrant such a strong pain medication, let alone a seven-time refill. She squinted and continued her descent down the page.

A high-pitched whine carved through her thoughts.

She glanced at the dog lying at her feet. "What's up, buddy?" she asked absent-mindedly. "You hungry?"

The dog whined again and got to his feet. "Hang on a sec," she said, reading. "Then it's home for chow."

The dog rose to his feet and barked. Maggie took her finger off the computer mouse and looked at him full-on. He was staring at the darkened stockroom.

"Just a bunch of boxes," she told him. "Nothing to worry about."

But the animal didn't seem convinced. He lowered his head and gave a low growl, a rumbling sound that reverberated from deep within his belly.

Maggie felt the hair on the back of her neck rise, her body raising the alarm. Despite Maggie's avoidance of emotion, she had learned to trust her instincts. She'd learned the hard way that ignoring them could lead to unpleasant consequences.

She backed away from the computer and walked toward the blackness that lay outside the ring of light cast by the monitor. In the semi-dark, she saw the familiar silhouette: a skyline of boxes, the corner of the eye-wash station, the mouth of the cubbies where employees stored lunchboxes and jackets.

Maggie approached the stockroom, feet gliding across the floor. She told herself to take it easy, to not let her imagination take hold, to breathe, for God's sake.

Her body wasn't having any of it. Blood thundered through her ears. Her breath came in shallow pants.

Maggie parted her lips to let more oxygen into her lungs and reached for the wall switch. She flicked. The room jumped into full relief, its emptiness exposed by the glare of Thom's unflattering fluorescents overhead.

Maggie released a lungful of air and looked back at the dog who had retained his post on Petrosian's ergonomic floor mat. "You ever hear of the dog who cried wolf?"

Her chuckle was interrupted by a vibration in her pocket. She plunged her hand inside and excised her phone. A text message from an unknown number. It was probably a solicitation, an invitation to make thousands working from home or advice about how to get rid of belly fat by eating one strange food. She moved to delete the message, but opened it instead. In the body of the text was a single photo.

Maggie squinted.

The image was of a nude woman. No, not nude. Wearing flesh-toned tights and a cream-colored top. She enlarged the photo, fear writhing through her insides like maggots.

Maggie gaped at the photo. In glorious high definition, she saw herself stride toward GymRatz.

The photo had been edited. Giant breasts and a spray of pubic hair had been crudely drawn with a doodling app. Her eyes had been scratched out. Hands clutched the hills and vales of her body. At the center of her forehead, a target served as a ringed beauty mark.

Maggie's stomach clenched and flipped. She backed out of the photo and searched the message for a clue to the sender's identity. The anonymous digits mocked her.

She steeled herself and re-opened the photo. She scanned her mutilated image in search of a clue. Then, she spotted it: the letters MM in the cleavage of the illustrated breasts.

MM.

Miles Montgomery.

Miles once again using a cell phone to target her. Miles once again harassing her. Miles once again sending a very clear message.

I see you.

I follow you.

I'll do whatever I want with you.

Maggie felt waves of retroperistalsis as her stomach readied itself to evacuate its contents. Maggie shoved her phone back into her pocket and fanned herself with her hands to reduce her temperature and the likelihood of losing what little she'd eaten that day.

She staggered toward the staff bathroom, her mind on Miles, the photo, the nausea that grew with each step.

A new sound invaded her consciousness.

A scritch-scratch of something—or someone—outside the door that led to the parking lot.

Her heart throttled up once again. Was debris from the dumpster being blown against the building? A stick drumming along to the winds' tempestuous gusts? Or was it Miles, there to make good on the hoped-for conclusion he'd drawn?

Maggie gathered her courage and a broom. Sure, she could call Constantine. Sure, she could dial 911. But what would she tell them? She'd gotten a creepy text message from an old coworker then heard a funny sound outside a pharmacy she wasn't supposed to be in? No, she had to handle this on her own.

Maggie inhaled deeply and charged the door, speed subbing for fickle bravery that waxed and waned with each heartbeat. She wrenched the doorknob and pushed the stockroom door. It flew open, steel and wood carrying it into the concrete wall behind it.

Maggie stood in the doorway, breath coming in hitches, shaking with adrenaline. She peered into the parking lot. Dumpster? Check. Studebaker? Check. Empty parking lot devoid of Miles Montgomery? Check and check.

False alarm number two.

She grabbed the door handle and began to pull it closed. A figure materialized from the building's shadow.

"I thought that was your car," a voice said. "What is it, a Valiant?"

She expected to see Miles's mocking smile. Instead Russ Brock stepped into her field of vision.

"What are you doing here?" Maggie demanded.

Brock gave a toothpaste-fired smile. "I had a feeling you'd show up here. Did you come back for a trophy? Or to cover your tracks before the police execute their warrant?"

Maggie looked around for the cameraman, for the sound guy. Indifferent stars winked at the otherwise empty lot. "No camera?"

Russ put his hands in his pockets and hitched his shoulders. "Sometimes old Russ likes to fly solo."

And sometimes old Russ likes to refer to himself in the third person.

Maggie tightened her grip on the door handle and began to pull. Brock put a tasseled boat shoe against the door. Maggie hated tassels. "Whoa, whoa, whoa. I'm here as a favor to you."

Maggie raised an eyebrow. "A favor?"

"An exclusive interview. So you can tell your side of the story. No cameras. No hubbub. Just you and me and my notepad. Maybe a candlelight dinner."

"I don't have a story," Maggie said, "and nothing to say to you." She gave him a long look. "You're trespassing, by the way."

The wicked grin returned. "That makes two of us." He flicked a card from his pocket, thrust it beneath her nose. "If you change your mind—and I think you might find that beneficial—I'm just a phone call away."

Maggie made no move. Brock let the card fall from his fingertips to the ground. "It's your funeral," he said.

Chapter 17

Constantine was waiting for her when she got home, Miss Vanilla in hand.

"Where have you been?" he asked, worry creasing the skin between his brows. "I called your phone seven million times, which is forty-nine million in dog calls."

Maggie threw her purse on the sofa and sank beside it. The dog jumped up and sat beside her. "Sorry, I thought I'd beat you home."

"When you weren't here and I couldn't get a hold of you, I just—" He placed Miss Vanilla in her cage and watched her round her wheel. A muscle in his cheek jumped as he worked his jaw.

Maggie grabbed his hand and pulled him beside her. "I'm fine, really, and I'm sorry I worried you. I just took a little drive."

"To?"

Maggie feigned interest in a couch cushion. "Petrosian's. To take a peek at the prescription database."

"Petrosian's? The drugstore that's sealed by crime scene tape, quite possibly the scene of a crime, about to be served with a search warrant and likely under police surveillance? That Petrosian's?"

"Well, yeah. But nobody was there. Except, uh, Russ Brock."

"Russ Brock?" Constantine's voice rose so high Maggie thought the dog might start howling. "The reporter whose favorite hobby is ruining your reputation?"

"He said he wanted to give me an exclusive to 'clear my name.'"

"Which might be a little more muddied now that you've added breaking and entering to Brock's list of Maggie's sins."

"I had a key. Besides, Brock was there, too, making him a possible target for a trespassing claim."

Constantine crossed his arms. "That's about as high on Brock's list of worries as overdue library books. I hope your field trip was illuminating."

Maggie pulled a strand of hair from her ponytail and twirled it. "Not really. I wanted to do a quick tour of the prescription database to see if I could find any commonalities in the meds the poisoning victims took."

"Didn't Petrosian do that already? And isn't that, like, a cop thing to do?"

"One, if Petrosian combed the database after our partial inventory following Colton Ellis's death, he certainly didn't share the results with me, and two, my history with Hollow Pine's detectives hasn't exactly filled me with confidence."

"They have fallen short of *Magnum, P.I.* status," he agreed. "Find anything useful?"

"Not really," Maggie admitted. "I didn't dive too deeply because of Brock's surprise appearance, but what I did see didn't raise any flags. It didn't look like any of the victims took the same meds."

"That's good news, right?"

"More like no news. They could have consumed any number of things laced with cyanide. Gatorade. Protein bars. York Peppermint Patties. All readily available at Petrosian's."

"Aren't there records of purchases other than prescriptions?"

"Yes, but I don't have access to those. Plus, the victims could have touched—or even inhaled—the poison." She shook her head. "I'm not sure what I was hoping I'd find. Something obvious, I guess. Instead I just walked away with more questions, including the possibility of drug abuse."

She summarized Colton Ellis's history of opioid use.

"Sad, but common," Constantine said. "It's a big problem."

"Huge. I'm just wondering why Petrosian didn't flag him as drug-seeking."

"Maybe he didn't notice? He could have been distracted. Between the new store and the lawsuit, he had a lot on his mind."

She worked at the skin at her thumb with the nail of her forefinger. "No matter how much Petrosian has on his mind, nothing gets by him. One time Francine came back from her break two minutes late, and he called her on it." She shook her head. "It just gives me a bad feeling."

"About Petrosian? The guy's an overgrown Boy Scout."

"It's just..." She ripped a shred of skin from her cuticle.

It was just that a potential addiction had been overlooked. It was just that Petrosian could have turned a blind eye in an attempt to sweeten a real estate deal gone sour. It was just that Colton Ellis was dead with no one to tell his tale. "I guess I have trust issues. Plus I had another encounter with Miles."

Constantine sat up. "Encounter? What kind of encounter?"

"The digital variety." She didn't mention the note in the car. She didn't tell him right after it had happened and felt awkward about bringing it up now. She pulled up the text message on her phone and handed over the device. He took in the image, the illustrations, the subtext. He handed it back, his face dark and dangerous.

"He has to be stopped."

"From what? Ketchuping my car? Sending nasty notes?"

"Harassing you. There are laws, you know, ones that can send him back to the big house. Tell Austin. File a report. Do whatever it takes to get that guy on the radar."

"You're right. I will." Maggie rubbed her eyes and leaned against Constantine. She was suddenly exhausted, fatigue pulling at her like gravity from a nearby moon. She closed her eyes, wanting to be swallowed by the blackness of sleep, the emptiness of mind, the...

Maggie jerked awake. She sat up and looked around, trying to get her bearings. She'd fallen asleep and Constantine had carried her to bed.

But why was she drenched in sweat, her heart threatening to beat its way through her chest? Had she been dreaming? Was someone in the room?

De Niro taunted from her phone. She went limp with relief. The call had awoken her. Miles again?

She fumbled for the device on her night table and closed her fingers around its cool, smooth case. She peered at the screen. Levon Petrosian's photo looked back, his eyes burning through the phone. She checked the time. Ten forty-five p.m. A little late for a social call.

She swiped to answer.

"Ms. O'Malley," he intoned, "please forgive the late hour."

Maggie glanced over at Constantine who was drooling onto his pillow. She slipped from beneath the blankets and crept into the hall. "No problem." She closed the bedroom door behind her. "What's up?"

"I'm afraid I have a bit of bad news." He paused.

Maggie filled the void with her fears. The Whitleys had died. There had been another poisoning. Petrosian had been arrested and used his one phone call to tell Maggie.

The silence dragged on.

"Yes?" she prompted.

"There's been another poisoning."

Door number two.

"Who? When?"

"I just got off the phone with Ms. Wren, the policewoman." Maggie sucked her teeth at *policewoman*. "Another victim was found in her home. She died several days earlier."

Maggie let that sink in. "How was she found? How did they know it was poisoning?"

"A welfare check, to answer your first query and lab analysis to answer your second. The victim," Maggie heard a shuffle of paper, "Claudia Warren lived alone, didn't have many friends. She'd been absent from work for a few days, didn't call in, which was unusual given her upcoming work trip to Tobago. Her coworkers eventually got around to notifying the police." He paused, his derision at the tardy notification underscored by silence. "The medical examiner had the foresight to check for cyanide poisoning, likely because it's top of mind for everyone in Hollow Pine."

Russ Brock and his media brethren had made sure of that. The drumbeat of the poisonings, the potential risk to the public and Maggie's propensity for being present when bodies cropped up had pealed across the tri-county area with the intensity of an emergency broadcast warning.

"Was she..." Maggie cleared her throat. "Was she a customer?"

"Yes," Petrosian said quietly. "She was. Filled her prescription for Levothroid every month."

Maggie consulted her mental database of pharmaceuticals. Lovothroid was a thyroid medication. Side effects included an elevated heartrate, which could pump poison more efficiently through Claudia Warren's body.

There was another moment of silence. Finally Petrosian said, "The police have their search warrant. They'll execute it tomorrow. I'm allowed to be present. I'm just not sure I want to be." It was a change of heart since his earlier eagerness, but she could understand it. Why would he want to witness his beloved pharmacy dismantled? "Hopefully, they'll find some answers. Hopefully there will be no more poisonings."

Your lips to God's ear, Maggie thought.

She ended the call and felt her energy drain as if she had opened a vein.

Part of her had expected another poisoning, the proverbial drop of the other shoe, the coda to a *danse macabre* set in motion by a madman.

Suddenly Petrosian's ignorance—or avoidance—of Colton Ellis's potential drug problem didn't seem so important. People had lost their lives. A daughter kept vigil at her mother's deathbed. Her boss's world was about to implode. And so was hers. How long did she have until Brock reported on the latest poisoning, the search warrant, the lawsuit he'd surely discover and Maggie's involvement he'd likely suggest?

She turned to open the bedroom door and found Constantine slouched in the doorway, his dark curly hair mashed against one side of his head, his eyes fogged by sleep, his bare torso creased with sheet marks. Maggie thought he never looked more gorgeous.

"I had a dream that someone woke me up," he mumbled as he rubbed his eye.

"And I had a dream that there was another poisoning victim. Unfortunately that turned out to be true."

Constantine stopped mid-rub. "Are you serious?"

"Dead. Unfortunately so is a woman named Claudia Warren."

"When?"

Maggie told him about her failure to arrive at work, which had been caused by her failure to breathe.

"And she's a customer?"

"According to Petrosian. I've never helped her, but apparently she came in every month for her thyroid medication."

"And none of the other victims took thyroid meds?"

Maggie shook her head. "Not that I saw. I didn't have time to get a comprehensive look at prescription history, but nothing jumps out as a prescription connection."

"Which, like we talked about, means a big fat nothing when you consider all the potential sources for contamination." He took her by the hand and led her back to the bedroom. He plopped onto the mattress and stretched his lanky frame on the rumpled duvet that Aunt Fiona had forced on them as a housewarming—which Maggie knew by her disapproving look was a living-in-sin-but-I'll-try-to-accept-it—gift. "So what's next?"

Maggie curled her body beside him and twined her hand in his. "The police will execute their search warrant and see if they can find a connection. I'm sure they'll do what I did: scour records of recent retail sales, try to see if anyone purchased the same thing. In the meantime, I'm betting they'll make an announcement not to consume anything that came from Petrosian's Pillbox. Proof or not, the fact that all victims patronized the same store points to something more than coincidence."

"True, but there could be other connections between the victims. You were looking for something pharmaceutical. Maybe there's something environmental, something...social."

Maggie stared at him. "You're absolutely right. We need to look at the victimology."

"Victimology? Guess I missed that class since I didn't major in murder."

"We need to see what connections exist outside the pharmacy." Maggie felt a familiar electric hum in her veins. It was the feeling she got when she was onto something, when discovery seemed imminent or at least achievable. "We also need to get serious about a suspect list. Who had motive, means and opportunity."

"I don't think we need to get serious about any of that since we're not the police and this isn't our case."

"Maybe not technically, but I am involved. Or at least I *feel* involved. So I'm going to get online, do a little social media snooping, see what I can find out about the victims, including any possible connections. Then I'll make a grid of possible suspects based on what I know and what I find. What do you think?" There was no reply. "Gus?"

Maggie looked over. Constantine was snoring deeply.

Chapter 18

Maggie made a pot of coffee and squirreled herself away in the home office. Her earlier exhaustion had dissipated like morning mist, pushing out the gloom that had settled in the whorls of her brain.

She'd research, construct hypotheses, analyze data and draw conclusions. God bless the scientific method.

She logged onto her computer. Two emails: a follow-up from Martha from Let Them Eat Cake! and a response to a query Aunt Fiona had made on her behalf about bridal bouquets. She'd deal with those later.

Maggie closed email and opened an internet browser. She began with her favorite research buddy of late: Google. As with her pharmacy foray, she started with the most recent victim.

Claudia Warren had a modest online presence. She was featured in the "Team" section of AdWorx's website as an account executive, her byline had graced a number of press releases on a client's revolutionary adhesive (sticky, but not too sticky), and she was relatively active on Facebook where she shared videos of baby goats sporting Shetland sweaters.

Claudia wasn't big on privacy. Her Facebook page and all of its attendant posts was open for anyone to see. A quick tour of Claudia's contacts told Maggie that she wasn't friends with any of the other poisoning victims, nor did she engage in high-stakes poker games or consume beef in the hopes of garnering a free t-shirt. Claudia's only connection with the other victims was her patronage of Petrosian's.

Claudia's posts bemoaning the single life sent Maggie to online dating sites. She found Claudia's profile on Christian Mingle, Plenty of Fish and Tinder, which made Maggie raise an eyebrow. Swipe right for murder?

Maggie went down the rabbit hole of searching the profiles of Claudia's potential suitors. Nothing obvious. Then again, few would include "poisoning" in their list of turn-ons.

Maggie changed gears and dove into the lives of Colton Ellis and the

Whitleys. No real surprises there, either.

Colton Ellis had amassed a wealth of Facebook friends thanks to his gregarious personality and eating exploits. He also used social media to test out bad jokes (expected) and hawk nutritional supplements (ironic). No mention of his legal troubles with Petrosian or his card games with the man who would soon own his property in The Estates.

As with Claudia Warren, he seemed to have no connection with the others.

Maggie sighed and wound her hair into a bun, then jabbed a pencil that she found on the desk through its tangled center. She made a silent plea to the patron saint of internet searches and input Riley and Mary's names.

Here, she hit internet pay dirt.

Mary was not only active on Facebook, Instagram and Twitter, she had a popular blog titled Riley's Road that chronicled her daughter's health struggles.

Maggie skimmed the posts and found herself impressed. Despite her mousy appearance, Mary was a fiery writer who peppered passionate posts with both biting humor and touching insight. Her stories were raw and powerful and funny and tragic—an authentic and compelling portrait of a single mother moving from town to town in search of salvation for her sick daughter.

Maggie spent forty-five minutes scrolling through Mary's social media contacts and blog followers. Despite her popularity, neither Colton Ellis nor Claudia Warren were friends or had followed or commented on her blog.

Maggie put her head in her hands.

Internet: 1

Maggie: 0

Maggie shut the computer. With failure, fatigue returned with a grudge. Her legs felt leaden as she trudged across the worn brown rug and stumbled toward the bedroom.

Tomorrow was another day. A day to re-examine what she may have missed. To search for suspects. To find the links she was certain existed.

Tonight belonged to sleep and whatever dreams—or nightmares—lay beyond.

Chapter 19

The scent of coffee tantalized Maggie's nose. Her eyelids fluttered then peeled open one at a time. She blinked and looked down. A steaming cup was beneath her chin.

"Thought you could use some vitamin C after your late night," Constantine said, nodding toward the heavily creamed mug of joe.

Maggie smiled and sat up. "And by vitamin C you mean caffeine or Constantine?"

"Both?"

She laughed and slid over. "Will you be this sweet when we're married?"

He sat beside her. "Sweeter, like a banana left too long on the counter."

Maggie wrinkled her nose. "Nice analogy." She inhaled the coffee's aroma and took a sip, relishing the warmth as it traveled down her throat.

"What did your insomniac pursuits net you?"

"Other than dark circles under my eyes? Not much. The victims' only connection seems to be the drugstore."

"And your motive/means/opportunity suspect list?"

She took another sip. "Under development. After I finish this and meet Ada at the gym. Hopefully this time I won't make a fool of myself."

He kissed her on her nose. "All part of your charm. See you when you get back."

Ada was waiting for Maggie at the GymRatz front counter, pulling her heel to her glute in a deep quad stretch. "I already checked you in. I've got two more guest passes for you then you'll have to commit." She rolled her neck, whipping her long, dark ponytail around. "My favorite is the SpinCycle. What do you think of it?"

Maggie thought of her previous exploits: underwear clinging to her tights, stationary cycles she'd sent crashing into each other in a spectacular cascade of metal dominoes. "I think I'll be lucky if they let me back in."

Ada laughed. "Don't worry. Sloane's cool. Couple more sessions and you'll be able to bounce a quarter off your ass." Maggie wondered about her odds with dimes and nickels and whether she could put coin-responsive musculature on a future resume. "Besides," Ada continued, "Spinning will get your mind off all the news coverage."

Maggie groaned. "Thanks for reminding me."

Ada laughed and looped her arm through Maggie's. "Don't worry. Everyone knows you're innocent." Maggie rolled her eyes. "Hey, I'm a cop in training. Trust me."

They strode past the locker rooms, around a snack counter laden with wheatgrass smoothies and gluten-free "bagels," and into the SpinCycle. "I'm going to refill my water bottle, check to see if that cute guy is lifting free weights. Be right back."

With the early hour, the SpinCycle was dimly lit, transforming the cycles into hulking, predatory shadows.

At least no one will recognize me, Maggie mused.

"Back again, new girl." Sloane slapped a meaty hand on her arm. "Great to see you."

Maggie resisted the urge to rub her arm. "Thanks."

"You're Ada's friend, right? Maggie? The one on TV." Sloane took a step forward, lowered her voice. "With the poisonings?"

Maggie with the Poisonings. Maggie thought that would make a great band name. "Um, I guess?"

Sloane bobbed her head slowly. "I thought so. Helluva deal. All those deaths. The pharmacy closing." She leaned even closer, the stale powdery smell of overworked deodorant encircling her. "The chance that we could have something poisonous in our medicine cabinets right now."

Maggie licked her lips. "Yeah, helluva deal." She looked over her shoulder. Where was Ada?

"And all that stuff about you," Sloane continued, "your past. Your exploits." Exploits. As if she were Ponce de Leon. "I just don't understand why they're not talking about that other girl."

Maggie concentrated on keeping her face neutral. "Other girl?"

The Boulder made duck lips, reviewed her form, anterior and posterior, in the room's mirrored walls. "Francine."

"Francine? Checker Francine? At Petrosian's?"

Sloane put a hand on her hip, inflating her bicep appreciably. "We used to train together. Body building." She flexed the bicep, which rippled beneath her smooth tanned skin, gave the mirror another glance. "That bitch has problems."

"What kind of problems?"

"Alcohol. Drugs. Trouble with the law."

"Drugs? Trouble with the law? *Francine?*" Maggie thought of her coworker's holier-than-everyone attitude. "Are you sure we're talking about the same person?"

Sloane barked out a laugh. "Oh yeah. I saw her the last time I was in Petrosian's, getting in some kid's face. I mean, kids can be a real pain in the ass, but you have to let 'em know who's in charge. Keep 'em on a tight leash, if you know what I mean." Maggie thought Sloane used the same philosophy in her Spin class. "Why a pharmacy would hire someone like her is beyond me."

Maggie opened her mouth to ask about Francine's run-ins with the law, to inquire about her coworker's drug history, when the room suddenly came alive with other cyclists.

Sloane gave Maggie a sympathetic look. "Listen, I'd like to dish more about Francine, but duty calls. Get ready to get your heart pounding."

Maggie was way ahead of her.

Chapter 20

Maggie was drenched by the time she crawled back into her car, her Dri-FIT shirt and tights falling short of their promise as they clung to her sweat-slicked skin. She waved at Ada as her friend pulled out of the parking lot. Maggie eased out onto the street and pointed the car homeward.

The idea: bring Constantine up to speed, dig into Francine's background, via the web and via Petrosian, then share whatever intel they unearthed with Gladys and Austin.

Bim, bam, boom.

Two blocks into her journey home, Maggie changed her mind. She felt a sudden, irresistible urge to turn the car toward the home of Levon Petrosian and, she was certain, concrete answers to troublesome questions.

She made a right onto Madison then another onto Jefferson, traveling the tree-lined street of the presidentially named neighborhood known for its brick-faced homes, expansive yards and dearth of construction. Once known as Doctor Row, the historic district had fallen out of favor among Hollow Pine's newest crop of professionals as nascent doctors, lawyers, tech gurus and entrepreneurs heeded the siren's call of *shiny! new! low maintenance!* espoused by The Estates.

Goodbye, stately old neighborhood. Hello, fancy new digs.

The result was faded majesty, block after block of tired-looking houses that wore their forgotten glory like an old letterman's jacket.

She coasted to a stop in front of the modest Federal-style home.

The house was easily the smallest on the street, but arguably the most well-kept. It was heralded by a rolling expanse of lawn, a low row of meticulously trimmed boxwood and freshly swept pavers. The blinds on every window were drawn. Despite the early hour, the porch light was illuminated.

Lights on, but nobody home?

Maggie grabbed a towel from her gym bag, dragged it across her face and beneath her arms. She shrugged into a hoodie she found in the backseat and slicked her hair into a ponytail. Not exactly high glamour, but hopefully her appearance wouldn't inspire Petrosian to don a HAZMAT suit.

Maggie climbed out of the Studebaker and jogged up to the house. Light seeped around the storm door and window seals. She knocked.

A deep emptiness echoed back. Maggie rapped again, louder this time, knuckles cracking against whitewashed wood. Nothing. Then a rustle from the other side.

The door cracked. A woman with a rectangular face and dark hair embroidered with silver peered back. She clutched the top of her red velour robe, cinching it like a bag against her throat. "Yes?" Her eyes flicked over Maggie's head and roved the middle distance. Looking for someone? Mapping out her escape?

Maggie cleared her throat. "Sona?" she asked, surprised at the facility with which Petrosian's wife's name fell from her lips. Maybe her brain was okay after all. "I'm Maggie. I work with your husband."

Sona released the neck of her robe and eased the door open. "I thought you were a reporter. They keep knocking on the door, asking for a comment."

"Is Mr. Petrosian available? I was hoping to talk with him about some things at work."

Sona shook her head, her skull a bobblehead atop her slight body. "He's out of town."

"Out of town?" Maggie asked more loudly than she'd intended. "Since when?"

Sona smiled, creating parentheses around her mouth, and shifted on slippered feet. Maggie caught a whiff of the warring scents of body odor and vitamins. It was a familiar odor, one that she had smelled on her mother.

"He decided to go fishing for a couple of days," Sona said, "take his mind off all this turmoil. He couldn't bear to be around for the search warrant. He said it would be like watching someone mistreat your child."

She wasn't surprised by the sentiment. Petrosian's unexpected trip out of town was another story. "If you talk with him, will you tell him I stopped by?"

Sona brought her hand to her throat and bowed her head. "Of course, but I doubt he'll phone. No land lines and cell coverage is poor up at the lake." She gave a rueful smile. "Which is why he's asked his sister to stay with me." She tilted her head toward the interior of the house. "Lev believes that cancer calls for a babysitter as well as a physician."

Cancer. Maggie had nosed out the truth, Sona's scent beckoning memory. Still, she was surprised. Petrosian was a private man, yet it was peculiar that he hadn't said anything about his wife's illness.

Maggie took Sona's hand, dry and papery as the page of an old book. Maggie wondered what story it could tell. "I'm sorry to have bothered you," she said.

"No bother. It's nice to meet the people Lev works with. I haven't been to the pharmacy in..." She looked away. "In a very long time."

"You make wonderful eggs," Maggie said suddenly, remembering the kindness of a meal Petrosian shared when Maggie was hungry. "And *nazook*. Mr. Petrosian has brought them in. So it's like a part of you is there."

Maggie felt the keen edge of grief as she remembered the enormity of Lev's small act of kindness, the crushing guilt of her suspicion. "I have to go," she whispered. "Thank you. And I'm sorry."

Maggie raced to her car, trying to outrun the feelings that threatened to engulf her. Petrosian's wife had cancer. He had been swindled out of a real estate deal. His pharmacy had become the site of cyanide poisonings. And all Maggie had done was question and judge and suspect. She dove into the shelter of the Studebaker and breathed deeply. Inhale hope. Exhale doubt. Inhale denial. Exhale suspicion.

Maggie's phone came to life, severing the greedy grip of her guilt. She checked the display.

Unavailable.

Gooseflesh prickled her still-damp skin. Not again.

She mustered courage, tapped to answer and put the phone to her ear. "This is Maggie," she said in her steadiest voice.

"Magnolia, this is Dr. Bartholomew." The neurologist who ordered her MRI and a man who rivaled pickled beets for personality. "I'm calling with the results of your imaging." He paused for approximately 1.5 million years. "The MRI showed that you don't have any structural abnormalities or bleeding, but with your symptoms I believe your brain was concussed and that you're suffering from post-concussion syndrome."

"Post-concussion—" she sputtered. "But I didn't even have a

concussion. Just a little bump on the head."

"After which you lost consciousness and experienced headaches, difficulty thinking, fatigue and irritability. That's a concussion."

"But the atta—the *injury*—was months ago."

"Everyone—and every brain—heals differently. Some people bounce right back. Others take months to improve. Even longer."

Longer? "What's the treatment?" Maggie scoured her memory banks for an appropriate medication for the treatment of concussion, past or present, came up empty.

"Rest, primarily," Dr. Bartholomew replied. "Avoid over-stimulation, get adequate sleep, good nutrition. Just take it easy."

Maggie had a feeling that "taking it easy" didn't include investigating a string of poisonings.

She thanked the doctor, promised to heed his advice and make a follow-up appointment, then cranked down the window. A breeze whispered over the red leather upholstery, carrying the scent of men's cologne. Sweet. Cloying. Soaked in memory. She looked up.

Miles stood three feet from the car.

"Hello, Maggie." He parted his lips, a shark's grin, sly, dangerous, so like his father's.

We're going to need a bigger boat, her mind quoted *Jaws* by rote.

"What are you doing here, Miles?"

Miles spread his arms, turned his face skyward. "Out enjoying this fine spring day."

"I mean out of jail. More specifically, here in Hollow Pine."

Miles clicked his tongue. "Such bad manners. You haven't even asked how I've been, what I've been up to."

"I know what you've been up to," Maggie said through her teeth. "Vandalizing and leaving notes in my car, sending me obscene text messages. Not to mention a ten-year stretch at the penitentiary."

"Ah, you've gotten my missives. Excellent. They're just one of the ways I like to keep in touch. As for my incarceration, it's all but eliminated for time served and good behavior. Oh, and for offering up information about my father."

Maggie stared. "You betrayed your father to save yourself?"

Miles shrugged. "I found out more about my father's activities after I was in-house." In-house. As if he were corporate counsel or had joined a fraternity. "If the situation were reversed, my father would have done the same."

Maggie was certain he was right. "Why are you in Hollow Pine?" She repeated. "Did you follow me here?

Miles gave a shark's grin. Maggie wondered how many rows of teeth queued behind the white veneers. "Follow you? Now why would I want to do that? I came here for a change of scenery." His eyes crawled over her body. "And you do make quite the view. You've inspired my artwork."

Maggie felt revulsion squirm through her. She started the car, jerked the gearshift into first. "Leave me alone, Miles."

He stepped to the car, put his hand on the doorframe, leaned in. His breath smelled as if it had passed its "best-by" date. His eyes once again roved her body, which had already crystallized with the salt of dried sweat. The smile dropped from the country club-handsome face. "Don't worry, Maggie. Alone is exactly how I intend to leave you."

Then he kissed the empty air between them and stepped away from the car.

Chapter 21

Maggie's hands shook as she steered the car from the curb, piloted it between the hash marks and fog line that marked the way home. She had expected fear. Miles's presence—and their shared history—was enough to elicit that. She didn't expect white hot rage that billowed deep within her gut. "How dare he?" Maggie seethed. "How dare he—"

How dare he what, exactly? Other than a vaguely menacing phrase and a Weinsteinian air kiss, Miles hadn't done anything except ketchup her car and proffer threatening-ish messages.

Still his presence both at the gym and outside Petrosian's home— in Hollow Pine period—suggested that he was watching her. Stalking her. Biding his time for whatever end game he had planned.

Alone is exactly how I intend to leave you.

She didn't know what he meant by that phrase. She knew she didn't want to find out.

Maggie took side streets that required clutch work but put her mind in cruise control and arrived home as the sun climbed to its mid-morning lookout high above the greening earth. She pushed through the front door, and the dog galloped up to meet her, his small body shivering with excitement. He gripped a chew toy that looked like a set of dentures between his teeth.

"Buying gifts for our guest?" she asked Constantine when he entered the room.

"Self-preservation until we find him a forever home. Caught him chewing on a flash drive, which four out of five dog dentists don't recommend. I put an ad in the paper and on Craigslist and canvassed the neighborhood with Found Dog posters to see if someone would claim him. So far, a lot of nothing." He pecked her on the lips. "How was Spinning?"

She knew she should lead with her run-in with Miles, her surety that he was hunting her, but Constantine's face was already pinched with worry. She also knew the story could wait.

She stowed her purse and gym bag in their usual spots. "Spinning was educational. The instructor knows Francine from another life. Let's just say her reincarnation into a better person may not have been complete."

"Meaning?"

"The instructor says that Francine was a former body builder with a penchant for fighting and an affinity for drugs."

"Francine? The churchy one?"

"Seemingly churchy. She's good at quoting scripture. Not so good at living it."

"A drugstore employee with a drug-using past. I'm sensing a blind spot for your boss, which doesn't look so good."

"It looks even less good now that he decided to go out of town."

Constantine gave her a long look. "Petrosian skipped town in the middle of a poisoning investigation at his pharmacy."

"He didn't 'skip town.' He went fishing. At least that's what his wife said when I dropped by to talk to him."

"Uh huh." He leaned against the wall, scratched a mosquito bite on his arm. "I realize that you like Petrosian with a mystifying daughterly affection, but you've got to admit that the signs are pointing to major weirdness. You've got a customer with a potential drug problem, a cashier with a shady past and desperation over a failed real estate deal."

Plus a flow of red ink running from the Petrosians' bank account to Sona's doctors, Maggie added silently.

"You're right," Maggie said, "but that's only because we lack other data." Constantine gave her a look. "I'm serious. We need to learn more, especially about Francine. She had means and opportunity to do the poisonings."

Constantine crossed his arms. "Motive?"

Maggie shrugged. "A drug deal that went south? A deep and abiding hatred for retail? I've done retail, Gus. I could see where she's going with that."

"I'm guessing this means you want to look into Francine's past?"

"Yes." She bent and ruffled the dog's ears. "And at other potential bad guys."

"You have someone in mind?"

She straightened. "Miles Montgomery."

Wariness crept into Constantine's eyes. "More love notes?"

"An in-person serenade outside Petrosian's house."

The wariness upgraded to alarm. "You saw him in person?"

She nodded. "He's out for good behavior, and for throwing his father under the bus."

"I hope that's not a metaphor." Constantine rubbed the back of his neck. "You ever file that complaint, tell Austin about the harassment?"

Maggie shook her head. Constantine had the grace not to scold. "Okay, Miles is out of the slammer. The question is, why is he here?"

"I asked him the same thing. He made a creepy reply. Typical Miles."

"Murderous Miles?"

She shrugged. "I don't know. I just wonder. I wonder why Miles is here. I wonder about his arrival and the timing of the poisonings. I wonder how far he'd go to punish me."

Constantine cocked his head. "Your theory: Miles murders customers at the drugstore where you work to make you look bad?"

"Maybe he figured he'd slaughter my reputation, then come back for the rest of me."

Constantine's face darkened. "Anything's possible."

"Everything's possible." Maggie took Constantine by the hand and began to lead him down the hall to the small home office. "And we're going to catalog the possibilities, starting with the letter 'M.'"

Maggie hijacked the desk, Constantine settled into the beanbag chair. She began with a simple Google search of Miles Montgomery. The search engine dutifully reported Miles's fate in the denouement of the Rxcellance story, but nothing else. No recent sightings. No scuttlebutt. No official statement or whisper of innuendo. Social media was similarly silent.

It seemed that Miles was a ghost who only haunted Maggie.

"It's time to involve the police," Constantine said. "Run your theory by Deputy Dog, tell him about Miles's escalation of harassment. Get everything on record and see if the cops can get a bead on how long he's been here, where he's staying, maybe encourage him to move along." He snapped his fingers. "Or get Ada on it. Isn't she with the police?"

"She's a cadet, but maybe she has some connections. I'd bet she'd be more willing to use them than Austin. He's strictly by the book."

Turned out Ada was, too.

"Sorry, Charlie," Ada said when Maggie called. "Can't risk it." Maggie heard the rustle of clothes, guessed Ada was getting ready for work—or the gym. "But I have friends who can. I'll ask around, see who feels like digging. Meanwhile, follow Constantine's advice. The guy's bad news."

Maggie thanked her and hung up.

"Now what?" Constantine asked.

"Now we do our own excavating, this time on Francine."

Unlike Miles' recently low profile, a Google search unearthed a wealth of information about the unfortunately coiffed cashier. As Sloane had suggested, Francine had spent some time on the body building circuit, flexing pecs and sass for cash prizes and kudos. It reminded Maggie of her brush with the beauty pageant circuit last year.

Maggie clicked through Google images. Save for the hair, Francine was unrecognizable.

The Francine of the past was buff and bronze, polished to a high gloss with copious amounts of self-tanner and oil. Her face, lean and chiseled like her physique, had a feline quality that suggested a steady diet of canaries.

Maggie zoomed in. Despite what some might consider superfluous musculature, Francine, like her fellows, was the picture of health. Constantine squinted up at the screen. "She doesn't look like a PSA about the dangers of drug abuse," he said.

"Maybe her drug of choice was the performance-enhancing variety."

Constantine nodded. "A great, albeit illegal, way to get a bulging leg up."

"Let's see if she has any other glamour shots." She searched Hollow Pine Mug Shots and came up empty. She widened her criteria for the county, then the state. "Bingo," she said, clicking a link.

A new image filled the screen: Francine looking disoriented and disheveled as she gave a wan smile to whoever was behind the camera. Maggie clicked again and read. "A couple of drunk and disorderlies," she said aloud. "Possession of marijuana and..." She tabbed through. "Assault."

A quick read of the report revealed that Francine Schatz, age forty-two, had struck a fellow contestant in the Ironwoman Championships after the victim, Jo Harper, had commented on Francine's footwear.

Constantine raised an eyebrow. "Fisticuffs over flip-flops?"

"More like War of the Wedges. Francine is the Imelda Marcos of Petrosian's. A different shoe for each day of the week."

"She's touchy about footwear and can't hold her liquor. That also describes half the women in my family."

"Francine is definitely not who she seems, but I'm not sure what that means beyond garden-variety reinvention. She did ask for time off when the Whitleys were discovered poisoned at Petrosian's, which is curious timing. We need to know more." Maggie tapped her finger against her chin, trying to dislodge a next move. She stopped tapping. "I have an idea."

Constantine gave her the side-eye. "Sounds dangerous."

Maggie's eyes glimmered. "Sounds fun."

Chapter 22

Maggie knew that Francine frequented a karaoke bar every Wednesday night. She regaled anyone who cared to listen—even those who didn't—with tales of her musical stylings at Café Humm where she eschewed alcohol but not the microphone. Her specialty: Christian rap, a genre Maggie had no idea existed.

Armed with an address and a desire to see what they could learn about Francine—musical or otherwise—they made the short drive to Old Town and parked in front of the café, which featured wrought iron tables and beret-ed wait staff meant to call to mind the streets of Paris or the sidewalks of Epcot Center. A bubblegum pink and mint green sign proclaimed it Eighties Night.

They pushed through the café's red-paned glass door and were immediately assaulted by Madonna's "Like a Prayer," performed by an eighty-something woman sporting a bustier beneath a gray cardigan embroidered with Siamese cats at play.

Constantine flashed a grin and opened his mouth. Maggie raised a finger to silence him. "Blend in," she whispered.

"But I forgot my fingerless gloves," he whispered back. She shushed him and claimed a table near the door. After a waitress clad in a rainbow sweater, stirrup pants and leg warmers took their order—Dr. Pepper for Maggie, coffee for Constantine—they settled in.

"I have some other news," Maggie said, chewing on her straw.

Constantine studied her face. "News?"

"I spoke with that neurologist I saw. The imaging looks fine, but he says I had a concussion."

"Had or have?"

"Both, sort of. Had a concussion. Have post-concussion syndrome."

He frowned. "Sounds serious. What's the treatment?"

"Rest," Maggie scoffed.

"Ah. And when do you plan to implement that?"

"Right after we talk to Francine."

They didn't have to wait long. After the elderly chanteuse finished her set, which included an enthusiastic version of "Like a Virgin" in which she crawled across the floor as her cardigan buttons scraped against the wooden stage, Francine sashayed to the microphone. She waited as two servers helped the elder singer to her feet, then claimed the spotlight when the stage was vacated. There was a smattering of polite applause.

Francine closed her eyes then cued the DJ. The opening strains of a-ha's "Take On Me" warbled from two large speakers. Francine warbled along, seeming to relish the departure from her usual rap routine.

Maggie fought to keep a straight face as Francine crossed the stage, crooning to anyone who dared to make eye contact. At one point, she serenaded a middle-aged man who had made the mistake of visiting the creamer station during the chorus. He purpled then slunk back to his seat without creaming his coffee. His lactose needs would have to wait.

Finally, the song ended. Francine concluded with a note two octaves too high and a couple of sharps off, then bowed deeply and gave a pair of left-right curtsies. Maggie's eyes ached from the effort of not rolling them.

Francine stepped off the stage, nudged her hair north, then wove her way among the tables toward the back of the room. Maggie reached out her hand. "Francine, hi!" she said with as much enthusiasm as she could muster. "Great job up there."

Surprise crossed Francine's face, followed by pride. "Oh, it was nothing," Francine said, pouring on the false modesty. "I just love giving people what they want."

"I don't think nausea is high on most people's list," Constantine muttered.

"Pardon?" Francine said. Maggie elbowed Gus in the side.

"Must be nice to have more time to devote to your, um, craft," Maggie said.

"My craft." Francine rolled the word around on her tongue. "I like that. And it is nice to have time away from the store. I get so sick of dealing with all that crap. The whiners. The fakers." She gave Maggie a hard look. "The shoplifters." She pulled down her shirt, white peplum with a bow at her neck. Her head looked like some kind of morbid gift. "But I guess you're not getting a lot of rest, being on the news and all."

Maggie felt her face flame. "Yeah, well." She gave a too-loud laugh. "Guess they need someone to blame."

Francine fanned out her hand and examined her crimson claws. "Maybe whoever did this is trying to teach a lesson."

Maggie and Constantine exchanged a glance. "What do you mean?" Maggie asked.

"Maybe whoever's behind the poisonings was tired of people turning to drugs instead of turning to God. So many people coming in for cures that medicine can't offer. Colton Ellis, killing himself with his diet. That girl and her mother, no backbone, no willingness to look outside a pill bottle for help."

"Well, Riley does have cancer," Maggie pointed out.

Francine waved away the diagnosis. "She needs more faith and less medicine. Maybe that's the lesson in this for all of us."

With that, she turned on her heel and walked off, her head held high, propped up on a pedestal of the justified.

Constantine opened his mouth, a retort budding his lips. He clamped his mouth shut and stared.

"What?" Maggie asked, following his line of sight.

"Oh, nothing," he said, taking a sip of his coffee. "Other than Francine chatting up Nigel Roberts."

Chapter 23

"What? Where?" Maggie whirled around, neck craned to see the back of the café, eyes scanning the crowd. Happy couples sprouted in clumps around low circular tables, heads together, arms entwined, cups bumping in caffeinated kisses.

She spotted a pair of ironically clad hipsters, a duo of young professionals in nearly matching suits, and a man and a woman with the small smiles and large silences of an awkward first date. Then: Francine sidling beside a small man with milk foam on his upper lip.

This was Nigel Roberts?

He was riper than middle age with a shiny pate, anemic mustache and a build that suggested a fearless dedication to couch-surfing. He sat hunched over his cup and glanced up occasionally at Francine, who appeared to be talking over him—figuratively and literally.

"I don't know about making time, but they do seem to know each other," Maggie said. "He's, um, different than I thought he'd be."

"Not exactly the image of the real estate tycoon, eh?" Constantine sipped his coffee, came away with his own foam milk mustache. "It's that whole looks can be deceiving thing. Trust me, he'd bite you off at the knees if he thought he could make a buck."

"That go for his poker games as well as his real estate deals?"

"I wouldn't be surprised. The guy likes his money. I imagine he protects it, no matter how it's earned."

Maggie watched Francine and Nigel. What was the born-again cashier/karaoke star doing with one of Hollow Pine's biggest movers and shakers? Better yet, what was he doing with *her*? She noted the distance between their bodies, the lack of physical contact. There was no hand on the arm, no accidental—or not so accidental—brush of hands.

"I'm not sure the relationship is personal," Maggie said, "but I do think it's interesting."

"Because they both knew Colton Ellis? Wasn't he everyone's almost-friend?"

Almost-friend. It was the perfect description for a popular man that no one really knew. Despite his relative renown, Maggie had heard that his funeral was poorly attended. Had Nigel Roberts paid his respects? Had Francine?

"I just wonder if there's any crossover between Francine's bad gal past and Nigel's high-stakes present," she mused.

"Birds of a felonious feather?"

Maggie shrugged. "Maybe Colton owed Nigel and couldn't pay. Or maybe Nigel wanted a clear shot at Colton's real estate. Poisoning Colton could take care of either problem—especially the second. It would be a way to not only eliminate Colton, but also Petrosian once the police decided he looked suspicious. Either way, Francine could do the deed."

"Once again, you've got means and opportunity, but no motive."

"That we know of. Maybe Francine likes cards. Maybe she's fallen off the wagon and Nigel knows people who can hook her up with performance-enhancing drugs—any drugs for that matter. That could be an area of commonality between Colton and Francine. Or maybe Roberts knew her from karaoke, saw someone with dubious morals and paid her to do the deed."

"Strangers on the Train in D Minor." He ran a hand through his hair. "Any way you look at it, it's a lot of maybes. When it comes to potential baddies, I still like Miles. He could have infiltrated the store and its drug supply. It's not like the counter is manned—or womaned—100 percent of the time."

Maggie chewed the inside of her cheek. "True, but Francine and Nigel are here now, and so are we. I say we talk to the odd couple and see what kind of vibe we get."

Maggie rose. Constantine followed. They squeezed through tables that had grown thick with crooners and listeners and made their way toward Francine and Nigel.

Maggie hoped for a casual farewell—and perhaps an impromptu conversation with the real estate mogul. Yet as she narrowed the gap between the unlikely pair, Nigel and Francine headed for the door.

Maggie grabbed Constantine's hand and pursued. A new singer came on stage, a local favorite judging by the murmur of excitement that surged through the crowd like a wave, and the patrons got to their feet to sway along with the music.

"Girls Just Want to Have Fun."

Maggie just wanted to get answers.

Pushed-back chairs became makeshift traffic cones. Maggie and Constantine slalomed around both wooden and human impediments, "excuse me" and "sorry" falling from their lips like a chorus. By the time they made it through the obstacle course, Nigel and Francine were gone and the second verse of the Cyndi Lauper cover had begun.

Maggie considered the options: 1) Follow Nigel and Francine, which seemed not only difficult, but slightly ridiculous considering that she had a pocketful of maybes and little else. 2) Go home and continue their digital snooping, which sounded like a recipe for a migraine. 3) Troll the streets hoping for a Miles sighting. 4) None of the above.

Maggie was leaning toward number four.

She massaged her temples and closed her eyes. When she reopened them, Constantine was staring into her face. "What?" she asked with a top-note of irritation.

"You okay? Your concussion syndrome or whatever it's called acting up?"

"It's not like a bum knee that aches when it rains," she snapped, regretting telling him about her condition. "I'm fine. Let's just go home."

At that moment, Nigel stepped back into the café. Maybe their luck was changing.

Maggie exchanged a look with Constantine and approached Nigel with her arms and smile wide. Constantine melted into the background. "Nigel! How are you?"

Confusion flickered through Roberts' eyes. "Oh, hullo. How are you?" BBC British accent. Forced-air warmth.

Maggie clasped both of his hands and leaned in for air kisses. "I haven't seen you in ages."

Roberts squeezed her digits and smiled. "Not since the...the..."

Maggie flattened her lips and closed her eyes. "Not since what happened to poor Colton."

It was a bluff, misdirection that she had a royal flush when in fact she had a pair of deuces. Roberts' smile faltered. "Yes, such a pity." He bit his lip and looked down, took the requisite moment of silence. "It's even poisoned my restaurant. Metaphorically speaking, of course. Fewer people are willing to consume food or drink they haven't personally prepared, although this place seems to be doing a brisk business." He paused to wallow in envy. "Even the doctors who frequent Palate du Gourmand are rattled, and you know what regulars they are."

He gave a jovial laugh and sawed his elbow at her ribcage. Sudden conviviality, an inside joke.

Maggie threw back her head and laughed knowingly. "You don't have to tell me." She added a chortle for good measure and then sighed into the dwindling laughter as if pining a premature death. She coughed into her fist. "You know, they think the poisoning may have been an inside job. One of the cashiers, or something." Maggie watched Nigel's face for a response. His face was the shade of Wite-Out. Then again, so was hers, so she couldn't be sure he'd paled with the mention of a poisoning cashier or always looked that way. "I also understand that they're looking into Colton's life, to see if anyone held any grudges," she pressed. "Or if he owed anyone money."

She cut her eyes to his face, watched for an uptick of pulse below his jowls, an increased pallor, eyes darting to avoid contact with hers. His expression was inscrutable. "Quite right, quite right," he said. "The authorities should explore every avenue." He looked over Maggie's shoulder as if seeking help on the horizon. "I'm chuffed to bits to have seen you, but I really must be running along."

Nigel performed a funny little bow then backed toward a door. She expected his commodious tweed-encased hips to nudge open the door. Instead he greeted a man who had just entered the café with a hand-sandwich handshake that defined hale and hearty.

Maggie studied the newcomer. Though he was halfway across the room, she felt a surge of familiarity. She'd seen him before, in the pharmacy, on more than one occasion. Was he a patient? A physician? A vendor? Someone who came in to use the bathroom? She couldn't remember.

Before she could map his face against the mental picture that began to form, he swept out the door, Nigel at his heels.

Chapter 24

Constantine edged to her side. "Did he make a full confession?"

"Not even when I suggested that police are looking at Petrosian's cashiers and people Colton owed money to."

"Sounds like a cool customer. Or maybe that's just the English thing."

"Maybe," she replied absently. "I recognize the man he left with. I've seen him before at the pharmacy."

"In the poison aisle?"

"That's just it. I suspect everyone but know nothing. All I can tell you is I've seen him at Petrosian's, but don't know why."

"It'll come to you. Meanwhile, any insight into Nigel's association with Francine, cashier and crooner?"

"None, but hopefully that will come, too." She stifled a yawn.

"You look beat. Let's call it a day." Constantine put his arm around her shoulder, and they stepped out of the time-warp of Eighties Night into the cool, fragrant evening.

Constantine drove home slowly, as if he had a new baby or wedding cake in the backseat. Maggie had a feeling that the vehicular crawl was for her benefit, which deepened her irritation. They idled past the old movie theater, renovated to its previous Art Nouveau glory, a convenience store and one of the town's lone multistory structures: St. Theresa's hospital.

Maggie sat up in her seat. "Turn in there."

"The hospital?"

"I want to check on the Whitleys."

"Now? You look exhausted, and according to you, someone recovering from a brain injury needs R&R. Probably other salubrious letters."

She clenched her jaw and ignored his armchair neurology. "We're right here and so are two witnesses. I visited before, but with a different agenda in mind. Come on. It'll be fun."

"Right. Like dental surgery."

Five minutes later, they were outside Room 325.

The door was buttoned shut. Maggie gazed up and down the hall, hoping a nurse would nod them in, granting both permission and assurance that they weren't interrupting an exercise in hygiene. The corridor was vacant.

Then the door to 325 opened and Deena appeared, wheeling a computer cart. The nurse's face broke into a wide smile. "Hey, Maggie, right? Back to see the ladies?"

Maggie nodded. "How are they?"

Deena pulled the door behind her. "Resting." Protecting patient well-being or shutting out an unauthorized visitor?

"I'm Constantine, by the way." He gave one of his dazzling smiles, the kind Maggie called the Constantine Special. Deena returned it with equal wattage. He had that effect on women. "So they're doing well?" he prompted.

Deena shifted from one orthopedic shoe to the other. "They seem to be heading in the right direction." Neutral tone. The Switzerland of information.

"I've been worried, especially about Riley given her medical history." Maggie looked at Deena from beneath her lashes, trying to gauge the nurse's reaction.

Deena's mouth twitched. She opened it. Closed it. Opened it again, as if finally relenting. "I decided from the time I was a little girl that I was made to help people, that my vocation—my *calling*— was nursing." She shook her head. "But Riley's situation is different. Complex. Nothing I do, nothing I've done, has been enough to help Riley." Deena blinked away tears and tried a smile, the motion hiking a tiny rhinestone riding atop Deena's left nostril. "The good news is that she's a fighter. She's doing better—her mom, too, in spite of everything."

"Well enough for company?" Maggie asked.

Deena considered the question, then bobbed her head slowly. "Actually some friendly faces might be a nice change of pace."

"A change from not-so-friendly faces?" Constantine asked.

"The police have been around a few times," Deena said. She folded her arms across pink scrubs. "A little disruptive, but nothing like the other guys."

"Other guys?"

"Reporters." Her face puckered as if she'd just bitten into something rotten. "Actually, reporter."

"Let me guess," Maggie said tightly. "Russ Brock."

"Bingo." Either Deena hadn't caught Brock's smear campaign of Maggie or was too polite to comment on Maggie's own struggles with the paparazzo. "He sneaked into the Whitleys' room and took pictures of them while they were unconscious. Can you believe that?" Maggie could. "Fortunately, the charge nurse caught him and confiscated the camera then 'accidentally' dropped it." A look of triumph splashed across her face. "Since then, we've tightened security. He hasn't been back. None of them have."

Maggie nodded, but wondered about the tightened security. She'd sailed to the Whitleys' room twice with no interference. This despite the fact that her face was all over the news, along with nouns like "cyanide," "murder" and "shooter." Maybe nobody at the hospital watched the news.

Deena moved her cart and cracked the door. "Anyway, I think they'd like to see you, especially Riley. She hasn't stopped talking about you since your last visit. I'll be at the nurse's station if you need me."

Maggie and Constantine hovered at the mouth of 325 then stepped over the threshold. "Hello?" She popped her head around the corner, hoping she didn't look like a deranged jack-in-the-box. "It's Maggie. From Petrosian's?"

She looked at the twin beds. Twin faces gazed back. Riley's split into a slow smile. Mary's, now disinterred from the tubes that once buried her, subdivided into a battery of emotions. Confusion. Fear. Curiosity. Finally: recognition. "You're the one who saved our lives."

Maggie flushed. "Well I don't know about th—"

Mary struggled to sit up, paste-white arms cantilevered over similarly hued bedclothes. She managed a few inches of height, collapsed, then pushed the button at her side to the let the bed's motor do the lifting. "It's so good of you to come."

Maggie gestured toward Constantine. "This is my fiancé." The word still felt funny on her tongue, like the taste of something she was still getting used to. "Is it okay if he—"

"Of course, of course." Mary waved them in and pointed to a chair. Maggie sat. Constantine stood.

"Thank you for finding us, for saving us—especially my baby girl." Mary reached a hand across the mote of linoleum between the beds. "She's been through so much."

"I've read your blog," Maggie said. "It sounds like you both have."

Mary's tears breached her lids and slid down a face mottled by illness and sorrow. "She's a brave kid. She makes me want to be brave, too."

"Seems like you have a great support system," Maggie said.

"It wasn't always that way." Mary took a great, laboring breath. Sheets folded with the rise and fall of her chest. "Riley's father left when she was just a baby. First sign of trouble, of sickness, he was out of there." She twisted a naked ring finger.

Maggie cleared her throat. "I'm wondering if you can tell me what happened before...before you lost consciousness."

"You mean if I consumed anything? Saw anyone lurking in the aisles wearing a trench coat or a gas mask?" Mary chuckled. The laugh dissolved into a paroxysm of coughs. She waited for the pleural storm to pass, took another shuddering breath. "The police asked me the same question. The answer is no. We didn't buy anything to eat or drink, didn't take any medication."

Maggie nodded. At least that answered the question about what had been consumed in hours leading up to the women's loss of consciousness. "And you didn't see anyone suspicious?"

"There weren't many people there, and the few we saw seemed like regular customers." A smile. "Whatever that is."

"Did you notice anything out of the ordinary? Anything at all?"

Mary shook her head and looked at her daughter, who mirrored the gesture.

Maggie felt a jab of disappointment. What had she expected? If the police had learned anything, they would have sprung into action, alerting the public, hastening the search warrant, seizing suspect drugstore items— and the perpetrator himself.

And yet she couldn't consider the visit a waste of time. She'd talked to the Whitleys herself. Seen Riley's smile. Verified the improvement of their health. Gotten proof that not all sick mothers leave their daughters to navigate the path to first periods and first crushes without a maternal cairn to mark the way.

She and Constantine drifted toward the door. "Thanks for talking to us."

"Thanks for being there when we needed you," Mary replied. She looked out the window for a moment, her eyes trained on the vast prairie with its pimple of a butte. "They're going to catch him, right? They're going to find him and make sure that he doesn't do this to someone else?"

"They will." They'd never caught the Tylenol poisoner. As much as she hoped for a different outcome, there were no guarantees in life. Or in death.

Mary's head dropped against the pillow, tension softening the rigor that tented the muscles of her face and neck. "Good." She closed her eyes, twin crescents against her plain, square face.

Maggie wiggled her fingers at Riley, who waved back. More hair had sprouted on her head, as if her body were responding to the lengthening days, the climbing mercury. "Come back again," Riley called as Maggie put her hand on the door.

"I will." This was a promise Maggie hoped to keep.

Out in the hall, Constantine said, "No closer to any answers."

"But the Whitleys are closer to being discharged, so it's not all bad news."

"Speaking of bad news." He nodded toward the head of the hall near the elevators. "There's the town crier himself."

Maggie followed Constantine's gaze. Russ Brock hovered over a coffee pot like a junkie waiting for his next fix.

Chapter 25

Brock's face was red with exertion, his hair hugging his skull in moist strips. Perspiration stains bloomed beneath the arms of his sports jacket in humid blotches. He'd either bounded up the stairs or was auditioning for an infomercial about the importance of wicking fabrics.

He seemed to feel her eyes on him and looked up. "Ms. O'Malley!" He came charging forward, his face contorted by exertion and excitement. "I have to talk with you."

Constantine stepped between them and Maggie felt anger flash through her. She didn't need chivalry. She needed Brock to leave her the hell alone.

She shouldered Constantine aside and stormed toward her tormentor. Maybe it was indignation. Maybe she wanted to prove to herself that the Whitleys' hero worship was not misplaced. Maybe she was tired of men trying to intimidate her. "Stop," she commanded.

To her surprise, Brock did just that. Then he pivoted on his loafers and darted for the stairs.

Maggie felt a surge of pride and a rush of power. With one word, she'd sent the great Russ Brock scrambling. Behind her, she heard the jangle of keys. She turned. Two security guards surged forward in pursuit of the newsman.

"Which way did he go?" asked the guard, a young man with long pointy ears that could double as antennae.

Maggie pointed toward the stairwell.

"Thanks." He lunged for the door, his brother-in-polyester inches behind him.

Maggie turned toward Constantine. "And here I thought I'd stopped the libelous presses."

"I'm sure you did. Security just sealed the deal."

Maggie stabbed the button to summon the elevator. "Brock's probably been casing the place waiting for the right time to try to interview the Whitleys. Maybe he saw me and figured he'd get a twofer."

"Between Brock and Miles, seems to me you've got a twofer on stalkers."

"Should we watch the fun? Looked like those security guards meant business."

Constantine eyed her. "Tempting, but I say we go home and watch it on the news. I'm curious to see how they spin it."

Maggie hesitated. She wanted to see Brock cuffed and hauled out of the hospital, but she could feel herself fading, a lack of food and a surplus of excitement catching up with her. As much as she tried to pretend otherwise, as much as she tried to deny away the diagnosis, she could feel the effects of her brain injury.

Finally she nodded, left Brock to the professionals and let herself be led away from the hospital and toward the sanctuary of home.

The dog and Miss Vanilla were waiting for them when they returned home, the former with his denture-like chew toy in his mouth, the latter staring at them through the grates of her wheel, nose twitching a rodent hello. "You still here?" Constantine asked the pooch sternly. Then he picked up the animal and carried him to the kitchen.

Constantine poured organic kibble in a dish and the dog attacked the food with the zeal of a dieter given free rein in a doughnut shop.

"Awfully fancy dog chow for a temporary guest," Maggie remarked.

"The bag said that it'll give him a healthy coat. I've been eating it and have already noticed a difference." He ran a hand through his dark curls to demonstrate.

"Impressive."

His phone rang. The theme to *Jaws*. He noted Maggie's expression and shrugged. "New ringtone. Seemed appropriate given our recent adventures—and luck." He pulled the phone from his pocket, frowned at the screen and turned it toward Maggie. Helena Papadopoulos's face gazed back.

"Hi, Ma." He listened, uh-huhed then said, "Okay, hang on." He took the phone from his ear and hit the speaker button. "Go ahead."

"Maggie!" Helena's voice trilled from the phone. "How are you, my dear?"

"I'm great," she lied. "How are you?"

"Fabulous, just fabulous." She hit the highlights of domestic life with Constantine's father, George, including a recent trip to the grocery store, a battle over which movie to see in the theater and various doctors' appointments for the treatment of bunions. She paused from the manic ramble then said, "The real reason I'm calling is to talk about wedding cakes. I understand there's some discussion about buttercream?" This said with the same tone one might use to describe a kind of fungus.

Maggie groaned inwardly. "Um, yes," Maggie said into the speaker, "but I think we're nearing a resolution." She imagined Polly and Fiona signing a document. The Icing Accord of 2019.

"Excellent," Helena chirped. "I would hate for things to get derailed over something so trivial." Maggie bit her tongue to avoid cataloguing all of the wedding preparations she found trivial. The tally so far: all of it.

"Hey, Ma," Constantine chimed in, "I have a quick question."

"About which priest is available for the sacrament? You've decided on Orthodox, yes?"

Feck, she thought, using the Irish-ized f-bomb her father—and therefore she—preferred.

Constantine hadn't broached the topic of a civil ceremony—or religion. He glanced at Maggie then averted his eyes. "Uh, no, about work. Your work." The phone filled with expectant silence. "You used to buy media."

"For twenty-seven years."

"And you know a lot about people in the news biz?"

"Of course."

"What can you tell me about Russ Brock?"

A snort on the other end. "That I refuse to watch him."

"Because he's smarmy?"

"Because he's a fraud."

Constantine exchanged a look with Maggie. "A fraud?"

"The man is a fiction," she said, her voice angrily underscoring both nouns. "Before he was Russ Brock he was Stanley Wurm."

"*Wurm?* You've got to be joking."

"If only. Stan started out as a cub reporter in Springfield, worked his way up the ranks. After a few years in print, he transitioned to TV. He made a name for himself as the guy who got the story. Turns out, they were just that: stories."

"Meaning what?"

"Meaning that he was doing fake news before there was fake news. Only one of his stories was a proven fabrication, a piece about the mayor paying off city council members to grease the political wheels, but there was gossip about other trumped up stories. The story fell apart when his source recanted. She said that the real payout was Wurm bribing her to lie."

Constantine whistled. "So what happened?"

"Wurm got fired then got arrested. He stalked his so-called source, harassing her at work, at home. She finally went to the police after he started leaving threatening messages on her car."

Maggie leaned forward. It seemed she wasn't alone in stalkers who relished leaving vehicular hate mail.

"Anyway," Helena continued. "That was the end of Stanley Wurm. Until it wasn't. He laid low for nearly a decade, doing God knows what, then came back on the scene with a new name, new hair and a new persona. Guess he fooled the folks over at Channel 4. The viewers, too. But those of us with long memories know the truth: Russ Brock is a lying man with a dangerous past."

Chapter 26

The conversation concluded with wedding queries, dietary recommendations and reminders of how much happier Constantine would have been if he'd become a doctor as he had originally planned. The love language of the Papadopoulos family.

Constantine uh-huh-ed his way into a goodbye then slid to the floor in a mock death. He pulled Maggie on top of him. "Good ol' Ma. How could I remember my failings without her tack-sharp memory? I call it my mom-onic device. You know mnemonic plus mom?"

Maggie rolled off of him. "Very funny. Have you been working on new jokes?"

"Just on days that end in Y."

"Interesting background on Russ Brock, aka. Stan Wurm. Sounds like the guy is bad news. And creates bad news."

"Speaking of Brock, I trolled TV and the interwebs for anything about Brock being escorted from St. Theresa's."

"And?"

"And nothing. Brock was reporting the news as if nothing happened. And maybe nothing did. He looked pretty spry for an oldish guy. He could've given security the slip." Constantine got to his feet, opened the fridge, retrieved a Tupperware of baklava that Aunt Polly had given him as a thank you for his recent handymanning exploits and loaded four dense triangles onto a small white plate. He pinched a piece of baklava between thumb and forefinger, handed it to Maggie, then snagged one for himself.

"It's odd that Channel 4 would hire Wurm/Brock, given his less-than-stellar track record."

"Like Ma said, people have short memories. A decade is a long time. If the guy did a good job of reinventing himself, the station wouldn't have been the wiser. Even if they were wise, they could have counted on their audience not remembering—or caring. There's a fair amount of apathy these days. Not including my mother, naturally."

"True." Maggie twirled her hair. "Now that we know about Brock's deep, dark past, I think Stanley Wurm deserves a closer look, starting via the internet.

Constantine popped another triangle into his mouth. "How many Stanley Wurms can there be?"

According to the Internet, there were fourteen Stanley Wurms. Constantine narrowed the search field and continued digging as Maggie sat atop the hill of beans that was the home office's beanbag chair. He whooped. She leaned in, read, then sat back with a sigh.

"Wurm's fall from grace was exactly as your mom said," Maggie said. "Guess she really does know best."

"Just don't tell her that." He double-clicked his mouse and enlarged the photo on screen. The apple of Russ Brock fell far from the Stanley Wurm tree.

The image was the kind of hard news publicity shot that required its subject to cross his arms and shoot eye-daggers at the camera. The intention was probably a photographic double-dog dare. Wurm managed to look constipated.

"Nice work with the Blue Steele," Constantine said, referencing the signature look of *Zoolander* in the eponymous film.

Maggie studied the image. Wurm/Brock rocked a seventies porn star perm, handlebar mustache and flesh-colored sports jacket. "Quite the style maven. The best part is the attitude. That shot screams overcompensation."

"Which lead to overstating. The guy wanted to climb to superstardom, didn't care whose light he put out on the way up."

Maggie reached over, minimized the photo and scanned the story. "Sounds like he'd been embellishing for a while. The story got too big."

"Just like his ego. Classic case of hubris." Maggie gave him a look. "My mom gave me a Greek Words in Everyday English daily calendar. I'm waiting to work ecumenical into a sentence."

Maggie sat back and put her hands on her knees. "So Wurm inflates stories to puff up his career, misjudges and gets caught, then decides it's a good idea to harass the woman he'd pulled into his mendacity." She flashed a grin. "I got my own word of the day calendar."

Constantine laughed then grew serious. "Wurm goes from foolish to felonious then reinvents himself, lands in a new town and snags a new job. Are you thinking he didn't learn his lesson?"

Maggie's eyes shimmered green in the blue light of the computer screen. "I say we find out."

Chapter 27

News Channel 4, For the News, For the People, was situated at the end of a strip mall next to a nail salon plastered with Photoshopped phalanges. Maggie parked in a space that marked its territory with the News Chanel 4 logo, which looked as though it had been crowdsourced. She twisted in her seat and looked at the dog, who snoozed with his nose between his paws.

"I still don't know why you insisted on bringing him," she said.

"Normally I'd bring Miss Vanilla, but there's some tension between her and the pooch." He dropped his voice. "Sibling rivalry. Anyway, I brought this for easy steerage." He produced a brown leather leash from his pocket.

Maggie raised an eyebrow. "Special food, dog toys and now this. A lot of supplies for someone who doesn't like dogs and who knows this isn't a long-term relationship."

Constantine snapped the leash on the dog's collar. "I like to support my local pet store. Besides, I don't want him running off. He goes crazy when he sees dogs in sweaters. It outrages him."

"Uh huh." Maggie opened the Studebaker's glove box and pulled out a magenta cloche hat. She plopped it on her head, smashing unruly curls into submission. "Think the news staff will recognize me?"

"Only if they have eyes."

They climbed out of the car and breached the front door of the news station as if it were an enemy basecamp.

A young man sat at the reception desk, eyes glued to the screen. In the lenses of his rimless glasses, Maggie could make out what looked like a video game: *Fortnite*. Maggie fingered the brim of her hat, obscuring her face with her hand, and wandered back toward the door where she pretended to study an artificial fichus, the dog tethered at her side.

Constantine marched to the desk and waited. The man paused the action on-screen and looked up at Constantine, a pleasant smile bisecting an acne-studded twenty-something face. "How can I help you?" His voice was deep and sonorous, a contrast to his slight physique. A brass desk plaque introduced him as Bradley.

Constantine smiled back. "We're supposed to meet Mr. Brock."

"I'm Mr. Brock's assistant. Something I can help you with?"

"He said we should only talk with him." Constantine leaned in. "Big story."

Understanding dawned behind the spectacles. "I work with Mr. Brock on a lot of stories." The eyes dimmed. "Well, I want to. Mr. Brock says I'm not ready yet, even though I put in my time at *The Gazette* in Saginaw." Bradley turned to his screen, gave the keyboard a few taps. "Looks like Mr. Brock left for the day. His calendar is clear." He looked up at Constantine. "No mention of any appointment with you, Mr...."

"Fletcher. Irwin M. Fletcher." Maggie tried to keep a straight face as Constantine channeled the character of his favorite Chevy Chase movie. "Will he be in tomorrow?'

More keyboard caresses. "He's blocked himself out for the day. But..." Bradley gave a conspiratorial smile. "I happen to know he's at Glass Half Full. He likes the Bloody Marys because they put lots of stuff in them. Last time it was four onion rings and a chicken wing."

"Sounds scrumptious. Thanks for your help."

"Not at all." Bradley's tongue snaked out of his mouth, moistened desiccated lips. "And, uh, I'd appreciate if you didn't mention that I told you where he is. He's always saying he'll do anything to get a story. I'm just not sure that includes interrupting happy hour."

"It'll be our little secret."

Glass Half Full was four blocks away. Maggie and Constantine clasped hands and walked, the dog trotting beside them. An image of domestic bliss—if they weren't trying to find a killer and spy on a potential stalker.

They paused outside the shake-shingled building and squinted at the door. Warnings against the admission of minors, an unenthusiastic *Passing* grade by the health inspector and a welcome for furry friends plastered the glass. Maggie took the two-out-of-three as good news and wrenched open the door. Three women, their lips still ringed with the telltale salt of margaritas, stumbled out then clattered up the street in towering heels, hips swaying to the beat of internal castanets.

Maggie spotted a man pressed into the shadows, his head turning to watch the trio of women walk by. She narrowed her eyes, straining to identify the man. He had a squat muscular build and long hair that puffed from beneath a beanie. Miles was taller and had a buzz cut. She averted her eyes and followed Constantine into the building.

They landed at the bar, a rustic slab of lacquered pine marred by the scuffs of thousands of glasses and the occasional pen knife. Maggie traced a love note gouged into the wood. *Janice + Jake 4Ever.* Not exactly Shakespeare, but it got to the point.

Constantine summoned the bartender, a man with biceps that looked like Christmas hams, and ordered vodka Collins for both of them. As they waited for their drinks to arrive, Maggie pulled down her hat and scanned the bar.

Despite the bar's hard-scrabble ambiance and *eau de frat house* odor of stale beer, Glass Half Full was populated by mostly middle-age men in varying stages of hair loss. Maggie peered across the sea of sports jackets, eyes hopping from one balding head to another, hoping to spy Brock.

"I don't think he's here," she said as she took a sip of the drink that had been planted before her with an authoritative *thunk*.

"Maybe he's at Glass Half *Empty*," Constantine said as his eyes roved the room. "Or the Choose Your Own Cliché Tavern."

Maggie took another sip, relishing the slow burn from gullet to belly. "Probably just as well. I'm sure he'd recognize me, and things would get weird. We should probably just—"

Maggie stopped mid-sentence as Russ Brock emerged from the men's room, wiping his hands on his khakis. He sauntered over to a table for two occupied by an empty glass topped with a half-eaten pork slider, checked his watch, folded several bills beneath his glass.

Maggie downed her vodka Collins in one gulp and tightened her hand on the leash. "Unsavory reporter at one o'clock" she whispered into Constantine's ear. "Looks like he's headed out. You pay the bill and I'll trail him. Then we'll text to meet up."

Before Constantine could answer, Maggie slipped behind a group of men crowded before a big screen TV tuned to Bloomberg Television. She hovered behind the suits and waited for Brock to leave. As soon as he vanished through the door, Maggie followed, dog in tow, Constantine waving frantically behind her. She turned and gave him an annoyed "I'm fine" wave then stepped into the street.

The temperature had dropped with the sun and Maggie zipped her thin sweatshirt to her chin, Aunt Fiona's voice whispering an admonishment about proper outerwear in her mind. She hugged her torso with her free hand and looked up the block. Beneath the indifferent glow of the streetlight, Brock waited at the crosswalk.

Maggie broke into a slow lope, closing the gap yet careful to keep a comfortable distance between her and her quarry. The dog kept pace, tongue lolling, nails scraping cement. The sound jangled Maggie's already frayed nerves. Dumb move, bringing the dog. In addition to the canine Stomp concert, the animal could slow her down. What was she thinking? The short answer: she hadn't been. Maybe it was the concussion. Maybe it was the vodka she'd just downed. Maybe it was both.

Brock crossed the street and looked over his shoulder. Maggie sank against the doorway of an apartment building, melting into a shadow guarded by two cement lions. She held her breath as Brock studied the dark, reading the gloom like tea leaves, then released a slow stream of carbon dioxide as he resumed his trek.

He approached a car. Maggie silently berated herself for not getting behind the wheel of her own ride. The Studebaker didn't exactly blend in with Hollow Pine's Hondas and Chevys, but wheels versus wheels was a better match than wheels versus feet. If he got in the car, she'd have no chance of keeping up.

Brock stopped in front a white Subaru, plunged a hand in his pocket. He jingled the contents. She expected him to pull free a ring of keys. Instead he popped a breath mint, wadded up the wrapper and threw it on the sidewalk.

Maggie made a mental note to add littering to Brock's list of sins.

Brock reached into his pocket again, yanked. From Maggie's vantage point, it looked like a piece of paper. He looked at it, gazed up at the large brick-faced building beside him, looked back at his hand. He continued to move down the street, repeating the regimen: a look at his hand, a look at a building, a look at his hand, a look at the next building.

Searching for an address?

She trailed him. A half-block later, Brock struck residential gold. He stuffed the paper back in his pocket, took one more long look over his shoulder then mounted four steps leading to a glass-paned door of a duplex.

The duplex was tall and slender with a faux Queen Anne vibe. It was so out of place among its neighbors, it looked as though it had been dropped by aliens with a penchant for turn-of-the-century architecture. Brock studied the numbers beside each door and selected the one on the right. He pressed a bell, its angry buzzer puncturing the silence, waited, then pressed again. Brock put his hands beside his eyes and pressed his makeshift spectacles against the glass. Then he stooped, slipped something under the door and trotted down the steps.

Maggie stepped from behind a gaggle of garbage cans and watched his retreat, considering her next move. Fish out what Brock had angled beneath the door, or follow him to places unknown? She squinted at the duplex, its door spotlighted by a porch light designed to resemble a torch. Too much illumination. Too much risk of exposure.

She gave the leash a gentle tug and continued to stalk the stalker.

Maggie felt a vibration in her pocket. She began squeezing the rectangle at her thigh, trying to mute the device's ringer that she had forgotten to silence. She half-succeeded. "You talkin'—" phone De Niro began.

Maggie froze, breath caught in her throat, waited for Brock to act. He stiffened, tilting his head to listen. A garbage truck lumbered around the corner, flicked on its reverse lights and ambled backward toward its plastic targets. Brock nodded—noise explained and disregarded—and moved on.

Maggie put the phone to her ear. "Gus? I can't talk right now."

"Where are you?"

Maggie craned her neck. "Not far from the post office. I'm following Brock, who seems to be a man on a mission."

"I'll be there as quick as I can." And then he was gone.

Brock walked. Maggie followed. Moments later, she realized that she had abandoned the semi-deserted street for a fully vacant alley. She stopped, turned, tried to get her bearings. Unfamiliar buildings in varying states of decay reached skyward, blotting out adjacent streetlights, dampening sound, narrowing possibilities for escape.

She looked down one end of the alley and then the other. Brock was gone. Or maybe he was hiding, waiting for her to come to him where the blackness was thick and alive.

Then a sound. A movement. Brock briefly illuminated in the blue-light glow of a cell phone as he fiddled with something near the base of a building, using the phone's flashlight to illuminate his work. Maggie held her breath as she watched him stoop low, handle an unseen object, look over his shoulder, repeat. There was a rumble at her side. She felt her pocket. Not her cell phone. The dog, emitting a low growl.

Feck.

Maggie reached down and stroked the fur between the dog's ears. The animal lowered his head, eyes pointing toward Brock, and growled again, sound waves bouncing against his ribcage.

"Shh..." Maggie soothed, but it was too late. The dog began barking, jaws snapping, teeth bared, hackles raised. Brock doused the light from his phone, gathered up whatever had held his attention and fled, throwing a long, searching look behind him.

The dog charged after him, heaving against the leash. Maggie's own chase instinct kicked in and she sprinted down the alley in search of Brock.

She collided with something solid. And human. She teetered from the impact and stumbled as she tried to regain her balance. She failed and hit the ground, crab-walking backwards, scrambling for the safety of the darkness.

She felt hands clamp on her shoulders. Tighten. She remembered the man in the shadows in front of the bar, the build reminiscent of Miles's, the long hair that could have easily been a wig. Panic, black and complete, rose in her chest and climbed up her throat. A low, guttural sound tore from her as she wrenched her hands free. Scrambled backward. Struggled to find her feet before Miles realized his advantage and leveraged it.

Then the world flickered. Fuzzed. A TV tuned to nothing. Maggie watched in wonder as the alley turned ninety degrees then vanished as her head hit the asphalt.

Chapter 28

Maggie awoke to someone licking her toes. "Stop it," she muttered. Her tongue was clumsy, her mouth cotton-dry. "Stop."

"Lay off, dog," Constantine said.

She heard claws strike floor, felt the cushion beneath her move as a thigh pressed against her side. "Mags?" Constantine sounded far away. "Maggie?"

She peeled open her eyelids, then shut them against the brightness of the room. Her head felt as if it, too, were stuffed with cotton. "What happened?"

"You passed out. Spectacularly, I might add. A recycling bin toppled onto you, coating yourself in packing peanuts. You looked like the next Marvel superhero." He put a hand to her brow. "You okay?"

She nodded. Felt a zing fire a warning shot across her forehead. "Where's Miles?"

"Miles?" Confusion in his voice. "Who knows? But I did see one Russ Brock hightail it down the street."

Maggie would have face-palmed, but she couldn't take yet another head injury. "So that was you I ran into in the alley?"

"The one and only."

She managed a smile. "Guess my brain was convinced otherwise, decided to shut down."

"Concussion fun and games?"

For once Maggie couldn't muster the energy to be annoyed at the mention of her injury. She had been experiencing symptoms. Plus there was that drink. What were the rules on drinking with post-concussion syndrome? She couldn't remember her neurologist specifically banning it, but he also hadn't advised her to avoid crack cocaine and bungee jumping. She promised herself to take it easy on everything. "Any idea where Brock went?"

"None. You catch him in any suspicious shenanigans?"

Maggie described Brock's alley skulking and message delivering. "I'd like to know who lives there."

"Your wish is my command."

Constantine grabbed Maggie's purse from the foot of the sofa and began to swish his hand inside.

"What are you—"

Constantine put up a finger, plucked out her phone, and thumbed through the apps. He opened Facebook, selected Location under Settings and clicked View Location History after re-inputting Maggie's password.

He pointed the screen toward Maggie and waved it triumphantly. "It's the spy in your pocket. You probably enabled it when looking for a Wi-Fi hotspot or checking in someplace. Anyway, it automatically records your locations, which comes in handy for times like this." He tapped on Location History and a map appeared, showing where the app had periodically logged her phone's location since their visit to Glass Half Full.

He determined the locations' addresses and began to search for their inhabitants. Fifteen minutes later, just as Maggie dozed off, Constantine said, "Holy shit."

"What?" she muttered, words slurred, mind sleep-drunk.

"That duplex you described is rented by Mary Whitley."

She was suddenly very awake. "Why would Brock go to their home when he knows they're still in the hospital?"

"See if someone else was home to interview?"

"Or something worse. Brock is known for stalking. Maybe his interest in the Whitleys goes beyond getting the story."

She sat up. The world cartwheeled. She leaned back. "We've got to get whatever Brock slipped under that door."

"Right after a quick jaunt to the emergency room to look at your head. You took a nasty tumble."

"I'm not going to the ER."

"Fine. Urgent care, then."

"No."

"I'm not going to argue, Mags," Constantine said quietly. "You know I'd do anything for you, including pretending to like romantic comedies, but I won't do something that puts you in harm's way." He smoothed back her hair. "Even if you're the one putting yourself there."

"Fine. I'll go. Happy?"

He put a hand over his heart. "Are any of us really happy?"

She rolled her eyes. "I'll go to urgent care on one condition." He eyed her warily. "We stop by the duplex first."

The building was just as Maggie had left it: silent and brooding. They crept up the steps, avoiding boards with nails that popped to the surface in a carpenter's game of whack-a-mole, and hovered at the door. Constantine reached up and loosened the porch lightbulb. The porch fell into darkness.

As Maggie had grudgingly agreed, Constantine would fish for whatever Brock had crammed beneath the Whitleys' door while Maggie played look-out. She stared into the street, watching for passersby, looking for hints that they'd been discovered hovering outside the home of Hollow Pine's most tragic family. Behind her she heard the grate of a coat hanger as Constantine slipped it beneath the door.

"Almost got it," he whispered. "Almost got...damn." He dropped the coat hanger with a clatter. They tensed, ready for the Neighborhood Watch to pounce, for a beat cop to come ambling up. The street's silence continued unabated.

Constantine angled the metal rod again. There was another rasp of metal on wood, the crinkle of paper, the long drag of something hauled from the depths. Constantine sprung to his feet, paper in hand.

He gave her a triumphant smile and a quick hug, then palmed the paper, remembering to play it cool. They sauntered casually to the Datsun and shut themselves inside its metal cocoon.

"What does it say?" Maggie hissed in the darkness.

Constantine hit the car's interior lights, smoothed the paper on the console between them. The anemic bulb illuminated a single sentence scrawled in pencil.

I'm coming for you.

Chapter 29

"I assume that's not a promise to take them to the airport," Constantine said.

"Sounds like a threat. Another checkmark in the Brock column."

"Seems like we have a lot of checks in a lot of columns. My vote: we hit urgent care then revisit this in the morning."

"Do you always have to be the voice of reason?" Maggie grumbled.

"No, sometimes I'm the voice of caution. I've also been the voice of C3PO, but that's only on weekends."

He started the car and pointed it toward the town's only twenty-four-hour urgent care. Two hours and an appointment for another brain scan later, they were home and in bed.

Maggie felt better physically. Mentally was another story. She was wrung out and defeated, no closer to answers to the questions that had begun to hound her, terrified that Brock would make good on his promise to come for the Whitleys.

Technically, the poisonings had nothing to do with her. Technically this was the Austin and Gladys show. Technically, she had no connection to the Whitleys despite the pull that kept drawing her into their orbit.

Technically, none of that mattered. She had begun to look under rocks. She wouldn't stop looking until she'd turned the one with spiders writhing beneath.

Maggie fell into a fitful sleep and was roused at five thirty by Robert De Niro. Only one person would dare to call so early. Maggie slid from beneath the sheets and padded into the hall, pulling the bedroom door behind her.

"Hey, Pop."

"Good morning, Maggie."

Good morning? Had Pop ever greeted her so formally before? "What's up?"

Her father coughed into the phone, then snorted and cleared his throat. In Maggie's experience, everyone had a tell. For some it was a series of rapid blinks. Others a reddening of the face or incessant babbling. For Jack O'Malley, it was phlegm.

Other than the occasional fib, Maggie's father never lied. Was the tell a lead-in to a difficult topic? Maggie steeled herself.

Jack O'Malley cleared his nasal passages again. "Maggie, I'm afraid I have some bad news."

It was the phrase he'd used when his preferred parmesan cheese vendor went out of business. It was also the phrase he'd used when he revealed that her mother's cancer had planted its flag in more organs, that her death was a certainty, inked on a cosmic calendar by the hand of God. *Upcoming event, date to be announced.*

It was a phrase that could mean everything or nothing at all.

"Uh huh," she said, clearing her throat, her own tell betraying her.

"I'm afraid I won't be able to make your wedding."

Maggie's mind skipped, a needle hopping the groove of a record. "I'm sorry if I wasn't enthusiastic about a church wedding or parking lot reception or—"

"No, no, that isn't it." A long silence wedged between them. "I've decided to go to CartCon. It's a food cart convention. Good networking potential."

Networking and potential. Two words she'd never heard other than to describe favorite news outlets and how Maggie wasn't living up to hers.

She shook her head. "I'm sorry. I don't understand. We haven't even set a date."

"Well, yes." Snort, cough, hack. "But I've gathered that it will be in the next year. CartCon is in six months, scarcely enough time for Fiona and me to prepare."

The implication was painfully clear. It wasn't that Pop couldn't go to the wedding. He didn't want to go. Maggie's father, her only living parent, the only other person left on the planet who understood the depth and breadth of the hole left by her mother, wasn't interested in coming to her wedding. Maggie felt as if she'd been slapped.

"Listen, if this is about the parking lot reception or fondant or—" she began again, suddenly desperate for the big wedding she despised.

"It's not that. It's..." The silence that followed was so complete that Maggie thought the connection had been broken. "I can't go."

Phone connection: fine. Their connection: severed.

Maggie mumbled a goodbye into the phone then let the storm that had been building behind her eyes, in her heart, break through the cloud cover of The Wall. Traitorous tears coursed down her cheeks. She wanted to curse, to ask why the father who had doted on her, guided her, cared for her in the winter that followed her mother's death had abandoned her at the gateway of her next journey. The lump in the back of her throat made it impossible to speak, to think.

Pop had always growled at Constantine. She had assumed it was all an act, that an underlayment of affection bolstered hollow complaints, empty criticisms. Now she wasn't so sure. Now she wondered whether he so disapproved of her spousal selection that he was willing to remove himself from her wedding—her married life—to show it.

Or perhaps he simply disapproved of her. Perhaps he saw her marriage as an opportunity to start a new life without the specter of the dead wife who looked so like Maggie.

Maggie felt something deep within her break, shift, die. She tried to cram the feelings behind The Wall. They oozed beneath like a poisonous gas.

So she encapsulated them. Buried them. Enclosed them in another cyst. Then hid that malignancy deep within her heart.

Maggie slapped the tears from her cheeks and let an internal Lent begin. She wouldn't think of her father or the wedding she didn't want or the marriage that might be doomed. She wouldn't let herself think about anything other than justice for the dead and solace for the suffering.

Chapter 30

Maggie made a pot of coffee, bitter succor for the spirit, poured a generous cup and walked to the living room. She flopped onto the couch and flicked on the TV: her first stop on the day's information-gathering circuit.

Maggie navigated to News Channel 4. Russ Brock filled the screen. He peered earnestly over his mike, expertly highlighted hair waving in the breeze. Behind him, a charred building stood wet and smoldering beneath the early morning sun.

Brock gestured grandly toward the ruined structure behind him, his mouth set in a grim little line. "Tragedy struck as it usually does..." His pregnant pause could have carried twins. "When least expected."

The camera followed Brock as he sauntered toward the burned-out shell. "This..." another grand gesture, "was the oldest building in downtown Hollow Pine. Abandoned by the community and bereft of hope for a renaissance, it has languished, unleased and unoccupied, for the past five years."

The camera zoomed in then panned up the face of the three-story structure. Broken out windows gaped like empty eye sockets. The front door, splintered and half off its hinges, sagged in a toothless frown.

Maggie sat up and placed her cup on a gouge in the coffee table, a fossil from Constantine's Pre-Coaster Era. She squinted at the image on screen, the hairs on her arms raising like tiny flags.

"It's a tragic turn for the once-vibrant district and a reminder that nothing is permanent," Brock continued. "Although no one was harmed in the blaze, many wonder if the fire could have been avoided with a stronger police presence. If those on the job were doing their jobs. If officers of the peace kept the peace." He took a breath, gathering momentum for his big finish. "If the men and women entrusted to protect and serve did just that."

It was a familiar rant, an oft-sung song in which a few notes changed, but the tune remained the same: Hollow Pine police were lazy and untrustworthy.

An assessment born of personal rancor? Past experience? Or had they become targets of Brock's rancor just as Maggie had?

Whatever the genesis, it didn't seem to hurt Brock's popularity with his base. Maggie imagined them nodding along at home, comfortable in manipulated outrage and manufactured indignation. Even Brock nodded with himself, his head bobbing to the beat of the righteous anger groove.

Brock looked grimly into the camera. "This is Russ Brock, in the field. Back to you, Doug."

The in-studio news anchor caught the verbal football and began extruding sound-bites to fill the blanks that Brock had left: fire under investigation, neighboring buildings reporting smoke damage, a reminder to check smoke and fire alarms.

Maggie hit mute and stared at the photo of the building behind the anchor's hairspray-fused head.

She closed her eyes. *Think*, she commanded her sluggish brain. *Remember.*

A glimmer of recognition materialized into a memory.

Her alleyway pursuit of Brock. Brock illuminated by the light of his cellphone. Brock fumbling with something, *doing* something. Brock silhouetted before a three-story building.

A building that looked like the one splashed beside Doug the Anchor.

Maggie picked up her cup and swallowed more of the tepid coffee. "Looked like" and "was" were miles apart. How could she be sure that Brock had been at the building devoured by greedy flames? How could she prove it? Wouldn't she and Constantine have seen him on their return visit to retrieve the note shoved beneath the Whitleys' door?

Maggie remembered Constantine's trick to determine who lived at the house where Brock had placed the note. She tiptoed to the bedroom and returned with her phone. She opened her Facebook app and digitally cruised by the previous night's locales, just as Constantine had, her pulse quickening as broken possibilities knitted into absolute certainties.

She logged onto the news stations website to double-check and triple-confirm. The address in the news story and the building in front of which Brock had loitered, had crouched and handled unseen objects, were the same

Maggie felt something twist in her stomach. Brock wasn't just faking the news. He was making it.

Chapter 31

She was at Constantine's side in seconds. "Gus," she whispered. "Gus, wake up." He grunted and turned over. "The server's down," she said more loudly.

He sat bolt upright. "Wha—? For how long?"

"For never. Come on, I have something to show you."

She grabbed his hand and pulled him from the bed. He muttered something about IT betrayal and stumbled after her. She pushed him onto the couch and used the DVR to rewind, wishing that life had a similar feature.

Constantine rubbed his eyes and yawned. "What is this, some kind of reality TV show about the effects of sleep deprivation?"

"It's a glimpse into Russ Brock's deeds as a newsmaker." She played the footage, showed him Facebook's digital breadcrumbs of her pursuit of Brock, then finished with the address of the building that had blazed hot and merciless and complete.

Constantine's eyes traveled from the TV to her phone. He leaned back and dragged his hand across his face. "Making fake news real. Talk about an overachiever."

"Makes you wonder what other news he made."

"Back when he was Herr Wurm?"

"Yes and the more recent past."

He looked at her, rubbed his face again and got to his feet. "I have a feeling that this conversation is going to call for some caffeine fortification."

Maggie followed him to the kitchen where he poured a fragrant Guatemalan blend into a mug, then turned it dingy white with a generous pour of half-and-half.

"I'm pretty sure I know what you're going to say," Constantine said. "I just wanted to chemically gird my loins." He sipped and spread his feet wide. "Okay, hit me."

"Brock's history suggests that he has no qualms about faking news—or about stalking women."

"Certainly seems like he was absent on the day they handed out scruples."

"If he set last night's fire to create a headline, there's no telling how far he'll go. Nobody was hurt, but it could have ended very differently."

"Suggesting that if he has such little disregard for human life, he'd be willing to take one—or more—if it meant a big story."

Maggie lifted a shoulder. "It's a thought. He's ambitious and ruthless. Like Brock's assistant said, Brock will do anything for a story. Maybe he wanted a shot at going national but wasn't getting the traction he needed to make the climb. He was the first to cover the poisonings, scooping everyone else. Add in the fanfare he created over his suggestions of police bungling—and my supposed role—and he rocketed to the top of the heap. The story could have been the break he was looking for."

"And you're saying that he created that break by poisoning four people at Petrosian's?"

"I'm not saying anything. I'm just suggesting."

Constantine swallowed a mouthful of coffee and then another. "It does make a certain amount of evil sense. He pegs my creep-o-meter almost as much as our pal Miles. I vote for a phone call to Austin and Gladys, you know, the people who are authorized to investigate this case."

"Yeah," she said grudgingly. "I guess that would be the right thing to do."

"If by 'right' you mean 'sane,' I totally agree."

Maggie grabbed her phone from the divot in the coffee table. She checked the time. Six o'clock. Too early for a phone call? Probably. She hoped her former relationship with Austin would grant her a little grace and dialed anyway.

She expected voicemail. Austin had become less available since the drama of the past year—and her engagement to Constantine. He picked up immediately. "Hey, Maggie," he said in a chipper voice. "How are you?"

How was she? Her brain wasn't working as well as she'd like, she was being maligned on television and stalked in real life, and her father had all but abandoned her. She guessed he'd prefer platitudes over the truth. "Great, and you?"

They exchanged pleasantries, discussing the weather, proposing get-togethers they knew would never happen. Finally Maggie said, "I'm calling about the poisonings."

"I figured as much," he said evenly. "Like I told you, it's an open investigation. I really can't discuss it."

"I know. I have something tell you."

She shared what she knew of Brock's past, her theory about Brock's desire to make news, whatever the cost, his skulking presence before last night's fire, how his coverage of the poisonings could advance his career. Austin was silent for a moment. Maggie imagined him shifting on his feet, digging his toe into the carpet. The sound of cellophane crackled over the line. No doubt the disrobing of a toothpick. "Gee, Maggie, I don't know. It all sounds kind of far-fetched."

"Far-fetched?" she said too loudly. She dialed back her volume and annoyance. "He has a history of inventing news. A record of stalking. I'm sure you'd hate to overlook a lead, especially if the poisoner is still out there, biding his time."

Austin sighed. "Okay, I'll look into it, and I'll talk to the fire chief. They're already investigating for arson. Wouldn't hurt to add more information—or supposition—to the heap. Anything else?"

Maggie considered telling him about Miles, asking if he knew about Petrosian's absence, divulging the six degrees of separation Nigel Roberts had with both Colton the deceased and Francine the cashier, maybe even throwing in the mysterious man conversing with Roberts at the coffee shop. She decided to keep those tidbits to herself. Better to keep him focused on Brock.

"Nope, that's it." She paused. "Unless you can tell me the latest with the search warrant?"

Another sigh, this one longer. "Once again, this is—"

"I know...an open investigation. I was just curious about how everything went and whether Petrosian's might re-open soon. I'm out of a job until it does."

Maggie played the sympathy card. Austin picked it up. "Gosh, I didn't think of that." The sound of teeth gnashing wood as Austin went to work on the toothpick. "I guess it's okay if I tell you that the search warrant was executed."

"And...?"

"And we bagged a bunch of stuff and sent it to the lab for analysis. Unfortunately," she heard a shuffle as Austin changed ears, "there's been a delay in processing. The lab had to close. Bomb threat."

"Bomb threat?" Maggie's synapses fired as she tried to imagine Brock calling in a threat or prowling around with packs of C4. She wouldn't put either past him.

"Everyone's pretty sure it's fake. Scuttlebutt is that the lab had to let someone go and there were some hard feelings."

"Disgruntled employee."

"Exactly. Problem is, we have to take every threat seriously. The bomb squad cleared the place, but the lab manager is freaked. He's worried about the employee coming back, doing serious damage."

"He has a point," Maggie said soberly. Too many headlines about gun-wielding revenge-seekers to deny that possibility.

"They're closed until we can make an arrest or determine that there's no credible threat. That means more warrants, more detective work, more time."

Time. Exactly what they didn't have. "Thanks for letting me know."

"You betcha, and thanks for the tip on Brock. We'll have to proceed with caution on that one. He's not exactly a fan of the police, and he has a big microphone."

Maggie ended the call and summarized for Constantine.

"I noticed that you neglected to mention stalker Miles," he replied.

Maggie crossed her arms. Uncrossed them. "I will. I just wanted to keep Austin's eye on the ball."

"Okay, then mention it to someone else." He ran a hand through his hair. "Meanwhile, we'll hang tight and let the detectives detect, watch them dig into Brock and see what skeletons they pull up."

Maggie finished her coffee and set the cup on the counter. "Or we keep moving and see what we can find out on our own, starting with you calling Brock about that bogus story you floated to his assistant."

"We're going to rely on my acting skills to garner information from a potential murderer while another potentially dangerous man skulks about town." He bolted the dregs of his caffeine infusion. "What could possibly go wrong?"

Chapter 32

"Mr. Brock's office, Bradley speaking."

Constantine goosed the volume button on his phone and angled it toward Maggie so she could hear. "Hi Bradley, we met the other day. I stopped in to talk to Mr. Brock about a big story and you directed me to Glass Half Full?"

"Oh yeah," Bradley said, his voice warming several degrees. "I'm sorry, but he's in a staff meeting right now."

"Damn it," Constantine said in a passable impersonation of *Star Trek's* Dr. McCoy. "Do you know when he'll be available? I'm guessing you practically run the place. The power behind the throne, as it were."

Bradley laughed. "You could say that, although I'm not sure Mr. Brock would. He says I can't do anything right." Russ Brock, equal opportunity jerk. Keyboard clacks echoed through the speaker. "Schedule-wise, looks like he's pretty tied up with the Petrosian poisoning thing. Like I said yesterday, he's blocked out his calendar for the day."

Constantine gave a low whistle. "The poisonings seem to be Brock's pet story. Other than last night's fire, they're all he ever talks about. It's like he's obsessed or something."

"Obsessed." Bradley drew out the word, gave the sibilant *s* extra attention. "That's the word for it, especially over that girl."

Constantine found Maggie's eyes. "The girl from the pharmacy? Maggie what's-her-name?"

"Uh, you know forget I said that. Forget I said anything. I get to talking, sometimes I can't stop myself. That's why Mom told me to go into the TV business."

"Makes great sense," Constantine soothed. "You're a natural."

"Naw, I talk too much. I shouldn't have made that crack about Mr. Brock and the girl. I wasn't serious, you know." He gave a laugh to show how serious he was about not being serious. "Just messing around."

"Right, right. It's just that all of us have been a little obsessed about the girl. About that Maggie at the pharmacy."

Bradley made a sound that was part scoff, part retch. "Not the pharmacy girl. The *girl* girl. The sick one who got poisoned. You know I put some money in one of those cans at the grocery store when she got leukemia? I even gave to her Go Fund Me."

"Is that right? Very nice. And what does Brock say about the girl? About the poisonings?"

Bradley plowed ahead as if he hadn't heard Constantine. "Plus I donated to that charity that grants sick kids wishes when I found out they were sending her and her mom on a cruise through the Panama Canal." Bradley paused. "Man, I'd love to see the Panama Canal."

Constantine closed his eyes. Maggie guessed he was praying for patience. "Uh huh. Yeah, me, too. Did Brock make donations for Riley Whitley? Contribute to charities that supported her?"

"Maybe. It's a good cause. That family needs help, and I'm always ready to lend a hand."

"That's great, Bradley." Constantine's eyelids fluttered closed again. "Maybe that's part of why Mr. Brock was so interested in their story. He wanted to raise awareness so they'd get the help they needed."

"Maybe." Bradley didn't sound convinced. "He was always tracking them. Following the story, he liked to say. Never mind that I suggested doing a piece on kids with terminal illness. He put the kibosh on that immediately, said it's too much of a downer." Derisive snort. "Like poison's not a downer."

"He say anything else about the Whitleys, the poisonings..." A pause. "Last night's fire?"

"Not really." Maggie could hear the shrug through the phone. "Just spent a lot of time out of the office chasing down the details."

Or creating them, Maggie thought.

"Thanks for your time, Bradley. You're awesome."

"I am? Thanks! Don't hear that very often around here." Another laugh, this one without mirth. "If you give me your name and number, I'll leave a message for Mr. Brock."

"That's okay. I'll just call him later."

Constantine poked the End button. "I'm not sure how helpful that was, other than propping up Bradley's confidence and confirming that Brock is infatuated with the Whitleys and the poisonings."

"The call also did one very important thing."

"What's that?"

"We now know that Brock won't be home for some time."

Constantine gave her a wary look. "I don't like the sound of that."

Maggie felt a jab in her chest. That was Jack O'Malley's most famous catchphrase. She pushed the feeling aside and made for the door. "Don't worry. You will."

Seven minutes later, thanks to light traffic, cooperative traffic lights and a heavy foot on the accelerator, Maggie pulled in front of ranch-style home on a block lined with similarly styled abodes.

The neighborhood radiated exhaustion. Trees, lightly clad in the pink and green of new flowers and leaves, stood stoop-shouldered in front of dingy homes. Paint flecked like dandruff onto drowsing porches. House numbers faded into nothingness by the steady thrum of rain and time.

Maggie circled the block twice searching for Brock's address. Process of elimination led her to a bandage-colored house with a tan brick edifice, rust-colored (or simply rusty) storm door and a sticker in the window claiming protection by a neighborhood watch program.

She parked a few doors down in front of a defeated looking house with crooked shutters, a sagging fascia board and a row of sunny daisies that embraced a cracked driveway. An old woman in a housedress stared at Maggie as she bent to retrieve the daily paper from her front stoop. Maggie waved. The woman smiled and returned the gesture. Kindness, like flowers, sprung up even in harsh environments.

Maggie and Constantine marched toward Brock's house. Maggie held a clipboard that she occasionally consulted, using a number two pencil to make check marks on the blank page. Maggie knew that the secret to going wherever you wanted was looking like you belonged there.

They arrived at Brock's and stood before the storm door. A *No Soliciting* sign had been affixed with a glue gun, but like the house numbers, the lettering had ghosted to near illegibility. Maggie knocked smartly then checked the clipboard, pencil poised. She pretended to make a notation. She and Constantine leaned toward the door and listened. Nothing from inside. A lawnmower fired up down the block.

"I'm going around," Maggie said under her breath.

"To do what?" He smiled pleasantly in case anyone was watching.

"Just look official and follow me." She gave the clipboard another look, flipped pages then walked to the side of the house.

Hastily stowed yard work equipment, stacks of flattened cardboard and a pile of damp scrap wood slowed their passage. Maggie eyed the clutter for signs of nefarious plans. All she saw was an affinity for messiness.

They rounded the southeast corner of the house and surveyed the home's rear-end. It had the same ambiance of resignation as the rest of the neighborhood, with a side of moldering takeout boxes for good measure.

"Maybe he's collecting them for a story on the dangers of cardboard," Constantine said, jutting his chin toward the boxes. "Environmental pollutant. Paper cut hazard."

"Fire fuel for an old building downtown," Maggie added.

Constantine folded his arms. "Now you're reaching."

"Okay, maybe. Just boost me up so I can see in this window."

Unlike the front of the house, which featured a large picture window framed by flabby drapes, the rear featured three small windows eight feet off the ground. Constantine laced his fingers to create a stirrup. Maggie stepped onto his hands and he hoisted her up with a grunt.

"What happened to the strength to carry me over the threshold every day?" she asked.

"I left it at home. Along with my better judgment." He panted and adjusted his grip. "Just hurry, will ya?"

Maggie dropped the clipboard and it landed on the balding lawn with a soft thud.

She put her hands up to the window's aluminum frame and put her nose to the glass. Her phone rang. She dug for it, shifting her weight as she rummaged in her pocket.

"Um, kind of a bad time to take a call," Constantine said between pants.

Maggie checked the screen. Forever Memories, the wedding photographer Fiona insisted Maggie contact. She imagined a photo of herself walking down the aisle without her father, his absence a void that would never be filled. She silenced her phone. No time for pain. Only time for focus. She peered through the glass once again.

Sink. Toilet. Shower. LL Bean catalog.

"Bathroom," she called down softly. "Can you skooch over to the next one?"

Constantine skooched. She repeated her maneuver. An old computer atop a monstrous oak desk, posters and paintings of classic TV shows and movies, a filing cabinet.

Brock's home office.

"Just hold it there a sec, okay?"

Constantine must have mumbled an affirmative, but Maggie heard only the growing tempo and volume of her heartbeat.

She pressed her nose hard against the glass, cold vitreous mating with warm flesh. In the void above Brock's desk, between a print of *Magnum, P.I.* and a cinema poster for *Broadcast News*, nestled a spray of photos. Each depicted a different moment, but all had a single subject: the Whitleys.

Mary and Riley in the parking lot of a doctor's office.

Mary and Riley eating ice cream.

Mary and Riley at Petrosian's Pillbox again and again.

"What is it?" Constantine asked, puffing between words.

"You can let me down," she said.

He lowered her gently to the ground. "You see something good?"

"Only if good means bad. Brock has a collage of the Whitleys plastered above his desk."

"Plastered in a creepy guy/serial killer kind of way?"

"Is there any other kind?"

"Good point."

"These pictures scream obsession and planning. From the volume and assortment, it looks like Brock's been following them for a while. He also seemed to have a special interest in their visits to Petrosian's."

Constantine raised an eyebrow at that. "So Brock stalks the Whitleys then tries to off them by poison to get the corner on a big story. Why them?"

"Sympathy. Outrage. The diet of today's news junkie. What better victims than a child sick with cancer and her beleaguered mother? Because of Mary's blog, they're well known in the community. The bigger the celebrity, the greater the response. And the more potential for a great story."

"Colton Ellis and Claudia Warren were collateral damage?"

Maggie nodded. "Unintentional casualties, unless we count the fact that the poisonings likely happened at the pharmacy where I work. It's no secret that Brock hates me. The poisonings gave him a great scoop and the chance to throw shade—and suspicion—on me. Plus he could leverage the subsequent investigation to continue to fly his flag of police incompetence. It's the story that keeps on giving."

"And Miles's arrival and stalking is, what, just coincidence?"

Maggie shrugged. "I guess so. All signs point to Brock."

"And now we point the police at him?"

Maggie dusted off her hands. "I'll call Austin again, tell him what we found. While he figures out what to do with the information, we'll keep on keepin' on."

"Keepin' on what?"

"Following Brock."

Chapter 33

Following was delayed by biology. Although fired by early morning caffeine, by the time the sun reached its apex, both Maggie and Constantine needed to refuel.

After leaving a message for Austin, Maggie pulled into the drive-in section of Dinah's Diner, and spoke into the smiling mouth of a giant plastic Dinah head, requesting two Beach Blanket Brisket sandwiches and a side of Saddle Shoestring Potatoes. Moments later, Dinah's doppelganger arrived, rolling toward them with bouffant hair, bobby socks and two white bags turned translucent by grease. Maggie felt her belly rumble in anticipation.

Maggie ate while she drove, steering with her knee as she glided the shifter up and down the column and licked mayo from her hand.

"Um, you know there are laws about distracted driving, right?" Constantine said, stuffing French fries into his mouth. "Not to mention driving with non-traditional limbs."

"Zartar used to apply eyeliner and mascara while she drove," she said, referring to a favorite former coworker. "Of course, she had an automatic transmission."

"Oh, then it's totally fine. In fact, I think they encourage it."

Maggie ignored him and pulled into a space across the street from the News Channel 4 studio. She relinquished her sandwich, dusted sesame seeds from her hands, and pulled a pair of miniature binoculars from her purse. She trained the binoculars on the studio's glass door.

"Very Spy vs. Spy," Constantine said, pointing to the binoculars. "Did they come with a trench coat and fedora?"

"I got them off Amazon, along with some new books for next semester's classes. Plus a case of Reese's Pieces, some of which are on board." She nodded to the glove box.

Constantine popped open the box and examined the cache of packages. "Surveillance food. Now all we need is witty banter and it'll be like we're in a buddy cop movie."

"Can you be serious, please? We're talking poisonings, the closure of Hollow Pine's oldest pharmacy, the targeting of an innocent woman and her sick child and—" Maggie stopped mid-rant and breathed in sharply. "There's the man of the hour now, heading God knows where to do God knows what."

Maggie and Constantine watched as Russ Brock strode toward a Toyota Tercel. He folded himself inside. Reverse lights blinked on.

Maggie lowered the binoculars and devoured the rest of her sandwich in two bites. She wiped her mouth on the shoulder of her shirt. "Let's see where Hollow Pine's newsmaker leads us."

Maggie had watched enough movies to have a vague idea of how to tail a car. In most of these movies, however, the tail was a vehicle that blended in. A sedan. A pickup truck. Maybe even an electric car. Not head-turning vintage wheels with shiny custard-hued paint and a crimson interior.

"Subtle as a dump truck driving through a nitroglycerine plant," Maggie muttered, half-quoting *Christmas Vacation*. "Let's just hope his vanity means that he only uses his rearview mirror to check his hair."

Maggie hung back, letting several cars between the Studebaker and the Tercel. The day was diamond-bright, the sun glaring down as if in disapproval of her plans. She rummaged in her purse, extracted a pair of sunglasses and slid the oversized frames onto her nose.

"I thought you couldn't hear as well with sunglasses on." Constantine raised a forefinger. "Oh, wait, that's me."

He sat up in his seat and elongated his neck as if it were on jacks. "Where the hell is he going?"

They had woven through the pedestrian-clogged streets of downtown, cruised past the big box stores that squatted at its periphery. Shopping oases gave way to verdant fields and deserted farm stands, which in turn gave way to empty thatches of land unencumbered by people or plow. Brock signaled and turned down a narrow gravel road.

Maggie checked her mirrors. The road was empty behind her. She slowed to a crawl then made the same turn. A sign at the mouth of the drive introduced the property as Restful Pines.

"Cemetery?" Constantine asked, eyeing a row of white tombstones that looked like teeth set in greening gums.

"Or a really weird day spa."

Ahead the drive widened into a parking lot. She pulled onto the shoulder and parked beneath a weeping willow with branches puddling the ground. "Let's see what—or who—brings Brock here. Judging by the number of vehicles, I'm guessing it's a funeral."

Constantine got out and eased his door shut with a click. "Crashing a funeral. Guess there's a second time for everything."

Although not far from the highway, the road noise was dampened by a dense screen of towering pines. Even when a gust of wind created a torrent of dust and debris, the tops of the trees gently swayed as if slow-dancing at prom. Restful Pines, indeed.

They slunk along the shoulder of the road, one foot on gravel, the other on the spongy forest floor, until they reached a column-fronted building that looked like the architectural lovechild of a Greek temple and a courthouse.

They stopped at the corner of the building and peered around. A small assembly stood with heads in varying degrees of convex angulation as a man in black read from a book. Overhead, a canvas canopy shielded mourners from sun and rain, but not from grief. Even at this distance, Maggie could feel sorrow radiating off the group.

After her mother had died, Maggie had sworn she'd never attend another funeral, that she'd never again smile and nod at proclamations of divine timing or watch someone's body be lowered into the fresh wound of an earthen grave.

How many times had she broken that promise to herself?

As if reading her thoughts, Constantine grabbed her hand then grazed her knuckles with his lips. "You okay?" he whispered.

"Fine," Maggie said, masking pain with irritation. "Just trying to figure out who the guest of honor is. Brock's there." She pointed. Constantine nodded as he spotted Brock's taupe-clad form at the front of the group, his head appropriately inclined like the others. Maggie's eyes roved the line of backs that stood before them. "Not the best view, but I don't recognize anyone else. I wish we could get closer."

Constantine tugged at his ear. "Brock doesn't know about me, right?"

Maggie shrugged. "His focus seems to be on me, but I wouldn't be surprised if he researched you, Pop and my third-grade teacher."

"I think this calls for a calculated risk." He kissed her cheek. "BRB. That's 'be right back' in keyboard."

Maggie was about to retort that she knew her digital acronyms, but Constantine was already gone, his long legs carrying him toward the small group. He drifted quietly to the back of the nebula. A tall woman with swimmer's deltoids turned his direction, nodded, then resumed the grieving position.

The man in black droned on. Minutes dragged by. Then, as if a spell had been lifted, the group reanimated and began to move about, embracing shoulders, kissing cheeks, shaking heads in the international sign for "what a tragedy."

Constantine turned to the woman next to him and said something. She touched his arm, nodded then dabbed her eyes with a tissue clenched in a meaty hand before moving along the reception line of misery. Constantine approached a man with a Budweiser baseball cap and a can-shaped physique. As the two chatted, Maggie saw Brock stride purposefully toward Constantine.

"Gus." She whispered his name, speaking to herself more than to him. "Gus, get out of there."

She watched in growing horror as Brock's strides closed the gap between Constantine and his newfound friend. Constantine did the sympathetic-head-tilt-and-nod as he listened to Budweiser Man. Behind him, Brock drew closer. Grew larger.

Maggie plunged her hand into her jeans pocket and rooted around for her phone, her forefinger already rehearsing its placement on Constantine's name at the head of her contacts list. She pulled the device free, fumbled, dropped it on a rock that jutted from the earth, shoveled it into her hands.

A cracked screen winked in the sunlight.

A damaged screen doesn't always mean disaster, she told herself. *It's what's on the inside that counts.*

She palpated the ruined screen. The phone was as unresponsive as Colton Ellis on the pharmacy floor. Evidently, the insides of her phone were cracked, too.

She looked up. Brock was at Constantine's shoulder, nearly touching it with his own.

Then, incomprehensively, impossibly, Brock walked on.

Maggie closed her eyes, lips moving in a silent thanksgiving. Then she realized that Brock was heading her way.

She spun around and raced along the side of the building, one hand against the cold white edifice for balance as her ankles turned on tiny hills and dales where grass regrew in uneven, variegated patches.

She darted around the far corner of the building and waited, muscles tensed, breaths coming in shallow pants as adrenaline dumped into her bloodstream.

Had Brock seen her? Was that why he was heading her way?

Maggie looked around for a makeshift weapon in case Brock discovered her. Came at her. She spotted an assortment of wildflowers.

Maybe he was allergic and she could throw them at him.

The sound of an engine cleaved the jackhammering of her heart in her ears. Maggie peered around the corner. Brock's Tercel retreated, spitting gravel in its wake.

Maggie put her hands on her knees and tried to recalibrate her limbic system. Brock was gone. They were safe.

She pocketed her phone and hurried toward the opposite end of the building.

The group had thinned, leaving archipelagos of mourners to remember the good times and rail against their end. She found Constantine talking to a middle-aged woman who kept looking over his shoulder like a guest trapped at a cocktail party by the talkative guy at the punchbowl.

She smiled at the woman, hoped she wouldn't recognize her from the news, and squeezed Constantine's elbow. "Time to go, dear. We only have the babysitter for another twenty minutes."

The woman told them to take care then backed away as though Constantine might drag her into a riptide of more unwanted conversation.

"Making friends?" Maggie asked, watching the woman hurry to her car.

"She said her son worked in IT, so we talked shop." He paused. "Or maybe I talked shop and she pretended to listen. Anyway, I have information."

"Tell me on the way," she said as she grabbed his hand and dragged him down the drive.

"On the way to where?"

"Wherever Brock's going next."

Back in the Studebaker, Maggie executed an eight-point turn, courtesy of the narrow drive and the car's wide turning radius, and smashed the accelerator. The Studebaker bucked then sprayed gravel.

Maggie winced as she heard rock hit fender and eased her foot upward. "Fingers crossed that he didn't get far or spot us."

She reached the main road and looked left, right and left again, as she had been taught in elementary school. Her second look to the left garnered a view of the Tercel's shrinking taillights. She turned to follow. "What did you find out?"

"It was non-denominational service for Claudia Warren."

"The woman found dead in her apartment?"

"And who has the dubious honor of being the last poisoning victim."

"At least so far." Maggie gripped the steering wheel. "I wonder if Brock went to Colton's funeral, too. Returning to the scene of the crime—or to its aftermath—is classic killer behavior."

"Keeping the thrill alive—or keeping tabs on the investigation. At least that's what I picked up from *CSI: Miami.*"

Ahead, Brock's Tercel squatted at a stoplight. Maggie changed lanes, slipping the Studebaker behind a plumber's truck that declared itself Number One for Numbers One and Two. Brock's form was silhouetted in the car's interior. He stretched, lowered the visor, then fluffed his hair with his fingers. The light changed. Brock finished his toilette, crept forward.

Maggie idled forward then continued her tail at a leisurely pace, one eye on the Tercel, the other on her rearview mirror to ensure that she hadn't earned the wrath of speed-minded drivers behind her.

Lanes widened. Buildings rose. Traffic congealed. Maggie's left knee ached as tendons and clutch worked overtime. A distant bell pealed in the back of her mind as she passed familiar streets and buildings. As foggy as her brain had become, there was no missing Brock's destination. He was heading to St. Theresa's.

The Tercel signaled at the hospital's entrance. Brock's etiquette rankled Maggie. He had no qualms about casting dispersions and murdering innocents. Traffic violations? That's where he drew the line.

Maggie watched him pull into a space abutting a small picnic area complete with wooden tables and a small fire pit. As if the hospital grounds were the ideal place for hotdogs and sack races. As if an impromptu cookout was the ideal way to kill time while waiting for a loved one to be wheeled from the recovery room.

Brock stepped out of his car, looked over his shoulder then hitched up his pants, exposing a Rorschach test of sweat stains on the shirt beneath his sports jacket. Brock was polished onscreen, but in real life, he was anything but shiny.

Brock peered into the back window of his car, tossed another glance over his shoulder then walked toward the building where hundreds recovered, hoped and died.

Maggie parked and cut the engine. "A visit to the Whitleys' home and now a pop-by at the hospital where they're recovering."

"The whole thing stinks more than your dad's haggis poppers."

She ignored the flash of pain at her father's name, pushed away the knowledge that she hadn't shared the news about her father's planned absence at their wedding, and took the key from the ignition. "Whether he's here to get a story or make one, it's bad news for the Whitleys."

Before Constantine could reply, Maggie was out of the car and striding toward the hospital. Constantine jogged to catch up to her. "Don't you think it's time for another call to your ex-BF and our current constable of the peace? At the least, Brock's trespassing. At the most, he's here to firm up funeral plans for the Whitleys."

Maggie pulled her phone from her pocket and turned its face toward Constantine, showing him the fissure that cleaved the screen. "Can't. Telephonic mishap."

"Give it a try anyway. I once ran over my phone and it still worked intermittently. Granted, it was in a heavy-duty case and I was in a light-duty vehicle. Anyway, if it doesn't work, you can just use mine."

Maggie shrugged and restarted her phone. It came alive. She looked at Constantine. "Me of little faith." She dialed Austin. She was rewarded with a computerized voice telling her that Austin's voicemail box was full. The phone giveth and the phone taketh away.

She pushed END and relayed the thwarted attempt to Constantine.

"There's always Gladys Wren," he said. "Or the rest of the police department."

"I'll give her—or them—a call later. Now I want to see what Brock's up to."

Maggie powerwalked toward the hospital then suddenly stopped short. Brock's car was just steps away, adjacent to a jade green Subaru papered with bumper stickers advertising the driver's voting and procreation records.

She darted to the other side of Brock's car. The Tercel was pristine, freshly washed and waxed, the tires so immaculate they looked as though he'd gone over them with an electric toothbrush then flossed the treads.

She cupped her hands around her eyes and peered through the glass, the second time she had peeped into Brock's windows. Plastic sheathed dry-cleaning hung in the rear passenger area—more neutral-colored suits, Maggie guessed—and two cloth grocery bags roosted on the backseat.

She circled to the back of the car and repeated her inspection. She began to turn toward the hospital, legs ready to power her through the double doors to wherever Brock was Spinning his web, when something caught her eye. She looked in the rear window and jiggled the latch on the hatchback.

Constantine cleared his throat. "I'm all for violating Brock's privacy—and his doors—but shouldn't we stop him from whatever it is he's doing inside the big white building with the vulnerable patients? Or, here's an idea, call the *actual* authorities?"

Maggie pulled out her phone and pushed it against the Tercel's back window. "Right after I document the evidence."

"Did he leave a McNuggets carton on the backseat?"

She looked at him. "Nope. Just poison."

Chapter 34

"Poison?" Constantine gaped. "As in 'Cyanide Poisonings at Local Pharmacy, News at Eleven'?"

She placed her phone on Brock's window, clicked the camera button. Nothing happened. Right. Intermittent functionality. She wondered how long before it would decide to start working again. If ever.

"Can I borrow this?" She boosted Constantine's phone from his back pocket, snapped several photos of the backseat, then attached the pictures to a text to Austin, along with an explanation. Hopefully he could still receive text messages.

She handed Constantine his cell and began to lope toward the hospital, cutting through the trying-too-hard picnic area, dodging landmines left by dogs. "Now we've contacted the actual authorities and given actual evidence. Come on."

Constantine was at her heels. "That's great, but can you tell me what's going on?"

"Brock has boxes and boxes of ant poison in the back of his Tercel."

Constantine caught up with her. "So he's not big on bugs. Me, neither."

Maggie reached the hospital doors and yanked on the handle, the cool metal solid as the idea forming in her mind. "Some pesticides, especially ant poison, contain cyanide. Brock has enough poison to decimate the ant population. Maybe all of Hollow Pine."

They ran for the elevator bank, ignoring the man at the reception desk who called after them, unperturbed by the baffled looks of patients and staff whose eyes followed their harried rush to the elevators' steel mandibles that clenched shut with an automated hiss.

Maggie pounded the call button and looked up, wishing that the hospital lifts had indicators that showed their progress like the green bar that crawled across her computer screen when she tried to save a large file.

Your elevator car is fifty percent of the way to you... eighty percent...ninety-five.

She glanced toward the door leading to the stairwell—the dreaded, deadly stairwell—calculating the PTSD/reward ratio of taking the stairs and reliving the past. The elevator arrived from the hospital's underground garage and opened to reveal a full car. Constantine stationed himself in the rear right corner. Maggie crammed herself between a woman with an up-do that looked like an abandoned bird's nest and a man in scrubs who seemed to be having a conversation with someone named "I See." The woman smiled at Maggie then coughed wetly into her hand. Maggie took a baby step away.

The elevator dinged at the second floor as if ticking off a checklist and again at the third floor. The doors slid open. Maggie and Constantine squeezed to the front of the car and stepped onto the worn carpet of the third floor.

To the left, a nurse restocked her cart. To the right, a patient used a walker to pull himself along the corridor. He took a step, stopped, fought for breath, then took another. He succeeded in making progress, but it was agonizingly slow. Maggie could relate.

Maggie and Constantine began to make their way to room 325 when the stairwell door swung open and vomited out a man. The trio looked at each other for a moment.

"Bradley?" Constantine asked.

The thin young man swept dirty-blond hair from a pimple-corrugated forehead knotted with confusion.

"I stopped by the station to talk to Russ Brock and you directed me to his favorite bar?" Constantine prompted. "Then I called back and we talked about Brock's obsession with Riley Whitley?"

Bradley's face reddened. "What are you doing here?"

"What are *you* doing here?" Constantine countered.

Bradley's eyes darted down the hall. "I, ah..." He clamped his mouth shut. His Adam's apple bobbed. "I followed Mr. Brock."

Constantine's face remained impassive. "Because you're concerned about his obsession with Mary and Riley."

Bradley's tongue arrowed out from between full lips, moistened his mouth. "I was worried he'd...I was worried he'd do something." His face caved in, the now moistened lips trembling. "I know he's not supposed to be here. He told me how he got kicked out last time, was almost arrested for trespassing. I, I..." He cast a sidelong glance down the hall then leaned in. "I called security. I didn't want to do it, but I felt I had to. I didn't want him to get in trouble, or do something that would make the station look bad."

The tears pooled behind Bradley's glasses then began to fall. Constantine clapped a hand on his shoulder. "You did good," Constantine said. "Did they escort him out?"

Bradley blinked, sniffed, wagged his head from side to side. "They haven't gotten here yet."

Constantine shot Maggie a glance. Brock was in the building, perhaps in the Whitleys' room, and security was nowhere in sight. Maggie and Constantine fell into step toward Room 325, Bradley snuffling behind them.

They didn't need to make a plan. They didn't have to discuss. Like twins separated at birth, Maggie and Constantine were tied by an invisible umbilicus that united mind and spirit, sensing what the other knew, experiencing what the other felt. It was a connection that had guided them through a baptism of fire. It also came in handy while playing Pictionary.

The halls were empty, filled only with the sighs of machinery tasked with monitoring and maintaining life. They reached 325 in moments. The door was closed.

Maggie knocked loudly, "Shave and a Haircut" in forte. "Mrs. Whitley?" she called as she eased the door open. "Riley? It's Maggie and Constantine."

A silence, deeper and more complete than the emptiness of the hall, echoed back. Maggie strained to hear the whir of machinery, the rustle of bedclothes over bodies and bedframes.

Nothing.

Maggie's stomach dropped to her knees. They were too late. Wurm had wormed his way into their room and finished the job he'd started, taking two lives, giving himself a shiny new headline. She imagined his satisfaction, pictured the front-page copy: "Whitley Women Succumb to Poison." She wondered how he expected to get away with it, then remembered people got away with murder on the daily. With a good lawyer, he'd welcome the publicity of a trial.

Maggie gave the door another push, the smooth laminated surface cool beneath her fingertips, and stepped into the room.

Riley lay in her bed, her face a waning gibbous. White. Diminishing. Luminous beneath the fluorescent lights. Mary, similarly wan, was seated beside Riley, the girl's slight form half on her mother's lap, a Pieta made of flesh rather than marble. The mother's head bent as in prayer, one hand on the girl's arm where the IV needle had bitten cruelly into her daughter's flesh.

"Mrs. Whitley?" Maggie said gently.

Mary's head jerked up, the hand that had caressed Riley's arm flying behind her back. Recognition dawned. The hand dropped to her side. "Maggie!" she said. "I didn't expect to see you."

"Mrs. Whitley..." Maggie began, "we're worried that you and Riley might be in danger."

The fear returned to Mary's eyes, pushing them wide. "What do you mean?"

"We have reason to believe that a reporter, Russ Brock, is—"

The door flew open. Maggie spun around, ready to confront, to defend, to do whatever it took to protect the critically ill girl, the recovering mother, the two-unit family with whom she felt an inexplicable yet unyielding kinship.

Deena poked her head around the corner. She saw the group and smiled. "Hey, a party! Looks like I'm just in time...." She looked at Riley's unmoving form, took in Mary's waxen complexion, and frowned.

She crossed the room in four strides, nudged Mary aside and performed the all-too familiar rite of assessment. Riley stirred in response to Deena's touch.

Deena looped her stethoscope around her neck and sighed. "Seems Whitley the Younger isn't doing too hot." Her frown deepened, creating fissures on her otherwise smooth skin. "With a case like hers, it's hard to know why." She looked at Mary. "You don't look so great, either. Let me check your chart and see when you're due for your meds."

Mary opened her mouth, but didn't have a chance to ask what cocktail of medications would be shaken and stirred, whether the hospitalist would be called to assess their worsening health, if they'd have to stay another night or three. The door once again opened and the quintet looked up in orchestral unison.

Russ Brock stood in the doorway, filling it with malevolent intent and lumpy polyester.

His eyes were red and sunken, the thin skin beneath purpled by insomnia. The rest of his face was ruddy and moist as if he'd been running. Whether it was due to his obsession with the Whitleys, an overabundance of work, or the rigors of arson, one thing was clear: Russ Brock was fraying around the edges.

He scanned the room, his eyes lighting on Deena, Constantine and Maggie before landing on Bradley. "You?" he snarled. "What are you doing here?"

Bradley shrank against Maggie. "I knew you were coming here. I wanted to stop you before you—"

"Before I what?" Brock's snarl grew to a growl. "You little shit. You disloyal, scheming little—"

Brock sprung forward. The door rebounded and hit him in the shoulder. At first Maggie thought he was going for Bradley. Then the reporter changed direction and charged toward Mary, batting aside Deena's cart, ramming the rolling food tray into the IV stand beside Riley's bed.

Brock stormed forward, legs pumping, mouth chewing unuttered words, one arm reaching into the straining pocket of his jacket.

"He's got a gun!" Bradley cried.

That was all Maggie needed to hear. She switched from defense to offense. She ducked her head, straightened her arms and ran for Brock. Constantine was right behind her.

They hit the reporter simultaneously. Brock reeled back, bouncing from Riley's bed to the displaced food tray to the room's small sink in a convincing imitation of a pinball, and fell to the ground.

The hospital room door banged open. A pair of security guards charged inside, eyes flashing, faces red with excitement and exertion.

"What the hell—" a stocky guard with mousy hair shouted, part question, part exclamation. "Freeze!"

Maggie's brain registered the command then, ignored it. Adrenaline was in charge now. Deference to authority figures had evaporated, along with any sense of self-preservation. The Whitleys were in danger. Brock wasn't freezing. Neither would she.

Constantine seemed to agree. Together they grappled with Brock, hands scrabbling against shoulders and elbows in an attempt to subdue the man and subvert his plan. Brock writhed and bucked. He shook them off and went for his pocket again.

"Gun!" Bradley yelled.

"Freeze!" the guard shouted again, his voice climbing into the upper registers of hysteria.

Maggie grabbed a pillow from the bed—what, was she going to have a pillow fight with him?—tossed it aside and searched frantically for an improvised weapon. She leapt across the bed and grasped a clipboard from Deena's cart and raised it above her head, eyes trained on the back of Brock's skull.

She heard a sharp report. Brock and Constantine reared back then came together as if in a brotherly embrace, Brock lolling atop Constantine. Between them a dark stain spread like night. Venous blood, ruby-red and precious, pumped onto the floor in time with a fading heartbeat.

Chapter 35

The scent of gunpowder filled the air.

Maggie rushed to the interwoven pair. She rolled the reporter off Constantine, her hands searching her fiancé's body for the source of the torrent of blood, desperate to stanch its flow.

Constantine was whole. She turned to Brock who gasped and gurgled as blood bubbled from a deep and secret well.

Russ Brock had tried to kill them, but that didn't stop Maggie from trying to save him. She pressed her hand over the hole in Brock's chest.

"You have to—" he wheezed, his voice barely audible. His mouth continued to work, but no sound emerged.

She began to recoil, horror at the dying man's nearness, at the scent of blood in her nose, the feel of warm liquid oozing beneath her hands. She stopped herself. Brock had something to tell her. Maggie brought her face close to his. "I have to what?"

The mouth worked some more. Blood trickled from its corner and ran to his chin.

"I said freeze, damn it!" The security guard's voice quaked, fear overtaking hysteria.

Maggie applied more pressure to the wound, aware that the same gun that had shot Brock could be turned on her and yet unable to stop herself. "What is it?" she whispered to Brock.

"You have to..." The words were little more than breaths. Maggie turned her head, angling her left ear, straining to hear. Brock closed his eyes then opened them slowly like a child trying to stay awake past his bedtime. "Watch out for the girl."

Maggie was way ahead of him. Though she barely knew Riley, she felt a steadfast protectiveness, a big sisterness.

Damn right Maggie would watch out for the girl. But why did the man who tried to kill her care? Final remorse? A deathbed confession?

The thought made Maggie lean in once more. "Why did you do it?"

she hissed into Brock's ear. "For the headlines? For the glory?"

"If you don't stop moving and talking, I swear to God I'll shoot you, too," the guard said.

Maggie finally complied. So did Brock. Permanently. Breath left his body. The gurgling ceased. He stilled for the last time.

The security guards approached, the man who had been shouting orders in the lead, his partner a few steps behind. In her peripheral vision, Maggie could see dun-colored hair and a matching goatee atop a blue uniform, a gun straight-armed before him

Guard One bent and eyeballed Brock. He ran a hand under his nose and sniffed loudly. "Shit." He straightened up and assessed the group. "You on the floor, stay right there. Nurse, attend to this man."

Maggie faced the floor, inhaling the smell of antiseptic and regret, and listened as Deena went to work on Brock and the guard muttered into his radio. Moments later, she heard the soft whisper of hospital shoes as physicians and nurses filed into the room, followed by the percussion of boots as police joined the throng.

The murmur of modern medicine at work didn't last long. Brock was pronounced dead almost immediately. The medical team was ordered away. Mary cried. Riley, roused from the stupor of illness, wailed like a child awaking from a bad dream. More officers filed in, shouting commands.

The cacophony ended with the purr of a woman's voice.

"Now, now," Gladys Wren said, her voice steel-strong beneath a veneer of calmness. "Let's all settle down." Wren's high-heeled boots came into Maggie's line of sight. She stooped down and met her gaze. "You can get up. That handsome fellow next you, too."

Maggie searched Constantine's face for signs of pain, of a lurking mortal injury. He nodded, giving the all-clear. She turned toward the lump on the floor. Brock lay motionless, the lake of blood still widening.

"Hospital security came just in time." Maggie rolled her neck, which had already grown stiff from staring at the floor. "Brock tried to attack the Whitleys."

"I didn't think hospital security carried weapons," Constantine said, dusting off his knees.

"New policy," Guard One said. He opened his mouth, inserted a thumbnail between his incisors, dislodged something and sucked vigorously. "Implemented last month to help reduce shootings."

"Right," Constantine said, "and I hear they give out drugs to help reduce drug abuse."

The security guard swallowed whatever his oral search party had netted. "I heard that guy say gun, so I pulled my weapon. I don't need you to—"

Wren held up a hand. "Whatever the hospital's policy, I'm sure an investigation will show that it was justified. Brock was on the attack. You put an end to it."

The guard bobbed his head once, a period at the end of Wren's sentence, and looked at his partner, who gave his own body language punctuation.

Wren shooed Maggie and Constantine toward the Whitleys, who looked as if they were trying to press themselves into the wall behind them. She squatted to get another look at Brock, who still oozed deep red liquid from an invisible aquifer that would soon run dry, then pulled latex gloves from a pocket and snapped them in place. She patted Brock's jacket pockets then performed an encore with his pants. "You said there was a gun?"

Maggie looked over at Bradley who'd raised the alarm. Bradley pushed back a mass of hair. His face was red and sweaty like an overcooked hotdog. "Pretty sure. I mean, he reached into his pocket." The conviction he'd voiced during the struggle had faded.

"I'm not finding it," Wren replied, peering beneath the bed, giving the room a once-over, "but if it's here, the techs will."

She pitched the gloves into a plastic-lined wastebasket as Austin strode into the room. He saw Brock and gave a low whistle. "Looks like someone's done making headlines."

Wren dismissed the security guards, who muttered comments about the necessity of the shooting, the difficulty of their jobs and careers they had turned down in favor of keeping the peace at St. Theresa's. Maggie learned that Guard One went by "Lefty" and had auditioned for every season of *The Bachelor* since the show's inception. He had failed to secure a spot. Maggie tried to imagine women vying for Lefty's attentions as he grunted and picked things out of his teeth with his pinky. Maybe the producers were onto something.

Wren then systematically emptied the room of civilians, instructing

Deena to relocate the Whitleys and asking Maggie, Constantine and Bradley to step into the Family Meeting Room for a debrief. Every order felt like an invitation, the directness of the requests softened by the lilt of Wren's Southern accent and her game show hostess gestures to move hall-ward.

Maggie trailed behind Wren and the men. She turned to bid 325 a last adieu. Stopped. Something flashed beneath the door to the hyperbolically-dubbed en suite bathroom.

Maggie approached, stooped. Another glint of light. Maggie stretched out her hand and felt something cool and metallic. She tugged. A metal coil crowned, followed by the birth of a small green notebook.

She crouched for a better look. It was palm-sized, smelled of dust and ink, and was scrawled with RUSS BROCK in blocky caps. Maggie turned to Wren, who stood at the mouth of the room. "Um, Gladys?"

Wren looked over her shoulder. A phone was affixed to her ear. She held up a finger: just a moment.

Maggie bit her lip and toed the notebook with the tip of her sneaker, hoping to "accidentally" open it. The notebook rotated like a board game spinner. She glanced back at Wren, who had planted a manicured hand on a slim hip then began pacing, her boots taking her further and further from Maggie.

Wren stomped into the hall. Maggie plucked the notebook from beneath the door and shoved it into her purse in one fluid motion. She folded her bag beneath her arm and stepped into the hall, smiling at Wren who high-stepped in front of the hospital room like a chalet cuckoo clock.

Maggie would share this important piece of evidence with her. Right after she had a good, long look at it.

Chapter 36

Wren's debriefing was plodding and purposeful. She spent three hours going over Brock's lie-studded career, the note shoved under the Whitleys' door, the discovery of ant poison in the back of his Tercel, the images of Riley and Mary plastered on the wall of his study.

Wren arched her eyebrow at the story of how Maggie had spied the photos at Brock's house. "You know that's trespassing, right? Not to mention interfering with a police investigation." Wren folded her hands. "I should also tell you that we received an anonymous call from a man who told us we should be looking at you for the poisonings."

"Me?" Maggie sputtered. "Brock probably made that call to throw suspicion on me. Or maybe it was Miles, an ex-coworker and former con who's been harassing me."

"We'll look into all of it," Wren replied noncommittally. She turned to Bradley. "What can you tell us about the events that transpired?"

Bradley added his narrative, and his suspicions tracked with Maggie's and Constantine's. The assistant reported his boss's months-long preoccupation with the Whitleys, his long absences from the office as he tracked their movements, his decreased hygiene, and his increased irritability which, Bradley noted with a reprise of sniffs, he took out on his assistant. Maggie couldn't help but notice that Bradley seemed relieved— and maybe a little delighted—by his superior's demise. She suspected many would share that sentiment.

After a quick spin through the Koffee Kiosk, Maggie and Constantine arrived home. Constantine unlocked the front door, ceremoniously carried Maggie over the threshold, then checked both pets for happiness and satiety before collapsing on the couch.

"You sure know how to show a guy a good time, Mags. First a funeral, then a shooting. Top it all off with a roll in the hay and we have the plot to the next Coen brothers' movie." He ran a hand over his face. "What do you think of that anonymous phone call accusing you of the poisonings?"

"Just like I told Gladys Wren: Brock throwing suspicion or Miles throwing shade." She reeled the notebook from the depths of her purse. "Let's review the private writings of Russ Brock, aka Stanley Wurm, and see if it offers any clarity."

Constantine sat up and leaned forward, squinting. "Brock's diary? Where'd you snag that?"

"The hospital. It must have fallen out of his jacket during the scuffle. You were quite manly, in a Colin Firth/Hugh Grant kind of way."

"Gee, thanks." He watched her turn the pages. "I appreciate the fact that you want to put an end on this little ditty by reading *Deep Thoughts by Russ Brock*, but isn't that evidence for the police?"

"And I'll turn it over. Later." She took a sip of hazelnut latte, a departure from her usual Americano. "I just want a sneak peek. They can be stingy with evidence."

"I can't imagine why." He put his arm around her and craned his neck. "Anything about me in there? Maybe about how I remind him of Han Solo?"

"Um, no." She knew they were being callous about Brock's death. Maybe the horror of the day had blunted their sensitivity. Maybe they had become hardened after witnessing so much loss of life. Maybe they were relieved that a murderer was gone. She glided her finger down a lined paged and turned it. "It mostly looks like story ideas."

"Made up ones or real ones?"

"Too soon to say." She set her coffee on the scarred coffee table and massaged her temples. A nascent headache had announced its attention. Her nerves had worn to fraying. She suddenly felt overwhelmed, a drowning woman trying to breathe through a straw. Repeated knocks to the head hadn't done her noggin any favors. Neither had the day's stress, lack of food or copious amounts of caffeine.

"You look like I feel," Constantine said, his eyes trained on her face. "What do you say to an early dinner out because the fridge is low on food and I'm low on ideas for meals made from mustard, three slices of bread and a half an onion." He put a hand on her shoulder, gave it a playful shake. "Come on. It'll be a good distraction. I'll even let you treat."

Dinner out felt like an unwarranted celebration. A man had died, after all. She gazed into Constantine's eyes, which were alight at the prospect of dinner at a venue that didn't feature a drive-through.

There were reasons to rejoice. The Whitleys were safe. The

poisonings were solved. She just needed to ignore the pain in her head, the growing agitation in her gut, and take a break from murder and mayhem. She folded the notebook. "Deal, but I get to pick the place."

The place ended up being the sole Mexican restaurant in town. They seated themselves in a corner booth, ordered cervezas and nachos, and set up camp reinvigorated by the change of scenery and the smell of beef, cheese and cilantro. Maggie's headache had even abated, going from a persistent throb to a low ache like phantom pain from an old injury.

Maggie splayed out Brock's notebook and looked over her shoulder. There was no reason to think anyone was watching, but she suddenly felt exposed. *I'm just being paranoid*, she told herself. Yet she couldn't shake the feeling of unseen eyes crawling over her, or the fact that Miles could be anywhere. Watching. Waiting. Planning.

Maggie turned to the page she'd seen at the hospital. Brock's handwriting was small and cramped, far worse than the dysgraphia Constantine teased her about. She traced the letters with her finger, feeling the indentation of Brock's pen, a relic of his movements. "Despite the Unabomber penmanship, Brock's thoughts are well organized. They're definitely story ideas, with an extra-large chapter dedicated to the Whitleys."

The cervezas came and Constantine guzzled. He belched energetically. "Words to go with his wall o' creepy pictures?"

"Basically. Looks like he was doing all kinds of research for a big piece on the Whitleys. Standard backstory stuff about their tragic lives, which would have dovetailed nicely with their tragic deaths."

She sipped her beer, made doodles in the condensation on the side of the glass. "Brock said something really strange right before he died."

"I didn't hear anything."

"He was whispering and wheezing, barely audible, but intense, like something he really wanted me to hear."

"Near-death confession?"

"More like near-death instruction. He told me to watch out for Riley."

Constantine's brows shot up. "He tries to poison her and her mother then worries about her well-being?" He scratched his ear. "Maybe he was trying to get on the good side of the Big Man in the Sky. And I'm not talking about Dale, the news-copter guy."

Maggie finished the face she was tracing on the glass then demolished it with a wipe of her thumb. "Maybe. He definitely spent a lot of time thinking about the Whitleys. Maybe research turned to obsession, which turned into something like love." She shrugged. "It happens."

"So what's the upshot on the Whitleys? Does he talk about their poisonings—or how he engineered them?"

She pivoted the notebook and turned the pages for Constantine. "Toward the end of the section, he talks about cyanide." She rewound the pages with a few flicks of her finger. "Most of his research covers Riley's illnesses, Mary's blog, the closeness of their relationship...your garden variety tear-jerker material."

Constantine read where Maggie pointed, narrowing his eyes to decipher the tiny blocks of text. "These two can't catch a break. Failure to thrive early on for Baby Riley, followed by abandonment by Mr. Whitely, who couldn't be located to pay child support—or, I'm guessing—care about his daughter's leukemia diagnosis." He shook his head. "Disgusting. Mary comes across as mousy, but she's got to be made of some pretty tough stuff. She put herself out there, made a living with her blog and got a community to rally around her daughter. That takes grit and guts."

"Which makes for an even more compelling story for Brock. Tragic beginning followed by inner strength to achieve success followed by a tragic ending. It's got everything."

"Everything but the ending Brock had intended."

The waitress ceremoniously delivered a mountain of chips, ground beef, cheese and beans that Maggie would typically be eager to summit. Now she grabbed a chip and scraped it against a slope of beans, her appetite dulled by the pathos of the Whitleys and the end of Brock.

Misfortune didn't seem to affect Constantine's appetite. He grabbed a chip in each hand and double-dipped, then crammed the whole mess into his mouth. He chewed, swallowed, irrigated his mouth with beer.

Then Constantine turned back to the notebook. "What other stories does Brock have in there? Anything about Colton Ellis or Claudia Warren?" He crooked a brow. "Or maybe some of our former favorite suspects, Nigel, Francine, maybe even Miles?"

Maggie flipped and scanned. "Looks like he was researching global warming, something about used car scams, a story about the broken child protection system, and an interview with female body builders and the pressure to be perfect—complete with his own illustrations of the female form."

She showed Constantine Brock's drawings and he mimed gagging. "At least they're anatomically correct." He crammed one more chip into his mouth and pushed himself away from the table with a groan. "Bummer there's nothing about Nigel in there. Definitely something off with the Nigel-Francine-Colton triumvirate."

Maggie grunted a distracted reply as she continued to pore over the pages.

"Find something more scintillating than dinner conversation with me, or are you just impersonating your dad?"

Maggie looked up. "Huh?"

He tapped the notebook. "Find something interesting-slash-incriminating?"

"No, just something strange." She took a sip of beer, wiped the foam from her lip. "In the story about female bodybuilders, there's a big section about performance enhancing drugs, particularly steroids. He interviewed a lot of different women, out of state and here in town."

Constantine nodded. "And?"

"And one of the women is named Sloane."

Chapter 37

"Other than Ferris Buehler's girlfriend, also named Sloane, I'm not getting the connection."

"Sloane, also known as the Boulder, is the name of the woman who teaches the Spinning class I've gone to with Ada."

"*The Boulder*?"

"As in mightier than the Rock."

Maggie watched Constantine try to keep a straight face. "Ah. Right. And this is interesting why?"

Maggie took another sip of her drink. "Sloane knew Francine before Francine found God and Aqua Net, back on the bodybuilding circuit." Constantine nodded. He remembered. "Brock's notes suggest that Sloane used steroids but quit when she got pregnant."

Maggie paused, digesting this. Sloane had never mentioned offspring, didn't display photos of her progeny around the gym, hadn't used her I-bounced-back-after-baby experience as an advertisement for her Spinning class. Not everyone publicized their childbearing status, but the fact that Sloane never talked about children, other than to suggest she found them to be a pain in the ass, seemed more than a little strange.

The strangeness was ancillary. She had to focus on the poisonings. Maggie reviewed Brock's notes again. "The timeframe is also right around the time that Sloane and Francine had a falling out."

"Sounds fascinating, but not sure how it's related to...anything."

"Sloane isn't just a former steroid-user and used-to-be friend of Francine's. She's also a pharmacy customer. With Colton Ellis's possible opioid addiction, that puts Francine at the nexus of something bad."

"It also puts Petrosian's at that nexus," Constantine pointed out. "No matter how you look at it, the timing of your boss's impromptu fishing trip is suspicious. Maybe Petrosian decided to hightail it out of town because he was hiding something that he worried would be revealed once people started poking around his store."

Maggie chewed on the inside of her cheek. "I don't believe that."

"Don't or don't want to?"

"I just want the truth. I can't access the pharmacy database, Lev is unavailable and Francine hates me. That leaves me with one path." She swigged the last of her beer. "And it's accessible by stationary bicycle tomorrow morning."

Daybreak came reluctantly, light reaching tentatively through the honeycomb shades of the bedroom then vanishing when passing clouds plunged Hollow Pine into a false night. It didn't matter. Maggie had been up well before the morning star and was on her third cup of coffee by the time she kissed Constantine's sleep-smoothed forehead and slipped out the front door.

Sloane's dawn SpinCycle class was sparsely attended, attracting insomniacs and diet diehards who hadn't let their New Year's resolutions melt away with the snow. Maggie hadn't asked Ada to come along to the gym. She knew her friend had to be at the academy early and relished the idea of talking with Sloane alone.

Truth was, if Maggie arrived early enough, she could have enough time to drop Brock's name. Enough time to bluff her way through a suggestion that she had been helping the reporter with his story on steroid use among female bodybuilders. Enough time to find out where Sloane had gotten her dope—and who had helped her procure it.

Maggie jogged through the gym's parking lot, eyes alert as always for Miles. She pushed through the front door, greeted the muscle-bound man behind the desk and forked over the final visitor's pass from Ada, still too commitment-shy to sign a one-year contract. Sure, she was engaged to Constantine, but till-death-do-us-part seemed less daunting than the prospect of twelve months of squats in a mirror-lined room.

Maggie tugged her tank top into place, checked her tights for hitchhiking laundry and walked past the weight room, which was lined with reflective surfaces and Adonises in training. She took a deep breath and stepped into the SpinCycle, a smile on her face, a conversation starter that didn't begin with "Say, tell me about your steroid use" on her lips.

The smile faded. At the head of the class, stretching by the instructor's stationary bike, was a woman she'd never seen.

"Hi there!" the woman said brightly. "I'm Lindzee! That's Lindzee with two e's and one z. Are you ready to get in the zone?"

Maggie tried to come up with something intelligent to say. She went with, "Uhh…"

Her response didn't seem to phase Lindzee. Lindzee bounced on her toes, sending her blonde ponytail skyward. "Awesome! Feel free to stretch out, get some water, whatever! We'll get started in a few!"

Maggie blinked against the onslaught of exclamation points. "Is Sloane here?"

Lindzee put an ankle on the bike's handlebars and stretched her torso over the kind of perfectly formed leg that accompanies articles like *Resize Your Thighs in Just Five Minutes a Day.* "She doesn't teach on Tuesdays. That's when she gets her manicures."

"Right." Maggie stuck her hands under her armpits to hide bitten-to-the-quick nails. "I was hoping to catch her because…" Maggie's mind chugged as she searched for a reason. "Because, um, because her protein powder came in. I placed an order for both of us."

Lindzee eyed Maggie's body for evidence of protein consumption. "Protein powder?" Lindzee switched legs and stretched again. "She's not using The Gun Show anymore?"

Maggie leaned in. "Not since she found out it contains corn syrup."

"Corn syrup?" Maggie might as well have said lead base with an asbestos chaser. Lindzee wound her leg back in. "My God, I had no idea. Are you sure?"

Maggie nodded again. "That's why I was hoping to get her order to her right away. You know how important protein is to Sloane."

"Absolutely." Lindzee put a hand to her heart in a silent pledge of allegiance to amino acids.

"Too bad I don't have her address," Maggie said, pouring on the nonchalance. "I could just run it by."

"I have it!!" Lindzee said, exclamation points multiplying with her excitement. "Hang on a sec!!" She bounded over to a large canvas bag slouched against the room's large mirror and removed a yoga mat, a pair of dumbbells and a day planner embellished with *BELIEVE* in pink glitter. She scribbled on a piece of scrap paper liberated from the bowels of the bag and walked the note over to Maggie. She checked her watch/step-counter en route. "She should be home now."

"Thanks." Maggie turned to leave.

Lindzee returned to her bike and mounted it with the elegance of an accomplished horsewoman. "Aren't you going to stay for SpinCycle? We're having a Spin It to Win It competition. You could win a gluten-free vegan brownie!"

"Thanks, but I'll take a rain check." Maggie paused in the doorway. "I'm already in my aerobic zone."

Chapter 38

According to Lindzee's fat cursive dotted with heart and star accents, Sloane Lewis lived at the corner of Fourth and Federal, approximately three miles away. Maggie shaved off two minutes from Siri's assessment of a seven-minute drive and pulled in front of a one-story house destined for the adjective "non-descript."

The house had a gray-brown body with off-white trim, a medium-sized yard and a layout that didn't appear to have taxed the architect's imagination. The only distinguishing characteristic: the two windows facing the yard had bars.

Cautious homeowner or someone with something to hide?

Maggie studied the house, pushing away her growing unease and the idea that dropping by Sloane's house to question her might not be the wisest decision.

There was no car in the driveway and the blinds on the windows were drawn, but that didn't mean much. There was a double-car garage, and some people were big on privacy. Especially people who put bars on their windows.

Maggie hopped out of the car and walked up the short concrete walk. Maggie rehearsed potential openers and decided to go with improvisation and see where that took her. She held her breath and rang the bell. The two-bell chime echoed through the house. Maggie waited the requisite twenty seconds for politeness then rang again. The tinny peal was lonely and bereft.

Damn it, she's already gone.

Maggie knocked, balancing "loudly" with "obnoxiously" and waited. Still nothing. She rotated on the ball of her foot and headed for the car.

Halfway down the walk, after a spray of pansies but before the lopsided birdbath that came before an invisible line of demarcation at the start of the Lewis property, Maggie heard a cry.

She froze, listening. A bird, perhaps, or even an exotic frog. Maggie had seen Facebook videos about—

The cry returned. Softer. Plaintive. The mewling sound of a trapped or injured animal. Yet Maggie knew with a certainty that she couldn't explain that the cry was human.

Maggie turned and again faced the house. The barred windows scowled in the early sun, seeming to say, "Forget what you heard."

But Maggie couldn't do that. Her mind was already turning back to Brock's notes. Sloane the bodybuilder. Sloane the narcissist. Sloane reformed by pregnancy to stop juicing and start living clean.

Maggie once again reviewed her knowledge of Sloane, looking for evidence of the spin instructor's motherhood. Had she ever mentioned the demands of parenting, the need to get back home to join husband and child or relieve a babysitter?

Not that Maggie could recall. Perhaps because Sloane didn't use a babysitter.

In her mind's eye, Maggie saw Brock's handwriting, indignation radiating from between the tight block letters. He was working on one story that featured Sloane, another about the shortcomings of the child protective safety nets. What if the story wasn't about steroids? What if the piece on Sloane and the failure of child protective services weren't two stories but one?

What if Sloane was the star of both?

Maggie ran back up to the house, rang the bell and knocked. She listened again, hopeful for the call of a bird, the cry of a kitten, something that would change her suspicion that the mewling was human-generated, that there was a child—alone? distressed? injured?—on the other side of the gray-brown walls, behind the cold, sure steel of the bars.

The crying ceased.

Maggie shook her head. *Stupid girl,* she chided herself. She had gone from fogginess to irritability to imagining things. What was next—pink elephants? dancing leprechauns? evil clowns holding red balloons?

The dread that had risen like a black tide ebbed away, leaving her feeling like a hand-hewed canoe, an empty vessel without purpose or passenger.

Then a new sound pinged against her ear drums, faint and persistent. *Beep! Beep! Beep! Beep!*

Maggie held her breath and focused on the sound. It was an alarm of some sort, with the tempo and urgency that suggested emergency.

Carbon monoxide. Burglar. Fire.

At this last thought, Maggie sniffed the air, and there it was: the pungent smell of burning wood.

Maggie pounded on the front door. "Hello? Is anyone home?" No response but that of an offended electronic device. She rang the bell and pounded simultaneously. "Hello? Sloane?"

Silence.

She bounded from the porch and ran to the barred windows. She put her face to the bars and looked in, a habit she seemed to be forming, but could see nothing around the dingy blinds that shielded the house against voyeurs like herself.

Maggie faced the street, looking for help, an answer, someone to corroborate her that she was wrong. That she was right.

Next door, she saw a lone poodle trying to tunnel his way under a chain link fence.

Maggie ran to the side of the house. It was windowless with an assortment of stored lawn care equipment that reminded her of Brock. Of course, the only fertilizing he'd be doing would be at the cemetery.

Maggie felt a surge of bile rise up her throat. She rammed down thoughts of death, of finding bodies and the inevitability of decay, and threaded her way between a wheelbarrow, a black plastic garbage bag and a tricycle with rainbow-colored streamers.

Maggie's heart clenched at the sight of the child's bicycle, and she kept running.

At the back of the house, the smell of smoke was stronger. Something burning slowly. Something burning green. And beneath it all, something rotting.

She spotted a sliding glass door and pulled. It held fast. She looked up. Dormer windows, but too high to reach without a ladder.

She swallowed a string of curse words that effervesced upward and raised her phone, hope overcoming rationality as she willed the phone's intermittent functionality to tip toward operational once again. She jogged toward the other side of the house. A root snagged her foot and she came crashing to the ground.

Her phone hit the dust, flying from her hand and skidding over a swath of earth scraped bare by last season's raking.

She stooped to retrieve the phone and spotted a slender rectangular pane—a *Laverne & Shirley* window—eighteen inches from the ground. She ignored the fallen phone, laid to rest beneath a stunted rhododendron, and gave the window a tentative push. It hinged inward with a gasp.

Surprised by this unexpected success, she pushed harder. The window creaked open to a one-by-two gap. An invitation and a taunt, barely able to accommodate a grown woman.

Maggie poked her head through the opening and strained to listen. The beeps had turned into long pulses during her transit from the front yard, a backbeat accompanied by the sigh of a house moved by an unrelenting wind that carried moisture and the promise of a storm.

In like a lion...

A high-pitch whimper joined the symphony, and certainty flooded through Maggie. She wasn't imagining things. There was a child. And an alarm. And the smell of smoke. She had to do something.

She shimmied her shoulders through the window, then her hips. Her body slid from the window's metal frame and she landed shoulders-first onto deep-pile shag carpet. Thank God for dated floor coverings.

She found her feet and then her bearings. The room was small, dark, dank. Blue-green carpet ran the length of the floor and halfway up the wall like a mold that thrived in the shadows. She blinked, letting her eyes adjust, and took in the furnishings: a washing machine and dryer, a patio umbrella embossed with yellow flowers and a *Sweet As a Daisy* headline, a plastic chaise lounge with broken struts that jutted out like fractured ribs, and a wall of cardboard boxes.

Maggie approached the boxes. Red printing tattled about the contents: corned beef hash, chili, canned fruit salad, Chips Ahoy! cookies. So much for Sloane's commitment to clean eating.

Maggie walked the perimeter of the cardboard wall and rounded the other side. She nearly collided with a dog kennel.

She squatted to see the dog in the half-light, to gauge its friendliness, perhaps even elicit a Lassie-like response to her query about a crying child. But there was no dog inside the kennel.

On a jumble of blankets lay a small child.

Chapter 39

"Oh God," she whispered. She didn't have time to think about who had put the girl in the cage or why. She'd read more articles than she cared to remember about parents who imprisoned their children. Sometimes with chains or in closets, sometimes with drugs or lack of food.

But now Maggie needed actions not answers. Maggie tipped forward onto her knees, prayer as much as posture, supplication that the child would be whole and warm with life. She studied the metal prison. It had been modified, the kennel door replaced with a hinged sheet of sturdy wires to accommodate the entry and exit of a human being. Maggie's fingers danced along the makeshift door, feeling for the latch.

It had been secured with a padlock.

Maggie yanked on the lock, rattled it back and forth, cognizant of the uselessness of her action, but powerless to stop it.

The child lay motionless, unmoved by the noise of metal on metal or the viciousness with which Maggie attacked the cage.

The hollow feeling returned to Maggie's stomach and moved its way up to her heart. Maybe she was too late. Maybe the child's whimpers had been silenced by smoke inhalation.

Do something, her mind bleated. *Move.*

Maggie shot to her feet to search for a key, to drag the kennel outside if necessary. Her hands roved the top of the cage then the small wooden shelf above the kennel, greedy fingers searching for palm-sized salvation.

"You won't find it there," a voice behind her said.

Maggie whirled around, ice in her veins, fire in her legs, ready to run or fight. A girl stood before her. "What?" Maggie could scarcely hear her own voice above the thunder of her heart.

"The key," the girl said. "She takes it with her now."

Maggie gaped at the girl, taking in the lank hair, empty eyes, the pale skin that glowed like moonlight leaking through the window like distant hope.

"I know you." Maggie said. Memories crowded into Maggie's mind. A girl in a dirty sweatshirt. A treat slipped into a pocket. Francine crying thief. "You were at the drugstore. You stole Zingers from Petrosian's."

"For me and Luna." The girl nodded at the motionless lump in the cage. "Sometimes she cries in her sleep." The girl ran a finger beneath her nose. "That trip to the drugstore was the last time I got out. Unless you count today." Victory flickered across her face then died, a candle snuffed out. She pointed at another kennel tucked beneath a staircase across the room. "New lock. She doesn't know I learned to pick this one, too."

Maggie's mind swam. Locks. Cages. A girl who steals for herself and her sister. An alarm. An alarm.

An alarm.

Maggie snapped to attention. "We've got to get you and your sister out of here."

Behind her, Maggie heard a girlish laugh. How many children were here? How many cages?

Maggie spun, ready to soothe. To save. Sloane stared back, newly manicured hands atop arms crossed in front of her muscle shirt.

Chapter 40

Sloane laughed again, a deep, throaty sound. For a moment, Maggie tried to imagine it on a laugh track for *Modern Family* or *The Big Bang Theory*. No good. Too sexy. No joy.

The Boulder uncoiled her arms. "What the hell do you think you're doing?" She took a step toward Maggie, her chest puffed out. Maggie wondered if she cultivated the same chest-forward strut when competing in bodybuilding championships. "You're trespassing," Sloane said, the volume of her voice competing with the alarm's. "Wanna know what I do to trespassers?" She laughed again then pulled a length of twine, goosing a bare bulb awake.

The bulb swung between them like a hypnotist's watch. Recognition appeared in Sloane's eyes. "You? *You*?" The laugh came again in gunfire-short bursts as she snorted to catch her breath. "The idiot from my Spinning class?" She obliterated the meager personal space between them. She smelled like coconuts, warm flesh and, yes, vanilla protein powder. "I don't know why you're here or how you got in my house, but I can tell you this much. You're not going to leave."

"But the fire alarm." Maggie's voice was thin, ragged. "We've got to get out of here. If not for them, for you."

Sloane gave Maggie a withering look. "That's not a fire alarm, you moron. It's a motion detector. I set it up to catch little people who go where they shouldn't."

Maggie lifted her chin. "Like outside their cages?"

"If they act like animals, they get treated like animals," Sloane shot back. "They need to *learn*."

"Hard to learn when you're unconscious," Maggie said pointing to the lump in the kennel.

"She's fine." Sloane rolled her eyes. "I give them Benadryl if I have to get a manicure or go to the gym. Keeps them out of trouble." She glared at the Zingers girl. "If they don't palm the pills or vomit the syrup. Point is..."

She paused as she searched her mental filing cabinet for the point. "You may have gotten the wrong idea about what you saw here. Maybe you'll tell someone." A sneer. "Try to *save* someone."

Sloane's hand shot out. Maggie flinched, but she wasn't Sloane's target. The girl was.

She batted the child aside, and Maggie saw pin-thin arms and legs fly into the air and land in a jumble in the corner. The girl didn't cry. She knew better. Sloane sprang toward the girl and snatched something from behind her. Sloane held up the object as if for Maggie's approval. A metal bat lay on Sloane's palms like a sleeping snake.

Sloane gripped the handle, choked up on it as if she were going to bunt Maggie's head. "You broke into my home," Sloane said, "invaded my domicile." A smile, pride at a new vocabulary word. "I have to defend myself. My girls."

Maggie widened her stance and lowered her center of gravity. How many times had she performed the same maneuver, been in the same situation? She trained her eyes on Sloane, taking her measure, evaluating her mettle.

Sloane raised the bat and swung. Maggie feinted left, darted right. The bat whooshed through empty air and landed beside Sloane's muscular thigh. Sloane pulled her lips back, part smile, part simian grimace, and cut the air again. Maggie ducked and rolled and landed beside Zingers girl huddled beside an overflowing laundry basket. Metal whistled above Maggie's head. A swing and a miss.

Sloane bellowed, an animal sound full of rage and fury and desperation. Maggie 1.0 would have been frozen with fear. Maggie 2.0 would not be cowed. She would not be intimidated. And she sure as hell wouldn't be killed by a 'roid-enraged Spinning instructor.

Maggie surveyed her surroundings. Her eyes had adjusted and the topography of the room jumped into relief. The laundry equipment. The shelves. The tower of cardboard, an altar of excess to feed Sloane's greed and deprive her children. No second bat. No easy way out.

That was okay. Maggie had let go of easy a long time ago.

In her peripheral vision, she caught sight of a dusting of snow near the washing machine. No, not snow. Laundry detergent. Even from a few feet away, Maggie could smell the lemon scent, cheap and artificial, reminiscent of the generic brand that joined other private label brands after the O'Malley household began to groan beneath the weight of medical bills.

She waited, biding her time. Sloane rocked back and forth on the balls of her feet. It was her turn to take Maggie's measure.

She miscalculated.

Sloane brought the bat back, ready to swing for the fences. Maggie dragged her fingers along the floor, nails snagging in the deep shag. She clutched a handful of stain-fighting salvation and flung it in Sloane's eyes.

Sloane shrieked and brought her fists to her face. She rubbed and then pawed at her eyes, frantic to stop the burning.

Maggie rushed forward and tackled Sloane at the knees. Sloane buckled and fell. She fought to release Maggie's grip, fought to scrape the searing powder from her eyes.

Sloane outweighed and out-muscled Maggie, but Maggie had the element of surprise, detergent and adrenaline. As Sloane struggled to free the laundry powder from her eyes, Maggie dug deep into an inner reserve of strength she only suspected she had. She grabbed Sloane by the legs and dragged her toward the base of the stairs.

Sloane made swimming motions with her arms and legs, but only treaded in the aquatic-hued carpeting. Maggie twisted Sloane's right leg against the grain. Sloane screamed and, for a moment, stopped.

Maggie took advantage of inertia. She shoved her hand in the pocket of Sloane's warmup pants. Her fingers closed around something small and metallic. She grasped the key and pulled it free.

Sloane re-enlivened and kicked at Maggie. Maggie grabbed a bottle of Spray 'n Wash that had fallen to the floor and sprayed it into Sloane's face, quashing an inane urge to mutter an Arnold Schwarzenegger-worthy one-liner like "Clean up your act."

Sloane began to claw her own face anew. Maggie pushed Sloane into Zingers girl's empty kennel, seized the lock and slammed it shut.

A scream of outrage tore through Sloane's throat, uncorking a stream of epithets about Maggie and threats about her future. Maggie tugged on the lock to ensure that it was secure. Then she grabbed the hand of Zingers girl, used the key she'd pulled from Sloane's pocket, unlocked the other kennel, and pulled the drugged toddler from her filthy warren of worn blankets.

Chapter 41

Roberta Kauffman, one of the two officers who responded to Maggie's 911 call made from a neighbor's house, tucked a girl under each arm. In the unforgiving glare of the sun, the girls looked paler, smaller. They allowed themselves to be corralled by Roberta's arms, but leaned away from her with their bodies, eyes searching the back of the squad car for signs of their mother.

In spite of it all, they sought the woman who had given them life.

Dusty Cleland, Kauffman's partner, tipped his hat back and scratched a patch of scaly skin near his ear, a pen poised above a notepad. "Go over why you broke into the house again?"

Maggie fantasized about wrestling Cleland to the ground and grabbing his pen to write the answer herself. "Like I said," she said as pleasantly as was possible through gritted teeth, "an alarm was going off and I knew a child was inside. I thought there was a fire."

"Which turned out to be someone burning yard debris next door," Cleland said.

Maggie gave a brittle smile. "Yes."

Cleland scratched the dry patch again. "And you knew a child was inside how?"

Maggie counted to ten and told herself that post-concussion syndrome was the reason for her irritability. It didn't help. "I heard a child crying inside."

Cleland nodded and scribbled. "And you believe that the mother," he consulted his notes, "left the girls alone while she went to get her nails done?"

"Alone and in cages," Maggie said, her tone underscoring the horror of it all.

Cleland shook his head. "That's effed up." An apt assessment. "Kauffman says the girls are fourteen and six. Guess they look younger because they're so small." His voice cracked. He cleared his throat. "Now remind me why you came to the Lewis domicile in the first place."

Domicile. The same word Sloane had used. Maybe she watched *Cops*.

Maggie repeated the lie she'd given Lindzee about protein powder and hoped Cleland wouldn't ask to see her cans of muscle-building dust. It was sometimes better to make up a lie than to reveal the truth.

It's the darndest thing, Officer. I stole a notebook off a dead man and decided to satisfy my curiosity about something that really has nothing to do with me. Isn't that wild?

Fortunately, Cleland seemed satisfied by the protein powder explanation. He scribbled, scratched, scribbled again. "We may need you to come down to the station, fill in some blanks about what you saw of the alleged abuse." Alleged. As if what Maggie had witnessed and what Sloane had confessed weren't enough.

"Of course." Maggie paused. "Were there reports of suspected abuse, maybe by a neighbor or teacher?"

Cleland shook his head. "Neighbors say they rarely saw the girls. They were home-schooled. And no record of suspected abuse." He chewed his lip. "That doesn't mean that someone didn't report to another agency. The right information doesn't always make it to the right people. Stuff falls through the cracks."

"So do kids," Maggie said, her mind turning to Brock's story idea about the challenges faced by child protective agencies, lapses in protecting society's most vulnerable. Had he found out about the abuse and reported it with no result? Did the state's inaction or apathy or incompetence spawn the story idea? Did he intend to use Sloane's girls as poster children of a broken system, hoping to bring attention not only to the girls' plight but the abuse of kids everywhere?

Maggie weighed the dual personae of Brock in her mind. Russ Brock, investigative reporter, working to shine a light on important social issues. Russ Brock, fake news-spinner, using others' misery to grab headlines and advance his career.

Maggie shook her head, trying to clear the images on her mental Etch-a-Sketch. The Brock she knew was ruthless and amoral. Yet over the past couple of years Maggie had learned that people were neither wholly good or entirely evil. There was plenty of gray in every aura.

Cleland tapped the notepad with his pen, interrupting Maggie's thoughts. "We're done, at least for now. You can go."

Maggie tilted her head toward his partner, toward the girls beneath her wings. "What's going to happen to them?"

"The mother, if you can call her that, has a sister. We called, but she's two states away so it'll take her some time to get here. Meanwhile, someone from social services is on the way."

Maggie nodded, swallowing the lump that knotted her throat. It was the answer she expected but didn't want to hear. Maybe the aunt would care for the girls. Maybe she was cut from the same cloth as their mother.

"Can I say goodbye?" Maggie asked.

Cleland frowned for a long moment. "I can't think why not." It was obvious he had tried. "But make it quick."

Maggie walked over to the group. She caught Kauffman's eye. The officer seemed to sense Maggie's intent and nodded. Maggie squatted to eye-level with the girl she had previously thought was a toddler, to chin-level with the girl who had pilfered Hostess snacks from Petrosian's. "I just wanted to say goodbye," Maggie said softly. She felt an impulse to gather the girls in her arms, to tuck the greasy strand of hair that had fallen across the eldest's forehead behind her elfin ear. She settled for a hand on each girl's shoulder. "It's all going to be okay."

"How's it going to be okay?" the older girl demanded. "You put our mom in jail. Who's going to take care of us? Where are we going to go?" The girl began to cry. "I hate you!" she screamed through her tears. "I hate you!"

Then both girls turned away from Maggie into the stiff polyester of Kauffman's uniform.

Constantine hadn't answered her phone call from the neighbor's house. He was probably on a conference call or on-location, tucked away in a client's utility closet. No matter the validity of his reason or the irrationality of her response, his unavailability rankled her.

It seemed he was never there for her. Not after her first terrible encounter with Miles. Not after the last. Not in the stairwell at St. Theresa's. Not last year when she had to make the decision to kill or be killed.

She jammed the key into the Studebaker's ignition and imagined Constantine spooning Lucky Charms into his mouth, searching eBay for Dr. Who memorabilia. A cold anger washed over her.

Maybe Pop was right to avoid the wedding. Maybe the whole thing was a mistake. Maybe someone like her, who seemed to do wrong every time she tried to do good, didn't deserve a happily ever after.

Maggie swatted away a tear that had absconded from the corner of her eye, another escapee from the capsule that had formed around her heart, trapping emotions like some kind of lethal pearl.

She rammed the car in gear and pulled into traffic, ignoring the bleat of a horn behind her. She stuffed down Sloane's daughters' hatred of her, chased it with her own self-loathing, her father's absence at her wedding, her growing fear that maybe she wasn't made to love or be loved.

Up ahead, a traffic light rewound the seasons, going from spring green to autumn yellow and red. She surveyed her surroundings, suddenly aware of where she had driven like a somnambulist.

She was back at St. Theresa's Hospital.

She had been pulled to the hospital by the magnetic power of opposites, the promise of a mother who had sheltered her daughter in her womb and then in her arms. Maggie, twice an orphan with her mother's death and father's emotional abandonment, once an orphan-er by ripping Sloane from her children, needed to see the Whitleys again.

Maggie zipped into a parking space and climbed out of the Studebaker. She knew her chances of seeing the mother and daughter were slim. They were ailing when Brock had tried to end them and could have been moved to a critical care unit. Or they could have rallied, improved dramatically, traded the whitewashed halls of the hospital for the comfort of home. Maggie didn't care. She had to see. She had to know. She had to yield to the magnet's pull.

She trod the familiar path from parking lot to elevator to the third floor. Unlike her last visit to the hospital, the halls were bustling with nurses. Shift change.

Maggie spotted Deena talking to man in scrubs whose head rose and fell like a cork on the ocean. Maggie stood a few feet away pretending to admire a watercolor painted by the hospital CEO's wife, hoping Deena would notice her. She did.

"Maggie! I didn't think we'd see you after what happened last time." She dropped her voice. "Are you okay?"

"I should be asking you the same thing. Not exactly a typical day at work."

"No, but we deal with plenty of drama here, too. That was just a variation on the theme." She looked at Maggie inquisitively. "You here to follow up or...?"

"I was wondering if the Whitleys are still here."

Deena threw a look at the man in scrubs. "I was just telling Ty. Riley has taken a turn for the worse. Fever. Lethargy. Confusion."

Maggie frowned. "Any idea what caused the setback?"

"I'd say someone poisoning her might have something to do with it." Deena's face hardened. "Hard to believe someone would hurt a child to further their own interests, but I've seen enough ugliness, witnessed enough cruelty, lost enough patients that nothing much surprises me. I just wish the doctors would listen to the nurses when it comes to treating the whole patient. Unfortunately, St. Theresa's is a boys' club." She glanced at the male nurse beside her. "Present company, excluded, Ty. I'm talking about the male doctors who think they're gods."

Ty grinned. "I hear ya, Deena. Sometimes it feels like we're invisible."

Deena gave Ty a grateful smile and turned back to Maggie. "Anyway, Riley's awake now, Mother Mary dutifully at her side. Room 310, if you want to pop in."

Maggie thanked her, nodded to Ty and was at 310 in moments. She tapped her code, as if the door were the entrance to a speakeasy rather than an infirmary, and Mary broke the seal, a cubist slice of face, filling the gap. She flung the door wide. "Maggie!"

Mary put her arms around Maggie and drew her into a hug. Maggie took in Mary's buff-colored sweater, the kind of pleated pants Fiona would call slacks, the smudges of unblended concealer that failed to mask the shadows beneath her eyes. She was holding up under the strain of her daughter's failing health and her own compromised well-being. But just barely.

Mary steered Maggie into the room, tucked her into a chair and supplied her with a paper cup of water poured from a metered carafe. A sick woman caring for a well one. Maggie sipped, her eyes wandering to the girl in the bed, the colorless complexion and skeletal face so like Sloane's daughters. She touched Riley's arm. The girl stirred but did not otherwise respond. So much for Deena's report that the younger Whitley was awake.

"They gave her something to help her sleep," Mary explained. "Hopefully rest will help her body heal."

"Do they know why she's not doing well?"

Maggie wondered about Brock's visits to the hospital, the possibility that he poisoned Riley and Mary while they convalesced in less-than-secure surroundings.

Mary pressed her lips together. "Do they ever know anything? Doctor after doctor, hospital after hospital, it's the same thing. They'll run some tests. They'll confer with another physician. They'll try another treatment. No answers, just hand-patting and head shakes. That's why I had to become an advocate, carting around Riley's medical records, doing research, fighting for her. Because if I don't, no one will." She poured her own cup of water from the carafe, drowned her anger and pain. "The truth is I don't know if it's the poison or the cancer or something else. Because it always seems like there's something else."

Maggie found Mary's hand, wrapped her fingers around the twigs that formed Mary's digits, squeezed again and again as if milking away the agony of a sick child, the exhaustion of caretaking, the fear of loss that followed like a shadow. Mary squeezed back. "I'm sorry," she said shaking her head. "I'm a little out of sorts."

Maggie gave Mary's hand another squeeze, hoping to bleed out the last of the psychic poison. "You have nothing to apologize for. You're a wonderful mom, and you're doing a great job."

Mary smiled sadly. "I kept hoping she'd be well enough for our cruise through the Panama Canal. Did you hear about that? Her wish is being granted by one of those charities." Mary looked at her daughter, lying white and still like a marble headstone. A tear brimmed at her lid, breached its banks. "Now I pray that *my* wish will be granted, that she'll be well enough to come home."

Maggie dragged herself from the room, the weight of Riley's illness sitting on her chest like a stone. The visit hadn't buoyed her spirits or restored her faith in humanity. It simply redoubled her anger at Brock and reminded her of the limitations of the doctors who had tried to save her mother and restore Riley.

She hit the elevator button and waited for the car to arrive. In her peripheral vision, she saw a woman motioning to her. Maggie turned her way. A middle-aged woman with a smart gray bob and sharp cheekbones waved at Maggie.

"Excuse me," the nurse called, one hand aloft. "Are you Maggie?"

"Yes?" Maggie replied as if she wasn't sure.

"Someone just called for you," she said, indicating the handset still cradled in her left hand.

"Who?" She clicked through her mental Rolodex, trying to think who knew she was at the hospital, who would be so desperate to reach her that he—or she—dialed the land lines of Maggie's recent haunts. Constantine? Aunt Fiona? Pop?

The nurse replaced the handset. "Someone named Miles. He said he wanted to make a reservation for you at the hospital. Said you'd need it."

Chapter 42

Maggie didn't know how she'd arrived back at her car. The elevator ride, the walk through the lobby, the traipse beside the hospital's sad little park, was as much of a blur as the rest of her conversation with the nurse.

Miles had already hung up, of course. He was done with his twisted version of his prank call.

Do you have Prince Albert in a can? No? How about Maggie O'Malley in a hospital bed?

She remembered that the nurse was pleasant but befuddled. "Not sure what that was about," she had said brightly. "We're not a hotel."

She had laughed. Maggie had not.

Maggie inserted the key into the Studebaker's lock and twisted. The lock popped and she slid into the car, eyes scanning the parking lot for Miles.

He was clearly following her, monitoring her movements, hunting his prey. She wondered if he had been at Brock's house when she and Constantine peered into the reporter's windows, whether he had lurked nearby when Maggie broke into Sloane's house and freed her daughters. Or perhaps he limited his stalking to the times and places that suited his schedule of harassment.

In either case, the frequency of his appearances had diminished, but the intensity had increased. He was growing bolder, maybe angrier and, if his query about the hospital bed was to be believed, preparing to exact his revenge.

Maggie locked the doors, put the car into gear and depressed the accelerator. She fishtailed around cones designating a new physician parking area and glanced in her rearview mirror. A man-shaped shadow leaned against a door near the hospital's entrance.. He raised a hand in a farewell salute.

A shiver slithered up Maggie's neck. She rolled her shoulders and leaned forward, pointing both body and car toward home, toward safety.

Two blocks later, Maggie realized home wasn't where she wanted to go. Miles could easily follow her, trap her, hurt her. She needed the safety of people. She needed space—literal and metaphorical—to process the day's events.

"Space" turned out to be a Starbucks.

She parked, cast a glance over her shoulder, the zillionth time she had executed that maneuver, and strode inside. She placed her order with a thirty-something man with a sleeve tattoo of a woman with hundred-dollar bills sprouting from her cleavage. He watched the news on a tablet, a media mutiny in a store that prized customer-employee interaction.

Maggie glanced at his screen, then peered closer.

News Channel 4 banner. Faux fichus. Two anchors, a woman with a smart bob and bright red lip and Bradley, moored to the news desk. Maggie blinked.

Bradley?

"Can I see your tablet for a sec?"

The barista shrugged and handed over the device. Maggie turned up the volume. Bradley turned to the camera and smiled.

The former assistant to Russ Brock had undergone a makeover. His glasses were gone, his greasy bangs styled into a Ken doll hair helmet, his pimples shellacked with a top coat of pancake makeup.

That was fast.

"I'm Bradley Dunham in for Russ Brock," he intoned, his voice an octave deeper than Maggie remembered. "Here's what's happening."

No mention of Brock's death. No reference to his stalking. No hint at the investigation into the poisonings that Maggie—and likely the police—believed he had masterminded.

Bradley's metamorphosis and the station's lack of candor were jarring. Rather than coming clean about Brock, the news station had propped up a new news anchor. It was like when the old *Bewitched* television show had changed Darren Stevens and figured its audience wouldn't notice. Or care.

Maggie watched Bradley commentate. He was smooth, polished, personable. Every inch the professional his boss said he'd never be.

Snippets of conversation between Constantine and Bradley drifted to Maggie's mind. Bradley's placement firmly beneath Brock's thumb. His inability to grow or advance in Brock's toxic environment. Dreams quashed by the malice—or perhaps the territoriality—of the man who was his senior in both age and position.

Brock's fall from grace and disappearance from the planet were the best things that could have happened to Bradley.

The anchors broke for commercial and Maggie traded the barista's tablet for a cup with 10 percent post-consumer recycled paper scrawled with "Mattie" in black Sharpie. She wove through the maze of tables and selected a round-top facing the drive-thru. She sat heavily on the wooden chair, memories of Bradley continuing to tumble through her brain.

Bradley had done more than badmouthed his boss. He'd watered her seeds of suspicion. He had tailed Brock to the hospital. He'd called security upon his arrival, and shouted "Gun!" during Brock's and Constantine's scuffle.

Any way she looked at it, Bradley seemed to not only benefit from Brock's death, but be at the center of its cause.

Had the young assistant engineered Brock's demise? Or was he simply at the right place at the right time?

Brock. Bradley. Sloane. Miles. There seemed to be no shortage of evil in Hollow Pine.

Maggie unshouldered her purse and rifled inside, batting aside her damaged phone, the Starbucks gift card she had forgotten to use and coupons foisted upon her by Aunt Fiona. Her fingers closed around the metal spine of Brock's notebook.

She exhumed it and began her dig for answers.

She wasn't sure exactly what she was looking for. Distrust of Bradley, perhaps, or an upside-down answer to the question "Is Brock a murderer?" Maybe it was scientific curiosity. Maybe it was her obsessive tendencies. Maybe it was a stubborn unwillingness to let questions go unanswered. She simply felt compelled to crawl inside Brock's mind and look around.

She placed the notebook on the table, flattened it with the blade of her hand. She flipped quickly through the book. No mention of Bradley. Plenty of college-ruled real estate for Sloane and the Whitleys.

She turned back to the section about Sloane, reading slowly this time, searching for clues that Brock knew about the children. The cages. The drugs to render them unconscious or compliant.

She found the mention of Sloane's pregnancy with a tiny "s" after the word. *Pregnancys*. Misspelling as proof that he knew that Sloane had more than one child?

Maggie continued to pore over the pages. Brock double-downed on his armchair diagnosis of Sloane as a narcissist and detailed the schedule she kept to maintain her appearance. Hairdresser. Nail salon. Tanning. Gym. Facialist. He noted that these appointments kept her from home for hours at a time and that no one came or went during her absences.

He followed this with multiple paragraphs about the impotency of the child welfare system. He pointed to inadequacies in funding, paltry follow-ups to open cases, the powerlessness of the courts to rescue children from drug-addicted parents more interested in their next hit than their child's next meal.

He cited case after case of babies broken by fathers who couldn't get their infants to stop crying. Toddlers burned into silence by stovetops and cigarettes. Children chained to beds, locked in closets and placed in cages.

"He had to know," Maggie said to the notebook. "He doesn't come right out and call Sloane an abuser, but he *had* to know."

"Huh?" asked the barista as he bused the table next to her.

"Nothing," Maggie muttered. "Just thinking out loud."

The man with the woman on his arm waltzed away. Maggie closed her eyes, thinking of innocence stolen and life lost.

The tone of Brock's notes about the challenges faced by the child welfare system was different than his excoriation of the police. He was frustrated, but also sympathetic, compassionate, concerned. They way Brock told it, child abuse was a scourge that was increasingly difficult to contain let alone eradicate.

For once, Maggie agreed with him. The statistics were staggering and inescapable. Media outlets and newsfeeds were clogged with tragedies and the data behind them, which Brock echoed in his notes.

More than six million children were referred to child protection agencies each year. Eighty percent of child fatalities involved one parent. Five children per day died from abuse.

Risk factors for child abuse included drug and alcohol use. Did Brock intend to highlight this deadly crossroads by tying in Sloane's previous steroid use to her current child abuse? Was Colton's opioid use connected? What about Petrosian's Pillbox? Did Brock fail to divulge his knowledge on the page and in real life because he wanted to get the abuse at its worst for maximum impact? Or had he called in to report the abuse and neglect of Sloane's girls only to be met with inaction, fueling his desire to maximize the story and excoriate its villains?

Maggie felt the familiar tug at the base of her skull. So many questions. So many headache-generators.

She turned the page. The heading: Mary and Riley Whitley. Their names were underlined with such force that the pencil had torn through the page. She hadn't noticed that before and wondered for a moment whether she'd done it herself, reading with pencil in hand, underscored without realizing, then forgetting she had done so. Clouds gathered with more frequency and ferocity in her mind. She couldn't be sure of anything. She couldn't trust her own memory.

Maggie turned back to the notebook. As with the rest of the journal, Maggie had read this section before. She took a mouthful of coffee, let it sit on her tongue for a moment, then swallowed, hoping a chemical reaction of caffeine and sugar would make her smarter and more adept at reading between Brock's cramped lines.

The comments and observations were as Maggie remembered. Brock had recorded the highs and lows of the Whitleys' lives with the detail and fervor of a man obsessed. He covered Riley's birth and her early illnesses. He detailed Mary's extraordinary efforts to obtain accurate diagnoses, her blog journaling their difficult journey and the sympathetic reaction by the communities in which the Whitleys lived. He chronicled the poisoning that threatened to take both of their lives.

It was the bones of a great story, the skeleton on which he'd climb to lift himself out of the grave he'd dug during his once shining career. But it had nothing in common with Sloane or drug abuse or Petrosian's.

Maggie began to close the notebook then paused. Something had caught her eye, an inconsistency, an error that irritated like a burr lodged in a sock.

She peeled the cover back once again, eyes roving to catch the words that had captured her attention. The phrase leapt from the page.

Cystic fibrosis.

Riley had been diagnosed with CF at age two. She couldn't gain weight. She had a nagging cough. She had chronic respiratory infections and a host of gastric troubles.

Cue the parade of doctors. The battery of tests. The baptism by fire into world of the chronically ill.

And yet Maggie remembered Deena talking about Riley's admittance to the hospital on a number of occasions for high blood pressure. People with cystic fibrosis typically had low blood pressure.

Maggie chided herself for seeing this discrepancy as suspicious. After all, Riley's cystic fibrosis was just the tip of her illness iceberg. The girl also had a metabolic disorder and, within the last year, an insidious form of leukemia that rejected treatment as it turned her body's own cells against her.

Perhaps Riley's cancer wasn't confined to her blood. Perhaps she'd developed a kidney tumor that had boosted her blood pressure. Or perhaps one of Riley's many medications was to blame for the life-threatening hypertension that landed her at St. Theresa's.

Maggie put her fingers to her now pounding temples and mentally transported herself to Petrosian's the night she'd broken in to review the victims' pharmacy records. She could picture the computer screen, the list of Colton's painkillers that had sent chills down her neck and red flags up her spine, but couldn't remember any specifics about Riley's medications.

They were numerous. They were varied. End of story.

Or maybe the beginning of one she had not yet considered.

Maggie brought her phone out from her purse, stared at its shattered screen, remembered its ruined insides. She powered it up, along with her hope. It responded, reanimated from a telephonic great beyond. A zombie phone.

She opened a browser app and logged onto Mary's blog. *Riley's Road,* it read, *The Path from Hope to Healing.*

The website was as she remembered. Plain and unadorned with its Times New Roman font and palette that called to mind Malt-O-Meal.

The only color: a bounty of photographs that showed Riley and Mary at various waypoints on their journey.

Riley shrunken and wan in a hospital bed.

Riley shaking hands with Cinderella at Disney's Magic Kingdom.

Mary pouring a green smoothie into two umbrella-topped glasses.

Mary giving a tearful thanks to a crowd of Lycra-encased joggers holding *Run 4 Riley* signs, Riley in the background with her walker.

Mary bathing her daughter's face with a Miss Piggy washcloth, her own face scrubbed clean, the image of makeup-free, plain-clothed, other-focused motherhood.

Maggie felt a tingling, the seed of an idea that needed the light of information to grow. She clicked Archives, a time machine that would allow her to go back to Mary's first blog post and Riley's first web-documented illness.

Maggie's phone rang. An image of Constantine's face obliterated Mary's. Maggie felt a flash of annoyance. *Oh, sure, now he calls.* Where was he when she was fighting for her life, when she was being stalked?

She answered on the second ring. "Hey there."

"What's wrong?" Constantine asked. "You sound funny."

There was no putting anything past Constantine. He knew her better than she knew herself. She felt her heart swell with love then contract with shame. How could she have blamed him for not picking up his phone? How could she have cold feet for the man who she loved since they met in the middle school lunch line when he topped tater tots with sour cream and proclaimed them "tater totchos"? What, exactly, was the matter with her?

She considered whether she should make an alphabetical list of her failings when Constantine interrupted her thoughts. "Mags? You there?" She heard the squeak of plastic and the soft shuffle of fabric as Constantine changed ears.

"I'm here," she said.

"Where's 'here'? I saw that you called while I was out troubleshooting a troublesome VPN connection. I won't bore you with the details—and don't say I already have." He waited for her to laugh, like an actor who knew all of the places to pause for the audience's reaction. When she didn't respond, he dropped his voice. "Really, Mags, are you okay?"

"I've had a really bad morning."

She gave her definition of "bad morning," which included finding two abused children, playing WWE with a woman twice her size and being tormented by Miles. She told him all that had happened, taking her time with the details, trying to distance herself from the events as if she were a reporter—Russ Brock or Bradley Dunham—recounting the details for anonymous viewers in their anonymous homes.

"My God," he breathed. "Did you call Austin?"

"Dialed 911 from a neighbor's phone about the kids. They sent over two uniforms who took Sloane away." She swallowed a lump that had lodged near her tonsils. "The girls, too. Who, by the way, hate me for ripping them away from their mother."

"You did the right thing, you know. With the kids."

Maggie thought of an aunt that was just like her sister. Of foster care. Of little girls dragging garbage bags full of clothes from one house to the next. Of the potential for more abuse by those entrusted to protect and care.

The right thing? Maggie wasn't sure that existed.

"I'm here for you, Mags," Constantine said softly. "For whatever you need. I'm here. Behind you and a little to your left."

Maggie took the phone from her ear and twisted her torso. Constantine stood in the doorway of the coffeehouse, his eyes dark and soft and worried.

Chapter 43

He was at her side in two steps, encircling her with his arms, burying his face in her hair.

"How did you know I was here?" she murmured into his chest, breathing in his scent.

"There's no place you could go that my love wouldn't find you." He put her at arm's length then flashed a crooked grin. "Plus I used the Find My Friends app."

"Smart."

He smothered her in another bear hug. She could scarcely breathe. She didn't mind. Constantine was the human equivalent of a weighted blanket.

"You sure you're okay?" he asked.

Her first reaction was to deny her pain, her fear. Admitting them would mean a confession of vulnerability, a lancing of the blister that had grown around her emotions. Instead, she leaned into him. "I am now. Except." Maggie smoothed the hair from her forehead and searched his eyes, as if she'd find confirmation of the idea that was beginning to take hold, absolution for entertaining its existence. "Except for this awful feeling I have."

"Stands to reason, seeing that you were attacked in a basement and have been the victim of a campaign of harassment."

"It's not just that. It's the Whitleys." She clasped her hands. Twisted. Released. "I think they may not have been poisoned—by Brock, anyway."

Constantine grabbed a coffee stirrer from the table and pretended to ream out his ear. "Beg your pardon?"

She sat heavily, pulled Constantine into a chair beside her. "After what happened with Sloane, I decided to take another peek at Brock's notes. I wanted to see what Brock knew and when he knew it." Maggie took a sip of her latte. "I think he was about to break a story about child abuse."

Constantine nodded. "Right. The research about Sloane. You're thinking he was going for some kind of 'roid rage angle?"

"More like a 'faces of abuse' angle."

Constantine tilted his head, reminding Maggie of the dog in the old RCA ads her father loved. "As in multiple cases with multiple abusers?" She nodded. He frowned. "How do the Whitleys figure in?"

Maggie traced the latte with a finger, letting the milk foam lace her skin. "I think Mary is abusing Riley."

Constantine's mouth formed a perfect O then collapsed into an upside-down U. "That's quite the reversal. Way you told it, Mary Whitley was up for mother of the year."

"I know, and an hour ago I would have been first in line to place the tiara on her head."

"What changed your mind?"

"A trip down memory lane."

She palmed her phone, flipped it on its back and opened it to Mary's blog. She touched a small square of horizontal bars layered like a club sandwich, navigated to the site's Archive section and began scrolling. "Mary began documenting Riley's health struggles almost since her birth." She flashed through photographs of a skinny, squalling infant with a red face and huge eyes. "As you know, Riley had problems right out of the gate. Low birth weight, failure to thrive, digestive issues."

More pictures. Grim-faced physicians. Emesis trays. An IV sinking into a tiny arm dotted with blue where phlebotomists had mined for hemoglobin gold. "She was diagnosed with cystic fibrosis as a toddler, but that was just the beginning of Riley's medical journey."

She flicked through the pages with her forefinger. "After the diagnosis, the real fun began. Riley had a cascade of health crises. Episodic pneumonia. Food allergies. A metabolic disorder. Cancer."

"Are you suggesting that this is more than medical bad luck?"

"That's exactly what I'm suggesting."

Constantine accordioned his arms across his chest. "Let me guess: Munchausen syndrome by proxy."

"Actually, I'm thinking more like malingering by proxy."

An eyebrow shot toward his hairline. "And the difference is?"

"Financial gain." She took a sip of her drink, made parentheses with her fingers to wipe the foam from the sides of her lips. "Both Munchausen and malingering are facetious disorders."

He shook his head. "Sorry, I forgot my set of encyclopedias."

"Basically people faking illness. With Munchausen syndrome, it's people who exaggerate or fabricate illness, usually for attention. With malingering, it's motivated by the possibility of some kind of gain."

"And 'by proxy' you mean it's imposed on someone else."

Maggie nodded. "Exactly."

He unfurled his arms and twanged the coffee stirrer with his finger. "No offense, Mags, but this seems a little cray-cray. First you have a total reversal of your opinion of Mary. Then you pull out a diagnosis of facetious whatchamacallit. What happened to Russ Brock, part-time stalker and poisoning hobbyist?"

Maggie felt the flash-boom of anger and frustration. Inhaled oxygen. Repeated with the latte. "He's still in the picture, but in a different way than I had imagined." She waggled the phone. "As I said, I went on Mary's blog to see if there was a connection between the Whitleys and Sloane. At first, I just saw a mother and daughter struggling with a child's medical conditions. Then I started to notice things. The variety of illnesses. The relentless lambasting of medical professionals. Moving around in search of answers for a kid who can't seem to get better despite the diagnoses, the medications, the repeat hospital visits."

She paused, took another swig of caffeine courage. "It all seemed perfectly innocent and unimaginably tragic. You don't have to have a master's in pharmacology to know that kids get sick—sometimes chronically so—and endure horrific tests and treatments in the quest for improvement. Then I remembered Deena."

Constantine's burgeoning frown bloomed. "Deena?"

"The nurse at the hospital. She said she had treated Riley several times before, often for dangerously high blood pressure." She leveled her gaze at Constantine. "People with cystic fibrosis typically have extremely low blood pressure."

Constantine tipped his chair back. "That seems a little thin, Mags. 'Typically' doesn't equal 'always'. And couldn't her other illnesses—or the medication she's on—explain a spike in blood pressure?"

"Absolutely, but once I started down this path of facetious disorders, things started to click. Mary could have manipulated Riley's blood pressure with medication. Ditto her other symptoms. Even physical characteristics, such as difficulty walking and dental discoloration and malformation, can be created and exacerbated by medical abuse. I also remembered the look on Mary's face when I sort of barged into their room and found Mary at Riley's side. At the time, I thought her startled reaction was from fear. Now I think it was guilt." Maggie paused to gather her thoughts. "I visited the Whitleys today. Riley's worse, possibly even drugged. Mary's pulling the suffering mother act."

"What if it's not an act?"

"What if it is?" she said hotly. "If I'm wrong, then I'm a bitch for thinking badly of a mother aching over the health of her child. But if I'm right, there's a girl who's being made sick by a mother who craves attention and all of the perks that go with it."

"Perks? Like what, hospital bills?"

"Donations. Cash. Gifts. Trips. There's a Go Fund Me button on the blog to create a trust for Riley, and it's not the first Go Fund Me she's done. There was also a trip to Disney World and an upcoming cruise, both courtesy of a wish-granting organization. Plus a free house through Habitat for Humanity and groceries from the women's auxiliary at the Whitleys' church."

"Okay, I can see the possibility—farfetched though it is—for a financial upshot. Then why poison Riley? Why kill the goose that lays the golden Go Fund Me accounts, along with innocent bystanders?"

"Maybe Mary was losing control over Riley. The older Riley gets the more difficult it will be to keep her quiet about the abuse. But I think it's more insidious than that. I think she enjoyed the attention, loved having people fawn over her, tell her what a great mother she was. If she worried that people were tiring of Riley's current medical conditions, feared they'd get suspicious if her daughter was diagnosed with yet another disease, poisoning would be the cure, catapulting her and Riley straight into the news—and new fundraisers. There may have been an upside if Riley died, a whole life insurance policy or trust account that paid out after Riley's death. By poisoning Riley, Mary would go from gaming the system to a grand slam."

"The unliklihood of an insurance policy and mixed sports metaphors aside, don't forget that Mary was a victim, too."

"To legitimize the poisoning. She had to make it look real and random. By ingesting cyanide, she added credibility to the crazed poisoner story and pointed the blame toward someone else."

Constantine gave her a long look. "You're saying that Mary poisoned herself in order to throw people off her scent? That's a pretty big risk. She could have died."

Maggie's eyes glittered beneath the can lights. "But she didn't. My theory: Mithridatism."

Constantine rolled his eyes. "Look, if I'd known there would be a vocabulary quiz, I would have studied."

"Mithridatism is when people consume poison in non-lethal amounts to develop immunity against it. It's sort of theoretical, but some say it has merit. Mary could have been dosing herself with cyanide in the months leading up to the poisonings."

Constantine perked up at that. "Like in *The Princess Bride*? 'I spent the last few years building up an immunity to iocane powder,'" he quoted.

"Exactly."

"So your new and improved theory is that this heinous crime was perpetrated by a single mom with a sick kid."

"Well...yeah." She nipped at the skin beside her thumbnail with her teeth. "Although Bradley, former assistant to Russ Brock, also had something to gain." She told Constantine her theory about Bradley's blind ambition and the benefits of having Brock out of the picture.

Constantine massaged the base of his neck. "I think I have whiplash from all the suspects you keep throwing out. I hate to say this, Mags, but it seems like you're chasing your tail. You keep coming up with new leads, fresh suspects, novel—and, just being honest here—slightly out-there theories. Is it possible that you're not thinking clearly? You have this post-concussion thing. You haven't slept. You've been assaulted, hounded and persecuted. Don't you think those factors might figure into your mindset? Inspired you to look into stuff that, strictly speaking, doesn't concern you? Spawned this game of musical suspects?"

"No, I don't," Maggie barked. She closed her eyes, focused on modulating her tone, volume and anger. "Riley concerns me. The closure of Petrosian's Pillbox concerns me. Truth and justice concern me. And I think each of the people I identified as potential suspects had merit. But we know more now. *I* know more."

"Okay, but even if Mary—or Bradley or Miles—had motive, how do you explain Brock's past, his current stalking, the photos in his house and the ant poison in his car, the fire?"

"It looks bad, but his actions could have been misconstrued. He could have been stalking the Whitleys for the abuse story. He could have ant poison in his car because he had ants. His house wasn't exactly an ad for

Good Housekeeping. And the fire story could have been legit. No word yet on whether it was arson, and even if it was, no evidence that it was set by Brock."

He counted off Maggie's theories on his fingers. "So you're saying Bradley could have done it to advance his career, Miles could have done it as an act of vengeance against you and Mary could have done it for fame and fortune, but Russ Brock, the guy who's cooling in the morgue because a security guard shot him in order to defend the Whitleys was actually innocent?"

"Out of all the scenarios I've considered, my money's on Mary. This isn't the concussion talking, Gus, or stress or injury. This is a hypothesis with serious merit."

"And an interesting one at that. But where's the evidence? The proof?"

She bolted the remains of her latte and wiped the foam from her lips. "Proof? That's where you come in."

Chapter 44

The dog greeted them at the door with one of Maggie's shoes in his mouth. He dropped the rubber-soled offering at her feet and panted a smile. She stooped and retrieved the shoe, which was unscathed but for a few tooth marks, then scratched behind his ear. "I appreciate the whole slipper-and-newspaper routine, but let's not make a habit of this, okay?" The dog's tongue lolled to one side. "Good talk."

She led Constantine to the home office. "It'll be easy," she called over her shoulder. "You're a genius."

"And easily induced by flattery." He ducked into the kitchen and emerged with a bag of Doritos Blaze and two Dr. Peppers. "Not to mention snack food. I'm going to write a book and call it *The Hacker's Diet*."

"Hack your way to scurvy?"

He opened the bag and stuffed a handful of bright orange chips into his mouth. "And a stronger VPN."

Maggie felt an intense and unexpected fondness. Constantine was brilliant, adorable, goofy and kind. Couldn't her father see that? Or did his disappearing act have more to do with her than her fiancé?

Tendrils of feeling began to creep beneath The Wall. Pain at her father's rejection. Grief for Sloane's daughters. Revulsion over the machinations she was certain Mary had put in motion since her daughter's birth. She bore down harder, pushing the feelings not just further behind The Wall, but sheathing them in alternating layers of denial and self-loathing.

She walked into the home office, balanced on the beanbag and turned her mind completely to the task at hand: proving Mary's guilt, saving Riley, solving the poisonings.

Constantine sat at the computer and cracked his knuckles. "Okay, Captain. Where to?"

Maggie leaned forward. "I'd like to get a look at Riley's medical records. With the advent of electronic health records, everything should be digital, right?"

"Digital, yes. Accessible, maybe."

"You're not scared of a little hospital security, are you? I've seen you scale firewalls like Spiderman."

Constantine puffed out his chest. "They ought to make a computer superhero. Byte Boy, or something. His catchphrase could be 'Byte me.' Anyway, gaining access might take some time. EHRs used to be sitting ducks for hackers looking to lift files to create fake identities, leverage credit cards, et cetera. Institutions are spending big bucks to update security protocols. I ought to know. A lot of the companies I work for implement and maintain hospital security systems."

Maggie sat up. "I wonder if any of them treated Riley."

She fired up her phone, wondered how long she could tempt fate with its intermittent functionality, how long she could make excuses to herself about why she hadn't yet dealt with it, and searched Riley's medical history on Mary's blog. She rattled off the names of hospitals and medical clinics that had seen the girl over the course of her time on the planet.

Constantine shook his head. "Haven't worked for any of those, but..." he turned toward the computer monitor, "Valley General is pretty small. Small institutions and those in rural locations sometimes lag in security updates."

"Which makes hacking easy."

"*Easier*. I just make it look easy." He bent his head and attacked the keyboard. He grunted, sighed, swore and ate four handfuls of Doritos, wiping the rust-colored dust on his jeans. Finally, he leaned back and decanted the bottle of Dr. Pepper into his mouth. "I'm in. What do you want to see?"

Maggie rose from the beanbag and brought her face to the screen. "Everything."

She scanned the sea of words, the colored boxes that floated like tiny life rafts. She learned that Riley's middle name was McKenna. That her birthplace was Fairview. That her father's name was Richard. She looked up at Constantine.

"This lists Riley's father's name."

He shrugged. "And?"

"And Mary told me that he left her when Riley was an infant. According to the chart notes during her visit five years ago, the father was at this appointment."

Constantine looked at her expectantly. "So she wasn't forthright about her relationship status. I could say the same of half of Facebook users."

"It reinforces my belief that Mary's a liar. It would also help explain how she manipulated her daughter's health. She would have needed her husband's cooperation, or his blind trust, to chase new diagnoses and foist tests and procedures on a healthy child."

"Allegedly healthy," he said, channeling Austin. "I've yet to see proof indicating she wasn't sick."

Maggie bit her lip. He had a point. She turned back to the screen.

The data was disappointing at best. Although the vast majority of hospitals had electronic health records, some were still basic, leaving holes in patients' medical histories, treatment plans, radiological images and lab tests. Maggie knew that less than a third of medical institutions acquired records for patients who received care elsewhere.

Bottom line: Riley's health records had gaps big enough to drive an ambulance through.

Discouragement flooded her body like a drug. The effect was soporific. Maggie slouched. She brought her arm to her body and flagpoled her head on her hand. She began skimming Riley's health records, her mind like a traffic cop after an accident. *Move along. Nothing to see here.*

She leaned over Constantine and clicked the mouse, this time centering the cursor over a box that promised a repository of laboratory tests. There was exactly one result. She stifled an urge to sigh yet again and clicked. Read. Then reread.

The lab was for a so-called sweat test, which measured chloride content as a means to diagnose cystic fibrosis.

Chloride greater than or equal to 60 mmol/L = cystic fibrosis

In all likelihood, anyway.

Yet according to Mary's blog, Riley was diagnosed with CF as a young child.

So why was a diagnostic test ordered? Anal-retentive double-checking? Loss of a previous result? A suspicious physician seeking confirmation?

Maggie clicked through for the results. It was blank. She moved her face closer to the screen as if her proximity could somehow intimidate the computer into delivering information. Nothing.

"Damn it." She pounded the desk with her fist then straightened up.

"No results."

Constantine was silent for a moment then bent over the keyboard. "It's possible the information was misfiled. Let me see what I can find with my shovel."

Hope began to bubble up. Maggie mentally clamped down. It was too soon to hope.

Constantine cursed then pushed himself away from the desk. "Two roads, same dead end. Either the results were never entered or they were somehow deleted."

"I guess we could try another hospital database." Her voice faded with the final word.

Hacking took time. If she was right about Mary, time was running out for Riley.

Constantine seized a pair of pencils from the desk and began to beat out the opening salvo to "Smoke on the Water." "I have an idea," he said. "Why don't we kick it old school?"

"Meaning?"

"Call the doctor who ordered the report and ask him why he ordered it and what he found."

"Right. I'm sure he'd be glad to violate HIPAA—and his patient's privacy—and spill the beans to some random woman."

Constantine beat out another riff. "So don't be random."

Chapter 45

Over the years, Maggie had pretended to be a lot of things. Confident. Ladylike. Self-possessed. She had even posed as a newspaper intern. This would be her first stint impersonating a physician.

She considered and dismissed a variety of aliases, most robbed from the starlets of classic film, before finally settling on Dr. Ada Duffy—a moniker mash-up of her friend's name and her mother's maiden name. She mentally donned a lab coat, blocked Constantine's cell phone number (figuring his phone was more reliable) and dialed the office of Larry Cohen, M.D, pediatrician. A woman with an after-hours timbre answered.

"Dr. Cohen's office," she purred. "This is Lola. How may I help?"

Maggie tried to deepen her own voice and promptly choked on her uvula. After the coughing passed and she stopped seeing hypoxia-induced spots, she swallowed hard and tried again. "Sorry. Recovering from bronchitis."

"Mmmm." Meant to express sympathy. Coming from Lola it sounded like a commercial for an adults-only phone line.

"This is Dr. Ada Duffy over at Hollow Pine Medical Center," Maggie said with as much authority as she could muster. "I'm calling about a patient. I'm curious about some past lab work and some blanks in her medical history. I was hoping that Dr. Cohen could answer some questions."

"Certainly, Doctor." More purrs then a pause. "Dr. Cohen is with a patient right now. May I have him call you?"

Maggie gave Lola a temporary phone number she had just purchased online. For those seeking anonymity, burner numbers were the new black. Then she ended the call and looked at Constantine. "Now we wait."

"And research?"

"Always."

Research meant more Dr. Pepper, salty snack foods and quality time with Mary, digitally speaking.

They returned to her blog and scoured each post and its replies with the thoroughness of a colonoscopy, trailing Mary through the labyrinth of her own posts and into the hinterland of other mommy blogs where she guest-wrote and shucked and jived her way into the hearts—and wallets—of sympathetic readers.

Maggie moved from the desk and returned to the corduroy folds of the beanbag chair. She steepled her fingers. "Nothing earth-shattering. Not so much as a tremor, unless you count the fact that Mary is a gifted writer."

"Or that Riley has been in and out of hospitals since the day she was born."

"All of which can look like a series of unfortunate events."

Constantine turned back to the monitor and performed a visual drive-by. "Of course there's the endless game of musical pediatricians. They change doctors like Aunt Polly changes hair color. Translation: a lot."

"A worried mother battling the heartless medical system and incompetent doctors," she said. "It's a great headline. Unfortunately no one's reading the fine print."

"Maybe the good doctor was and that's why he ordered the sweat test."

De Niro blared from Maggie's pocket, rocketing Maggie's pulse skyward. She pulled it free and checked the screen. Ada. Probably about Miles. She considered answering it, but she was expecting a call from Dr. Cohen. She'd talk to Ada later.

Maggie silenced the phone. Moments later, Constantine's phone chimed. They exchanged a glance. *Good timing.*

Maggie checked the screen. Blocked number. She looked at Constantine. "Speak of the devil." She swiped to answer. "This is Dr. Duffy."

"Dr. Duffy, Larry Cohen here." Booming. Affable. No titular assignation to function as verbal ego wall. Just "Larry." Maggie liked him already.

"Thank you so much for calling me back," Maggie replied.

"Ms. Cooper said that you had a question about a patient." Ms. instead of Lola or—as men of a certain generation sometimes said—"my girl." Another tick in the good guy column. Larry chuckled. "It's nice to get a phone call instead of an email. Makes things so much more collegial. Now what can I do for you?"

"I have a new patient. A sixteen-year-old girl with a history of chronic illness." She paused. "I read through her medical history and saw that you treated her several years ago. I was hoping you could offer some impressions."

"Impressions, huh." The sound of rustling papers came crackling over the line. "Now you've got me curious. Who's the patient?"

"Riley Whitley."

Maggie heard a slow release of air. A bicycle tire losing pressure. "I've been waiting for this call for five years."

Chapter 46

Maggie's heart had climbed into her throat. "I'm sorry?"

"I hoped this call would come, even prayed despite my Thank-God-I'm-An-Atheist membership card." Larry tapped something in the background. "What did she come in for? Pneumonia? Diarrhea? Delayed puberty?"

"Leukemia," Maggie replied.

"Leukemia." This said like a foreign phrase. *Pardon me, but can you direct me to leukemia, please?* "And you have questions..." He paused. "Suspicions?"

"Both." Maggie's eyes roved Riley's medical record. "I saw that you ordered a CF sweat test when Riley was in your care but didn't see the results. I was hoping you could fill in the blank."

"Blanks," Larry corrected. "Emphasis on the 's.' That kid's chart looked like it was out of a book of Mad Libs. You know, 'noun: strange symptom' or 'verb: losing weight.' I didn't see all the holes at first. All I could see was a sick little girl and her worried mom. The dad, too, the one time he came along. Then I started to notice a pattern."

"What kind of pattern?"

"Riley got sick as soon as the attention surrounding her most recent medical emergency waned. She'd be doing better, responding to treatment. As soon as the television segments ended and people rolled up their Save Riley posters, she'd land right back at the hospital. With symptoms that had nothing to do with her cystic fibrosis, I might add."

"Which was why you ordered the test."

"That and the fact that the mom tweaked my antenna. Too involved. Too knowledgeable about medicine. Too...everything. So, yes, I ordered the test, and the result was as I suspected: negative. No cystic fibrosis. But by that time, the dad had split and Riley and Marlene were long gone."

"Marlene? The mother said her name is Mary."

Another shotgun laugh. "At least she's consistent with her

consonants. After I got the results, I called child protective services. I'm no expert in Munchausen by proxy, but my gut told me that this woman was making her daughter sick, and the data seemed to back me up—or at least invite closer investigation. But they vanished, right along with the CF diagnosis."

"You tried to track them down?"

"We all did, but they had disappeared. At one point, I picked up their trail in Kentucky. They had changed their last name to Williams. More alliteration. It's interesting that they're back to Whitley."

"Maybe they believed the trail had gone cold. They showed up at my office with Riley's medical records in hand. Mary said that past clinicians were incompetent. She'd learned that if she wanted to do something right...well, you know."

He grunted, tapped some more. "What tipped you off?"

Maggie cleared her throat. "Inconsistent symptoms, idiopathic responses to meds, repeated hospital visits, incomplete records—" she paused, thinking, "possibly doctored by the mother. I felt it was worth a call."

Another grunt, approval if Maggie's curmudgeon decoder ring was working correctly. "Good call on the call, Doctor. What are you going to do now?"

Maggie's mind turned to Riley. The hundreds of hospital visits. The countless tests. A childhood ebbed away by the current of her mother's greed. She clenched her jaw then tore the last of the cuticle beside her nail. "I'm going to stop her mother."

Chapter 47

"Don't you mean 'we'?" Constantine asked when Maggie ended the call. "As in your fiancé and the authorities?"

"You, absolutely. The authorities..." she cocked her head. "Eventually. I already have a voicemail and text into Austin. I'll follow up after we get more data."

Constantine rose from the desk chair where his hind-end had taken up residence as Maggie had stood during her impersonation of a physician. "So, what, you're going to wrestle Mary, aka Marlene, to the ground and force her to confess?"

"Of course not. We're going to catch her in the act."

St. Theresa's parking lot was clotted with cars, most of which hovered around the SurgiCenter entrance as if waiting for good news about their owners.

Maggie and Constantine snaked around mid-sized sedans, wagons and coupes dusted yellow with pollen, and jogged lightly into the hospital.

They bypassed the reception desk and the thicket of flower arrangements that obscured the ancient man at its helm, claimed an elevator and rode in silence to the third floor.

Moments later, the doors parted. Maggie stepped out, pausing in the small foyer that formed a miniature narthex that seemed to demand penitence and reflection. She ran a hand over her hair, as if stroking the struggling bun would smooth the cuticles of her frayed nerves. "My mom always told me that visiting the sick was an act of corporal mercy. Today it might also be an act of justice."

"God—and mouse—willing."

Constantine hoisted a vase shaped like Mickey Mouse's glove and inspected the spray of daisies within. A square smaller than an SD card winked beneath a swatch of pink cardboard calligraphed with *Thinking of*

You!

Standard issue get-well flowers with not-so-standard issue spy camera, procured from Constantine's cache of accessories for security-minded clients.

He gave a grim smile. "Now we plant the plant and catch the monster, although I'd like to go on record that I still think this is a job for the authorities."

Despite the crowded parking lot, the medical floor was deserted, nurses' carts abandoned in the hall as if their drivers had been ferried to heaven during the rapture. Their steps ate up the stain-resistant carpet as they hurried down the corridor. Chances were good that the Whitleys were still there. Riley's condition was poor, no doubt aided by her mother's interference. But there was no reason to dawdle. They had to stop the woman who was mothering Riley to death.

The door of 310 hung open, a metal mouth agog in surprise. Maggie exchanged a look with Constantine. After so many visits to a room barred with the halfhearted limbo of a door set ajar, the openness made Maggie feel uneasy. Exposed. She grazed the smooth white plastic with her knuckles then crossed the threshold without waiting for a reply.

Mary hovered near Riley's bed. Her head whipped around at the sound of Maggie's steps, a furtive and startled response that reminded Maggie of her last visit to the hospital room. "Maggie!" she said. "What a pleasant surprise."

Maggie pasted on a smile and slid into the room, Constantine a breath behind her. "Thought you ladies could use some cheering up."

Maggie stepped aside and Constantine presented the Mickey Mouse vase like a fine wine. Mary's head cocked to one side, lank brown hair brushing her cheek, and moved away from the form on the bed that lay as still as a secret. "How nice," she said, pond-colored eyes lit with avarice. "A gift."

Mary spread her fingers to accept the offering, grasped it, then brought it to her face for inspection. The smile slipped at the corners. Perhaps she didn't find the gift card she expected. Perhaps she was allergic to daisies. She recovered, crimped her lips upward at the corners. "Thank you so much."

Mary placed the vase on the laminate abutting the room's sink. Maggie gauged the distance between the flowers and the wilted girl in the bed. Too far. She picked the vase from the larder of toiletries that surrounded it and relocated it to the window that smiled down on Riley. "The woman at the gift shop said it needs full sun," Maggie explained, angling Mickey's fingers toward the sleeping girl. "It's alive, so you can plant it when you get home."

Mary frowned at the botanical newbie that had relegated larger, more ornate flower arrangements to backup singer status then shrugged. "Great," she said without luster. "That'll be nice."

The trio stood looking at one another for a moment. Constantine broke the awkward silence. "Well, we should let you rest. You take care now."

"Thank you so much. You have no idea what this means."

"Oh, I think we do," Constantine replied, easing open the door then holding it for Maggie. "Enjoy."

The door shushed behind them, metal latch smooching metal tang. Constantine slid his hand across Maggie's palm in a silent gimme-five and they sauntered down the hall toward the Family Meeting Room. Constantine grabbed a round veneer table in the corner of the room and set up shop, drawing his phone and a set of ear buds from his pocket. He pinched and prodded the phone into obedience until the correct app launched.

Maggie looked over his shoulder at the phone. The Whitley's hospital room appeared in Movietone black and white. From the camera's vantage point, the room bloomed and fish-eyed under the harsh hospital lights. A funhouse without the fun. Constantine plugged the earbuds into the phone and handed Maggie half of the listening pair. Maggie fit the nodules into place. The white noise of machinery whirred the song of the hospital lullaby.

On screen, Mary moved about the room. She peered into the mirror above the sink and, perhaps finding her reflection dull enough, nodded with satisfaction. She sank into the chair beside Riley's bed. Crossed one leg. Then the other.

The moments struggled by like a wounded thing. Maggie found her eyes wandering to the scuffs that marred the table in front of her, indelible marks to match those illness and injury would leave behind.

Movement on screen captured her attention. Mary walked to her own bed, dragged a bag from it, rooted around inside and wrenched something free. Maggie squinted. It looked like sandwich-sized Ziploc bag.

Mary cut her eyes to the door. She slunk toward it, inched it open.

Maggie watched the back of her head as she gazed into the hallway. The back of her hair was neglected by comb and brush. Keeping up appearances, but only partly.

Mary pushed the door closed and glided across the room, Ziploc bag still in hand. She stood by Riley's bed, gazing down at the human she had grown inside her body. Then she opened the baggie and grasped the IV that twisted into her daughter's arm.

Maggie heard a sharp intake of breath. Realized she had made the sound.

Constantine looked over at her, his face a reflection of what he felt, what they both felt.

Fear. Revulsion. Fascination.

Behind them, the glass door banged open. It cracked the wall beside it, vibrating with the rebound. Maggie jumped to her feet, her heart lodged somewhere between her wisdom teeth and her breastbone.

"Aw shoot. Guess I don't know my own strength." Austin stood red-faced and grinning in the archway, thumbs hooked like commas into his pockets. "They ought to put a doorstop on this thing."

Maggie and Constantine stared at him gape-mouthed. "What?" he asked looking at his shirt, then his trousers. "Did I spill salsa again?"

Adrenaline bled from Maggie's nervous system. "What are you doing here? Did you get my voicemail and text?"

Austin shook his head. "Nope, phone's been acting up." Technology woes seemed to be catching. "Gladys asked me to check on the patients to see if they had anything to add to their statements." He eyed her. "What are you doing here?"

Maggie searched her mind for a suitable explanation, decided to go with the truth. "We're spying on Mary."

Austin's eyes saucered. "What would you want to do that for?"

Maggie told him, one eye on Constantine's phone. Austin doffed his hat, shimmied a hand through a russet thatch of hair. "I dunno about this."

"Just watch and you will. Please, Austin. Trust me."

She held his eyes, a silent plea for him to remember the past, to secure a sick girl's future. A muscle at Austin's jaw tightened, but he nodded and closed the door.

The three turned toward the tiny screen. Mary hadn't moved during Maggie's momentary standoff with Austin. She seemed to be wrestling with something. Maybe herself.

Then a shift. An uplifted sternum. A jut of the chin. Determination rolled off her in waves through the murk of mediocre resolution.

Maggie's throat closed as she watched Mary release the IV, open the Ziplock baggie and extract a hypodermic needle from its thin plastic shroud. She pushed the needle into the IV port. Her thumb hovered over the plunger.

Maggie's vision swam. She realized with some surprise that her cheeks were wet. Beside her, she could sense Austin spooling up, Constantine rising to his feet. But she was already standing, scrambling for the doorknob, missing, cursing Austin for closing the damn door behind him, then flinging it open and tearing down the hall.

The hall, which had been a ghost town, had come alive while they'd been sequestered in the Family Meeting Room. The corridor crowded with nurses bustling from room to room. Patients taking tentative steps with walkers or canes. Room service delivering steaming trays of whatever passed for food at St. Theresa's.

Maggie dodged past confused patients, irritated medical professionals and an outraged custodian. The hall seemed to elongate, her feet moving but not making any progress as the Whitleys' door receded, as if she were watching a dolly camera move in *Rear Window*.

Then she was at Room 310, hand held before her like a traffic cop, like a shield, like a weapon.

She punched the door. The portal hushed open, sighing along hydraulic hinges. Mary whirled around and locked eyes with Maggie.

"What—" was the farthest Mary got.

Maggie covered the room in two hungry strides, her mind on all that Mary had done to Riley, the plan grown like a toadstool in shadows where the mother's soul should have been. Maggie pulled her hand back, unsure whether she was going to bat the woman's hand away, strike her or wrest her from Riley side.

Her fingers parted, made contact with the arm of the woman who dared to call herself a mother, then contracted around the fleshy part of her upper arm. The flesh dimpled. Unlike Sloane, Mary could do with a tricep press or two.

Maggie could feel Constantine and Austin at her back. Constantine put a hand on her arm, perhaps to steady, perhaps to contain. Austin vocalized his concern over her actions with a sharp, "Maggie! Stop!"

But Maggie wasn't going to stop anyone but Mary.

She wrenched Mary's arm, yanking her away from the IV port, ignoring Austin's warnings to let Mary be, heedless of Constantine's pleas to calm down and let the authorities handle things. The woman yelped, a cry of indignation and surprise, and released the syringe, which dangled on the IV like dying fruit on a poisonous vine. Riley stirred on the bed, lifted her head, the corona of hair that had graced her pillow falling into her eyes.

Mary's grunt became a growl. She wound her free arm back and swung. Maggie lost her balance with the weight shift, regained it, pulled Mary in like a dance partner. She could see every pore on the woman's face, a veil of sweat misting her upper lip, worry lines quilting the dermis between and beside her eyes. Maggie guessed that the worry lines were anxiety about being caught. They certainly weren't about her daughter's health.

Maggie clasped Mary with her other hand, cinching her with freshly grown muscles. "You're done," Maggie whispered, her voice quaking with rage. "You're done hurting Riley. You're done hurting anyone."

Understanding bobbed into Mary's eyes. She lowered naked lids to half-staff. "You don't know shit," she spat.

"We do know shit," Constantine said, concern over Maggie's manhandling of Mary fading as his anger rose. "We also know shit's cousin, proof." He waggled the SD card. "Footage of you playing doctor. I'm betting dollars to tongue depressors that you've got something very nasty in that syringe."

Reflexively, Mary flicked her eyes to the needle then at the Ziploc baggie. "It's homeopathic," she said lifting her head. "An organic blend to help Riley."

"Cyanide's organic, too," Maggie said.

Mary's face closed shop. "I have no idea what you're talking about, but I do know I want a lawyer. I'm going to sue every last one of you."

"Now, now," Austin soothed. "No need to talk about suing anyone." He eyed Mary. "But you do have the right to an attorney. And to remain silent."

Mary cut him off with a scoff. "You're arresting me? This is outrageous."

Behind her, Riley sat up. "Mom?" Her voice hitched, turning the word polysyllabic.

Mary glared at Austin then at Maggie before softening her face and turning to Riley. "It's okay, pumpkin. Everything is going to be okay."

Austin watched the exchange, his head tennis-matching between mother and daughter. He leaned into Mary, his ginger hair almost brushing her silver-threaded bangs. "I can take you in without the...uh..." A glance at Riley. "Without the bracelets. You just need to cooperate."

Mary studied him, his pockets, which likely contained cuffs, then dragged her eyes to the girl attempting to disentangle herself from the sheets. Mary dropped her head, her body deflating as if whatever bilious humor that had filled it was escaping into the ether. She gave a slight nod. "Call my sister. She'll take care of her." Another aunt to the rescue.

Riley won the battle of the bedclothes and walked shakily to her mother's side. She encircled her mother's waist with a thin, needle pocked arm. "What's happening?" the girl wailed. "Why are they taking you away?"

Mary gave a beatific smile her virginal namesake would covet. "It's all right, my angel," she cooed. "Maggie thinks I've done something wrong, but it'll all be cleared up in a couple of hours."

Riley turned wounded eyes on Maggie. "Is this true?" The girl pushed out her lower lip. It was cracked, the inner rim caked by the leavings of an oral medication. Or perhaps its opposite.

"Riley, I—"

"I hate you!" Riley croaked then turned and sobbed into Mary's puce-colored sweater. "I hate you! I hate you! I hate you." She unleashed her hatred and pain into the woman who had tried to kill her, but her target was the girl who'd saved her.

Pain budded in Maggie's chest, divided, a rending of the heart during a Lent of the spirit. "Riley, I—"

"Get out!" Riley's voice was ragged with emotion and the insult of intubation. "Get. Out."

Maggie was transported back to Sloane's basement. A liberation from abuse that meant a separation from a mother.

Maggie gave one last pleading look at Riley. The girl burrowed further into her mother's belly, against the place she'd grown in the darkness of her mother's womb. Then Maggie walked silently to the door and out into the hall.

Chapter 48

Maggie took a mouthful of coffee from the carafe perched on the hospitality table in the family conference room. It was burned and bitter and hot, and Maggie welcomed the punishing scald. The ache in her chest had migrated to her eyes and she felt the dangerous sensation of tears gathering in the green room of her ducts. She screwed her eyes shut. She would not cry. She would not feel. She would not cry. She would not—

"Mags? You okay?"

She opened her eyes. Constantine was inches from her face. She lifted her chin, dipped it. Shook her head. She was not okay. Not even close to okay. And she was exhausted by pretending otherwise.

Constantine pulled her to his body. She leaned into the hardness of his chest, the softness of his faded tee, inhaling his scent of soap and laundry detergent and something likely laced with MSG. She knew the gesture was a mirror of the embrace she'd witnessed moments ago between Mary and Riley and squeezed her eyes against the image inked on her mind.

The sound of a throat being vacated of phlegm broke them apart. Gladys clasped her hands in front of her navel as if in prayer. "Sorry to interrupt."

Maggie brushed a recalcitrant lock from her eyes. "No interruption at all." She smoothed a finger beneath each eye, wiping any would-be evidence of a runaway tear. "How did you get here so quickly?"

"I was already in the hospital talking to the administrators about Brock's shooting. Austin radioed me. Here I am." She flashed picket fence teeth. "Austin said you have some kind of video footage?"

Constantine grabbed his phone, opened the app and played the footage after an explanation of its genesis and a warning about its quality. Gladys Wren watched without reaction or comment. When the video ended, she said, "We'll need the file of course, and likely your phone to ensure that the content wasn't manipulated."

Constantine grimaced at the thought of losing his phone—even momentarily—then nodded. He handed her the device.

Wren zippered open her messenger bag, plucked out an evidence bag and dropped the phone inside. Constantine looked as if he'd missed the last life raft off the Titanic.

"Don't worry, you'll get it back," Wren assured him. She turned to Maggie. "I'd read you the riot act about interfering, but it's always nice to catch an abuser."

"And a murderer," Maggie replied.

Wren blinked.

"I believe Mary is behind the poisonings."

If Gladys was surprised, she hid it. The only hint of emotion was the elevation of both brows, which were joined by a horizontal line in a hirsute game of connect the dots. "So now Mary's a murderer."

"*The* murderer. I—" She looked at Constantine. "*We* think she poisoned Riley as a ploy for sympathy and donations, or if Riley died, to get her hands on insurance money or Riley's trust fund."

"Does Riley have life insurance or money in trust?"

Maggie held Wren's frank and appraising gaze. "I don't know, but it wouldn't be hard to find out. I do know that Mary had fabricated—maybe even created— chronic medical conditions to drum up attention, not to mention money, trips, even a house. She needed to up the ante for a bigger payout—emotionally and literally."

Gladys's brows remained high and tight. "And the other victims were collateral damage, air cover for a story about a crazed killer poisoning Hollow Pine?" Maggie nodded. Gladys's lips tightened. "What about Russ Brock? What you told us about his past transgressions, the allegations of stalking, his planned assault on the Whitleys before security took him out?"

"I think Brock was interested in the Whitleys because he suspected abuse and wanted to prove that Mary was making Riley sick. He was working on a story about child abuse. You heard about today's arrest of Sloane Lewis for keeping her children in cages?" Wren hadn't. Maggie filled her in. "I now believe his interest in them was professional rather than personal."

Wren frowned. "You're saying that Brock came to the hospital to *interview* the Whitleys?"

"Or to confront Mary," Maggie replied. "You never found the gun

Bradley claimed he saw, right?"

Wren pursed her lips, said nothing. It was answer enough.

"I have a feeling his assistant, Bradley, was all too glad to throw suspicion on Brock," Maggie said. "He may not have planned for Brock's death, but he benefitted from it. He's now anchoring the nightly news."

Wren folded her arms and battened down her lips even more tightly. "Okay. We'll look into the abuse angle. And the possibility that Mary poisoned four people in order to keep abusing her daughter." The edge of her voice was tinged with skepticism. "The crime scene techs will be here soon to process the hospital room. They'll find out what was in Riley's IV and those needles Mary smuggled in."

"The lab's up and running again after the bomb threat?" Maggie asked.

"As suspected, it was a hoax. Probably someone who didn't want to go to work."

"Or someone who wanted to buy time," Maggie replied. "No lab. No testing. No murder weapon. Of course, with Mary's arrest, you have probable cause for a search warrant of her phone and her duplex. A lot could be discovered during a search. Evidence of a phone call to the lab. Evidence of medical child abuse. Evidence of murder."

Wren bristled. "You may have uncovered an abuser, maybe even a murderer. Or you could be dead wrong. Either way, we don't need you to tell us how to do our jobs. Leave search warrants and investigations to the professionals."

She dropped the evidence pouch into her canvas bag and marched from the room, tucking her navy blazer around her middle like the mantel of her office. Maggie watched through the glass door as she floated down the hall and slipped through the elevator doors, which parted before her like the Red Sea.

Maggie plunked onto a loveseat upholstered in a palette reminiscent of bodily fluids and put her head in her hands. The small couch shifted as Constantine sat beside her. Their bodies slid into the caldera he had created.

"For someone who just saved a girl's life and possibly solved a murder—hell, two murders—you look as happy as your dad on Tax Day. Any day, really."

She looked at him. His voice was light. His face was dark with concern. "I saved a girl's life and ruined it in one fell swoop. That's three for three in the family wreckage department. In one day, no less."

"Riley lashed out because she's angry and scared, but she had to know her mother was making her sick."

Maggie tilted her hand in a maybe-yes-maybe-no. "Maybe. Or maybe she believed that Mommy Dearest was doing the right thing."

"*More* wire hangers?" he asked, half-quoting *Mommy Dearest*.

"Maybe. It's not unusual for abused kids to excuse and even defend their abusers, even when they've suffered unthinkable trauma." Maggie thought of cages, soiled bed clothes, needles and scalpels. "The parent-child bond is tough to break, no matter how many times it's been cut."

Maggie's phone De Niro'd. She checked the screen. An 800 number. Miles going corporate? Maggie goosed the device awake with her thumb and put it to her ear.

"This is Maggie."

"Maggie O'Malley of Petrosian's pharmacy?" The voice on the other end was male and congested. He sounded as if he were auditioning for a nasal spray commercial.

She felt her guard go up. "Yes, that's right."

"This is Dave from HazMail," his adenoids replied. "How are you today?"

Pretty shitty, Dave, and you? She thought.

"I'm fine, thanks," she said.

"Great," Dave monotoned. Maggie heard the clack of a keyboard. "The reason I'm calling is that your sharps container was due to our facility for disposal, but we haven't received it." Every word was slowly released like news from a tickertape. "Do you need us to send a new pre-paid mailing box?" Before she could reply, he pressed on, "Or if you'd like to change your shipping schedule, I can help you with that." More keyboard clacks. "We could switch you to our quarterly program?"

Maggie closed her eyes, thinking. Then it clicked: Petrosian had asked her to be the contact person for all of Petrosian's vendors when she first started interning, including a disposal service for used sharps employed during pharmacy vaccinations.

"How late is our shipment?" she asked.

"About a week. Petrosian's has always been like clockwork, so we wanted to reach out. You're happy with the service, I hope?"

A week. Just before Petrosian's closed. Just before the poisonings. "Yes. We'll get the container out to you just as soon as we can. Thanks for the call."

"Package problems?" Constantine asked after Maggie hit the End button.

"Our biohazard disposal service didn't receive our sharps container."

"Because Petrosian's is closed?"

"Thom takes shipments to the post office because it's on his way home from work. I can't be sure, but I think he took the sharps container from the pharmacy a couple of days before the poisonings."

"So the company should have had it by now."

Maggie nodded. "Which means the police could be missing a crucial piece of evidence." She bent over her phone and scrolled through her contacts. "I didn't think about it until now, but anything administered via hypodermic needle could have been the mechanism for poisoning."

She furrowed her brow. "The Whitleys were planning a Panama Canal cruise. Claudia Warren had been preparing for a work trip to Tobago. And now I remember Colton Ellis talking about traveling to Columbia for some kind of eating contest. Petrosian's offers Yellow Fever vaccinations. The supply could have been contaminated. I didn't even think of mentioning vaccines to the police."

"And as far as we know, neither did Petrosian," Constantine reminded her, "or any of your other coworkers, including doubting Thomas."

He was right. The guilt wasn't hers alone, yet she felt its keen edge nick her insides.

She found Thom's phone number, pushed to dial, hoped her intermittent phone would continue to cooperate. The phone rang in her ear. And rang. And rang. Eight rings in, the phone picked up. So did Maggie's heart.

"Hi, this is Thom," voicemail Thom said. "I can't come to the phone right now..."

Naturally.

Maggie waited for the requisite beep and left a message to call her. She ended the call and pocketed the phone.

"Shouldn't you have mentioned the sharps container?"

Maggie got to her feet. "Nope. Because we're going to ask about it in person."

Chapter 49

The home of Thomas Henry Dutton was a half-mile past the *Welcome to Hollow Pine Where Neighbors Are Friends and Friends Are Neighbors!* sign that marked the seam where outskirts ended and city began.

"Thomas Henry Dutton, huh?" Constantine wrinkled his nose.

"You don't approve?" Maggie lifted her foot from the accelerator as the speed limit dipped and the buildings multiplied.

"Too serial killer-y. All the best serial killers have three names."

"Lots of people have three names."

"Yeah, but these three names are hinky."

She gave him a look at "hinky"—someone had watched *The Fugitive* again—then turned her attention back to the road.

Siri suggested turns. Maggie obeyed. She coasted to a stop in front of a lone house in a new subdivision that advertised *Dream Homes at Dream Prices*. She squinted at the neo-bungalow, which sprouted from the ground in Sherman Williams earth tones.

Constantine opened the door. "What's the plan?"

Maggie thought for a moment. "I'm thinking the no-plan plan."

Constantine put his hand to his throat in mock-horror. "The scientist is going to wing it? Hang on while I record this for posterity." He mimed writing on his hand. "Dear Diary..."

Maggie clambered out of the car. She tucked runaway hairs into her makeshift bun and ran her hand over her coral t-shirt, then caught a glimpse of herself in the car window. She looked as if she'd taken a ride in a clothes dryer.

She ignored the riotous hair and straightened her spine. Together she and Constantine marched up the crisp new sidewalk to Thom's crisp new house like a two-person army.

She rapped on the door, a fiberglass number in the ubiquitous medium brown found in new developments nationwide. For the second time that day, her summons was met with silence.

She reconsidered her no-plan plan and took the opportunity to rehearse her speech to Thom. Should she lead with the lost syringes, which may or may not have contained cyanide, or with the fact that they'd gone missing on his watch? Either way, she doubted she'd be invited in for coffee cake.

Maggie knocked again. Nothing. She tried the handle. It turned easily.

Constantine put his hand on top of hers. "I don't mean to be a stick in the mud, but I gave up burgling for Lent."

"We're not burgling," she whispered as she pushed the door wide, "and didn't you tell me you gave up skydiving?"

"Well, yes, but that was for the first few weeks."

She poked her head through the door. Wine-colored shades were drawn, creating an interior dusk. She took a step inside, pulled Constantine beside her. "Thom? It's Maggie."

She felt as if she were watching a rerun of her earlier activities. Knock. Break in. Find something terrible. Repeat.

"Thom?" she called louder this time. "I tried to call but couldn't reach you."

She took another step, skating across faux wood flooring, distressed to look realistic. She stopped, tilted her head. Listened. Was she imagining things or did she hear violin strains?

"Is that Tchaikovsky?" Constantine whispered.

She was definitely not imagining things. At least not this.

She nodded and pointed down a narrow hall that jutted from the foyer. Constantine held a finger aloft then jogged to a living room furnished with a La-Z-Boy chair and a sixty-five-inch big screen, then out of sight to what Maggie imagined was the kitchen.

He returned seconds later, panting lightly. "Nothing of interest, unless you count a keg, a tower of pizza boxes and a half-eaten ham sandwich that's become a science experiment."

Maggie wondered how long it took for a sandwich to rot, why Tom would leave it to molder.

They moved down the hall, their feet squishing on new carpet in a slightly lighter shade than the house paint. Two pairs of footprints debossed the rug, one large, the other small. Maggie looked for speckles, for smears of brown and rust. The carpet and the adjacent walls were pristine.

Halfway down the corridor, the hall elbowed into two small bedrooms, both empty, both shadowed by the sleep masks of vermillion shades. At the hall's terminus, a door stood closed, tightlipped.

Violin strains seeped beneath the door. Something else, too. Something for the olfactory senses.

Maggie caught a whiff of perfume, sweet and cloying, a female complement to Miles's signature scent.

Beneath it, something organic. Pungent. Loamy. Rotten.

Maggie's stomach lurched. She clutched a fist to her gut, concentrated on keeping her latte where she'd put it. She could feel Constantine behind her, waiting, ready to help. But she didn't want help. She wanted to do this on her own.

Maggie reached forward and depressed the rubbed bronze lever that poked from the door like tongue. The room belched out a foulness Maggie recognized immediately.

Decay.

Decomp.

Death.

Different words. Same end.

Maggie moved her fist to her face and spread her hand to shield her nose and mouth. It was ritual borne of habit, but without effect. The scent engulfed her, oozing into her nose, her mouth, her brain.

She staggered forward, eyes sweeping the room. The bed: empty. The chair: empty. The floor: empty.

She spotted a closet, doors slid shut. She lumbered toward it, put her hand into a small brass niche that functioned as its handle and tugged.

The closet door opened and shared its secrets: two battered suitcases, a basket of dirty laundry. And the decomposing body of Thomas Henry Dutton.

Chapter 50

Austin strode from Thom's house, degloving his hands of two layers of nitrile. He wadded the gloves and disposed them in a small plastic bag before joining Maggie and Constantine at the curb.

He regarded the vehicles that arrived on the scene, two to process the scene, one to transport the body, then turned his attention to Maggie. Whether by oversight or by design, Austin always managed to ignore Constantine.

"He's been dead for some time," Austin said, stating the obvious. "The ME will be able to determine time of death—or hopefully come close—but I'd guess several days. Maybe a little longer." Austin smoothed a gingery patch of hair above his ear. "Any contact with him after the pharmacy closed?"

"None."

"Anyone you work with see him after it closed?"

"No idea."

"And you came here because..."

Maggie felt her hackles rise. Why were the police so intent on making her repeat herself? "Like I told you on the phone, I'm trying to find out what happened to the box of sharps Thom was supposed to ship to the disposal company. It's possible the pharmacy's vaccines were poisoned."

"Right," he said again. He hitched his thumbs through his belt loops. "Well if the box is here, the techs will find it, along with some answers as to why Thom took his own life."

Maggie raised an eyebrow. "You're convinced he died by his own hand."

Austin unhooked his thumbs and made a wide sweeping motion. "You saw him hanging in that closet. I very much doubt it was an accident."

Before Maggie could offer up an alternative reason that began with "foul" and ended with "play," a new figure emerged from the house. Gladys

Wren strode toward them, arms tucked to her chest like wings. She landed a few feet from Austin, nodded at Maggie and Constantine.

"A few surprises inside," she said without preamble. "And I'm not talking about the body." She eyed Maggie. "What do you know about Thom's personal life?"

"Nothing. Thom's part-time, sort of keeps to himself."

It sounded like every neighbor's account of the serial killer next door.

"Maybe he keeps to himself with his coworkers. Customers...well, that seems to be another story."

"I don't understand."

"It seems that Thom had a relationship with one of Petrosian's patrons."

"Relationship?" Maggie repeated, as if it were a word she'd never heard.

She thought of Mary, of a plan to Mrs. Robinson her way into Thom's life and gain access to the pharmacy. Mary was no femme fatale and yet Maggie could imagine her fostering a friendship with Thom, playing on the young man's sympathy, using her sexuality to crack open his defenses and get at the yielding flesh within. She imagined it wouldn't take much to turn Thom's head, to convince him to let her help clean behind the counter during an afterhours visit or romantic encounter.

It was perfect. It was evil. It was a shame it didn't occur to her sooner.

Wren untucked her arms and produced a small framed photograph. She held it out to Maggie to inspect.

Maggie leaned in. In the photo, she could make out two faces clinched, cheek to cheek, in a sideways embrace. She zeroed in on the subjects. The man was indeed Thom. She moved her eyes to the woman, expecting to see Mary, mid-nuzzle against Thom's twenty-year-old face.

But the woman in the photo wasn't Mary. In fact it wasn't a woman at all. It was a girl.

Riley Whitley, clear-eyed and bird-bodied, stared at an unseen camera from the harbor of Thom's arms.

Chapter 51

"Is that—?" Constantine began.

"Riley Whitley?" Gladys supplied. "Yes, it is." She shuffled through an assortment of unframed snapshots.

The duo sharing a milkshake.

Riley on Thom's lap, head on his chest.

Thom and Riley side by side, hands entwined.

Maggie did the relationship arithmetic: sharing food + cuddling = probable couple

Gladys proffered the final item in her arms. A rumpled piece of paper, large, loping handwriting scrawled across the page. Y's became smiley faces. I's were footnoted with hearts.

You are my morning.
You are my night.
You are my life.
You are my light.
You are my one.
You are my all.
You know my heart.
You'll catch my fall.

Maggie turned wide eyes onto Constantine. "My God."

"I know," Constantine said solemnly. "That has got to be the worst poem I've ever read."

Gladys gave him a withering look then straightened the pile in her hands, slit open an evidence bag, and popped the paper and photos inside. "I probably shouldn't have shared this to you. I just wanted you to know the truth about Riley, see the result of careful, *professional* investigation."

Maggie ignored the dig. "Riley had a relationship with Thom," she said more to herself than anyone. "Despite her illness, despite everything."

"Extraordinary, isn't it?" Gladys mused. "If you're right about Mary, she controlled every aspect about her daughter's life, except one."

"I don't understand," Maggie said. "Where did they rendezvous? How were they able to carry on without raising Mary's suspicions? How did Riley have the strength to have a romantic liaison?"

"Unfortunately, Thomas Dutton isn't available for an interview," Gladys said flatly. "We'll have to question Riley."

"'Question'?" Maggie's voice had grown thin and high. "That sounds an awful lot like 'interrogate'."

Gladys pulled her mouth into a garrote smile. "You're protective of the girl. That's understandable, given her circumstances. Still, she's a witness in what's becoming a very strange case."

"She's not a witness. She's a victim, first of her mother's abuse, then of Thom's. No matter how consensual their relationship looked, he was several years her senior, and she was under eighteen. If they had sex, Thom would be committing statutory rape."

"That's correct," Gladys said coolly. "Unfortunately it can't be proven or prosecuted because the alleged perpetrator is dead. What I can do, what I *will* do, is look into the common denominator: the alleged victim who's connected to not just one death but three."

"Alleged?" Maggie's voice thickened, rising in volume and octave. "We have video proof of Mary's medical abuse."

"Which still needs to be verified by the experts. Besides, victimhood is no guarantee of innocence. Some of the worst crimes have been perpetrated by those who themselves have suffered."

Maggie opened her mouth. Closed it. Opened it again. Gladys was right. Abuse victims sometimes became abusers themselves or lashed out at the society that had failed to protect them.

"A few years ago," Gladys began, her voice turning storyteller, "a girl murdered her mother after enduring years of medical abuse. The mother had a feeding tube inserted into her daughter's stomach, forced her to use a wheelchair, came up with all kinds of diagnoses to explain her daughter's symptoms. All fake. All designed to stroke her best-mom-in-the-world ego."

"Gypsy Rose Blanchard," Maggie murmured, her mind turning to the articles she'd read, the true crime shows she'd watched. "I remember the story."

"Then you also remember that Gypsy had a secret boyfriend, someone she convinced to kill her mother."

Maggie said nothing.

"The secret boyfriend killed the mother while Gypsy hid in another room. Then they posted anonymously on the mother's Facebook wall, pretending to be an unnamed assailant, claiming that Gypsy had been abducted during a home invasion in which the mother had been murdered."

"The mother had a name," Maggie said. "Dee Dee." The dead deserved respect, even when they did terrible things while alive.

Gladys studied Maggie for a moment. "Yes, Dee Dee."

Maggie lifted her chin. "You're suggesting that the same thing happened here? That Thom and Riley became involved, that Riley confided about the abuse, that the two conspired to end the abuse—and Mary—along with innocents who had the misfortune to come in contact with their murder weapon?"

Gladys straightened her jacket, ran a hand along the strands of her caramel-colored hair. "I don't have to suggest it, Ms. O'Malley. You did a beautiful job of doing it for me."

"You're wrong. You're wrong about Riley, about this copy-paste of the Blanchard case. You're wrong about it all."

"Why? Because Riley's incapable of it? Unwilling? Long term abuse does things to people. So does desperation."

Maggie couldn't argue with Gladys. Riley has been an offering to medicine, a sacrifice in the temple of her mother's insatiable hunger for money and attention. Her childhood had been burgled. Her adolescence ransomed. Weakened and isolated, Riley had become as much a prisoner as Sloane's daughters in a cage wrought by manufactured illnesses and their cures.

Maggie imagined forced ingestions of sodium. Secret injections of fecal matter. Tests administered by physicians who'd become unwitting jailers. At first, Riley was too young to know anything different. When she grew old enough to understand, she was likely threatened or physically altered to play along.

Maybe Mary gave the rack another turn, began a new regimen of torment that Riley couldn't imagine enduring. Maybe Riley fell in love with Thom and saw that she was more than her mother's voodoo doll.

Maybe Riley had decided to do whatever it took to break free.

Had Riley acted in desperation? And if she had, wouldn't her culpability be mitigated by circumstance? Wouldn't it be shared with the mother who had turned her into Frankenstein's monster, one stitch, one poke, one pill at a time?

She thought of Brock's dying words.

Watch out for the girl.

Maybe it was a warning to beware rather than a supplication to protect.

Maggie shook her head. No. Impossible. Every instinct told her it wasn't true, couldn't be. And although she didn't trust her feelings, she had learned to trust her intuition. Even after last year. Even after it had failed her.

"And Thom just went along with it?" Maggie asked. She'd meant it as a challenge. It came out watery.

"It wouldn't be the first time someone killed—or planned to kill—to protect a lover. Did Thom have access behind the pharmacy counter?"

A "no" leapt to Maggie's lips. Then she remembered. The lights. The ghastly fluorescent bulbs that Thom had installed behind the counter just days before Colton breathed his last.

She had wondered what had inspired him to choose lighting that jaundiced anyone bathed in its sallow glow. But she hadn't wondered why he had replaced perfectly functional bulbs. Until now.

Explanation: swapping bulbs allowed Thom access to a restricted area of the pharmacy so that he could contaminate vaccines with cyanide.

Other explanations: Maggie would have to come back to that.

She cleared her throat. "Not typically, no, but he did replace some light bulbs behind the counter."

Gladys's eyebrows reached up on tiptoe to kiss her hairline. "Shortly before the poisonings?"

Maggie shifted. Nodded.

"He could have allowed Riley back there to fill pill bottles with cyanide."

"Or syringes," Maggie said dully. "I believe it's possible that all of the poisoning victims had injectable vaccinations in advance of tropical vacations. We'd have to check the pharmacy records to be sure."

"Interesting." Gladys smiled tightly. "The techs are scouring the crime scene. If there's a box of used syringes, they'll find it." She fished her keys out of her bag, twirled them on a slender finger. "Something drove Thom to his death. My bet: guilt by what he had done or by what he had allowed to occur. Whether Riley convinced him to execute her plan or joined him behind the counter to taint medications without his knowledge,

Thomas Henry Dutton could no longer live with himself. The person at the eye of this storm is Riley Whitley."

"I don't believe it." Maggie shook her head vigorously. She could practically feel her brain sloshing against her skull. "It could have been Mary. She could have found out about their relationship, become enraged by Riley's secrecy, her disobedience, and decided to stop it—and her daughter—permanently."

"Anything's possible," Gladys said, her voice surprisingly gentle, "but I prefer what's probable."

Gladys placed the evidence bag in her attaché. She patted it like a cherished child, looked over at the house. The door opened to expel two men carting out the zippered remains of Thom. "We'll see what the evidence says. In the end, it doesn't matter what you believe or what I believe. In the end, it's all about science."

Chapter 52

Maggie stared at the receding taillights of the police and emergency vehicles. She walked over to the Studebaker, listed against it, drawing comfort from its custard-colored paint as doubt poked her. Chided her. Mocked her.

Riley's not a victim, it whispered. *You were wrong about her. You were wrong about everything.*

"No," Maggie said aloud.

Constantine sidled beside her, took his place at the fender. "No, what?"

"No way Riley did this."

Constantine lifted his hand toward the now-naked street. "The lead detective made a pretty convincing argument."

She toed the asphalt, found a jagged edge, lifted it with the tip of her shoe. "I'm not buying it. Riley's only fault was being born to the wrong mother."

Constantine leaned against the Studebaker, toed the same jagged puzzle piece of asphalt. "I know you like her, Mags, but I think you're letting your feelings color your opinion."

Maggie laughed, a sharp, brittle sound. "Since when have my feelings ever been a factor? Yes, I care about Riley, I think she's a great kid. But this is about reason, not emotion."

"You sure about that?" he asked, eyes on a sky crowded with charcoal clouds.

His phone interrupted her retort. She looked at him. "I thought you gave your phone to Gladys Wren."

He shrugged. "I did. But I always carry a backup."

Constantine checked the screen then put the phone to his ear. "Hey, Ken. Yep, glad you called my second number." He mouthed "Kenny Rogers" to Maggie. "What's up?"

Maggie felt a cold dread seep into her bones. Constantine's aunt's health was fragile. Maybe her boyfriend had called to report she'd fallen. Had become ill. Or worse. Maggie held her breath as Constantine murmured into the phone.

He ended the call and stowed the phone in his jeans. "Car trouble. They were on their way to salsa dance lessons and ran out of gas. Kenny does most of the moving while Aunt Polly stands there looking regal. Anyway, they had been making out the night before and left the engine running." He made a face.

Maggie gave a quick prayer of thanksgiving. "They want you to ride to their rescue?"

"Like a knight in shining sheet metal. Timing works out, though, because I've got to check on a server I installed at an insurance company down the street anyway. Two birds, one me. I'll grab my car, do the deed, then we can get dinner and talk about..." He indicated the house behind them. "You know."

She did. Oh, how she did.

The clouds continued to labor during their drive home, building to a peak as they pulled into their driveway. A gust of wind tore the door from Maggie's hand as she opened it, wrenching it against its hinges and sending a bolt of pain up her shoulder.

Constantine jogged around to the driver's side. "Shit. Another blast of wind like that and this thing will set sail." He touched her arm. "You okay?"

How many times would he ask that? How many times would he need to?

Maggie bit her cheek. She found her most believable smile and nodded. "Give Polly and Kenny my best. I'm going to get inside before Mom Nature grounds me."

Constantine kissed her. "Be back as quick as I can. Oh, and I bought a different flavor of dog food for Chewbarka. Evidently he's more of a chicken-in-gravy guy."

"*Chewbarka*?"

Constantine shrugged. "What? I thought he needed a name besides 'Dog.' Plus he looks like a little Wookie."

"I thought you didn't like dogs. And that he was a temporary guest."

"Well." Constantine scratched his ear. "He's good company for Miss Vanilla. They just pretend to not like each other. And no one's claimed him so I figure he can hang with us for...ever." He gave her another peck on the lips. "Anyway, he likes one-and-a-half scoops with a few tablespoons of water for maximum gravy-ness. Have fun and don't do anything I wouldn't do. Which is pretty much anything."

Maggie smiled then dashed through the front door as Constantine headed for the shelter of his Datsun. The newly christened Chewbarka greeted her with raised doggy eyebrows and one of Maggie's running shoes. She eased her sneaker from the mutt's mouth. "Another one? We need to get you a new hobby."

Chewbarka twisted his head and barked then followed her to the kitchen.

She rummaged through the pantry and found Constantine's new bag of gourmet dog food. She ripped it open just above a tagline that promised to connect the buyer's canine with its lupine ancestors and checked the price tag. It was higher than most of the items in their pantry. "Not a dog person. Right."

She poured brown bits shaped like tiny cutlets into a red plastic bowl, then prepared her own meal, layering meat, cheese and vegetables between thick slices of rye, halving the completed tower with a sharp knife. She smelled her creation, inhaling the tang of meat and mustard, and waited for her stomach to respond. It soured, causing her mouth to water in anticipation of a gastric event rather than delight.

Maggie wrapped the sandwich and put it in the fridge. Death had killed her appetite once again.

She opened a cabinet abutting the fridge and rooted around, shoving aside bottles of extract, cans of soup and a package of sloppy joe mix, and pulled out a bottle of wine. She checked the label. Non-alcoholic cabernet. She kept rummaging. Nothing in the adult libation department. They must have killed the last of the booze.

Maggie shrugged and poured the alcohol-free wine into a goblet that she had rescued from a thrift store clearance bin, grabbed glass and bottle, and walked to the living room. She plunked onto the living room couch, leaned against the cushions, stared at the popcorn ceiling speckled with a constellation of glitter. With her luck, it was probably nice, sparkly asbestos.

She closed her eyes, trying to shut out the ceiling, the world, the possibility that Riley was a murderer. No luck.

Gladys was right. Riley had a motive for trying to kill her mother. She had means and opportunity by virtue of her relationship with Thom and his access to medications behind the counter.

But Riley, a killer of innocents as well as the guilty? Maggie couldn't believe it. Or perhaps she wouldn't.

Maggie sat up and swung her legs to the floor, hair curtaining her face. Gladys had suggested that emotion had colored Maggie's perception. Constantine had seconded it. She had to prove to them—to herself—that logic and reason still held sway.

Think, O'Malley, think.

She lifted her goblet from the coffee table, gulped it to low tide, grabbed a discarded envelope from Constantine's archipelago of debris. She flipped the envelope, grabbed a pen from beside a half-empty bag of Cheetos and began to write what she knew. *Just the facts*, she told herself, channeling her inner Joe Friday.

Three poisoning victims (four if she counted the perpetrator)

Cyanide poisoning

No means of administration/murder weapon found

Missing sharps

Sharps previously in custody of Thom

Thom dead

Thom and Riley in a romantic relationship

Maggie lingered over this last point, recalling the photos and love note Gladys Wren had paraded beneath their noses. The imprint of smaller footprints in Thom's carpet. The barely discernable scent of stale perfume that floated through Thom's rooms like a wraith.

Could Riley have killed Thom?

Maggie poured the last of the wine down her throat. No matter how she looked at it, Thom and Riley were at the center, and Riley was at its very heart. Yes, Thom could have planned to kill Mary of his own volition, without Riley's knowledge or encouragement. But Riley had the most to gain from her mother's demise.

Maggie stared at the list inked on the envelope, invoking her scientific brain to take over. Was she missing anything, or was it all as it seemed?

Her eyes landed on the second item in the list. Cyanide.

She needed to start with the elemental. Or in this case, the compound.

Chapter 53

Maggie picked up the pen again, words flowing as the data she knew about the poison flooded her brain.

Cyanide could be in a gaseous form as hydrogen cyanide or cyanogen chloride, or in a crystal, such as sodium cyanide or potassium cyanide. It was present in various pits and seeds, cigarette smoke, pest control products (such as ant poison), and used in some medical and clinical applications.

Maggie stopped writing. Medical and clinical applications. Why hadn't she thought of pursuing this angle before?

Maybe because you have a brain injury and have been preoccupied by wedding planning, family drama and people trying to kill you? she reminded herself.

She flipped the envelope over yet again and began to write above the address, making a list of cyanide's medical uses.

Laetrile, a dangerous and unorthodox cancer treatment not recognized by the FDA, contained cyanide. Method of administration: ingestion or injection.

Did Mary give Riley Laetrile as an alternative therapy for the leukemia she didn't have? Did Mary or Thom—or Riley—contaminate Petrosian's Yellow Fever vaccines with Laetrile?

Maggie continued to think through the possibilities.

Sodium nitroprusside, which contained cyanide, was used to measure urine ketone bodies for people with diabetes. Maggie was familiar with this application. In fact, Rxcellance had been working on new testing kits when she was there.

Her mind turned to her old employer, her old coworkers.

Miles, hulking, arrogant, dangerous, stood front and center in her consciousness.

He had tailed her to her adopted hometown. He had harassed and threatened her. He had handled a compound that could have been twisted into the instrument of death for Colton Ellis and Claudia Warren.

In the pantheon of potential suspects Maggie liked Miles best because she hated him most.

But that was emotion, not reason.

Other than a revenge killing perpetrated to ruin Maggie, Miles had the least to gain from the poisonings. There was also the question of access. Thom—and by extension Riley—would have most easily infiltrated and contaminated the pharmacy's vaccines.

She poured three fingers of ruby liquid into her glass, sipped, added another finger, continued thinking and writing.

Sodium nitroprusside, sold under the brand name Nitropress, was also used to decrease blood pressure during hypertensive emergency and as a vasodilator during heart surgery.

Hypertensive emergency. In the back of Maggie's mind, a bell pealed.

Riley had been admitted to hospitals several times for malignant hypertension. Had sodium nitroprusside been administered? Could Mary have somehow spirited the drug from the hospital? Could Riley have done the same?

Maggie abandoned her glass on the island of a magazine subscription card, got to her feet and walked to the home office. Dust kited through the room's artificial sunlight. Maggie dropped into the chair before the keyboard. Chewbarka sat on her feet and yawned.

She hovered over the keyboard then bowed to the digital oracle, once again typing the URL of Mary's blog. She read.

Since moving to Hollow Pine eighteen months ago, Riley had been to St. Theresa's twenty-three times. Four of those visits were for hypertensive emergency.

Maggie again marveled at the fact that no one wondered why a girl with cystic fibrosis, which typically presents with low blood pressure, had life-threatening, brain-cooking, organ-killing high blood pressure. As with Riley's office visits, her symptomatology defied logic and yet no one looked closer or put the sick girl and her mother beneath the microscope along with samples robbed from Riley's small body.

Maggie scrolled through Mary's posts, her teeth aching from the saccharine description of the mother's love for her daughter, the girl's fight for her life. True to Munchausen-type mania, Mary dove deep into the medical details, celebrating the minutia of each test and every procedure.

Medical bottom line: Riley had been given Nitropress each time she visited St. Theresa's ER for sky-high blood pressure.

That in itself was curious. The drug had fallen out of favor in recent years, perhaps because a side effect, though rare, included cyanide toxicity.

Had Mary suggested its use, perhaps telling the medical team that Riley had responded positively to it in the past, was allergic to alternatives? Had she inserted herself behind the scenes to gain access to the drug? Or, as Gladys Wren would surely propose, had Riley been the pilferer of Nitropress, swiping a vial from a tray, concealing it within the folds of her hospital gown, squirreling it away as she planned to end her mother and whatever unfortunate innocents happened to get in the way?

Both scenarios were possible.

Maggie clasped the computer mouse, preparing to navigate to a new page, when a photograph caught her eye.

In the throes of Riley's crisis, Mary, as usual, had taken the opportunity to snap a few selfies. Her pained face was front and center, worry lines cratering her downturned mouth and the edges of her tear-brimmed eyes. In the background, Maggie could make out Riley's prone form and a team of professionals at work to save her life.

In the middle of the group: Deena, nurse extraordinaire.

Maggie clicked to the other entries, the other photographs. They also featured action shots that caught a girl hanging in the balance as medical professionals worked feverishly to tip the scales in her favor.

Once again, Deena was part of the medical team.

That wasn't unusual. Nurses were omnipresent, the heart of patient care and central to the well-being of those they served with grace and compassion. It made sense that Deena would be front and center when Riley was in crisis, especially since she'd mentioned previous stints in the emergency department before becoming a floater often assigned to the medical floor.

Deena's presence was logical. Normal. Easily explained and readily dismissed.

Then why did it gnaw at Maggie?

Maggie shut her eyes, the zillionth time she had done so to find her inner quiet.

On the blank screen of her mind, conversations with Deena replayed themselves.

Deena's anguish over Riley's poor health.

Deena's near-idolatrous attention to her young patient.

Deena's declaration that Riley's mysterious turn for the worse was due to someone poisoning her. Brock was dead. Who else could she have meant?

Maggie thought back to her last conversation with Deena. "Hard to believe someone would hurt a child to further their own interests," Deena had said. Could she have been talking about Mary?

Maggie shook her head. She was being ridiculous. Constantine was right. She wasn't thinking clearly. She was coming up with implausible ideas, her typically scientific brain muddled by injury, stress and too little sleep.

No, Mary remained the most viable suspect, with Thom and Riley close at her Keds-clad heels. The notion of a killer nurse was insane at best and reckless at worst. By all accounts, Deena was a saint. A paragon. A salve for those suffering in body and a boon for those suffering in spirit.

And, a voice inside her head reminded her, *the person with the easiest and most continuous access to Nitropress.*

Maggie mentally bore down to drown out the voice. Stopped herself.

Despite all the reasons to doubt her mind, her instincts, her abilities, she knew she was capable of dispassionate discernment. She also knew that breakthroughs didn't happen when people let their internal editors take the reins.

Why not think through the possibility? Why not put the idea of Deena-as-architect-of-mass-poisoning under her mental microscope? After all, experience had taught Maggie that people weren't always as they seemed.

Maggie turned the theory—and the woman—over in her mind.

Strip away Deena's sunny personality, her time-honored profession, her evident devotion to her patients, and there was a woman with means and opportunity.

But motive? That was more elusive.

Maggie considered the possible purpose behind the poison. Deena could have suspected Mary of medical abuse and used the poisonings to point the authorities toward the malevolent mother. Or she could have sought to free Riley from her body, an angel of mercy sending a sick girl home to Jesus.

Maggie's stomach turned. Most healers followed the Hippocratic Oath to do no harm. But as a true crime aficionado, Maggie knew that sometimes doctors and nurses took lives rather than saved them.

Former physician H.H. Holmes was perhaps the most notorious example, transforming hotel rooms into chambers of horror during the 1893 Chicago World's Fair. There was also pediatric nurse Genene Jones who killed sixty children under her watch, Kirsten Gilbert who caused patients to go into cardiac arrest and then revive them with varying degrees of success, and Kimberly Clark Saenz who injected bleach into patients' dialysis lines.

Their motives varied. Some gunned for glory like arsonist firefighters who got high on heroism. Others wanted to spare patients further pain. Still others had predilections for control and violence that coincided with job descriptions that put them in contact with agents of death.

Maggie loved nurses. She adored Deena. But she couldn't ignore Deena's proximity to Nitropress, their conversations, her own admission that she'd lost patients over the years. Maybe she'd helped them to the great beyond.

Maggie pushed her chair back. Chewbarka lumbered to his feet and looked up at her expectantly.

"I won't be long," she told the dog as she stroked his silky ear. "My personal hacker is otherwise occupied, so I'll have to go on-site for a little hospital recon. I'll be back before your evening Milk-Bone."

With that, Maggie snagged her purse, her car keys, her sometimes-functional phone and headed out the door into the darkening gloom.

Chapter 54

The rain predicted by meteorologists and foreshadowed by a brooding sky and lashing winds turned out to be an overachiever.

Instead of the promised intermittent showers, the heavens cleaved and let loose a torrent of water like a long-held grudge.

"It's enough to make Noah jealous," Maggie muttered, her hand slipping and skidding against the rain-slicked car as she tried to put the key into the Studebaker's lock. "Good thing Pop bought me all-weather tires for my birthday."

Maggie felt the all-too familiar pang at the thought of her father, the ache of something that used to be, like an old injury activated by overuse. She got into the car and focused on the task at hand and the road ahead.

She pulled onto their street, drove two blocks, then eased the Studebaker onto the main drag. Her heart accelerated as she thought of her visit to St. Theresa's, her half-formed plan to interview Deena's colleagues, her hope and worry that Deena would be there. Maggie's foot responded in kind, depressing the gas pedal, speeding toward whatever fate awaited.

The car hydroplaned then fishtailed as it gained purchase on the glossy road. Maggie lifted her foot from the accelerator and leaned forward, gripping the steering wheel.

Up ahead, Maggie saw a rotating beacon of red and blue, a police car lighthouse guiding vehicles to safe passage. Maggie tapped the brakes and flicked the windshield wipers to high. Intermittent clarity offered a view to the reason behind the flashing lights: a four-car accident blocking the street ahead.

Feck.

Maggie eased to a stop behind the growing phalanx of cars, which grumbled and snorted in the murk. Maggie craned her neck and spotted a gap fronting a side street. She signaled, maneuvered around the line of idling vehicles and turned onto the street. She squinted into the gathering dark. Empty. Exactly as she liked her streets.

She increased her speed, slowly this time to avoid losing control, and turned her thoughts to Deena, to Mary, to those entrusted to heal and help.

Mary had betrayed the office of motherhood. Maggie wondered if Deena had forsaken her position of trust as a nurse.

She mentally skipped ahead to her visit to St Theresa's. She imagined walking into the hospital. Donning an abandoned set of scrubs lifted from the staff room. Paying the role of new employee. Asking questions about Deena that would lead to insight and information.

She considered what she'd say if she encountered Deena in the hall or in the elevator, how she'd pose questions and mine for the mother lode of information she was certain was just below the—

Bang!

Maggie felt the car bottom out and lurch to the side.

Maggie yanked on the steering wheel, overcorrected, crossing the street's yellow hash marks like a kindergartner coloring outside the lines.

Stay in your lane.

She tugged the wheel to the right. The car responded with a distinct lack of enthusiasm then began to complain.

Thwap. Thwap. Thwap.

Maggie swore under her breath. Flat tire, likely the memento of a pothole.

Winter chewed on roads in Hollow Pine, sucking marrow from beneath the asphalt's crust. Summer would bring road work crews and their rock and tar quilt-work. Unfortunately, summer and road work were still months away.

Maggie pulled to the side of the road and cut the engine. She pushed the door open, struggling against the push and yaw of the wind.

Rain blasted her face like a fire hose, filling her nose with water and the pungent scent of grass and pine. She jogged around to the Stude's trunk and popped it open. The interior was a pit of black that seemed to absorb all light.

She de-pocketed her phone and pressed the flashlight app. Nothing happened. She repeated the motion, more deliberately this time as if to show her phone that she meant it.

The result was the same.

Double feck.

Whatever phenomenon that had allowed her cracked phone to work had ceased. It was her own fault. Distracted by an unrelenting desire to unmask a murderer, she had failed to have the phone repaired or replaced.

Maggie dragged her hand through the trunk in search of the spare tire. Her fingers skipped along the carpet's nubby nap. Back. Forth. Back again.

Then she remembered: she'd taken out the spare tire to make room for the wedding items Aunt Fiona had foisted on her post cake-tasting. She had temporarily stored the spare tire in the garage, intending to return it after she had gone to a seamstress and determined how to stitch together past and present. She had forgotten. She had forgotten so many things.

Maggie groaned and trotted toward the driver's side. Her foot found another pothole and plunged into it, twisting her ankle and filling her shoe with water. Maggie choked back a yelp and pulled her foot free. She reached one exploratory hand to her ankle and canvassed the geography of the injury. It had already puffed like a Poppin' Fresh Dough biscuit. She wouldn't be running for a while.

Maggie hobbled to the driver's side, shoes squishing a symphony of wet and nylon, pulled the door against the whip of wind and rain, and collapsed inside. She slammed the door shut and cradled her head in her hands. She wasn't just stranded. She was stranded in a rainstorm. On her way to unmask a murderer.

A potential murderer, a voice in her head reminded her.

Maggie considered the possibilities: hoof it back home, hope her phone would be in the mood to communicate once again, hope for the kindness of strangers, like Blanche DuBois in *A Streetcar Named Desire*.

But Maggie wasn't much for waiting. Or hoping. Or relying on anyone but herself.

She unbuckled her seatbelt and prepared herself for a long, soggy walk.

She heard a sound outside the car.

Maggie froze, adrenaline sparking through her body. She peered out the window, listening. Her own reflection stared back, gaunt and dejected.

She heard the sound again, sneaky and sly.

She raised her hand to depress the locks. Before she could make contact with the button, her door flew open.

Miles stood before her, his hair clinging to his head like a skullcap.

Chapter 55

Miles showed his teeth. "Why, Maggie O'Malley. Fancy meeting you here."

He slipped into the car, sickeningly-sweet cologne billowing behind him. He slammed the door shut and hinged his body to face her. "I've been hoping for some alone time." He reached out a hand, traced the air above her cheek. "Some *us* time. That's why I've been following you."

Maggie's fought against the memories, the blackness, the knowledge that she had multiple opportunities to report his behavior, the certainty it would have done no good. "Get out," she growled.

Miles laughed. "I don't think so. I've waited too long for this, worked up an appetite. Revenge may be a dish best served cold, but I like my dishes hot." He brought his finger closer, made contact with her skin. "Like you."

Maggie flinched as if she'd been burned and shrunk against the car's blood-red interior. Her mind stuttered as previous theories, considered and disregarded, shuttled through her brain.

Had Miles followed her to Hollow Pine to exact a personal revenge, to take his pound of flesh literally, painstakingly? Or had he been more global, more clever in his approach, poisoning Petrosian's patrons, casting doubt's shadow on Maggie, letting her thrash and flail as she tried to solve the crimes and redeem her reputation?

She shrunk against the door, felt the door's window crank at her back.

Maggie's instinct was to flee into the wind and the rain that rocked the car like a cradle. But that would mean turning her back. That would mean running and hiding. That would mean avoidance rather than defiance.

That would have meant a retreat to Maggie 1.0.

Maggie straightened, leaned toward danger rather than away. She knew who was behind the poisonings and why. She didn't have time for Miles's shit.

She smiled and brought her face close to Miles. His eyes widened in surprise, then delight. She reached out as if to return his touch. Then plunged her fingers toward Mile's eyes.

Miles was too fast. He parried, darting his head away, snaring her wrist in his hand. "Nice try," he sneered, "but this isn't a punishment so easily avoided. You're going to pay for destroying my career. My life."

He twisted her hand, bending the backs of her fingers toward her wrist. Maggie cried out in pain and tried to pull her hand free. Miles increased the pressure, his eyes shining with pleasure at her pain, then he pulled up and back, cranking her hand behind her back, lighting up the nerves from fingers to shoulder where the wind had earlier wrenched the car door from her hand.

He pinned Maggie's arm against the seat, raised his free fist and brought it to her cheek. The blow sent her head rocking to the side. He repeated the action from the other direction, pushing her head the other way.

Blood erupted from Maggie's cheek, flowed in a red tributary into her mouth. She spat, bucked against the seat and thrust herself forward to ram her head into Miles's chin.

She missed. He laughed. "Kitty wants to play," he said.

Then he stopped laughing and brought something shiny from the back of his pants. He pushed a button. A blade sprung free.

Miles widened his smile, his wet, white teeth competing with the knife for gleam. He brought the blade back, preparing to plunge or to slash or to slice. Behind him, the passenger door sprung open.

Framed by the Studebaker's window, Deena stood powerful and silent in the rain.

Chapter 56

Deena reached into the car and grabbed Miles by the collar of his polo. She twisted the fabric, tightened the textile noose around his neck, then knocked his head into the dashboard.

Miles screeched then flailed. Deena frowned and repeated the maneuver. Miles sagged against the passenger seat, consciousness ebbing with the blood that oozed from his temple.

Deena grabbed Miles and heaved him from the car, her face twisting with effort. She had lots of practice—and muscles—from moving patients on their hospital beds.

She pulled Miles onto the deserted street, then climbed into the car, slammed the door and depressed the locks that Maggie had failed to engage.

Deena pushed back her hood, releasing a puff of fragrance. She forked her fingers through her blue hair. Dark furrows revealed swaths of sodden scalp. She looked at Maggie. "Looks like I'm just in time."

Maggie opened her mouth. Nothing came out. She was dazed by Miles's attack. Deena's sudden appearance. The fact that she was alone with a woman who was very possibly a murderer. She found her voice. "You should probably call the police." She nodded toward Miles. "He won't be out for long, and my phone's dead."

Deena quirked her head toward the unconscious man outside the car. "He won't be a factor for a while. Besides, the storm's messing with my signal. No bars." She didn't show Maggie her phone. Instead, she gestured out her window. "You know that guy?"

Maggie nodded. Her mind whirred as she contemplated her next words, her next move.

"You can't trust anyone." Deena shook her head sadly. "I was detoured by the accident and hopped onto this side street. Then I spotted your car. I've seen you park it in front of the hospital. Very distinctive."

Maggie wondered if Deena had watched her from a hospital window or seen her in the parking lot. Both options were within the range of normalcy, and yet Maggie felt the insistent crawl of unease scuttle down her spine. Maybe Deena had followed Maggie from her home. Maybe Deena had been watching her, hunting her, just as Miles had.

"Anyway," Deena continued, "I thought I'd stop to see if you needed a hand. Turned out I was right. I'm glad I was there for you."

"Did you follow me here?" Maggie asked, giving voice to her growing suspicion.

"No," Deena scoffed. Her head bobbed once before changing to a horizontal trajectory. "Like I said, I was detoured by the accident, turned onto this street and happened to spot your car. I'm glad I ran into you, and not just so I could stop this creep, but also so I could congratulate you."

Maggie wagged her head, uncomprehending. The conversation was following the night's events, going from strange to stranger.

"For catching a monster?" Deena prompted. "Mary?"

Right. That monster.

Deena leaned toward Maggie, her perfume, sweet and familiar, wafting between them. "I had my suspicions, you know. Mary was so *involved*, suggesting all these tests and procedures, standing by while her daughter suffered then simpering about it on her stupid blog." Deena wiped the corners of her mouth where spittle had collected and smoothed the rain-speckled coat with her palms.

"Did you voice your concerns?" Maggie asked.

Deena gave a bitter laugh. "At St. Theresa's, doctors' voices are the only ones who are heard. It doesn't matter that we provide most of the care, that we hold our patients' hands when they're scared, cry for them when they don't make it. At St. Theresa's, the doctors are gods and Mary was a saint." She put her hand to the passenger window, fingertips tracing a caduceus, the medical cross, into the condensation. "I even set up a camera like you did. It caught Mary taking Riley to the bathroom, then Riley becoming violently ill." She looked at Maggie. "I said it was abuse. The doctors said it was coincidence. I even called the police. They took my statement. Nothing happened."

"So you took matters into your own hands." Maggie stared at the rain-streaked windshield, the trees bent low by the will of wind and water. "You decided to poison Mary to stop her from hurting Riley."

The accusation was a test. An assay by Maggie O'Malley, scientist. A trial to gauge the reaction to an irritant. Maggie knew it was reckless. She was injured, vulnerable, alone with a potentially dangerous woman. But she was emboldened by outrage, a sudden surge of repressed emotion, by non-alcoholic wine that offered an unexpected liquid courage.

Deena stared at Maggie then cackled. "That's the craziest thing I ever heard."

"You tried to hide the target of your murder by making the poisonings look like mass murder," Maggie pressed on. "You stockpiled Nitropress from the hospital. Infiltrated the vaccine supply of the pharmacy you knew the Whitleys patronized. Then waited for Mary to die, hopeful that her COPD, diabetes and other medical conditions would leave her more susceptible to the toxin."

"You're crazy," Deena scoffed. "I care about that girl like a sister, like a daughter. Why would I put Riley at risk by poisoning her?"

"Maybe because you believed that Riley's multiple exposures to Nitropress offered some immunity. More likely because both women were your patients and you were in control of who received the antidote—and who received more cyanide. While you nursed Riley back to health, you poisoned her mother, who was in turn trying to sicken Riley. You were convinced you'd win, that you'd stop Mary for good. And it worked, if you don't count the innocent people who died and the fact that Riley's been accused of the crimes you committed."

The smile that had played at Deena's lips fell away. Her eyes clouded over, a penumbra crossing her face as an internal storm gathered to match the squall outside. "What do you mean?"

"The police discovered that Riley was secretly involved with Thom, the custodian at Petrosian's Pillbox. They figured Riley wanted to get out from under her mother's thumb and had Thom taint the pharmacy's vaccine supply. They'll arrest her."

Deena swallowed her lips. "That can't happen."

"It's going to. The police are building their case now. Once they have enough evidence to obtain an arrest warrant, they'll collect Riley from her aunt, cuff her tiny wrists and put her into the back of a police car."

"You're lying. You're making all this up."

"Wish I were, but it's the truth. Now if you tell *your* truth, what really happened, the girl you say you care about will be free. She'll finally be safe."

Deena shook her head. "Even if what you say is true, no court in the land will convict Riley. She'll get counseling, maybe do community service, but she'll walk, and now that her bitch of a mother is out of the picture, she'll do it without the aid of a walker."

Deena leaned forward, bringing her pretty, pointed face inches from Maggie's. "I'm not worried about Riley. I'm worried about you. You're out here all alone." She pointed out the window. "Well, not alone. With a man you've had some kind of altercation with, who wishes you harm, who could easily overpower you. Harm you." She leaned closer. "Murder you."

Maggie could feel her pulse throbbing in her neck, making its way from her carotid artery to her jaw and temple. It had quickened, double-time becoming triple-time, her heart an engine revving in anticipation of a drag race.

She knew she should stop talking, stop provoking Deena. But she was feeling dangerous as the anger roiled behind The Wall and within the callous.

What was the boiling point of anger? Today it was Miles and Deena.

"You killed Thom, too," Maggie said. Her body was vibrating, sending shock waves through her words. "You knew about his relationship with Riley and used him to gain access to the pharmacy's vaccine supplies. You guilted him into silence, telling him that he was complicit in the poisonings. Then you waited until it was safe to make your move. You went to his house. You convinced him to let you in. You followed him to his bedroom where he kept the biohazard container. You killed him by your own hand while making it look like he died by his. I saw your footprints. I smelled your perfume. I know your intent."

It was all conjecture. It all had the ring of truth.

Deena hung her head. Her shoulders slumped forward in defeat as if cut low by the scythe of Maggie's accusations. Then suddenly, she was on Maggie. Deena's hands wrapped around Maggie's throat, bony knee pinning her hip against the driver's door. Maggie's fingernails, blunted by constant chewing, scrabbled against the vise of Deena's fingers, which clamped against her larynx until her breath became a series of ragged ellipses.

Maggie brought her arms between the V formed by Deena's hands and brought them down against the other woman's limbs. The seal between them broke.

Maggie twisted her body and sprung toward Deena. Caught off balance by the counterattack, the nurse reeled back, hitting her head against the dashboard, a mirror image of what she had done to Miles.

The sound of flesh and bone against glass reverberated through the air, a timpani to the rain's snare drum rhythm on the car. Deena brought a hand to her head, took it away. It was smeared with bright-red blood that continued to pump from a meandering gash near her temple. She and Miles had twin injuries.

Deena roared, a low rumble that began somewhere deep within her belly and exploded from up her throat. She hurtled herself toward Maggie, curling fingers into fists. She struck Maggie in the forehead—a head injury tit for tat—then the cheek. Maggie heard the crunch of bone, like heavy footfalls on gravel, felt pressure then pain at the epicenter of the crater Deena had created on her face.

Maggie's hands flew to her face. Pain veiled her face and head, settling into the crevices created by Deena, perching atop the peaks where flesh had already begun to swell after Miles's assault, punctuating the damage already exacted by her concussion. She was dizzy, disoriented and bloodied. She was beaten. But she wouldn't be beat.

The old Maggie was a survivor. The new Maggie was a fighter.

Maggie turned her wrists inward, shielded her face, then reached out her hand and slapped Deena with an open hand.

The act seemed silly, a cat fight maneuver that called to mind cinematic stereotypes of bosomy cheerleaders who spontaneously disrobed. But the slap had the effect Maggie was going for.

Deena stopped, wide-eyed at the halfhearted assault, then laughed. "That's all you got?"

It wasn't.

Maggie flexed the nascent muscles she'd worked to build under Ada's insistence and smashed the heel of her hand into Deena's throat. Deena wheezed and reeled back. Maggie put her fist into Deena's soft, yielding gut. A gust of air whistled through Deena's lips and she dropped against her door, cracking her head against the glass.

It was a lucky break. Maggie would take it.

Maggie looked at the woman, her unconscious form an echo of the girl they had both tried to save. Maggie could hurt her. She could even end her. She didn't want to do either.

Maggie reached over the seat and rummaged around the backseat. Her hand landed on a mass of tulle and ribbon, leavings from her mother's wedding gown.

She dragged the material forward and put one knee on Deena's chest.

The woman groaned, moved, then stilled. Maggie cuffed Deena's wrists with tulle and ribbon in a hideous mint green tourniquet. Cruel and sartorial punishment.

Deena moved, consciousness announcing itself in her musculature. She blinked at Maggie and then at the makeshift cuffs. She moved again, winced, then, to Maggie's astonishment began to cry.

The woman who had tried to kill her, who had succeeded in killing three people, had dissolved into a puddle of saltwater and regret.

"I had no choice," Deena sobbed. "That woman was torturing her daughter, killing her. And no one was doing anything. I had to do it. I had to stop a murderer."

Maggie looked at her, disheveled, bleeding, earnest in her desire to protect the most vulnerable of patients. "I know," Maggie said quietly. "And now I have to do the same."

Chapter 57

"You're sure you don't mind?" Maggie asked Constantine as he pulled out of the driveway.

"Are you seriously asking if I mind squiring the most beautiful girl in the world to the ball?"

"I'm not sure driving me to work while my car's in the shop is 'squiring,' and I don't think anyone has ever called Petrosian's 'the ball,' but I appreciate the sentiment, especially the implication that I'm a princess."

Constantine grabbed her hand. "I'm just glad you kissed this frog."

He made the familiar turns to Petrosian's and coasted to a stop in front of the drugstore. "You're sure you're okay?"

Maggie touched the base of her orbital bone. "No need for surgery, remember? Just ice and rest."

"And avoid getting punched in the face multiple times."

"That, too."

Constantine cupped her chin in his hand then brushed the area beneath her eye with his lips. "What about the rest of you, the parts not mapped out on an anatomical diagram?"

Maggie straightened her spine. "They're fine, too. Haven't you heard? We're stronger in the broken places."

"Then you're one of the strongest people I know."

Maggie shook her head. "I think that title belongs to Riley. Abused by her mother, accused by the police. And yet, she endures."

"What happens to her now?"

"She lives with her aunt, figures out who she is and what she wants. Heals from a pain that doctors and hospitals can't cure."

"Speaking of hospitals, I take it Deena's trading St. Theresa's for the state penn."

"If the DA has his way. Deena is cooperating. She's made a full confession, said she didn't want to put Riley through any more."

"A criminal with a conscience." Constantine scoffed. "How novel."

"She thought she was doing the right thing. She was desperate to help Riley. She decided she'd do whatever it took to free her from an abusive mother."

Constantine shook his head. "You know what they say about the road to hell, Mags. She could have tried harder to involve the authorities, gotten the staff of St. Theresa's to rally around her theory, done a lot of things besides poison innocents to kill the guilty."

"She's got to have a screw loose to do what she did." Maggie looked out the window at nothing. "She talked about losing patients in the past. Maybe St. Theresa's should look into the deaths of her charges."

Constantine stared at her. "Angel of mercy moonlighting as an agent of death?"

"She wouldn't be the first. Besides, everything's possible, remember?"

"I guess." Constantine was quiet for a moment. Finally he said, "What made Deena suspect medical abuse?"

"The same things that alerted me and Dr. Cohen—maybe others: multiple visits that didn't add up, an overly involved mother, something 'off' about the whole thing. My guess is that the plan was hatched after Deena witnessed repeated exposure to Nitropress. She knew the drug had fallen out of favor because of the potential for cyanide toxicity and newer, perhaps better, options. She figured she'd turn medicine against the medical abuser, who was in worse health than the daughter she trotted out for pity and payola. Deena planned to put herself into a position where she'd be in charge of the Whitleys' care, care for Riley and continue to poison Mary. People would call Riley's recovery a miracle and Mary's eventual death by poisoning a tragedy. I watched Mary decline. Now that I think back on it, her symptoms coincided with Deena's visits to the hospital room."

"It's a tidy hypothesis, Mags. But there are still unanswered questions. How did Deena ingratiate herself into the Whitleys' care? How did Mary gain access to the vaccines, or the pharmacy for that matter?"

"I think once Deena became obsessed with Riley, she kept tabs on her visits to the hospital. After Riley was admitted, she could have volunteered for a shift. The hospital's chronically short-staffed. It wouldn't be hard for her to pick up shifts and find herself caring for her favorite patient. And to answer your second question: Thom. He was part-time at Petrosian's, part-time at the hospital, which was likely how he met Deena and cultivated his relationship with Riley. Deena could have become aware of Thom and Riley's relationship and convinced Thom to replace the vaccines with her own supply, telling him that they contained an experimental drug that would help Riley."

"Which supports your theory that Thom didn't die from a case of conscience. Eliminating Thom would mean getting rid of a witness."

Maggie nodded. "Deena didn't admit to helping him to the great waiting room in the sky, but that's my bet. Remember, these are all just theories. We'll know more when she gives her full statement."

"I'm not sure we can count on full-disclosure from a self-proclaimed murderer."

"No honor among thieves?"

"Thieves maybe. Murderers, not so much." He shifted in his seat. "What about our pal, Miles?"

"Back in the big house. Violated parole for moving without telling his PO."

"And for stalking and assault."

Maggie smiled, but the light didn't touch her eyes. "That, too."

"And Brock? Has he posthumously been knighted a hero or a villain?"

"Neither. He's just...human. I saw on the news, which is still anchored by Bradley, by the way, that the cause of the warehouse fire was oily rags. Brock was not an arsonist. And it seems that he did contact CPS about the abuse he suspected. When he didn't get any traction, he decided to turn lemons into a career-building lemonade stand and run an exposé on the faces of abuse and lapses in the system. Never mind the fact that he let the abuse continue while he honed the story."

"Neither wholly good or entirely evil. Sounds like that describes quite a few people."

"Mmm."

Maggie gazed at Petrosian's storefront. Through the plate glass window she could see Francine filing her nails and Nan running a broom in front of the check stands. Business as usual or pretending that Thom's permanent absence didn't leave a hole in more than just the duty roster?

"Any closure on the whole drug abuse angle or the connection between Francine and Nigel and maybe even Sloane?"

"Nope."

"Ah."

No witty remark, no smart aleck comeback. For once, Constantine had nothing to say. Neither did Maggie.

Maggie opened the car door and climbed out. She closed the door and leaned through the open window, inhaling a tree-shaped air freshener that smelled like cherry cough drops. "Pick me up at five thirty? Maybe we can go to dinner."

"Or we skip dinner and elope. Like, tonight. For realsies."

Maggie smiled. An elopement. No dress. No decision about fondant versus buttercream. No wondering whether Chewbarka would walk her down the aisle rather than her father. "Are you propositioning me?"

A smile lit his face. "Absolutely."

Maggie leaned across the seat, kissed him hard. The cold feet that had begun with her father's cool attitude toward the wedding warmed. Constantine was her North Star. Her heart would always point his way.

She ducked back out the window and waved goodbye, then strode toward the door. The closer she got to the entrance, the more she wanted to escape, to turn around, to hide at home and in the shelter of Constantine's arms.

She should be happy. She'd unmasked an abuser, caught a murderer, righted wrongs without the benefit of an invisible airplane or the Lasso of Truth.

She couldn't remember the last time she'd felt so low.

Innocent lives had been lost. Riley had not returned her many calls. According to Austin, Sloane's sister had reneged on her promise to care for her nieces, meaning foster care—and likely separation—for the girls. And now she was returning to work, employed by a pharmacist who had turned a blind eye to potential opiate abuse. Worse, her reluctance to share her suspicions of drug abuse, her continued presence at the pharmacy despite this knowledge, meant tacit approval. Maybe even collusion.

Maggie pulled the door open, was greeted with an olfactory stew of germicide and cleaner. She stood for a moment before the row of check stands, letting her eyes—and perhaps her ethics—adjust.

Nan's broom stopped inches from Maggie's running shoes. "Hey, Maggie. Glad to be back?" Behind her, Francine glowered over her emery board, sawing the nail on her middle finger, perhaps preparing it for deployment.

"Good to see you, too." She left the question unanswered. Too many lies already. "Where's Mr. Petrosian?"

Nan pointed her answer. Behind the counter, his inner sanctum.

Maggie thanked her, nodded at Francine who studied her cuticle as if it were the Holy Grail, then walked the plank of Aisle 5, her mind on the girl with the Zingers, the mother who abused her, the oblivion that surely lay ahead.

Maggie walked past the Hostess rack, the Vienna Sausages, the heat-and-eat trays of mac and cheese, her feet gliding over the floor's polished tiles.

She stopped.

She couldn't do it. She couldn't go back to her job, pretend nothing was wrong, act as if she didn't know—or at least suspect—that the man she'd grown to admire, had come to respect, had betrayed his position. His ethics. Her.

The days of duty, of slavishly following what others wanted her to do, were gone. Because that Maggie was gone, too.

Maggie pivoted, her arms already pistoning her toward the front of the store and the person she was meant to be, had almost forgotten existed. Behind her, the front door banged open and boots clanged on the tile. She turned. Three men clad in the kind of business casual that brought to mind plainclothed police charged toward her.

Maggie stepped toward a steeple of granola bars. The men sprinted by. One muttered into a cell phone held like a walkie-talkie. The other nodded at her.

What the—?

Maggie spun back around and followed them.

They landed in front of the pharmacy counter and flanked a bespectacled man with a tin of Altoids in his hand. Maggie felt the same zing of recognition she had felt at the karaoke café when she spotted Nigel Roberts talking to a man. This man.

Petrosian looked down from his pharmaceutical pulpit and nodded at the officers. "Ah, yes," he said, mouth flatlining, eyes sparking. "I believe you're looking for Dr. Wells."

Dr. Wells. The recollection was complete. She'd seen the doctor in the pharmacy a handful of times and had come across his name in the pharmacy database.

The doctor's jaw fell open, a trapdoor to his esophagus. He snapped it shut. "What is this about, please? I'm very busy." He shook the Altoids tin, as if indicating that his hectic schedule allowed only for fresh breath.

The man who had been using his phone as a walkie-talkie said, "Dr.

Wells?"

"I believe that's already been established," the Altoid-user huffed.

"Agent Li, DEA."

Maggie started. Not police. Federal agents.

"These are agents Boyce and Brown." Li pulled a sheet of paper folded in thirds from the innards of his suit. "We have a warrant for your arrest for the unlawful distribution and dispensing of a controlled substance without a legitimate medical purpose and without a proper medical examination."

Li handed Wells the document. Wells grasped then released it. The paper fluttered to the ground.

Wells' oral trapdoor re-opened, releasing a whoosh of air. He gulped oxygen. "This is outrageous."

"We agree," said Agent Brown as he retrieved the fallen warrant and gathered the doctor's hands behind his sports jacket. "That's why we're here."

"This is outrageous," the doctor repeated. "Absolutely outrageous." He was out of synonyms, as well as time. "I want my lawyer."

"You'll have him," Li replied. "You can call him on the way to the field office."

"Field office?" Wells' voice cracked like a middle schooler's. "What is that? *Where* is that?"

Li began to nudge Wells down the aisle. "You're about to find out."

Wells' voice crescendoed down the aisle then dimunuendoed as he passed through the front door to the fate that awaited him.

Maggie turned slowly to face Petrosian. "What was…" The question died on her lips.

"That," he replied, brushing nonexistent dust from his impeccable lab coat, "was the result of six months of work with the DEA."

"*You* are working with the DEA?"

"Was. I alerted them to a doctor I suspected was illegally distributing opioids. They asked for my help to bring him in."

Maggie tried to absorb this. Petrosian hadn't ignored Ellis's drug use. He wasn't being paid off so that he could cover Sona's doctor's bills. "You knew about Colton Ellis? Used him to catch Wells?"

Petrosian frowned at that. "Certainly not. Ellis was part of the operation, along with Francine."

"*Francine?*"

A curt nod. "Undercover agent."

Maggie's world gyrated. Petrosian was working as an informant with Colton and Francine as part of an undercover sting operation. What next? Petrosian as government operative? The pharmacy as a cover? Her boss's stint on *The Voice*?

Maggie processed the news about Francine, remembering her checkered past, her born-again hypocrisy, her aloof demeanor.

Stay in your lane.

"Francine had a history of substance abuse," Maggie said. "Steroids. Marijuana. Alcohol. Probably more. Plus petty crimes. The feds flipped her, made her one of their own. That's why she was so horrible. To create distance, to establish boundaries."

"You're correct about her being 'flipped,' as you say." The corners of Petrosian's mouth curled. "But I'm afraid Francine's superiority and standoffishness is personal as well as professional. It's just who she is. Although," he looked at her over his glasses, "she did want to keep her distance based on your past...history."

Right. Working with a nosy amateur sleuth wasn't exactly helpful during a sting. Maggie thought about the roles that Francine, Petrosian and Deena played, some authentic, others manufactured. Things—and people—weren't always as they seemed.

"Why the pharmacy? Why not snag Wells at his clinic or home?"

"Discretion. Convenience. Take your pick. I set up a meeting with Wells, told him I knew something was going on and that I could help him. In short, I tantalized him with forbidden fruit, and he bit. Now we'll see if he gives up his business partner, Nigel."

"Of course," Maggie said, the picture crystalizing. "Nigel provides patients to Wells, then takes a cut of the action. They were long-time acquaintances from Nigel's poker games, which catered to moneyed clientele including Dr. Wells. Pleasure became business. From what I heard, Nigel was always looking to expand his empire."

Petrosian nodded. He almost looked impressed. "Very good, Ms. O'Malley."

"How did you become suspicious of Wells?"

Petrosian made an expansive gesture with his hands. "Experience. Wells was an enthusiastic prescriber of hydrocodone and OxyContin, even more so in the past year."

"After Nigel Roberts opened his restaurant/poker club."

Petrosian nodded. "When he started prescribing fentanyl, that got my attention. I looked back through my records. Over the past year, the vast majority of Wells' prescriptions were for opioids. Unusual for a family practice physician."

"How did Colton Ellis become involved?"

"He was a patient of Dr. Wells and knew him from Roberts' poker club. I asked him to offer Wells money in exchange for a prescription for hydrocodone in order to test my theory. Ellis was amenable because he was tired of his doctor beating him at poker. Ellis and I were also trying to close the real estate deal and he wanted to play nice."

Maggie gaped. "So the real estate deal with Nigel Roberts was just a cover?"

"Yes, it was a way to get closer to Nigel Roberts, to ingratiate himself into Roberts' world. Ellis and Roberts bonded over poker, alcohol and real estate. By the time Ellis asked Dr. Wells for hydrocodone, trust had been established. Wells told him to see Nigel Roberts then come back to the office."

"A prescription from a drug lord, then one from his physician."

Petrosian's eyes sparkled. "Precisely. Drug-seekers would pay Roberts, Roberts would pay Wells, Wells would break out his prescription pad. After Ellis told me about Wells' pay-for-play practice, I contacted the state police. The FBI and the DEA contacted me. Then the game was afoot."

"The local police didn't know about the operation?"

Another headshake. "Only the DEA and FBI. At first, the agencies feared that the poisonings were a result of the operation. I feared that, as well. Fortunately, you discovered the truth and helped save a girl's life. Other lives, too." Petrosian smiled. It was a rare event, a reverse eclipse that shone light on all in its path.

Maggie returned the smile, happiness seeping under The Wall, lancing the boil in which poisonous feelings had been allowed to grow and fester. She felt a letting go, a lightening, an abatement of the haunting by young girls torn from their mothers. At least for the moment.

Petrosian laced his fingers. "I must apologize for my lack of availability after the poisonings. The agents were worried about increased scrutiny and advised me to leave town and minimize contact."

"And I'm sorry about your wife, about Sona. She told me about her illness."

Petrosian nodded but said nothing. No further details. No prognosis. Maggie wondered if that was typical Petrosian privacy or the symptom of a bleak outlook.

"We can speak more later," Petrosian said, drawing himself up. "Now it looks as though you have a visitor."

Petrosian nodded to someone behind Maggie then turned and passed through the turnstile of the pharmacy counter, disappearing among the plastic shelving.

Visitor?

Maggie rotated. Her father stood, hat in hand—literally—before her.

"Pop?"

"Sorry to bother you at work, Maggie dear." He took a breath as if to say something more, wrung his hat.

"That's okay. Um…" Should she go for small talk? Demand to know why he'd let his only daughter, his last connection to the wife he'd buried, walk down the aisle alone? "What's up?" A cop-out, but at least she was verbalizing.

Jack O'Malley looked up at the ceiling as if taking her question literally, then down at his shoes, buffed and polished for Mass. "I've been an ass," he said without preamble. "I told you that I wouldn't go to your wedding because it wasn't going to be in a church. Told myself the same thing. But that was a lie."

He reached out to her, let his hand drop to his side. He gave the hat another twist. "The truth is, I couldn't stand the idea of losing you." His voice wavered. He coughed into his fist. "The truth is, I thought if I didn't go to your wedding, you wouldn't go through with it. Things would stay the same."

Maggie felt a frisson of anger. "You wanted me to choose you over Constantine."

"I wanted to stop time. I wanted you to be the little girl who held my hand, who helped me fill the parmesan shakers, who reminded me I had a reason to get up every morning after your mother died."

He rounded the blood pressure machine, sat at its miniature desk. "Then I realized I couldn't stop time any more than I could bring your mother back. And that the surest way to lose you was to keep doing what I was doing."

Maggie stepped forward. "Pop—"

"Now, now, don't get all mushy on me." He struggled from his seat.

"You have a wedding to plan, and I have a tuxedo to rent. I want to look good when I walk you down the aisle." He grabbed her hand and pulled her into an impromptu waltz. "And when I show my moves on the dance floor."

Maggie laughed. Jack released her and plunked the hat on his head. "I'll call you later. Maybe we can go to lunch. Catch up."

As far as Maggie knew, her father had never gone to lunch and considered "catching up" a luxury akin to two-ply toilet paper. "Sounds good."

She watched as her father marched down the aisle, her mind imagining it flocked with white and adorned with flowers.

Maybe she and Constantine wouldn't elope. Maybe Maggie would have a church wedding after all.

Jack O'Malley would walk her down the aisle. Chewbarka and Miss Vanilla would be ring-bearers. And Constantine would be waiting for her, eyes shining, hand outstretched as he beckoned her into the life they had always been meant to share.

Maybe Maggie would have her happily ever after, after all.

© TaguePhoto.com

KATHLEEN VALENTI

When Kathleen Valenti isn't writing page-turning mysteries that combine humor and suspense, she works as a nationally award-winning advertising copywriter. *Protocol* is her debut novel and the first of the Maggie O'Malley mystery series. Kathleen lives in Oregon with her family where she pretends to enjoy running.

**The Maggie O'Malley Mystery Series
by Kathleen Valenti**

PROTOCOL (#1)
39 WINKS (#2)
AS DIRECTED (#3)

Henery Press Mystery Books

And finally, before you go...
Here are a few other mysteries
you might enjoy:

A MUDDIED MURDER

Wendy Tyson

A Greenhouse Mystery (#1)

When Megan Sawyer gives up her big-city law career to care for her grandmother and run the family's organic farm and café, she expects to find peace and tranquility in her scenic hometown of Winsome, Pennsylvania. Instead, her goat goes missing, rain muddies her fields, the town denies her business permits, and her family's Colonial-era farm sucks up the remains of her savings.

Just when she thinks she's reached the bottom of the rain barrel, Megan and the town's hunky veterinarian discover the local zoning commissioner's battered body in her barn. Now Megan's thrust into the middle of a murder investigation—and she's the chief suspect. Can Megan dig through small-town secrets, local politics, and old grievances in time to find a killer before that killer strikes again?

Available at booksellers nationwide and online

Visit www.henerypress.com for details

THE SEMESTER OF OUR DISCONTENT
Cynthia Kuhn

A Lila Maclean Academic Mystery (#1)

English professor Lila Maclean is thrilled about her new job at prestigious Stonedale University, until she finds one of her colleagues dead. She soon learns that everyone, from the chancellor to the detective working the case, believes Lila—or someone she is protecting—may be responsible for the horrific event, so she assigns herself the task of identifying the killer.

Putting her scholarly skills to the test, Lila gathers evidence, but her search is complicated by an unexpected nemesis, a suspicious investigator, and an ominous secret society. Rather than earning an "A" for effort, she receives a threat featuring the mysterious emblem and must act quickly to avoid failing her assignment...and becoming the next victim.

Available at booksellers nationwide and online

Visit www.henerypress.com for details

PUMPKINS IN PARADISE
Kathi Daley

A Tj Jensen Mystery (#1)

Between volunteering for the annual pumpkin festival and coaching her girls to the state soccer finals, high school teacher Tj Jensen finds her good friend Zachary Collins dead in his favorite chair.

When the handsome new deputy closes the case without so much as a "why" or "how," Tj turns her attention from chili cook-offs and pumpkin carving to complex puzzles, prophetic riddles, and a decades-old secret she seems destined to unravel.

Available at booksellers nationwide and online

Visit www.henerypress.com for details

MURDER AT THE PALACE

Margaret Dumas

A Movie Palace Mystery (#1)

Welcome to the Palace movie theater! Now Showing: Philandering husbands, ghostly sidekicks, and a murder or two.

When Nora Paige's movie-star husband leaves her for his latest co-star, she flees Hollywood to take refuge in San Francisco at the Palace, a historic movie theater that shows the classic films she loves. There she finds a band of misfit film buffs who care about movies (almost) as much as she does.

She also finds some shady financial dealings and the body of a murdered stranger. Oh, and then there's Trixie, the lively ghost of a 1930's usherette who appears only to Nora and has a lot to catch up on. With the help of her new ghostly friend, can Nora catch the killer before there's another murder at the Palace?

Available at booksellers nationwide and online

Visit www.henerypress.com for details

CPSIA information can be obtained
at www.ICGtesting.com
Printed in the USA
LVHW100235151218
600413LV00013BA/93/P